13/1/14

The Arrow of Sherwood

The Arrow of Sherwood

Lauren Johnson

First published in Great Britain in 2013 by
PEN & SWORD FICTION
An imprint of
Pen & Sword Books Ltd
47 Church Street
Barnsley
South Yorkshire
S70 2AS

9781783030019

A CIP catalogue record for this book is
available from the British Library

Printed and bound in England
By CPI Group (UK) Ltd, Croydon, CRO 4YY

Pen & Sword Books Ltd incorporates the Imprints of Pen & Sword Fiction, Pen & Sword Aviation, Pen & Sword Family History, Pen & Sword Maritime, Pen & Sword Military, Wharncliffe Local History, Pen & Sword Select, Pen & Sword Military Classics, Leo Cooper, Remember When, Seaforth Publishing and Frontline Publishing

For a complete list of Pen & Sword titles please contact
PEN & SWORD BOOKS LIMITED
47 Church Street, Barnsley, South Yorkshire, S70 2AS, England
E-mail: enquiries@pen-and-sword.co.uk
Website: www.pen-and-sword.co.uk

The Arrow of Sherwood

'As the earth grows dark when the sun departs, so the face of the kingdom was changed by the absence of the king… All the barons were disturbed, castles were strengthened, towns fortified, ditches dug.' – Richard of Devizes

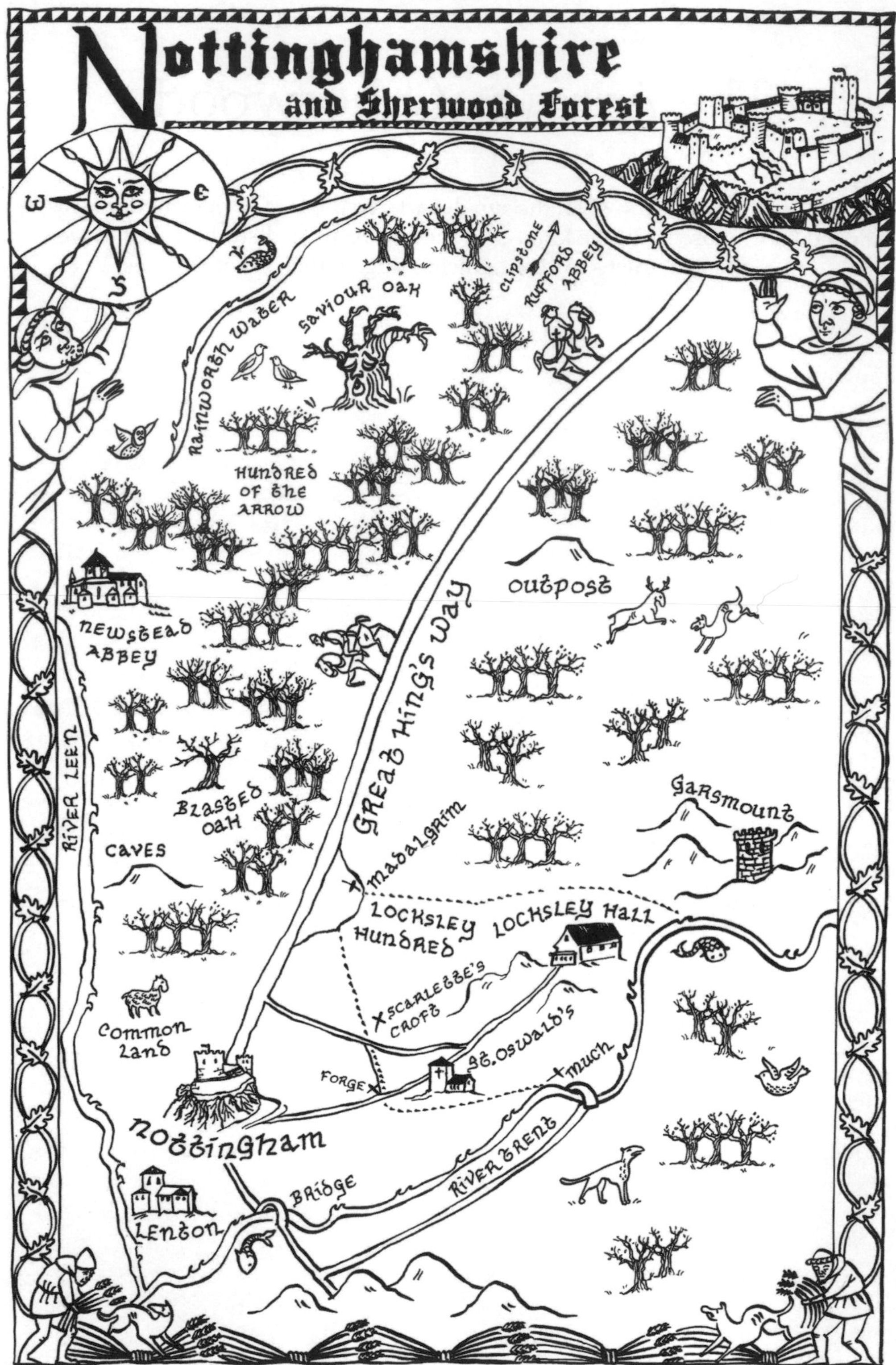
Nottinghamshire
and Sherwood Forest
W
E
S
Rainworth Water
Saviour Oak
Clipstone
Rufford Abbey
Hundred of the Arrow
Newstead Abbey
Outpost
Great King's Way
River Leen
Blasted Oak
Caves
Madalgrim
Garsmount
Locksley Hundred
Locksley Hall
Scarlette's Croft
St. Oswald's
Common Land
Forge
Much
Nottingham
River Trent
Bridge
Lenton

1193
Candlemas

Candlemas dawned on Nottinghamshire in a crush of frost. A green land, they called England, green and pleasant, but in winter there was hardly a flash of green to be seen. White sheets of snow lay across the hillsides, and where weary ploughs had churned the earth black soil too was rimed with white. As a churchbell chimed for Matins three fields away a crusader turned his horse down a forking path into the valley. Farmers emerging from their smoky homes swathed in wool barely glanced at the man. Just beyond the miller's brook the crusader's horse was startled as a pig shrieked through an open gate. The swineherd called a warning. The crusader scarcely twitched as his horse skittered away from the animal. The horse was wide in its haunches, strong in the legs, and the lad took a moment to look up from it to the rider.

'Sorry, my lord,' he said instinctively.

Afterwards he wondered why. The man had not been dressed richly, and his face was darker than any lord of England he had seen. It was something about the way he sat his saddle, perhaps. Straight upright and secure. The swineherd shrugged and started off again after the pig. Better to be safe than sorry these days. Some lords would have you strung up for looking at them wrong.

The crusader plodded on. It had been a long ride home, but he was accustomed to lengthy journeys. Snowflakes stirred in the grey vastness of the valley. The crusader glanced at the sky, clouds scudding overhead. It had been years since he had seen skies as pale as this, gleaming white and heavy as over-stuffed feather bolsters. His back twinged, yearning for the comfort of a good bed. He pressed the sensation down, closing his eyes for a moment and exhaling, breath misting in the air.

As he opened his eyes, he smelt it. Horses, horseshit, market stalls, brazier fires, great kitchens, dank stone, dust. Nottingham. And there it was. The jagged puzzle of battlements and towers on Castle Rock, smoke drifting in plumes from it, a muddle of smaller buildings sprawling in the town beneath. There would be celebrations, no doubt. Yesterday's fasting would be forgotten in today's feasting. The crusader considered. He ought to press on to Locksley Hall and deliver his news in person. But the bustle of Nottingham drew his eye. He had a shuddering remembrance, a flash of anxiety and excitement that he had not felt since the last time he was within those walls, four years before. He found he had nudged his horse towards Nottingham Bridge before he knew his own decision.

The crusader watched the town's sights pass him as through a warped lens, or a reflection on rippled water. How often in far-foreign dreams had he seen these same streets enclosing him? But as he neared the inner walls he saw that something had changed. Banners fluttered from the ramparts, crimson, or – red and gold. Those were not colours he recognised. Instinctively his fingers reached for the sword pommel at his hip. Guards stood at the gatehouse into the middle bailey, wearing tabards of the same alien colours. He slowed and nodded briskly. A soldier's greeting. One of the men nodded in return, the other, fairer, frowned then stepped into his path.

'Stop please,' he said. His English was thick with an accent not altogether familiar. Like the banners, it sat strangely in this so-known place. 'What business do you have here, my lord?'

The crusader paused. He had no business at all. 'I am here to pay my respects to the sheriff.'

The guard was unconvinced. 'It would be faster to go to the hall,' he said. 'Please get down.'

'As you like,' the crusader replied, making sure to emphasise his own accent. He dropped from his horse and pushed back his hood. As he did so the two crossed palms sewn to his chest gleamed light under his dusty cloak. The darker guard's eyes widened.

'You have come from the Holy Land, my lord?'

'I have.'

'Do you know anything of the king?'

'No more than you, I think. He won a truce with Saladin. Now he rests a prisoner in Germany.'

'The wickedness of the German Emperor,' muttered the fair guard. 'He is worse than the Saracen, taking another Christian hostage.'

'I am sure the sheriff will welcome news from Jerusalem,' said his companion. 'He has been holding an Assize today with the Lords Vipont.'

'I have not heard that name in Nottingham before.'

'You have been gone too long. They are friends to the king's brother, come from Normandy.'

'True noblemen,' added the fair one.

'You are welcome,' said the darker, 'to enter the castleyard, my lord, but if you seek hospitality you should head for the hall.'

The crusader did not know which hall they meant, and was in no mood to loiter in the windswept yard of Nottingham Castle. He would press on for home, he decided, and made to turn his horse. But the next instant he was stalled at the sight of a figure crossing the yard. It was a lady, her long auburn hair bound in two plaits that hung down her back. The vivid red of her gown and crisp white of her linen veil stood stark against the muck and shadows of the bailey. She was tall, too tall for beauty, her features too angular, her chin too prominent. But in the decisiveness of her stride there was something so familiar to the crusader it caught his breath. He knew the curt nod she gave the carter, the definite placement of her hands, the slight angle of her head as she tried to be modest but cast furtive glances around her defiantly. A glance fell on him, she met his eye, she looked back to the ground, she slowed, she glanced again, she scowled, she stopped, she turned and looked and stared, and her defiance was gone. He twitched his horse's bridle and strode towards her.

'Marian,' he said, and it was a name that had not crossed his mind in years.

In the Sepulchre of Jerusalem he had seen a woman kneel before the tomb of their saviour with a look of awestruck disbelief. He saw the same look now on the lady's face, and it was strange to see it so uncertain. He remembered his courtesy, and bowed his head. She did not remember hers, and kept staring.

'I hope you are well.'

When still she did not speak he suppressed an all too familiar feeling of irritation.

'My lady,' came a voice, so close the lady Marian jumped. An Englishwoman, well dressed, plump and wrinkled, addressed her. 'Lord Vipont is in the solar.'

The lady held up a hand to silence her, and turned to the crusader. 'Is it you?'

A stupid question, the crusader thought. But yes, he said, it was.

'How long have you been in England?'

'Long enough to ride from Dover.'

'You crossed the sea in January?'

She sounded disapproving. He felt his patience fail. This, too, was familiar.

'Yes. Perhaps you will excuse me. I was only passing on my way to my father at Locksley. You will send my regards to your father, I hope. I daresay I shall see you again soon.'

He bowed again and turned to mount his horse, but a pressure on his arm stopped him. The lady's hand. She seemed as surprised as him to find it there. She withdrew it, but did not step away.

'You go to see your father?'

'As soon as I leave here.'

'His father?' The Englishwoman squinted at him. 'Doesn't he know?'

'Hush, Gytha,' the lady Marian said. 'You can find your mother at Locksley,' she told the crusader, 'but your father is not there.'

'Then I will see my mother.'

He mounted his horse.

'Robin –' the lady bit off her sentence, annoyed to have called him that. 'My Lord Locksley, you must know that your father was unwell?'

'I did not, my lady. Excuse me.'

She stepped into his path.

'He was unwell. He caught the sweating sickness two summers ago. Hundreds died across the county.'

He could not see why she laboured this point.

'I will pray for them.'

'Your father –' she hesitated, breathed deeply, avoided his eye. 'Your father was one of them.'

The crusader stopped. He felt his horse beneath him, shuddering with tiredness. He felt a wind sharp as ice whip through the yard. He felt the woman Gytha's pale eyes watch him with sadness. More than that, he did not feel.

'I – I am sorry to tell you. A message was sent to you, but it must never have arrived.'

Robin knew he should reply. 'It did not.'

'We did not expect a response from you, or we might have tried to write again. But we had word from a servant of the Earl of Derby that you died at Acre.'

'The earl died. I did not.'

'Your mother still lives,' said Gytha, with an attempt at comfort.

That sounded about right.

'Yes,' said Marian, 'you will find her at Locksley Hall.' She seemed on the point of saying more, but checked herself and murmured something to Gytha. 'You should go to her. She will be so glad to know the news from Acre was false. I will come with you.' She called for a groom to ready her horse.

'That is not necessary.'

'You will see why I come when we get there. Gytha, call for Edgar and Waltheof. Nottinghamshire is not so safe as it was when you left,' she added by way of explanation.

'I have travelled safely enough these past days.'

'Crusaders may do that. Ladies cannot.'

His patience was wearing thin. 'Then perhaps you should stay here.'

She said nothing as Gytha wrapped a cloak around her shoulders and the two attendants approached with her horse. But between her eyebrows there was a crease that told him what she thought. In her eyes, he was obdurate and foolish, rude and boorish, but he was a man and a lord and she could not tell him so.

'There is no question that you are Robin of Locksley,' she said. She tried to smile as she said it, but the irritation in her voice cut through.

She mounted her horse and waited for her attendants to do the same. Robin looked around the yard to avoid meeting her eye. At the top of the castle steps a pale man with neatly arranged black hair was standing. Robin did not know him, but recognised a nobleman from his dress. He watched Marian as she loitered with a crusader in the yard. Marian did not look in his direction, but Gytha bowed her head to him. He spoke to a page wearing the same crimson-or of the banners, and the page headed for Marian.

'We should set off,' she said and spurred her horse ahead of Gytha's.

Robin did not argue. As he passed beneath the gate he heard Marian speaking low to Gytha. 'Tell him I did not see him,' she said.

They rode in silence, Robin leading the way, the Englishmen bringing up the rear. Visitors to the market squares and churches – and not a few beggars – slowed their journey, and Robin did not know if he was glad to have time to prepare or if he was eager to press on and reach his home. Either way, they reached it in the end. Without his father's lordship he had expected to find the hall changed, but there it still stood, solid as ever. The outer wall, the gatehouse, the great kitchens tucked away behind the inner yard, the stables brushed and the kennels shining.

Marian dismounted and waited on the steps leading into the hall.

'You should give thanks for your safe arrival,' she said, nodding towards a shrine in the corner of the doorway. 'I will prepare your mother to see you. It will be a shock.'

That was an understatement, he thought. She went inside and he regarded the poor shrine welcoming visitors to Locksley. It seemed absurd to bend his knee before the rain-rubbed crucifix when he had travelled through deserts to the walls of Jerusalem. He had felt the sun scalding the earth where Jesus lived and died, and here he stood before a grey stone block, his father dead and unable to see that he had paid his penance. He knelt anyway. Thank you, God, he prayed, for reminding me that you enjoy nothing more than making a fool of man. When Marian's man, Waltheof, came to accompany him inside he crossed himself with every outward sign of calm devotion and followed him in.

Outside Locksley Hall might look no different but inside everything had changed. There was not a trace of the life that Robin had known. His father hated – *had* hated, he corrected himself – excess. His mother, in their greyer moments, had chided her husband that he should have been a monk, not a lord. A lord was expected to deck his halls with tapestries, the floors with tiles and sweet smelling rushes, to have cushions of silk and velvet. Clearly, a lord who enjoyed being a lord had decorated his father's great hall in Robin's absence. A roaring fire and hot wine had always greeted any guest of Lord Robert, but not tapestries dancing with mythical beasts and walls painted with flowers.

He knew the way to his mother's chamber, but even if he had not he could have found it by following the shouts. His mother was born under a full moon, when the stars were in Cancer and all the female traits are heightened. She had never been one to stay calm in a crisis.

'What will we do?' he heard her shrieking. Her voice dropped to a burble. Marian must be trying to soothe her. A fool's errand. 'But the lands are gone… He will kill me… He will…'

The door had been left partly open. Through it Robin saw his mother pacing back and forth, tears streaming down her scarlet face. She wore a loose gown, had clearly only just got up. His father would not have permitted such slothfulness. He pushed the door aside and knelt in the frame.

'Mother.'

He lowered his head so he could not see, but he could still hear her alarm. She gave a stifled gasp. Her feet tap-tapped over to him. She seized his arms, forced his eyes to hers.

'Your sister is dead,' she cried through sodden gulps.

That news struck harder than word of his father's death. Not long before Robin left his sister had married. He remembered how full she had been of hope and expectation. The intervening four years had been cruel to this family.

When he said nothing, his mother faltered between clasping him into an embrace and pushing him away. 'Your nephew is taken,' she said. 'They took him, they bought him, it was not my doing, everyone said it was for the best, poor orphan child. The lands were his, what could I say, your father was not here to guide me. I listened to others, of course I did.' She released him, paced about again.

'I did not know I had a nephew.'

'We could not tell you. You were dead as far as we knew. Do not reproach me. I lost both my children, and my husband.'

'You have not lost your children,' said Marian, attempting to calm her. 'Your son is here.'

'You know nothing of what I have suffered,' she said, not listening. 'You have not watched your dearests die.'

She collapsed into a chair and sobbed. Robin told one of his mother's attendants to fetch some wine. That generally brought his mother out of her hysterical fits. And if she did not drink it, he certainly would. Marian stood awkwardly in the middle of the chamber, not wishing to intrude on a family's grief, but she could not leave when her duty was to help Lady Joan. Robin sat on the edge of the bed and addressed her.

'When did my sister die?'

'Not long after your father. In childbed. Her husband was already taken in the sickness.'

Now he understood his mother's words about the lands. With his father dead and Robin presumed the same, his sister's son was heir to the whole Locksley estate. Buying the wardship of such a child guaranteed a great estate to a lord – an estate they could use as they wished until the child reached his majority. That day was still over a decade away.

'My mother said my nephew was taken. Where does he live now?'

'Jocelyn's wardship was bought by Lord Eudo de Vipont. He lives with the family in Nottingham Castle.'

'Vipont. I keep hearing that name. They are friends of the king's brother?'

'Good friends. They knew the Count of Mortain in Normandy and came to England when he was given ownership of the castle. He made Eudo his seneschal. It was the count who sold them Jocelyn's wardship.'

'Is the count allowed to sell wardships when the king is abroad?'

Marian's lips pursed but she did not reply. Her face said clearly enough what she thought of the business. Lady Joan's attendant had returned with wine. She drank a cup of it eagerly. Robin took one and held it in his hands. Marian hesitated, then joined him. When the wine had done its work and calmed his mother, Robin asked a final question.

'If this Norman lord holds the Locksley estate how is it that you still live here?'

'Lord Eudo let me stay. It is mine by rights anyway, my dowry. Your father promised me I should have it when we met at the church door.'

'Although widows' dowries are not always safe these days.'

Marian muttered the words. Realising she had been heard she blushed and changed the subject. 'There is something else you should know.' She looked pointedly at Lady Joan.

Robin's mother put down her cup. 'I – yes. Your father… Since we believed you dead, we wanted to keep the tie between our family and the Peverills alive. Of course you could not marry Marian, so her father proposed that he marry me instead.'

A characteristically cool-headed scheme from Sir Walter Peverill.

'My father and I moved to Locksley Hall after the marriage,' said Marian. 'Your mother did not wish to leave. We still visit Peverill Tower sometimes. If you wanted to live in the hall yourself now you are returned I am sure my father would respect that wish and withdraw us to the tower.'

Lady Joan was not happy about that. 'Marian is betrothed to someone else,' she said, with a flush that suggested she was eager to deny her stepdaughter moral superiority. 'Lord Eudo's nephew, Guy. We arranged it this year, we are just waiting for the contract to be agreed.'

Marian stared with concerted effort at the floor. Robin put aside his undrunk wine.

'If I had known everything was so well organised with me dead, I would have spared myself the expense of coming back. Will you excuse me? It is too hot in here.'

Before Marian could say he should not leave or his mother grasp him again he strode from the chamber. He needed air, he thought. Not the cloying perfume fug that hovered over the whole hall now. He marched outside into the sharp cold morning. It was somehow of a perfect piece that Marian was the one to bring him here. She had always been eager to please their parents, running to them to report his wrongdoings. He had told her that would stop as soon as they were married – he would not have a wife who told tales to his mother. There was one mercy, he supposed. If Marian was to marry this Vipont nephew, he was free of one duty his parents had chosen for him. He regretted leaving his cup of wine inside. A desperate thirst had suddenly come over him.

He was on the verge of walking to the kitchens himself to fetch a jug of ale when he remembered his promise to his father. On his return to England, he had sworn to behave as a good lord should. He would pass no more time with brewers and butchers and bastards. He had not asked about Will Scarlette, he realised. Had the sickness taken him too? Since his mother would not stand to be asked about her husband's bastard, Robin would have to find out in the town. No, he thought, his mind turning again. No, he would not. He had sworn to avoid the company of his brother on his return, and somehow he suspected that even dead, his father would know if he broke that oath. If he was not to see Will it did not matter whether he knew if he was alive or not.

A noise echoing across the frozen earth distracted him. At the gatehouse, the watchman had stepped out to talk with a group on the manor's boundary. They were dressed in ragged russet, shredded fleeces giving them a weird look, like sheep walking on their hind legs. Sickly sheep at that. One was a woman, pushing forward a boy with arms thin as sticks. They looked like the pilgrims he had seen in Jerusalem, bones shining through their flesh after months of travel without enough food. Waltheof passed him on the way to the well. Robin called him over and asked about the beggars.

'They are here for alms,' Waltheof explained. 'Scraps from the dinner table.'

'Surely dinner will not be served for another hour.'

'That is why there are so few of them. By the time the bells chime for Terce there will be dozens.'

'Why do so many come here for charity?' He found it hard to believe his mother was lavish in her giving.

'They do not just come here. It is the same at every manor in Nottinghamshire. On a market day you are lucky to get near the castle during dining hours. Ever since the Count of Mortain was granted Nottinghamshire there have been more of them. Many of the old lords have left for their Norman lands and demand money instead of service as their rent. In their place, many of the count's friends from Normandy have come here and imposed duties that had long been forgotten for most men. Merchet, heriot, lerywite. Now there is a ransom to be paid for our king on top of the demands of the lords and the count, the crowds will just get larger.'

Waltheof made no attempt to conceal his anger. Robin was surprised. When he had last been in England common men had not shown such open disregard for their rulers.

'You speak very freely.'

'Forgive me, my lord. The lady Marian does not mind it.'

'Nor do I. But you will find other lords do, I expect.'

He thought of the pale-faced figure on the steps of Nottingham Castle. No doubt that was Marian's new intended. He had looked proud, and proud men did not often seek advice from their inferiors. Waltheof nodded and was silent. Robin watched the beggars at the gates. Sure enough, more sickly stick figures were clustering. He remembered that his father had always made sure to dole out extra alms to children on Candlemas. He sighed.

'Come inside with me. I should grovel to my mother, or she will not let me eat at her table.' He caught the eye of the child in his mother's grasp at the gate. 'And have a loaf sent out for every beggar under twelve.'

The news of Robin of Locksley's return spread through the county fast as fire. It was greeted with disbelief, and then a sweeping change of opinion. The youth who had committed murder and fled justice was condemned. The man who had done so and died at Acre was held to have redeemed his soul: life for life. The crusader who survived years of Saracen attacks, campaign fever and returned home again unharmed must have divine blessing. This once unworthiest of men was now seen as blessed for some higher purpose.

Robin noticed it when he rode to St Oswald's Church for the celebration of Candlemas that night. People stared openly as he passed by with the Peverills' household in rank around him. One old woman, the butcher's widow if he remembered right, called down God's blessing on him. The last time he had seen her she had screamed for him to be hanged. Others, too, smiled and reached up their hands to him – whether to touch him, and Jerusalem by association, or to offer obeisance, he did not know. After that first trip he removed the crusader's palms from his tabard. He put them in a wooden box, beneath the altar in what had been his father's chamber. He resolved that like everything connected with his penance, he would put the palms from his mind. Those years in the East seemed like a fever dream now. It was hard to think, as he walked the icy length of the church where he had been baptised or sank into the mattresses he had slept on for all of the years of his youth, that only a matter of months before he had stood in swirling sandstorms, facing down pots that burst fire and men whose eyes bled murder. The distant past seemed to scrub the recent from memory. When his mind wandered back to the Holy Lands, he thought of the palms in his father's chamber and remembered his oath. He would be a true lord now.

All the same, when he told his new stepfather of his intentions he was regarded with suspicion. Sir Walter Peverill had been appointed sheriff in the second year of King Richard's reign and two years later he still took his responsibilities as the king's representative in Nottinghamshire seriously. As sheriff, he told Robin sternly, he could not permit any leniency within his own household. Those closest to him must be punished more harshly for their misdemeanours even than a stranger, for a man who could not control his family was unworthy to lead the county. Robin suspected more bluster than truth in these words – Sir Walter had always let his heart rule his head, otherwise his precious Marian would have been married years ago – but the sheriff's sense of biased justice might explain how so few of the Locksley servants seemed to have kept their positions under his lordship of the hall. Robin found scarcely any of his father's, or his own, old attendants still there. He set out to put his new stepfather's mind at ease. The last thing he wanted was to be watched and followed by suspicious Peverill servants everywhere he went.

'Please believe me,' he told Sir Walter over supper that first night, 'I swore to live a better life when I returned to Nottinghamshire and I will. I will give you no cause to punish me, as sheriff or lord.'

That had pleased Sir Walter. He had nodded his bushy head and set his chin.

'Then whatever you need from me, Robin, you just ask and I will help you. When you meet the Viponts you will see that they are not unreasonable men. If we are all of the same mind, I am certain we can put all this…' He gestured into the air. My father's death, thought Robin, or word of my own? Or perhaps my nephew and estate being handed over to strangers? Sir Walter did not find the words. 'All of it behind us. A *good lord* will be sure to have no trouble with the law.'

The meeting with the men who had bought his lands from under him was soon in coming. As they walked from Mass a few days after his return, Robin's mother told him in sombre tones that the Viponts were to receive their hospitality that morning.

'Walter has arranged it all for you,' she said, her voice softening over *Walter* in a way it never had for Robin's father. 'The Viponts will dine with us, so you must wear your finest clothes. None of your musty foreign stuff. And bathe, for Jesus's sake. If only they had come yesterday, I would have had one of our pigs stuffed, but since it is Friday eel and trout must do. I do not want you putting them off the meal with your stink. I swear sand still clings to you.' She dusted an invisible mark on his shoulder, then paused, suddenly wistful. 'You look so much more like your father since you came back. You make me feel quite the old woman.' She shook the thought away. 'Eudo de Vipont said that the next time the king's brother visits his estates, he will introduce us to him. Imagine the honour if he joined us here – the Count of Mortain within these walls.'

Beaming again with vain imaginings, his mother went to make up her face and chastise her maids. The bath had already been prepared in Robin's chamber, rosewater scented and floating in herbs. It was a luxury, and he would have taken his time in it, but one of Sir Walter's men had been assigned to bathe him and would not stop chattering questions about the East. At one point Robin honestly thought he would have to describe the cushions King Richard had sat on to treat with Saladin. That was sufficient for him, and the water still warm, he rose from the sponge seat to dress.

The appointed hour arrived. The hall waited for the household's dinner, while Robin and his new family sat in Sir Walter's solar. His mother had thought it better to give the Viponts the choice to eat either in the hall with their attendants or in the privacy of a smaller chamber. Time trickled on. Evidently the Viponts liked to make their hosts wait for the honour of their presence. Marian twitched in her chair. She had never been good at sitting still in one place. Her body was too long, thought Robin, casting a baleful look at her. Lady Joan leant over and rearranged Marian's hands.

'You should have let me powder your face,' she said, her mood soured by the delay. 'You are red.'

'Just a little flushed, I think,' said Sir Walter, patting his daughter's hand tenderly. 'A lady is allowed that when her betrothed comes to visit, hm?'

He grinned at Lady Joan, but Marian had only gone redder. Robin would bet five pence she was biting her cheek so as not to respond. At last there was a flurry of noise in the courtyard. Lady Joan rearranged herself, rearranged Marian, and stood as their long-awaited guests arrived.

'Welcome, friends,' said Sir Walter, raising his arms in greeting. 'We are so glad to have you with us on this happy day.'

The Viponts were all pale-skinned, dark haired and clad in various tones of crimson. One of them stepped forward, his mantle cut long in the old fashion, his chin bearded and flecked with grey.

'Lord Eudo,' Lady Joan whispered to Robin. The head of the family.

'It is our honour to join you, good Sir Walter,' said Eudo, embracing his host. 'My lady Joan, lady Marian. And this must be the Lord of Locksley.' He turned sharp eyes on Robin.

'By birth,' said Robin, smiling dryly. 'Although not currently in land.'

Eudo laughed. One of his relatives, larger and less carefully groomed, stopped smiling abruptly. Robin suspected that had they been alone, he would have dealt Robin a stinging word – or, looking at the size of his arms, a blow.

'It is a joy to me,' said Eudo, 'that Lady Joan has had her son restored. And that young Jocelyn may know his uncle. Jocelyn!'

He called behind him and from the stairwell came a child. Robin's heart lurched. Jocelyn was the image of Robin's sister as a child: dainty, red-cheeked, straight-nosed and with eyes large as a doe's. Jocelyn knelt in greeting to his family. Eudo waved him up and put his hands on the boy's shoulders in a gesture both proprietary and paternal.

'I hope that we have done nothing that would displease you in raising him so far,' said Eudo to Robin. 'We flatter ourselves that even had the regrettable misunderstanding over your death not arisen, you would still have been content to let Jocelyn pass his youth in our household. Perhaps you have heard that we are fortunate enough to enjoy the good graces of Prince John, Count of Mortain? We are happy to use what influence we have with the count to Jocelyn's advantage. Perhaps his marriage might be arranged to one of the great heiresses of England? In time, of course.'

Robin knew a politician when he met one. Eudo clearly had a gift for manipulating those around him, and his mother and Sir Walter beamed at him as if he were a prince himself. But it was a cruel trick to bring the boy with him on this first meeting, to suggest however subtly that by wanting the restoration of his rightful estate Robin would disadvantage his own kin.

'Surely the marriage of wards,' said Robin, 'is a matter only the king can arrange?'

'The king and his government,' said Eudo, 'that is certainly true. But while the count is not regent, he has such good will among his barons and the justiciars of England that whatever he asks is sure to be granted. Perhaps, being so long abroad, you have not had the chance to understand how things in the king's lands now stand? We –' he gestured to his family '– knew the count in Normandy for many years, and have seen how excellent a lord he is.'

Perhaps that was so, but Robin had heard stories only of the count's failures. In the king's army the word had been that his brother was not made regent because he could not be trusted with any real power. The title of Mortain and the promise of a rich wife had been all that King Richard was willing to allow him. Nonetheless, perhaps it was not wise to debate such matters on a first meeting. As long as the count was in England and the king was not the Viponts had it in their power to keep the Locksley estate if they wished. If Robin was to have any hope of regaining it he must put aside personal displeasure and be as subtle and falsely charming as Lord Eudo.

'I have not had the honour of being introduced to your family,' he said, turning to the glowering fat man.

'Ah yes,' said Eudo. 'This is my brother, Ranulf. And his son, Guy.' Sure enough, it was the pale man Robin had seen at Nottingham Castle. Guy bowed his head with less successful guile than his relatives. 'And my own son, Serlo.' A slender mirror of Eudo himself. 'Many of our attendants you will doubtless come to know. My steward, Lanfranc –' a stocky presence to the rear of the group '– is trusted throughout this county. The others you may meet in time. But I fear the ladies here have waited too long to dine, and are slim enough that they should not miss a meal lest they shrink away entirely.'

Lady Joan blushed appreciatively. Sir Walter took the hint and called for dinner. They ate, surprisingly to Robin, in the hall among their men. The Viponts all brought their own knives to the table, and Serlo wiped his hands disdainfully on the linen napkins Lady Joan had provided. Obviously he was used to better quality. Robin had hoped to have the chance to speak to Jocelyn, but whether through protective design or out of rigorous adherence to etiquette, the boy was placed far from him, at the outer edge of the table next to Guy. After grace was said, hands washed and the first course laid before the host, everyone fell to their meals. For a time, all was idle chatter in the hall. But when the second course was on the table Eudo turned to Robin.

'Let us speak plainly with one another. You wish to regain those lands that were your father's for yourself. And I have no desire to keep a man from what is his by right – your family have accepted that you are Robin of Locksley, and so I accept that also.'

'Good,' said Robin. 'Then it is a simple matter. I will take them at your earliest convenience.'

'However,' said Eudo, smiling politely, 'more than your own rights are at question here. What of Jocelyn's rights? What of my own, and my brother's, and our sons who expected to succeed us to our estates? We purchased Jocelyn's wardship in good trust that the Locksley estates would be ours to use until he reaches his majority. Now, are we simply to step aside and hand over those lands to you, without going through the proper channels? Without compensation?'

Robin was about to offer compensation himself, if money was all that was in question.

'The truth of the matter,' continued Eudo before he could speak, 'is that we bought the lands at a very favourable rate – favourable, I mean, to the count. After the king granted him the county of Nottingham and he honoured me by appointing me his seneschal here I, of course, wanted to repay him for his trust and financial assistance seemed the obvious means to do so. The count needs to maintain the court of a prince and with the additional cost of financing the king's endeavours he has often found himself in debt. As a result, if we were to return the Locksley estate to you at the rate we purchased them I fear you would be repaying us for many years to come. The estate yields little in financial terms, alas, due to poor harvest and other matters only God can affect. If we return the lands at a lower rate, we shall ourselves lose out. And that is to say nothing of the rights of your mother and her husband. They expected to live their dotage in Locksley Hall and Peverill Tower – I have heard them speak of it – and you would deny them that right by claiming the whole estate for yourself.'

'So what do you suggest, Lord Vipont?'

'I think it would be wisest to proceed through the courts. I know a little of the laws of England, so I can offer my advice?'

'Certainly.'

'Your first decision must be which claim you make on the estate. You must send to Westminster for a writ, either of novel disseisin, suggesting we have illegally usurped you – which I hope you do not feel we have done – or perhaps for that of mort d'ancestor, given that you may claim the lands as those of your late father. But I fear you can choose only one writ, which you must submit to the sheriff, your stepfather, for him to empanel a jury to decide if the case has merit and then it will be passed on to the royal justices. If at any point the writ you choose is questioned you would have to begin your suit all over again.'

Eudo spread his hands wide, palms up. He had more than 'a little' knowledge of English law, Robin thought ruefully. He had never had much patience for the intricacies of the law himself. If he were to get much further in this suit it was clear he would need to employ the services of a good clerk as quickly as possible.

'Whichever course I take, whether mort disseisin –'

'Mort d'ancestor,' corrected Eudo with a smile.

'Yes, that is what I meant. However I proceed, it will be months before the estate is restored to me.'

'I am afraid so. We had a visit from the royal justices after Epiphany. Their next circuit of this county will not be soon in coming.'

Robin suppressed a wave of frustration. If Eudo had wanted to overwhelm him with the challenges of his case, he had succeeded. He speared a slice of meat on his plate then changed his mind and laid down his knife. Across the hall Jocelyn looked between the empty plate in front of him and the communal bowl of meat on the table. When Guy turned away to talk to Marian, his little fingers reached into the bowl and seized a ball of pastry, stuffing it into his mouth before anyone could tell him off for bad manners. Robin smiled.

'What about my nephew?'

'While we hold his wardship we have a moral obligation to bear the expense of raising the child. But my family have also come to truly care for him in the time he has been with us. Serlo has a child only slightly older. They are like brothers to each other.'

That stung. Jocelyn had had a hard start to life, losing both parents and his male relatives before he was even out of infancy. For all Robin might want the child to join him at Locksley Hall, it was cruel to force another upheaval on him before Robin had the estate to care for him.

'If he is happy with you and you with him, he should stay in your home. But I wish to meet with him now and then. Does he ride yet?'

'He has ridden once or twice on Serlo's son's training pony. He fell once, but it has not deterred him.'

'That will be my sister's blood in him,' Robin smiled. 'She was stubborn as a mule.'

'You may visit your nephew when you wish, provided we have some warning of your coming. I would wish to give the Lord of Locksley proper hospitality.'

Eudo raised his cup, offering it towards Robin. He raised his own, and together they toasted the agreement. It only occurred to Robin later that Eudo had managed in one meal to persuade him to live as a dependent of his mother for as long as it took the royal justices to visit Nottinghamshire again. For all his charm, he should not be underestimated.

Time moved slowly at Locksley Hall. The days were an endlessly repeating round of sedentary activities. Morning mass rose them, the household broke its fast on bread and cheese – Lady Joan and Sir Walter on a lot of cheese – and idled the morning away. Dinner lasted hours with only the briefest of afternoon pauses, then the sheriff and his lady insisted on drinking wine and taking bread before Evensong. As light failed the candles were lit, supper was served, then they gambled a little, more prayers were said and at last, just as Robin's threshold for boredom was reached, Sir Walter announced that the two of them would leave for the nightly audit. This at least necessitated conversation with the hall's servants, discussing expenditure and reporting any wrongdoing. Robin's father had been wont to punish all manner of minor sins – gaming for money, swearing, late arrival at Matins – with a seat in the ewery during meal times, enjoying nothing but bread and water. Sir Walter inclined to fines, fines and more fines. The only real discussion was how much the fine would be, or for how long the servant's wages should be docked. At last, the gates were barred, the household offices shut up and the porters went out to keep their watch. Even then, Robin found little peace. He lay in his bed, painfully awake, mind turning over and over the unimportant details of the day, restless while his body grew fat on inactivity. He had no brother, no male cousin or friend at hand to accompany him riding or hunting. With all the sitting and drinking forced on him it was a miracle he did not piss himself by Evensong.

Robin remembered now why he had so often disappeared during the cloying rituals of his parents' day. While the service areas rumbled with life, the servants everywhere running through their tasks without rest, the rhythms of a lord's day were as treacle. He watched from the mist-smeared window of the solar as rain swept across the flat meadows, soaking the earth and striking the forest beyond. The trees of Sherwood shivered in the downpour. He remembered how, in parts of the forest, the trees crowded so close together that rain hardly seemed to fall at all. They had been so cold, he and Will, as they huddled in a hollow trunk for warmth, hiding from the sheriff's men and their families. He smiled. In the Holy Land he had drawn on that memory – of the aching cold, deep in his bones and the dribble of water from his nose to his chin – when he tried to stave off heatstroke. It was hard to say when he had been more uncomfortable: when dripping in sweat or soaked in rain. Now, he thought, and almost spoke aloud. Beside the fire his mother snored as she dozed and Marian squinted into her sewing. Sitting in this hour-sapping chamber is worse than rain or sun. And the knowledge that he was doing as his father wished was no comfort to him at all.

Shrovetide

In the depths of the forest, Robin had known peace. Away from fretting family and the whirling world, all that existed was the sun shining shards through the fluttering emerald leaves. The soft rustle of animal life and low creak of ancient roots. The breath of the wind soft on his face, cooling the patches where the sun did not light it. He held out his arms, felt the air dance through his fingers. His eyes were closed but he could still see the movement of the trees as flickers of light shone grey and red in his blinkered vision. This was God's true cathedral, he thought, and inhaled the incense of the cool damp earth.

A raindrop landed between his eyes and woke him from his reverie. He pulled his hood further down over his face to protect it. It was winter still and the forest would be dark and full of scratching sticks.

'The weather in England has not improved.'

Sir Walter laughed. 'No, you can always be certain of rain in Nottinghamshire.'

They rode towards St Oswald's hall, where the Hundred Court of Locksley was assembling. Howling winds whipped along the valley floor where the road ran, and their horses' hooves stuck in the cloying clay. Robin glanced through the lashing rain at the men and women digging up the earth, pulling out stones and weeds in a bid to ready the soil for spring crops. It was early for such tasks, but there seemed little else to occupy them. The last Lenten season Robin had spent in England saw lambs birthing and goats bleating all over the county, but there were no signs of such life now.

'Has it been a poor year for the flocks?' he called to Sir Walter.

'Not bad,' said Sir Walter. Noticing Robin frown he continued, 'Many animals had to be slaughtered for the count's household when he stayed in Nottingham at New Year. And we had the royal justices and auditors here after Epiphany. It was an honour, but an expensive one.'

Robin watched one of the workers – whether man or woman, he could hardly tell – stand up straight and stretch their back. The figure noticed the sheriff's party and bent the knee, face disappearing into a rain-soaked hood. The prospect of spending a day dispensing justice to men whose pigs had trampled another's field or lords who believed their boundaries had been infringed by a neighbour's huntsmen was far from enthralling, and the foul weather had done little to raise Robin's spirits. But he needed to prove his willingness to knuckle down to such tasks, if only to ensure that when a writ requesting the restoration of his estate went before a jury of local lords they would not reject it. The sight of the poor souls scratching the earth in hope of future food at least served as a reminder that his own misfortunes – a cloak that did not keep out the cold, a home he could not call his own – were small indeed by comparison.

'How many will attend the court today?'

'A few dozen. The usual lower born men who generally hold this court with the bailiff, and then some of the local lords. These larger assemblies of the Hundred Court with the sheriff only happen twice a year. They never last long. We are just ensuring law is being followed as the king would wish. Watch your purse when we reach St Oswald's. Thieves and vagrants always flock to the church when the lords come to hold court.'

Robin looked disbelievingly at the escort of attendants who rode in a protective ring around them. A thief would be lucky to get at a purse through them. Sir Walter followed his gaze.

'Believe me, Robin, these days you cannot be too careful.'

Sure enough, around the walls of St Oswald's church where the Hundred Court assembled a bustle of ragged figures churned back and forth. The horses lifted the sheriff's party above the melée, but Robin could easily see how on foot you could lose your possessions to a cutpurse. That moment a face in the crowd caught his eye. A mirror of his own, but the chin sharper, the eyes darker, the clothes patched and poor where Robin's were new bolts of wool. He pulled at his reins in surprise and his horse flinched.

'What is wrong?' asked Sir Walter, gesturing to one of his men in alarm.

'Nothing,' said Robin hastily. 'Someone I thought I recognised. I was mistaken.'

But there had been no mistake. Will Scarlette had seen him. No doubt he wondered why, with news of Lord Locksley's return echoing through the county, he had not received a visit from his half-brother. Robin set his eyes towards the gate into the yard of St Oswald's, not looking back until the gate was closed behind them. An antechamber had been set aside for those attending the court to remove their sodden mantles and boots and leave their weapons in the care of their attendants. St Oswald's was not a large church, nor a particularly rich one, but the chapterhouse was warm, with a ring of seats surrounding the central space where those accused of wrongdoing would stand before their local lawgivers. Robin was not surprised to see that Eudo de Vipont and his family were already there, exchanging greetings and good humour with their fellow lords, paying little attention to the lesser men of the Hundred. Eudo came to meet the sheriff and Robin with arms outstretched.

'It is a pleasure to have you join us, Lord Locksley. I fear the faces you see today may be rather changed from the last time you attended a local assize. Many of the old lords of this county have departed. A number, I know, went with you to the Holy Land.'

'And have not returned,' said Ranulf, with a bleak smile that suggested it would have been no great shame if Robin had been among those unfortunates.

'More I fear have had to leave to defend their lands in other counties. There were rumours in the New Year that England would be attacked by the French King Philippe,' said Eudo. 'So all those lords with lands on the coast went to protect them.'

'The rumours came to nothing,' said Sir Walter reassuringly.

'But now there are fresh whispers that King Philippe invades the Norman lands of your lords. The Count of Mortain has gone to Normandy himself to hold the French king back. I do not doubt it will only be a matter of weeks before he returns with your good lords of Nottinghamshire.'

'Since your own lands lie in Normandy,' said Robin, 'why have you not gone with the count to defend them?'

'We have brothers there who are doing it,' said Ranulf.

Of course you do, thought Robin. Doubtless the Viponts are legion.

'You speak of changes to our assize,' said a voice behind the Viponts. The sound of it sent a shudder down Robin's spine. 'But I see our Lord of Locksley is a changed man too.'

A thin figure stood up to meet them, red hair thinning above a sharp-witted face.

'My lord Geoffrey D'Alselin,' said Robin. He bent his knee lower than he had to anyone since he returned.

'Rise yourself, my lord,' said D'Alselin. 'You and I now are equal in the eyes of this assize.'

He looked Robin up and down, his left eye squinting as it always did when he concentrated. The last time those eyes had focused so intently on Robin it had ended in his exile to the Holy Land.

'My son is gone to Normandy to defend our lands,' said D'Alselin. 'It is a difficulty your family have been spared, since you have no lands there to defend. Nor any in Nottinghamshire at present.' He laughed. The hairs on Robin's neck bristled with anger but he did not rise to the bait. d'Alselin leant closer. 'Tell me how my friend the earl of Derby died.'

'There is no need for that now, Geoffrey,' said Sir Walter brusquely.

'I will gladly tell Lord D'Alselin anything he wishes to know,' said Robin. He forced a smile that emerged as a grimace. 'The earl had camp fever.'

'A poor death for a good man.' Lord D'Alselin crossed himself and stepped back, apparently content. 'I am pleased to find you spoke true, Sir Walter. It seems Master Robin has finally learnt to control his temper.'

He turned his back to Robin, giving him time to look about. D'Alselin was one of the few faces he recognised. The old Earl of Derby and the Lord Furnivall had gone with him on Crusade, and neither returned. Presumably their sons were in Normandy now, along with the other absent lords. But there were also faces that were new to him, men who spoke with the same slight accents of the Viponts and regarded Robin with disinterest. He went to sit at the sheriff's side but his way was blocked by Guy.

'I hope you do not feel I have stolen anything from you.' His face was wide-eyed and serious. For some reason it reminded Robin of a child. 'I refer to the lady Marian, of course.'

Robin barked a laugh, then realised he should not have. Guy looked affronted.

'No,' said Robin swiftly. You've taken something I didn't want, he thought.

But said instead, 'I wish you both joy. When do you marry?'

'There are still some legal matters to settle.' His eye darted in Eudo's direction. Legal matters, Robin thought. That meant the Viponts were holding out for more money. 'But we hope by the year's end.'

'We', Robin noted. Had Marian managed to find a husband who viewed her with affection, who looked to her as a true partner? That was a fortunate abnormality in arranged marriages.

'I look forward to attending.'

Robin sat before Guy could press any further conversation on him. Sir Walter was calling the court to attention. The bailiff of the Locksley Hundred, responsible for keeping the peace and reporting all crimes before this court, stood to present the various cases that still needed to be settled before they retired for Lent. Most of the cases brought forward and penalties awarded were so simple as to require almost no concentration from the men in attendance. A butcher had carried away a pail of blood and entrails by day rather than night. Six pence fine was demanded. A horse had been left standing in the marketplace on a market day. A penny fine in recompense. A bailiff had been rebuked by a local woman. A shilling fine to be paid to the bailiff directly. A saddler had thrown hides over the Trent Bridge to shave them. Half a mark, as it was his second offence.

Robin's head slumped in his hand halfway to sleep when there was a shuffle of movement near the door and the bailiff's words roused him suddenly to alertness.

'I wondered when you would arrive, John Blunt.'

Robin turned towards the door. He knew that name very well. It had once been as dear to him as Will Scarlette's.

'Blunt is the chief tithing-man for St Oswald's,' Sir Walter whispered. 'He is responsible for reporting the crimes of this tithing. It is not like him to be late.'

'Forgive me for my delay,' said John, reverencing to the chamber. His French was stilted. He had never been good at it. 'I was not allowed admittance by the steward Lanfranc.' He looked to the Viponts, whose faces were all innocent amazement.

'Master Blunt told me he had a very important matter to raise before this court,' said the bailiff. 'If the sheriff will permit it?'

Sir Walter nodded his permission and John Blunt stood to address the chamber. His eye lingered on Robin in momentary surprise. Robin looked away. He did not want to remind the lords present of his old familiarity with the common-born man before them. To express himself clearly, John made his report in English.

'I was one of those appointed to circuit the Hundred of Locksley at Michaelmas and declare all the moveable property of those living here. I then gave this information to law-worthy knights – men in the household of Lord Eudo de Vipont, overlord of this Hundred. My declaration, and that of other trusted men in this Hundred, was used to assess the level of tax we all had to pay through Lord Eudo to the Crown. But when the demand for taxes came, it was wrong. The information we had provided had been changed, so it appeared all those living in this Hundred owed more than we had to give. We had to pay, and so we did. Yet when these taxes were made over to the royal tax collectors by Lord Eudo's men, they claimed there was too little. Somehow, these knights had miscalculated twice. Firstly, in the amount collected and secondly in the amount given to the Crown. This is not the only case of such trickery I have heard. Across this county other hundredmen have reported the same thing happening, but always on the lands of Lord de Vipont. I appeal that this court fines Lord Eudo for the same amount of money that was taken from his tenants and appoints the knights of a different lord to collect the taxes and deliver them to the royal officials in future.'

When John fell silent the whole chamber watched for Lord Eudo's reaction. He sat back in his chair, with no apparent signs of either guilt or concern. Sir Walter asked him for his response to the accusation.

'My response? My response is that this Englishman lies.'

'I do not lie,' said John angrily. 'And I have oath-takers from across the Hundred willing to swear that what I say is true.'

'Twelve of them?' Sir Walter asked.

'Yes.'

'And Lord Eudo, can you gather twelve men to swear to your innocence?'

'As many as you wish. I shall have both the knights this man has accused and my clerks summoned to whatever court pleases you, sheriff.'

'This is too serious a claim to be settled today,' said Sir Walter. 'It shall be heard before the county court when Lent is over. Both of you must bring your oath-takers to it.'

And with that the court's business was concluded. Robin deliberately avoided John Blunt, not wanting to be drawn into conversation with the man who accused Eudo de Vipont of extorting money from the Crown. Whether Eudo had or not – and it was not unlikely, given how often in the past Robin had heard stories of corrupt tax collection – he needed the support of the Viponts more than he needed the friendship of John Blunt at that moment in time. When he went to the antechamber where he had left his mantle and boots, he was told they had been removed to a smaller chamber, away from the bustle of departing hundredmen and lords. It was some relief to be out of reach of all those inquiring eyes and mouths. He tugged his boots on, still damp despite their time by the fire. A shadow falling over him made him blink, then an arm was around his neck and a vice grip tugged him into the darkness of a closet. As he writhed against the assailant, reaching for the sword that was still with his servant, he heard a laugh that stopped him. The grip relaxed, and hands black with dirt pulled him to his feet.

'I thought you'd be quicker than that.'

Robin looked up to that sharp chin and twisted smile again.

'What in Christ's name are you doing, Will?' he cried, rubbing at his neck.

'Oh, so you do know me then?'

Robin scowled. 'Yes I know you. But what are you doing in here? This is a private chamber. If you were found breaking into an assize of the court you could be arrested.'

Will shrugged. 'Wouldn't be the first time.'

'It might be the last.' Robin tugged at his mantle to put it back in order.

'Why haven't you come to find me? You've been back long enough.'

'I did not know where to look.'

'I haven't moved.'

Robin would not be drawn now. The last thing he needed at his first Hundred Court since his return was for Sir Walter or one of the other lords to see him hiding in a closet with Will.

'I need to go. Sir Walter will send someone to find me.' Will stood in the way of the door, folding his arms as a challenge. 'Move aside.'

He nudged Will, intending to march past him, but Will shoved back.

'I don't care to move aside. Like I was a dog or a woman. I'm your brother.'

'Bastard brother,' said Robin.

Even before the words were out of his mouth he regretted them. He started to speak, to take them back but Will was already stepping away from him, his face contorted in disgust.

'That's how it'll be, is it? You'll be calling my mother a whore next I expect. Have her flogged through the streets for ribaldry, pull her along by her hair.'

'What are you…?'

'All I'd expect of the Lord of Locksley. All I deserve from him. You're your mother's son now, and I'm mine, and our father's dead. There's an end to it.'

Will turned his back on Robin. Robin reached to take his arm, but Will shook his hold away. Robin reached again, and Will tried to slip from his grasp, pushed Robin, and Robin pushed back. It did not feel a heavy blow, but Will had not spent years in mail, swinging a sword and marching on fortresses. He was weaker now than Robin. The push knocked him backwards and he lost his footing, falling heavily out of the closet and onto the hard floor of the antechamber. Robin did not put out a hand to help him. Will staggered to his feet, staring at his brother. He was startled, perhaps by the fall, perhaps at finding the two of them unequal now in strength. He stumbled backwards, righted himself, gave a sneering bow and ran from the chamber.

Robin clenched his fists, fighting the urge to kick something or throw whatever was at hand into the fire. All he had were his own clothes and the chair in the chamber, neither of which would be wise. Why did Will have to be so bloody-minded? Why could he not have waited, the fool? What was he doing sneaking into the church, approaching Robin as if the past four years had never happened? Robin pulled at his mantle again, tugging his hood up. The worst thing was he had missed his brother, he truly had, and if Will had only waited a few more days he probably would have gone to find him out. But now there was no question. He could not trust Will to be subtle, or to do what was wise.

Sir Walter appeared at the doorway to the chamber.

'Is all well?' he asked. 'I heard a noise.'

'I tripped over my mantle,' said Robin. 'Can we get back to the hall? I need a drink.'

He led the way back into the driving rain, hoping the rough ride home might beat his vexations out of him.

Try as he might, Robin could not put Will from his mind. The bastard wheeled and turned through it so that he could get no peace. Back at Locksley Hall Robin's mother could be heard from halfway down the stairs loudly instructing a servant about the Shrove feast they were hosting that night. They had guests arriving, she was saying, and everything must be perfect. The very last thing Robin wanted to do at that moment was have his mother instruct him on his clothing and manners. He would go where she would not look, and where he might actually find some sensible conversation. He headed for the kennels.

The master of the hounds was one of the few old servants who Robin still recognised. Wulfstan was his name, and there was a good deal wolfish about the rest of him too. There was a quick, dark grin in his balding pate, and sinewy strength in his crinkled limbs. Wulfstan had always been good to Robin, covering for the lad when he knew him to be out making trouble and giving him the best puppies of any litter with a wink and a quiet. 'This one's for you, Master Robin.' He met the new Lord of Locksley with more warmth than anyone else, going to tousle his hair before stopping himself.

'No mustn't do that,' he said, holding up his hands. 'Master Robin's a lord now. He's full growed and uglier than ever.'

Wulfstan showed him around the oak beds and carefully arranged leashes of the kennels. The smell of the place set Robin's blood singing. They were not far from the stables, and the scent of the horses and hounds, the straw and leather, reminded him of the first hunts he had been on with his father. The first time he had been sick with fear, and only his determination not to let anyone see it had got him through the day without puking.

'Do you remember the puppy you had from that old hound of yours?' asked Wulfstan. 'The sighthound.'

'Husdent. Yes.'

Wulfstan unleashed a hound.

'This is him.'

The pup was now an adult hunter, muscular and lean with a silver coat. He did not recognise his old master, but was excited enough at sight of a new face to run around his knees. Robin dropped onto his haunches to calm the hound.

'You must take him out for a run,' said Wulfstan. 'There won't be a hunt for a while with this weather. The hounds are getting fat.'

'You and I both,' said Robin, scratching Husdent under the chin.

The sound of hooves and calls echoed from the courtyard on the other side of the stable. Lady Joan's guests must be arriving. Robin rubbed Husdent's ears. At least he had an excuse to stay in the kennels longer. His mother would not be best pleased if he greeted their guests in the courtyard reeking of dog and covered in slather. But Husdent stood up suddenly and began barking. Robin felt him quiver and before he could stop him the hound flashed past, baying towards the courtyard.

'Back, Husdent,' called Wulfstan, starting after him.

'I'll go,' said Robin.

He ran through the shadows to where Husdent was shouting, at the edge of the courtyard. It was not like a hunting dog to bark at horses. But the next instant all was clear. Husdent had his jaw at a lapdog pup's throat, mouthing threats while the pup leapt for his ears. The pair tumbled over one another as they fought, wheeling towards Robin. A woman's voice called but the pup ignored it.

'Come here. Come – now.'

With a sigh, the woman approached. Robin seized Husdent's collar and yanked him from the pup, but still the smaller dog jumped and yapped.

'Where have you gone, naughty pup?' The woman stepped into the shadows and Robin could not avoid being seen. 'Oh excuse me,' said the woman – the lady – wrapped up in furs against the bitter wind. Robin bowed his head and scooped up the pup.

'This must be yours.' He handed it to the lady, who gathered it into her cloak, wiping dust from its head.

'He is always causing trouble,' she said, smiling apologetically.

'How old is he?'

'Three months.' She gripped the pup's neck to stop it wriggling. 'Old enough to know better.' She nuzzled it, allowing Robin a moment to look at her. He did not recognise her, and she was striking enough that he did not think he would have forgotten a meeting. Her skin was parchment-pale, her cheeks flushed from the wind and ride. Her hair was dark and neatly tucked back beneath her veil. The pup nudged a lock out of place in his twisting. She sighed again.

'Let me help you,' said Robin, stepping forward to take the puppy, one hand still at Husdent's collar.

'Thank you,' she said, and took the chance to look at him as he had her. A smile of recognition crossed her face. 'You are Lord Robin. You will not remember me, I suppose. We met some years ago, when I was a child. I remember that scar.'

She touched her chin softly, mirroring a pale slice through Robin's own. And drawing his eye to her slightly parted lips.

'You must forgive me,' said Robin, not as smoothly as he wanted.

'Elaine Peverill,' she said. 'Sir Walter is my uncle.'

Robin had a flash of memory: a dark haired girl sulking with Marian around the walled garden at Peverill Tower. She had certainly changed since they last met. Having tucked the lock behind her ear, she took back the pup. Her hands stood stark white against Robin's travel- and kennel-smeared skin.

'I heard Marian is marrying someone else now,' Elaine said. 'A Vieuxpont?'

'Vipont, yes.'

'You do not mind?'

Robin was surprised by the directness of her questioning. 'No. We are not well suited to each other.'

'She said that also.'

Elaine smiled, and Robin sensed he was being mocked. He found he did not mind. A man's voice called from the yard.

'I am here,' Elaine called back. 'I should go inside and meet everyone properly. Shall I pretend I did not see you by the kennels?'

'That might be best.'

Elaine curtsied. 'Then it was delightful not to have met you again, Robin.'

She turned her back before Robin could bow in kind. He glanced at Husdent, who gazed up at him with a baleful expression.

'Yes,' said Robin to the hound. 'Isn't she?'

Having washed and changed out of his travelling clothes, Robin joined the party for their Shrove Tuesday feast. Elaine and her attendants had already greeted the rest of the family by the time he arrived.

'So this must be the Lord of Locksley,' she said when she saw him, curtsying demurely. She shot him a mischievous grin. 'I would hardly have recognised you.'

The table was laid with three courses, six dishes in each. There were birds of all kinds, boiled and stuffed and minced and sliced; in sweet wine sauces, and thick blanched ones; in tarts and custards and pastries. As one of the servers sang grace the memory of the beggars at the gates flashed across Robin's mind. Not many men in the county would be feasting tonight. He wondered if Will and his mother had enough to eat. He had looked thinner, poorer than Robin remembered.

'You are serious,' said Elaine, puncturing his glum thoughts.

'I was just thinking of a friend. Forgive me.'

'What is there to forgive? It is only right we think some serious thoughts tonight.'

She passed a piece of pheasant under the table, where her lapdog was wriggling back and forth. She smiled at Robin conspiratorially. He smiled back. On the other side of him Marian was picking at her plate.

'Not hungry?' said Robin.

Marian cut a piece of venison slowly. 'Not particularly.'

'Eat, Marian,' cried Sir Walter jovially. 'You will regret it when we are abstaining.'

'The more that is left,' said his daughter with a sidelong glance at Lady Joan, 'the more may go in alms tonight.'

'I intend to make the most of this opportunity to eat what I like,' said Elaine, trying to cheer the mood. 'I cannot refuse piglets and stuffed poussins and – what is this again, Uncle?'

'Blandyssorye,' answered Lady Joan. 'Almond milk and ground chicken.'

'It is all delicious,' said Elaine. 'I would not think of leaving it. Marian, you may give me yours if you like.'

'Alms are really meant for the poor,' Marian muttered.

Before she could say more Robin reached over her, speared the largest piece of meat on her plate and deposited it on Elaine's instead. Elaine laughed out loud. Marian stared at the empty space on her plate in resigned silence. Robin grinned at her, knowing that she would not get up from the table until Sir Walter did, no matter how much she wished to. And thus, with Elaine for company and twenty dishes in front of him, Robin found he could pass the evening without once thinking of Will Scarlette again.

The third Sunday of Lent blew the clouds from winter's gloom and dawned with a sky cold and blue. The sight cheered Robin's spirits as he rode towards the parklands of Nottingham Castle, a falcon on the arm of the attendant next to him. Alan was the man's name, and Robin had chosen him from the sheriff's household because he was sombre and inclined to silence. Eudo de Vipont had given permission for Robin to meet with Jocelyn that day and enjoy some pursuits beyond the confines of chambers and halls. Since Jocelyn was still too young to ride out hunting hares and roe deer, Robin had chosen hawking instead. True, he would have to pay penance in alms for defying church strictures during Lent, but he would rather do that than sit in a solar with the child, passing the hours at backgammon.

As Robin reached the shadow of Nottingham's walls he heard a shout behind him. He turned to find Elaine, Marian and their attendants cantering towards them. Elaine drew up her horse alongside his, beaming and breathless from the ride.

'I hope you do not mind if we join you? It is such a fine day we could not bear to waste it sitting in our chamber.'

'We?' repeated Robin, casting a glance at Marian.

'Marian enjoys sunshine as much as any lady,' said Elaine, putting her hand on her cousin's warmly. 'And she is fortunate, for she does not burn like I do. However, I decided I could risk freckles for your sake, Lord Locksley. As long as you do not mind? I so wish to meet your nephew.'

Robin said he did not mind at all, and the party continued to Nottingham Castle together. In the courtyard they found Eudo and Guy in conversation with their grooms.

'Then it was not false report,' said Eudo as he noticed the ladies in the party. 'My daughter-in-law told me she had received a message from Locksley Hall promising additions to our gathering. I am delighted to see it was true.'

He reached out a hand to Elaine to assist her from her horse. Guy did the same for Marian. Robin swung from the saddle himself.

'You have brought your own bird, Lord Locksley,' said Guy, raising an eyebrow while he tucked Marian's arm into his own. 'There was no need. We had many of our finest falcons sent from Normandy so we would not miss our favourite sport.'

'I understood English birds to be the best,' said Elaine. 'Does not the Count of Mortain prefer an English peregrine when he hunts crane?'

'Very true,' said Eudo genially. 'But we think our Norman falconers have the better of the English in training. Them we have also brought with us.'

'Well I shall happily make use of your mews, if you are willing to share your fine beasts with us ladies?'

'It will be our pleasure,' said Guy. He offered his free arm to Elaine. 'And you may choose one for Jocelyn from our number, if you wish.'

The trio proceeded ahead of Eudo and Robin to the mews while their attendants saw to the horses. Robin tried not to glare at the back of Guy's head for depriving him of Elaine's company when he already had Marian to entertain him. The mews was a new construction, daub walls and thatched roof still fresh scented. Inside there were peregrines and sakers, lanners and goshawks, even sparrowhawks for clerical visitors.

'This one we are still training,' said Guy of a creature seeled on its perch.

Noticing the bird, Eudo added, 'Our falconer has only this morning had a wild bird caught for us to train. Perhaps you wish to watch the seeling? I have never seen it done.'

His guests agreed. Eudo led Robin to a space at the rear of the mews, where the seeling could take place in darkness and quiet. The falconer already had the bird swathed in a moist cloth, its wings pressed firmly into the body without stifling the beast's breathing. When Eudo nodded for him to proceed the falconer handed the bird to an assistant who grasped its feet, the talons gleaming sharp as knives in the half-light. The falconer pulled out a round needle, linen threaded, and carefully pushed it through the bird's lower eyelid, taking care not to perforate the thin membane there. Drawing the needle through the eyelid, the falconer pulled the thread up and over the falcon's head, towing the lower eyelid with it until it was drawn all the way over the upper. Then he repeated the process on the other eye, so that the bird could see nothing. It had been hooded with its own lids. He tied the ends of the thread carefully atop its head, moving feathers to cover them so that the falcon did not scratch them free. The falconer took the bird back from his assistant and presented it to Eudo.

'There, my lord,' he said. 'Now I must blunt its talons and fit the jesses.'

'Is it not remarkable,' murmured Elaine, 'that so keen a predator can be tamed simply by closing its eyes?'

'I have seen this done by an Arab,' said Robin, watching the bird sit quite still on the falconer's arm, head slightly cocked as if listening. 'But he used a leather hood to blind the bird.'

'It might work as well,' said the falconer. 'Perhaps I shall try it when I man the next one. With my lord's permission, of course.'

'Perhaps,' said Eudo. 'We will leave you to your work.'

The ladies having chosen a bird each, and Robin refused the offer to give Jocelyn a Vipont falcon, the group remounted their horses and rode to the sward beyond the castle at the edge of the forest. There, the rest of the Viponts waited in a ring around Jocelyn, who sat on a low trotting pony. Spying his uncle, Jocelyn bowed in his seat.

'My lord,' he said, sober as a bishop. 'I trust you are well today.'

They certainly taught their manners well, these Viponts. Serlo's son, Roger was mounted on a slightly higher pony near what must be his mother. He was a slender creature, looking little older than Jocelyn despite having two years on him. He beamed proudly as a hooded falcon was placed on his arm, but within moments his hand trembled with the effort, much to the amusement of his relatives.

'You are certain,' said Serlo's wife, 'that they are not too young for this sport?'

'Calm yourself, Idonea,' said Serlo. 'The boy is fine. Aren't you, Roger?'

Roger smiled with gritted teeth.

Robin rode closer to Jocelyn.

'Do you know how to hold a falcon?' he asked. Jocelyn held out his arm unsurely. Robin corrected it, laying it at a right angle to his body, the wrist aligned. 'Put your thumb and forefinger together like this. Tuck away the rest of your fingers. My bird has not bitten or scratched in years, but he grips hard.'

He put a glove on Jocelyn's arm and gestured Alan to hand over the bird. Jocelyn's eyes widened but the falcon sat placidly enough. Robin took the bird back onto his own wrist with a smile.

'Good arm,' he said. 'You may fly him when we are closer to our quarry. I will take him for now. He gets restive during a journey.'

'He is a beautiful creature,' said Elaine. 'What is he called?'

'Fleet.'

'An English name?' said Guy in surprise.

'For an English bird.' Robin smiled. 'What are we hunting today?'

'Heron,' replied Serlo. 'They nest down by the river's edge not far into the forest.'

The party set out, regrouping in a pattern much more pleasing to Robin, who rode to one side of Jocelyn while Elaine rode the other. The boy was not talkative, answering in a word the questions of his companions, but Robin suspected all children behaved so. Besides, it afforded Robin a chance to speak to Elaine without interference. After riding some time in silence, Jocelyn looked up at Robin.

'Lord Locksley,' he said.

'I am your uncle, Jocelyn, you may call me Robin.'

Jocelyn frowned and glanced at Serlo. Clearly the Vipont family were not so familiar with their elders.

'Uncle Robin, how many Saracens did you kill in the Holy Land?'

Robin was surprised. He felt Elaine's eyes on him while he considered an answer. 'As many as wished to kill me.'

'Did a lot of them want to kill you?'

'Not all of those I met.'

'You must be a great fighter. Lady Idonea said that all crusaders fight with God's arms.'

'God's arms would be strong indeed.'

'Can I see?'

'See what?'

'See you fight, uncle.'

Robin smiled but shook his head. 'Guests do not draw swords in their host's presence.'

'A pity,' said Elaine. 'But perhaps your host will not mind? Shall I ask him?'

Robin met her eye. He suspected he could not deny Elaine's wishes, if submitting to them would earn her admiration.

'When we return to Nottingham,' he said to Jocelyn, 'I will show you the guards of a knight.'

'That is not fighting,' said Jocelyn, disappointed. 'I wanted you to fight against someone.'

Eudo heard the boy. He reined his horse closer to Robin. A ripple of interest spread throughout their party.

'Is our crusader going to give us a display of arms?' he asked. 'That would be diverting.'

'Since I have no arms but my sword it would be a poor display,' said Robin.

'It is still one I would wish to see,' said Ranulf, bringing his great horse to a stop in front of Robin. 'Perhaps a lord of England fights differently from one weaned in Normandy.'

Ranulf's tone suggested he knew who would come out better in such a contest.

'Guy, you have fought in tournaments. You can face Lord Locksley.'

He swung a hand carelessly. Robin met Guy's eye. Despite his surprise, Guy did not look displeased at the prospect.

'We are not dressed to fight,' Robin said. 'It would be bad manners for me to dirty my host's fine clothes with this mud.'

'I think he is afraid of you, Guy,' laughed Serlo.

It was not the first time a man had tried to incite Robin to an unwanted fight with hints at cowardice. Robin knew his own courage and ability. He had no need to prove it before these men. But it had been months since he had fought a man, months since his lazy body and mind had worked itself against an opponent, and the thought of it made his fingers flex in anticipation. Elaine's eyes glittered.

'Take Fleet,' he told Alan, passing the bird and dismounting in one movement. At the edge of hearing Marian was whispering to Guy anxiously. He held up a hand to her and dismounted in turn. As the party drew back their horses from a patch of slightly drier earth Guy watched Robin, his sword already drawn, a dark look on his face. Whatever useless emotions clogged his body – jealousy, perhaps, or anger – he was eager to vent them on Lord Locksley.

'Are you certain you wish to fight me, Guy?' Robin asked. 'Marian will not thank me if I break your nose.'

Guy scowled. 'What makes you think it will be my nose getting broken?'

The Viponts laughed. Robin smiled wryly. 'Experience,' he said, and drew his sword.

They faced each other across the damp earth, Guy working himself into a starting stance in the mud. Robin set his feet securely, held his sword beside his head in a roof guard, and waited. Guy moved first, swinging his sword in an arc towards Robin's flank. Robin blocked it with a downward sweep then struck back hard against Guy's raised blade, stepping into the blow, then again and again. Guy was forced backwards by the force of these repeated strikes, skittering at the end into short steps, his sword at his side. To give him his due, a lesser man would have slid on the slippery earth under the force of those blows.

Robin did not pursue Guy, but smiled at him mockingly. Jocelyn clapped his hands. Guy was not finished. He struck again, this time thrusting towards Robin's belly, a stab that Robin leapt away from. He caught the edge of Guy's sword with the cross of his own, dragged it high into the air, felt both swords lock together, and swung it down to the other side of Guy, pinning his arms awkwardly under Robin's own. He and Guy were thus wedged into a form of embrace, faces inches from each other. It would have been the easiest thing in the world to butt his own head into Guy's then, to follow through on his promise of a broken nose, but at the edge of Robin's vision he saw Jocelyn, and had just enough sense of avuncular honour not to show his nephew such an ungallant move.

'I told you,' he hissed into Guy's face, 'that I wish you and Marian joy. If you fight me because of her, then believe me, I have no longing for her.'

Guy struggled to free his sword. 'You think that makes me less inclined to fight you?'

'It should, if you had sense.'

Before he could say more he felt something connect with his stomach, a blazing pain, the breath knocked out of him. Guy had elbowed him hard in the belly. He struggled to grip his sword and raise it before Guy brought his own stinging down on his back. But before he could do so there was a shriek from the party behind them. Idonea, her arm raised to point, moved towards Roger and Jocelyn in alarm.

Both Robin and Guy turned to where she pointed. Emerging from the cover of the forest was a group of figures – dirty figures in poor clothes – making for the hawking party. There must have been a score of them at least, carrying the arms of farmers and workers. The Viponts moved to cut off the infants and ladies from the path of this common horde. Their attendants moved towards the men, drawing weapons against them.

Robin blinked in amazement, uncertain if his guts were affecting his vision. As the figures drew closer he made out faces he knew: Thurstan, the blacksmith's son; Lefchild, the farmer pale as snow; John Blunt the fletcher, who he had seen only days before in the Hundred Court. Half of the faces before him he remembered from his youth. Men he had drunk with when he should have been at his father's side. And now they walked towards their lords, grim as a war party. John Blunt was at the head of them. When they were close enough to speak to the lords they did not bend the knee, or lower their eyes.

'My Lords de Vipont,' called John in hesitant French. 'We come here to entreat a message for the Count of Mortain. As the lords of our Hundred, we plea for your assistance.'

Serlo started towards them with his sword drawn but Eudo stopped him.

'We are not errand boys,' Eudo called. 'You trespass on our lands, and our time. Leave now, or we will give you reason to.' He gestured to his men, who waited only on his command to charge the hundredmen.

'Wait,' said Robin, struggling upright. 'Let me speak to them a moment. I know English.'

'There is no need to speak to them,' said Serlo in disgust. 'They stand in defiance before us, they threaten our family…'

'They have offered no threat,' interrupted Robin. 'I will hear them. Hold your men for a few moments more.' Without waiting for a response, he walked to the group, sheathing his sword.

'Our Lord of Locksley,' said Lefchild, looking amused. 'It's good to see you again. Will told us you wouldn't seek us out, but we've found you anyway.'

'You should leave,' said Robin in English. 'Whatever issues you have can be brought to the sheriff at the county court. If you stay here,' he said more quietly, 'there will be trouble.'

'We don't want trouble. But we've spoken to the sheriff, we've attended the courts, we even found a man to write to Lord Eudo, and all our pleas have been ignored. We can't be bled dry.'

'Is this about Lord Eudo's men demanding the wrong taxes?' asked Robin, looking at the Viponts. They stood in a circle muttering to each other. Lanfranc the steward was dispatched away from the group, back in the direction of the castle. To gather more men perhaps. 'Because you've heard what the sheriff said. He'll decide the case at the next county court.'

'We all know what will happen there,' said one of the other hundredmen bitterly.

'This isn't about that,' said Lefchild. 'That was Michaelmas, now Lady's Day is coming and more taxes are being called in. Not just for the king, but for the count as well. These collectors come so often for our money we can barely survive from month to month. Our fuel has been taken, our flocks, our livelihoods, they can't have more money.'

'No one ever wants to pay their taxes,' said Robin, following Lanfranc with his eyes. The Viponts had turned to watch them.

'My lord, you do not know how it is,' said John. 'We have nothing to pay the taxman with. All we ask is that our lords protect us. We ask that they tell the Count of Mortain to leave us this one time, to allow us to sow our crops and tend our flocks without them being stolen from us. Master Robin…'

'Don't call me that,' cried Robin. 'You've got no right. Put these pleas at the next county court, and justice will be done. Now if you have any sense, you will leave before you are beaten out of the forest.'

John Blunt looked at Robin. It was the same look that Will had given him after the Hundred Court. The same look his father used to have when he learnt about Robin's misbehaviour. Robin could not stand to see it. He drew his sword.

'If you stay any longer,' he said loud enough for the Viponts to hear, 'I'll beat you out myself. Go.'

Reluctantly, the group dispersed. John Blunt was among the last, and just before he disappeared into the forest, he turned his back on his old friend with a shaking head.

The hawking party dispersed in low spirits that day. No herons were caught, the birds were not exercised, and Jocelyn did not get to try his arm again. By evening the sky rumbled the threat of thunder as Robin sat at one of the last unshuttered windows of Locksley Hall.

'Your mother has been crying,' said Elaine as she joined him in the windowseat. She sounded amused. 'Apparently you challenged Guy to a duel today, and the Viponts will never forgive you.'

'God's eyes,' said Robin. 'Where does that woman get her thoughts?'

Elaine shrugged, her face dancing in the candlelight. 'There is a benefit to it at least.'

'What is that?'

'If she is crying in her chamber, she is not here to disturb us. Of course, I could go and tell her you did not fight a duel, but I rather like the idea of you duelling. It makes you sound like the knight Yvain, come out of King Arthur's Court to…'

'Fight a dwarf?' Robin did not care much for such romances.

'Do you have a quarrel with Guy?'

'No. I think he has a quarrel with me.'

'I wonder why that might be.'

Elaine let her eye fall on Marian, who was sewing by the hearth. Feeling herself watched, she looked up, questioningly. Elaine smiled.

'Perhaps I should leave you to your thoughts.'

She moved to get up. Robin caught her hand before she could leave. 'Stay,' he said. 'Talking to you is one of the few pleasures I have had today.'

Elaine blushed slightly, pleasingly, and sat down again. She kept her hand in Robin's.

'I hope that is not true. Or your life is truly to be pitied.'

He laughed. The sound startled Gytha, who had been snoozing near the fire. She glanced up, heavy-lidded, then slumped back into slumber again. She did not make much of a chaperone. Elaine threaded her fingers through Robin's and edged slightly closer.

'What do you wish to talk about then, my lord? Since it is such a pleasure.'

'Not Guy. Or dwarves.'

'But that leaves almost nothing to discuss. We could talk about Constantinople, or Jerusalem? I hear they are the most beautiful cities in the world.'

'Perhaps they are.'

'Are you going to say that their beauty is nothing compared to mine? For men have said that to me before.'

'No,' said Robin, although he had been about to. 'And which men have said it?'

'I cannot even remember their names. It was a game we played, when I visited the queen – the old queen I mean – at Winchester years ago. They competed to pay the best compliments.'

'What did they win?'

'A kiss. Of my hem.'

'Poor recompense I'd say.'

'If you had won I would have let you kiss my hand.'

'Still poor.'

'My cheek then?'

She turned her cheek towards him. Her neck was lengthened by the movement, becoming long and white as a swan's. He longed to lean forward and kiss it, feel the pulse rippling beneath her skin. When he did not speak she turned back.

'You know, you and I are almost cousins now. Since your mother married Marian's father you and her are brother and sister, and as I am her cousin so I must be yours.'

Robin did not see the consequence.

'When I say goodnight to Marian I kiss her upon the lips. Perhaps that is what I should do for all my cousins.'

Before Robin could speak Gytha startled herself from sleep again with a snort.

'Your poor woman is tired, Marian,' called Elaine, loosing her fingers from Robin's. 'It is time we retired.' She stood and curtsied to him. 'Good night,' she said, 'cousin.'

In a dream that night Robin found himself back in Nottingham's alehouse. He was dressed plainly, as he always used to dress, his woollen tunic muddied and ripped. He looked down and found a pot of ale in his hand. There was a blow to his back and he spun to meet the attacker only to see John Blunt's laughing face.

'Good reflexes on a lord, aren't there?' he said. He raised his cup high in the air. 'Here's a health for Master Robin, buyer of the ale. Waes hail.'

'Drink hail,' cried the chamber at large, downing its cups.

Robin raised his own ale in thanks and looked around the chamber through his future eyes. Slumped on a barrel was Lefchild, his pale eyes red from the effects of alcohol. He was never able to hold his drink, that lad. He looked up at Robin, raised one unnaturally white hand in greeting then pulled it through his long, fair hair, drawing the whole lot over his face as he let himself slide to the ground. Will moved to pick him up, but Thurstan stepped in.

'I wouldn't bother,' he said. 'Let him sleep it off.'

Thurstan was built like an ox, but his brawn was deceiving. In that alehouse, no man save Will was sharper. But perhaps Thurstan even had the edge over Scarlette. He had had the sense to stop poaching since he married Aedith. With her brewing and his smithing they had little need of the extra funds stolen hareskins and venison haunches brought them. Aedith refilled her husband's jug from the barrel under which Lefchild had slipped. He kissed her full on the mouth in thanks. Even watching them now in this dream haze, Robin felt a pang of jealousy. An arm fell around his shoulder. John Blunt's bearded face grinned next to his smooth one. John never got as drunk as the rest of them.

'You don't look as if you were enjoying yourself, Robin?'

Robin heard himself speaking.

'My father has set a date,' his younger voice said. He must be seventeen, eighteen at most. He sounded absurdly young. 'The Monday after Easter, I'm getting married.'

John wrinkled his nose. 'There are worse women you could marry,' he said.

'But I don't want to marry her,' Robin said petulantly. 'I want to be able to choose my own wife.'

'Funny,' called Will, half falling from his stool. 'Usually it's beggars can't be choosers.'

He threw his head back and laughed. Robin downed his drink. He did not like being the butt of a joke, even Will's joke.

'You've at least got a few weeks left,' said John, trying to cheer him. 'You can enjoy your freedom until Lent is over.'

Lent, thought Robin. And suddenly he knew which night this was, and exactly how it ended. The alehouse darkened around him as time shifted. He was being shoved out of the door, rolling into the muck of the street. Will leapt after him, dodging the fist of Alnoth – or was it Acard? Robin could not remember. He had let his mouth run away with him, that much Robin knew. Will pulled Robin back to his feet. Despite the drink he felt steady as a rock. Their pursuers spilled out onto the street and, sure enough, at the front of them was Geraint. Thurstan's little brother had all his brawn and none of his wit.

'Are you running away?' he called. 'That's what I've heard about Lord Locksley's bastards. All prick, no spine.'

'At least I've got a prick,' shouted Will.

Robin felt sick. He did not know if it was the dreaming version of himself, knowing what was coming next, or the drunk youth full of ale.

'Prick but no balls,' laughed Geraint. 'Might as well have an eel in your hose.'

'Leave it be, Geraint,' cried Thurstan, following them into the street. 'Don't be an arsehole.'

The sheriff rode past. Robin was usually afraid of him but he was so drunk the sight of the man just amused him. He was shouting something about keeping God's season, or praying – whatever it was Robin and his fellow brawlers ignored him. Robin felt the world spinning, the shouts echoing off each other, men moving around him, a glint in the darkness, a cry that brought him reeling back to his senses, and then he lunged.

Geraint sank to his knees in the earth. Will pulled at Robin, trying to drag him away, half throttling him in tugging at his collar. Robin could not move his legs. He stared as Thurstan grabbed his brother, as his hand came away slick with blood, saw the look he gave Robin, a look Robin could not forget even if he drank all the wine in Gascony. Robin glanced at his own hands, found blood there too. And just as he turned to follow Will the darkness was punctured by a blast of light, shrieking through the black night towards him, striking him dead between the eyes.

He threw himself sideways, tumbling heavily out of bed. His fall was broken by the legs of the servant sleeping on a mattress on the floor next to him. The man stifled a howl. Close to the dwindling fire a figure raised itself in alarm.

'Lord Robin?' called Alan. 'Are you unwell?'

Robin staggered upright, shaking and sweating in the darkness of his bedchamber. His bedchamber. Robin looked about to reassure himself. He was not in the Holy Land, nor in the street with bloody hands.

'Yes,' he said huskily. 'I had a bad dream.'

'You are awake now, my lord,' said Alan. 'Is there anything you need?'

Peace, thought Robin. But he would not find that here.

'No,' he said. He sat back in bed. 'There is nothing I need from you.'

Alan lay back by the fire. The servant grumbled and twisted on his mattress. Robin stared out of his bed, between the open drapes. Long after the other men around the chamber were breathing deep in sleep, Robin was still sitting up in the darkness, keeping watch over his memories.

Passiontide

The middle bailey of Nottingham Castle was deceiving. Though it did not stretch as high as the inner bailey, mounted already on Castle Rock and with a keep reaching skyward, it was where the important work of the castle was done. In the time of the last king a great hall had been built there, magnificent as any church, pillared and painted, gilded stars picked out in the ceiling. But Robin's eyes were fixed on the floor. The floor was wide flagstone, rush strewn and scented, with a tiled dais for the lords at the high end, but even this he did not see. He was thinking of Elaine, the sweet perfume that filled the air when he was with her. It was not the cloying musk of the made-up courtiers but a scent light as mist. It reminded Robin of the jasmine on the walls of Jaffa in the last light of evening, just as the white flowers released their final burst of scent. He remembered how he had inhaled that floral air into his lungs during the long nights in the East, held it there as long as he could before breath overtook him and he let it sigh out. When it was gone there had been nothing to distract him but the hot stones cooling and night soil growing, and the lost memory of that sweet perfume. It was not good, he thought, to let his mind turn to poetry like this.

'Sir Walter,' called a voice from a doorway in the side of the hall. Eudo appeared, followed by the other men of his family. He embraced the sheriff and Robin where they stood. 'My apologies for keeping you waiting here. Thank you for joining our small court.'

He led them to the table on the dais, where wine and glasses were being placed by a servant. They sat, all on one side, facing down the columned length of the hall.

'And forgive me the mystery surrounding your invitation. I know usually a lord holds manorial court alone – after all, how can my tenants be of interest to a nobleman who has his own? But your judgement will be welcome today, if you will attend a little longer?'

'Certainly,' said Sir Walter. 'Robin and I are eager to assist in any way. Eh, Robin?'

Robin smiled by way of an answer. For all Eudo's fine words this seemed an unnecessary effort for them all. The sheriff's county court was the final court of law before the royal justices, and any matter raised on the Vipont lands that was serious enough to require Sir Walter's attention today would eventually end up there. What was the purpose of him hearing the same case twice?

Eudo called for Lanfranc the steward to open their court. The Viponts fell to talking among themselves while they waited and Sir Walter leant towards Robin.

'Your mother and I have been talking,' he said in a low voice.

Nothing good could come of that, thought Robin.

'When Marian marries, perhaps it would be wise for us to look to an alliance for you.'

'You want me to marry?'

'It is high time, Robin. Your mother and I have forged this bond between our families. It would be a shame, would it not, to let it die with us?'

'But Marian will marry Guy.'

'Yes, yes, that is all settled. Your mother thought perhaps a union with my niece. With Elaine. Would that be displeasing to you?'

Robin was astonished. His mother had actually read a situation well.

'No. Not displeasing.'

Sir Walter smiled, gave Robin a paternal pat on the shoulder and sat back as the first men to face the court entered the hall, flanked by Vipont guards. At sight of them any thought of Elaine was driven from Robin's mind. John Blunt. Lefchild. Thurstan. Other faces Robin had known years ago, and those he had seen only days before, appealing for intercession in the forest. When he had told them to appear before the court he had not expected them to be shackled, sallow and – in John's case, not to mention a few others – bruised and limping. He struggled to say nothing, to show nothing. He did not want to appear either partial towards these men or against them.

Eudo leant forward, over the table.

'I am afraid this is the reason for my secrecy, Sir Walter, and why I felt it important that you attend this court today. You will recognise John Blunt, who made claims that I had perverted local taxes for my own enrichment. These other men are, I believe, among those who he was to call on as oath-takers in the county court. But they have proven themselves in sight of witnesses to have no respect for the law. Lord Locksley, I fear you may know some of these men too.'

Robin had sunk back in his seat, trying not to be observed. He sat up in surprise, looking between the faces of the Viponts and the chained men, unwilling to admit to any knowledge until he knew why they stood before him.

'They are all from the Hundred of Locksley,' Eudo continued. 'So although now they are my tenants and villeins, by your birth they ought to receive your justice. That is why I thought it best to have you here today as well. I did not wish to offer offence before your estate is restored.'

'No offence taken. Continue as if I was not here.'

He wanted no part of this case. He could not stand in judgement of those men. Not of John. Not of Geraint's brother.

'Have these men been accused of some crime?' Sir Walter asked.

'All have been seen committing offences. Not only did they trespass on the forest of the Count of Mortain, but they have been seen stealing, harbouring other felons, receiving and selling items they knew to be stolen and poaching.'

Sir Walter shook his head. 'These are crimes indeed. You have the witnesses to them here, I presume?'

'Yes.'

'Bring them forward then.'

'They are already here.'

Eudo gestured to his guards and servants, who stood around the hall attentively. That gave Sir Walter pause. It was highly irregular for so many to be convicted on the word of witnesses sworn to the lord accusing them.

'There are no other witnesses? No other hundredmen or women who saw these crimes committed? Their neighbours perhaps?'

'They can be found, my lord,' said Lanfranc, 'if you wish.'

Robin bet he knew what that meant. Strong-arming these men's neighbours into speaking against them.

'There is another witness among us whose veracity could not be questioned,' said Eudo. 'My steward suspected that a number of these men were villeins, born unfree, when they threatened us in the forest while we were hawking. As you know, it is illegal for such men to bear arms, and on further investigation Lanfranc learnt that these men had indeed done so in direct contravention of our laws. Is that not so, Lord Locksley?'

'Pardon?'

'You were with us in the forest when these baseborn men perverted justice by bringing arms before us.'

'I…They carried the tools of their trade, certainly.'

'Scythes,' said Serlo contemptuously. 'They carried scythes and cudgels and knives.'

'Knives?' repeated Sir Walter. 'Is that true, Robin?'

In the aisle of the hall John Blunt looked at him from under his black eye and bleeding brow. Robin did not want to say anything that would condemn him.

'I was not the only lord there…'

'But you,' said Eudo, 'are a native of this county. Your word must count for more than that of us outsiders.'

Clever, thought Robin, wanting to strike Eudo in his politic face. Very clever.

'Yes,' he said at last, because it was only the truth. 'I believe some of them had knives. But most men carry them. And I do not think they ever intended harm against us…'

'Nonetheless,' interrupted Eudo, 'they could have, if they were pushed to it. Now, Sir Walter, will you hear the witnesses describe the crimes of these men?'

'I better had.'

Sir Walter settled himself in his seat as the first of the Viponts' spurious witnesses was brought forward. Robin could barely listen to them. His eyes were drawn again and again to the sorry huddle of men he knew. It was beyond convenient that these felonies had been uncovered between the day that John Blunt accused Lord Eudo of crimes and the county court assizes when those crimes were to be investigated. Sir Walter clearly thought the same, but he could hardly admit as much without discrediting every single servant in his ally's household who made these claims, and whether he spoke out now or later the effect would be the same: he would as good as call the Viponts liars. For the peace of the county and personal ambition Sir Walter could not do that. Neither, Robin had to admit, would it serve his own interests in the Locksley estate if he did. He was resolved. He would take no part. Whatever decision was reached by the sheriff, he would abide by it.

Eventually the last witness completed his testimony and the decision could be left no longer. The men's guilt had been attested by more than a dozen allegedly honest witnesses. Sir Walter had to follow Eudo de Vipont's thinking and admit that the men were guilty.

'What punishment do you intend?'

'Hang them,' said Ranulf. 'That is the penalty for poaching.'

'Unless any of them prefer to have their eyes and testicles removed,' said Serlo.

'That is an extreme punishment,' said Robin. 'Not all of them were seen poaching. If you wish to punish them all together you should mete out less harsh justice.'

'Stealing can also be punished by hanging,' pointed out Serlo.

'A fine would be kinder,' suggested the sheriff. He took in the men's ragged and patched clothes. 'Not a large one. Perhaps their families and neighbours can be responsible for finding the money?'

'And if they do not?' said Eudo. 'We cannot very well keep them in the cellars of the castle indefinitely, eating food that honest, hard working men have made.'

'Hang them,' insisted Ranulf. 'It is a clear enough case. These men have mocked the law twice. Firstly by wrongly accusing my brother and secondly in committing crimes that under the law of this country demand death.'

'Sheriff, I think the decision must lie with you,' said Eudo. 'Whatever you demand, we will abide by.'

Sir Walter let out a heavy sigh. He had gone too far down this path with the Viponts to turn back now.

'A fine of half a mark on every man, to be paid by the Tuesday after Easter. If the fine is not paid for a man, then he will hang.'

'The right decision, I think,' said Eudo quietly. He waved his hand to dismiss the men. 'And of course they will now be unable to speak against me in the county court. Even if the fines are raised, these men are no longer trustworthy enough to act as oath-takers.'

'You are right, Lord Eudo. What a happy coincidence.'

Robin watched the men as they shuffled out of the hall, the clanking of their shackles echoing in the courtyard beyond. He should have spoken for them, he thought, tried to persuade the sheriff out of his decision. But what good would his lone voice have been against a dozen Vipont men swearing that their version of events was the true one? He would only have engendered resentment against himself, and the hundredmen would still have ended with the same punishment. He thought of Elaine. He thought of Jocelyn. He thought of the lands that he should be administering, resting still under the control of strangers. Those were the concerns of a good lord: marriage, heir, estate. He knew he would have achieved nothing by defying the Viponts, and yet still he wished that he had.

The days were warming, the light creeping through the chinks of the shutters earlier, the dusk falling later. There were more chances for Robin to escape the confines of Locksley Hall and explore the forest edge, to fetch Husdent from the kennel and give him a run after hares. On one such morning at the kennel door he found Elaine, cloaked and gloved to ride.

'I thought I would join you this morning,' she said. 'I had a message from my mother yesterday that she has begun arrangements for my marriage. So I thought you could show me the estate I will be mistress of?'

She smiled. There was something of Wulfstan's good-tempered mockery in it. Robin would have agreed to a morning in her company even without such an excuse.

'You do realise,' he said pointing, 'that at the moment my estate is that horse and this dog.'

'Only at the moment.' Elaine rubbed Husdent's head. 'Besides, he is not a bad dower.'

Robin helped Elaine onto her horse and glanced around, expecting to be joined by an attendant. There was no one else in the courtyard and no other saddled horses.

'No Gytha?'

'She has a cold. I have told one of my own ladies to attend me.'

Elaine waved towards a window in the hall, where a pale face looked out on them. The attendant nodded in greeting and turned back to a piece of embroidery in her hands.

'She must have very good eyesight,' said Robin.

'Exceptional.' Elaine nudged her horse out of the yard. 'Shall we go before Sir Walter sees us?'

Despite the stated aim of their ride they saw hardly any of the Locksley estate. They ambled aimlessly, lost in conversation. It was with surprise that Robin saw they had reached the edge of the forest, where it tumbled into Sherwood and towards the Viponts' lands. At sight of it Elaine's face darkened.

'What became of those men we met when we were hawking?'

'They have been arrested. At Hocktide they will hang.'

'Good. I have never known men so bold as that. On my father's estate those men would have been taken immediately and whipped.'

'That might have been a kinder punishment.'

'Less permanent, I suppose.' Robin felt Elaine's eyes on him as he contemplated the earth at his horse's feet. 'You do not seem comforted by the thought.'

'I am not. I knew those men when I was young. It does not give me joy to condemn them to hang.'

'Then why did you?'

'Because Eudo de Vipont trapped me into it.'

Despite himself, Robin told Elaine the details of the Vipont court, of how Eudo made Robin speak on his behalf despite his better instincts.

'You could have spoken against him?'

'Not just against him – against his whole family. And what then? If I displease the Viponts they might put up a challenge to me regaining my estate. They might demand lawyers sit on the case for years in Westminster. They could bleed the estate dry with their own lawyers' fees, with bribes to royal justices, and deny me access to Jocelyn so the family can never regain our lands.'

'If you trust them so little why do you not employ a clerk yourself to look into the case?'

'I know none. And I do not have the coin to pay for one even if I did.'

Elaine set her lips in thought.

'I know of someone who could help you. There is a clerk who used to work in my father's household, now he is part of the chancery of the sheriff. He was trained at Oxford and has spent time in Westminster. You might argue that as the sheriff's stepson, by working for you he is still within his remit and therefore needs no other payment? Peter is his name. I can introduce you to him.'

Robin seized the bridle of Elaine's horse to draw her towards him and kissed her.

'If that is my thanks simply for telling you about a clerk I wonder what will happen if Peter regains the lands for you.'

'It is more help than you realise. You have given me the best counsel I have had since I returned.'

'That is only right. For all I said, I do not really want to be Lady Locksley of the hound and horse. If I can help you to regain these lands I will.'

Robin met with Peter the clerk the following day. He was indeed a useful ally to have. He was as shrewd as Elaine had suggested and eager to assist the sheriff's family even when warned of the need for discretion. He was only too happy to palm off the rigours of tax receipts for the county's Easter audit in exchange for penning writ requests to the clerks of Westminster. Robin left his meeting with Peter in high spirits.

As he neared the courtyard of Locksley Hall on his return he saw a cloaked figure near the stables, walking back and forth with linen parcels. He dismounted his own horse and left it chewing grass by the hall's wall. Silently, he crept closer, keeping to the shadows so as not to be seen. The figure looked around nervously and Robin caught a glimpse of its face. Marian. Waltheof emerged from the stables with her horse, loaded down with heavy saddlebags. She nodded to him and he moved stealthily across the courtyard in the direction of the kitchens. Marian slunk behind her horse and prepared to mount it. Robin's curiosity was piqued too far to let this slide. He tiptoed around the courtyard until he was directly behind her and addressed her loudly.

'Marian Peverill, what are you up to?'

She jumped, and as if that were not a clear enough sign of a guilty conscience, blushed and said, 'Nothing. It is no concern of yours.'

Robin reached his hand to her bridle, his arm barring her way up to the saddle.

'Am I not your brother now, dearest Marian?' he said with a teasing smile. 'Is it not my duty to keep you safe from harm?'

Marian drew back from the horse and pulled at her gloves. She refused to meet his eye. 'Stop mocking me. It is like being twelve again.'

He let go of the bridle, threw the reins back over the stable ledge and leant against the wall. 'Then tell me what you are doing.'

Marian looked at him reluctantly. 'You said that now you are back you wish to be a good lord.'

'I am being a good lord,' he said, bristling.

'I did not say you were not –' Marian sighed. 'We cannot ever speak to one another without arguing. How am I supposed to trust you?'

Trust. Why would she need to trust him? Now he really wanted to know. 'What *are* you up to?'

'I will tell you, if you promise that you will not speak back, and you will not say anything to my father or your mother. Or Guy.'

Robin was intrigued. Perhaps he could agree to such a promise and break it later. Promises to a woman were not the same as to a man.

'Swear it on your honour as a lord,' said Marian, 'as I am a lord too.'

Jesus, it was as if she read his mind. Perhaps they knew each other too well for deception. She watched him closely.

'You are not a lord,' said Robin. 'But I will swear it.' He crossed himself, and touched his heart. 'Now what is your secret?'

'I may not be a true lord,' she said, speaking softly and looking about her, 'but I wish to behave as a true lady, as one who has obligations to my tenants and the people of this county.'

Robin suspected an aspersion against his mother, but did not rise to the bait.

'You do not know how bad it has been. None of the lords do. They drift off to London and Normandy and Winchester, or just to follow the Count of Mortain. And while they are gone everything here gets worse. The men who stay behind steal – not just the common men, the knights too – and lords abuse the law courts to extract money from those who can hardly afford it…'

'Which lords?'

'All of them when they have the opportunity. Even the church takes more than it is entitled to these days.'

So John Blunt's accusation against Eudo was far from a singular occurrence.

'And what has this to do with you?'

'I cannot sit on a council or in the courts, but I can try to stop children from starving.' She opened the saddlebag on the horse. It was full of bread, preserves, smoked fish and cheeses.

'You are stealing from our kitchens?'

Marian recovered the bag with a snap.

'I am only giving what we would send them in the end anyway, if only more alms came from our table. And I try to help the families who I know commit no wrong, but are punished because their kin or other men in their tithing committed a crime and they must pay the fine.'

Despite himself, Robin thought of the fines on John Blunt's kin. He wondered if, had Marian sat in that court she would have spoken up for the hundredmen. It was easy enough to complain of a system you had no part in.

'How long have you been doing this?'

'A few months. At New Year the castle was held by the count and with all the rumours swirling about, his men did what they pleased. I started taking the food out myself then.'

'And what happens if your father notices the food has gone missing and dismisses one of the kitchen boys for it?'

'He has not noticed yet, and nor have you – you have both been doing the nightly audits. I used to help him with them now and then, before you came back. He said I would need to know how to do it when Guy is away from home. I used to change the sums slightly and give the remainder to Waltheof to pass to our tenants.'

She could not hide her pride at tricking the system.

'You are stealing from your own family, Marian.'

'Charity is a Christian duty,' she said coolly. 'I would have thought you knew that.'

He barked a laugh. 'What, because I have been to Jerusalem? There is not much Christian charity to be found there. Not much Christian anything now.'

'It does not matter if you agree with me. You have sworn not to tell anyone, so you cannot. And I will keep helping people, because I believe that is what makes a good lord.' She pushed past Robin and leapt into her saddle. Just as she was about to spur the horse on, she paused. 'If you truly want to know why I do this, come with me.'

'Now?'

'Unless you have other business to attend to? Visiting the kennels? Riding out with Elaine perhaps?' She smiled sweetly. Of course she knew what he had been doing. She always had before.

'Very well.'

He went to fetch his horse from the patch of grass near the wall and returned to find Waltheof attaching one more saddlebag to Marian's horse. And so they rode out together: Robin, Marian, Waltheof and a horse laden with self-stolen charity.

The croft's shutters were broken. Through holes in them came flashes of light: the fire within, around which the whole family and its animals would be gathered. It was a watte-and-mud building not much larger than Locksley Hall's kennels, the thatch on the roof darkened by damp. They picked their way through the ditches and hedges surrounding the building, past the remains of what had once been a mill. A child appeared in their path, back laden with firewood. She – Robin thought it was 'she' – knelt in alarm at sight of the horses. Marian dismounted.

'Where's your mother?' she asked in English. 'I've brought something for her.'

The child led them on to the croft. At the door she darted inside and called for her mother. A woman appeared in her place, wiping blood from her hands.

'My lady,' she said, bending the knee.

'Mistress Tova, I brought some food for your family. But before I give it to you, would you let me show Lord Locksley inside your home?'

'Lord Locksley?' Tova's eyes widened with fear. 'Why, my lady?'

'He wants to see how those on his lands live.'

'If – if he likes. But we haven't cleaned it today.'

'That won't matter, mistress.'

Robin dismounted and followed Marian inside the house. If the outside had reminded Robin of his kennels, the interior was more like the stables. The ground was nothing more than packed clay, sacks of straw covered in coarse blankets and sheepskins forming the beds piled in one corner of the croft. Scrawny animals were scattered around the single chamber, with children tending to them as one prepared a thin stew over the fire. The family stepped forward to greet their guests. A teenage boy who had been wrapping the legs of a cow in shreds of linen stood up.

'Forgive me, my lord,' said Tova. 'We've been bleeding the cow for blood pudding.'

'They keep the cow alive rather than kill it,' Marian whispered to Robin in French, 'because they can use the milk and blood for longer than they can save the meat.'

'I know why they do it,' said Robin. He addressed Tova, 'Don't worry about your home. I've slept in far worse myself.'

'Thank you, my lord. These are all our animals, you see. And these are my children. Goda, Tholf, Tovild, Godwin and Murdoch.'

She touched each of them on the arm as she spoke. The last gave Robin pause. He looked Robin in the eye, fearless.

'People call me Much, my lord,' he said. 'Are you here looking for servants? I could work for you.'

'That's not why I'm here.'

'I'm strong, my lord,' the lad continued. 'And I can run fast. Do you need a messenger? Or a groom? I could do both. Or work in the kitchens.'

'Peace,' said Robin. 'If I need servants in the future I'll remember you, Much. I can't take any now.'

'Because you don't have your lands?'

'Yes,' said Robin. 'You are well informed.'

'We miss your father, Lord Locksley. He was a good man. The lords we have now aren't so kind.'

'Hush,' said Tova, striking the boy on the head. 'You don't speak so to your lord.'

'It's all right,' said Marian. 'Lord Locksley likes to hear people speak well of his father.'

'Where is your father, Much?' Robin asked.

'Dead, my lord.'

'The sweating sickness?'

'The noose, my lord.'

'Your father was a criminal?' Robin looked at Marian. So much for her claim of only helping the innocent.

'That's what the sheriff decided,' said Tova quickly. 'We wouldn't question our lord Peverill.'

'Of what crime was he accused?'

Tova hesitated. Even Much hesitated. 'They said he stole from a chapel,' he said at last. 'But he didn't – my father was a godly man, he never would have…'

This earned him another smack around the head.

'It doesn't matter now,' Tova said harshly. 'Whether he did or didn't, he is dead. And I beg you, Lord Locksley, not to think that we question the sheriff or any of his men.'

'I can see you don't. We shouldn't keep you from your supper.'

Robin led Marian back outside. The air smelt fresher for being in the croft. Waltheof had unloaded some of the food from Marian's saddlebag and handed it to Tova.

'Bless you,' said Tova, kneeling before them, 'my lord, my lady. May St Nicholas and St Anne and the Blessed Virgin watch over you in thanks.' She kissed Marian's hand and went back inside.

'They are among the better off,' said Marian as the croft receded into the distance behind their horses. 'At least they have a roof and their livestock still. I have seen children out in the forest gathering acorns from the floor because it is all the food they have.'

'They seemed unduly afraid of your father,' said Robin. 'He is not quick with the hangman's noose.'

'He is quick enough. But he is not the worst. The Viponts are not much loved in these parts, nor the other Norman lords who have arrived with them.'

'And yet they will be your family soon. I suspect Guy will not be best pleased to have his wife wandering the countryside with her servant handing out herrings to the poor.'

'I would hope,' said Marian more seriously, 'that he would listen to my appeals to help the people of our estates so I would have no need to wander the countryside. Some husbands do listen to their wives.'

Robin ignored that barb.

The visits lasted all afternoon. At every stop Marian insisted Robin look into the homes of those given charity. He had seen poverty before, the point did not need labouring to him, but what was surprising was how far some of those crofts he had known from his rides around Nottinghamshire years before had deteriorated. Fences were patched with scraps of wood where someone had trampled them, livestock stood sickly and trembling in their pens, the daub of many buildings had scrubbed away to reveal the willow weave beneath. In every patch of gritty earth people worked, women weeding, children collecting stones and scaring crows, men fighting their ploughs. In places there were piles of green planks next to fresh-dug ditches, assembled suspiciously like a palisade. The lords' buildings, too, had new walls, more guards, fiercer dogs. Where wealth allowed they had towers, crenellated and watched.

'Your father,' said Robin as another tower appeared on the horizon, 'told me that the French king's invasion never happened. Why have men taken such pains to defend themselves against a baseless threat?'

Marian was watching the tower too.

'I have heard that if King Richard does not return from captivity his brother will move to seize the throne. Not everyone views the Count of Mortain as favourably as the Viponts. Some lords will resist him. People have been muttering about civil war for months.' Marian bit her lower lip. 'I have never known war. Plundering back and forth, quarrels between lords, but never true war.'

'It is not to be wished for, that is certain.'

'I am afraid,' said Marian, and she stared at the tower as if she could see the conflict playing out around it, 'that if war comes to Nottinghamshire it will destroy it. I had a dream about flames not long ago, the whole county burning. I pray it had no meaning.' She glanced at Robin. 'Don't laugh.'

'I was not going to.'

'You already have experience of such things. I must sound like a foolish woman to you. A coward.'

'There is no shame for a woman in cowardice.'

That answer did not seem to satisfy her. They rode in silence for a while. The saddlebags were almost empty now. There would only be one more stop before they returned home. It was another ruined croft, but looked to have been damaged only recently. There were cinder marks in the thatch and one of the shutters had been torn down and still lay shattered on the earth. Marian paused in front of this building and held out her hand for Robin to do the same. Waltheof leapt from his saddle and rapped at the door. A face appeared, a livid bruise on the mouth standing stark against the woman's pale features. Waltheof embraced her, then turned her chin to see the injury better.

Marian dismounted slowly and picked up the last parcels from the saddlebag. As she passed Robin she said quietly, 'This is Waltheof's sister. I will tell you more inside.'

Robin followed her into the croft, which was virtually bare. In one corner a pile of broken pots and shards of clay had been gathered. Waltheof helped his sister to a stool next to a pile of blankets that looked to contain a baby then fetched a sheepskin for Marian to sit on.

'God save you for coming, my lady,' said the woman. 'And you, my lord.'

She smiled at Robin through eyes red from crying.

'Aelfeva, this is Lord Locksley,' said Marian. 'Will you tell him what has passed since I last saw you?'

'If I can, my lady.' Aelfeva shifted herself, tensing suddenly at a pain somewhere beneath her clothes, then moving again to be more comfortable. 'My husband, Thorfridh, went with John Blunt and some others a fortnight ago to appeal to our lords for a relief from the next collection of taxes. We have nothing to give the collectors. Everything we had was taken at Michaelmas and New Year. They got no promise of relief, and Thorfridh said he thought he was followed on his way home. We thought no more of it, but last week Lord de Vipont's men came here while Thorfridh was away and demanded to know where he was. They said that he'd been seen stealing in Lowdham and poaching in the forest.

'This cannot be true, my lady, for Thorfridh never goes there. On market days we go to the Priory and sometimes into Nottingham but never much further. I told them there must be a mistake and that they should speak to John Blunt, who is our chief tithing-man and can call for a jury to answer the charge. But they refused. They were angry with me, cursed me, said I lied to them and my husband must have fled the shire. I said it wasn't true, but they struck me for speaking and started smashing my home – they said they were looking in case Thorfridh hid here, but they took everything I own and broke it against the walls. I was so afraid for my child, my lady. I feared they'd harm her too. But thank Jesus they didn't.

'They left me here with all my broken things and when Thorfridh came back I told him what had happened. I told him he must go to John Blunt, but he said John was already taken by the lord's men. Then I said he should flee but he would not risk a fine being placed on our family and our home seized if he was declared outlaw. He went to Lord de Vipont's steward of his own free will and said he would answer whatever questions they had for him. But they just – just beat him and – and now he is in jail and I – I can't… He will hang…'

She broke down in tears. Waltheof moved to comfort her. Marian looked at Robin. He expected censure but there was only pity in her look. She was as involved in this case as he was. It was her future family who had subverted the law, she had been there the day that John Blunt and his men confronted the hawking party. But even as he thought this Robin knew he lied to himself. It was not in Marian's power to defy the Viponts and it was not her words that had condemned the accused men.

'Do you know,' Marian asked Aelfeva, 'how much the fine is for Thorfridh's release?'

'Half a mark,' said Robin, surprising them. 'I was in the Viponts' court when they were condemned.'

'I can't pay it, my lady,' said Aelfeva. 'Not even a quarter of it.'

'There is no need for you to,' said Marian. 'I will give you the money for his release. You don't have to repay me. Think of it as Maundy alms a little early.'

'You cannot give them the money,' said Robin in French. 'The Viponts know these men have no coin. If one of their wives can pay for release, they will assume the money is stolen. She might be arrested too.'

Waltheof understood his words, although Aelfeva did not. He frowned at Robin.

'What do you suggest I do, Robin?' said Marian. 'Allow an innocent man to hang?'

'He may not be innocent.'

'He is,' said Waltheof.

'If you are determined to help them,' said Robin, 'then you must pay for this man's release yourself. Openly and with the knowledge of all those involved, so that no one can question his wife.'

Marian nodded, but hesitantly. Her father would not be pleased at such a show of defiance.

'I'll pay the fine,' she told Aelfeva, 'and see that the sheriff releases your husband to you. If you have any further visits from Lord de Vipont's men you must send word to me as soon as you can.'

Robin doubted that would do much good, but kept silent. Marian handed Aelfeva the food parcels and was thanked meekly. Perhaps she also did not really believe good would come of Marian's promise. He and Marian left Waltheof to bid his sister farewell in private.

'Do you really believe you can protect this family?' Robin asked as they mounted their horses.

'Their home is on the border of Eudo's estate. Perhaps if I speak to Guy he can appeal to his uncle to be lenient in the future. It will be more trouble to him to have them before his manorial court again than it will be to let them keep working his lands.' She was about to put up her hood, then left it down. 'No point trying to hide now I suppose. My father will know where I have been soon enough. If you wish, Robin, I can keep your name out of this.'

'What, after you have introduced me to half the poor of Nottinghamshire?' Robin smiled. 'I think my name is in this whether I want it or not.'

'I can explain how it was. There is no need for us both to be out of favour.'

Robin watched Aelfeva as she waved her brother farewell at the door. If any man had treated his sister as she had been treated, he thought, he would have killed them. He would put money on it that had his sister been alive now she would have been the first to join Marian in her illicit charitable endeavours. Putting right the wrong that her brother had done in the first place. That had often been her way.

'Tell your father I wanted to help. And if he ever lets you leave the hall again, I will carry half the food next time.'

Holy Week

The hart was almost the colour of the oaks that surrounded it. When it darted between the trees it seemed to disappear – no mean feat for so large a beast. Above it, the branches snapped away from its antlers leaving telltale signs for the huntsmen to follow. It heard the horn blast again, answered by the call of the hounds. It had been sniffed out – the scenthounds had done their work – the sighthounds were taking over the chase. The hart leapt from the undergrowth. The lords spurred their horses after it. A muddle of men and horses and dogs crashed through the forest, shouting and blowing horns, running and galloping. The hart charged ahead. Robin had it in his sights. It lunged sideways just ahead of him, over a thicket. He cleared the obstacle, heard another rider clear it too, then confusion behind as others missed the jump and turned their horses about. The huntsmen blew their horns. At his side was Serlo de Vipont, nudging his horse ahead of Robin's, twisting the spear in his hand. He sat up, took aim, threw, missed. The hart had changed direction again. It was being driven back towards the hunting party.

Robin's blood roared in his ears but his mind was silent. The babble of thoughts that had troubled him for weeks was crushed in the focus of the hunt. Instinct held his spear beneath his arm and pressed his horse towards the quarry. The game was almost up. The deer would soon be brought to bay. He and Serlo were quite alone when it bounded into a thicket and struggled out the other side. Robin leapt the thicket, Serlo was a heartbeat behind. The hart had disappeared from view. The forest was denser here, the tree roots treacherous for careless hooves. The hart was no fool, seeking out such shelter. Robin had the advantage over Serlo now, slowed his horse to listen for the sound of his prey. In a patch of clearing some way ahead of him, a fawny shape rustled – two shapes – three? There could not be three harts. One of the shapes unfolded from the earth, growing tall and thin on two hind legs. It was not a hart. It looked about, gave a cry, seized something from the earth and leapt away. The second shape unfolded and jumped, the third moved slower. Robin reacted quickly but not as quickly as Serlo.

'Poachers.' His horse lunged ahead of Robin's. 'Run them off at the other side.'

Robin spurred his horse, charging to the left of the group. He just had time to see the carcass of a deer on the earth, unmade and part butchered. Habit made him grip his spear, prepare to strike. Instinct told him to ride the prey to bay. He could see one of them ahead, ragged and hooded, tearing through the forest with a bundle in his arms. In the undergrowth a man might outrun a horse, but this man would not. He could hear the horse bearing down on him, redoubled his efforts. His hood fell back from his face as he turned to see how close the chase was. Robin's concentration was broken. Only for an instant – a moment long enough to confuse his horse – for the man to leap a root – for the horse to lose its footing – to stumble. Robin kept his seat and the horse did not throw him, but the poacher was gone. He knew he could not catch him now. He would not run down Will Scarlette.

Robin turned his horse. All the joy of the chase was gone, the silence punctured. What in Christ's name was Will doing poaching? In the daytime, in royal forest? He had always been a fool but this was virtual self-murder. If Serlo had been giving chase instead of Robin he would have been speared to a tree by now. A cry in the distance. Perhaps that was the fate of the other poacher. Robin rode towards the noise. Back by the deer carcass in the clearing Serlo was dragging a man by his collar. Since Serlo was still on his horse the man stumbled and jerked, half-strangling himself in his struggle to keep up.

'You did not catch yours?' Serlo said, shaking the poacher as he came to a standstill.

'My horse tripped on a root. He was clear by the time I recovered.'

'Do me a service then and ride back to the party to fetch Lanfranc. This creature can stand trial for his crime.'

The poacher struggled upright. He looked at Robin. Jesus wept, when would God stop mocking him? Robin knew him too – the gangly form, the overlarge dark eyes. It was Tova's son, Much. His hands were bloodied where he had been butchering the deer. His face was bloodied too. Perhaps he had fallen when Serlo caught him. Perhaps.

'My horse is still unsteady,' said Robin. 'It will be quicker if you go back. I can watch the boy.'

Serlo scowled. First his sport was ruined by poachers, now he was expected to run messages like a squire. He unlooped a dog leash from his belt and threw it to Robin.

'Tie his hands then. He is a slippery bastard.'

Robin dismounted and took Much's hands. Much started to struggle.

'Don't,' Robin hissed in his ear, 'move a damn muscle.'

Much let his hands be leashed behind his back. Robin took him by the shoulder and pushed him onto the ground.

'Sit there.'

'I will not be long,' said Serlo. He looked down at Much and said, in deliberate English, 'You will hang for this.'

He turned his horse. Robin and Much were left alone in the clearing.

'You fool,' Robin said, kicking Much in the leg. 'What are you thinking of, poaching on royal lands?'

'These aren't royal lands,' Much said defiantly.

'They are under the lordship of the Count of Mortain, the king's brother. That makes them royal.'

'Before that they were part of our common lands. The king declared them forest and now we can't take the meat we always had before. How is that justice?'

Robin shook his head, sat on a rock, listened to Serlo's horse grow more distant. This boy would hang, he thought. His mother would lose her husband and her eldest son to the noose. If Marian did not bring her food next month and there was no meat from the forest, what would become of her? Of Much's brothers and sisters? They could not live forever on the bleeding of one cow.

'How old are you?' he asked.

'Fifteen.'

A horn was blown, not far away, not as far as Robin had expected. They were coming back. No, he thought. This he could not allow. He pulled his knife from its pouch, seized Much by the elbow, sliced open the leash, pulled his horse by its bridle and held out the reins to the boy.

'Take my horse,' he said.

Much stared at him.

'There's no trick to riding. Take him to the edge of the forest and before you reach open ground jump off and run.'

'You're – letting me go?'

'If you hurry up.'

Robin pushed Much towards the saddle. He struggled into it awkwardly.

'Cut your hair when you get home and if you can, darken it. Charcoal, wine vinegar, whatever you have.'

The horn blew again. Robin could hear hooves on the earth. He slapped the horse's haunch and it lurched forward. Much barely managed to hold on. He slumped over the animal in a desperate clinch. Robin called out before Much disappeared from view, 'And tell Will Scarlett I'll be calling.'

The horses were close now. Robin had not thought this plan through. His heart pounded. Despite himself, he smiled. Acting first and thinking second. It was just like old times. He threw the leash and knife at the ground, ran his hands through his hair, slapped his own cheek and pulled at his clothes.

'Stop!' he cried as the horses thundered towards the clearing. 'Thief!'

At the last moment he kicked up the mud where the horse's hooves revealed a track. Then Serlo and Lanfranc were before him. They looked about in confusion.

'Where is he?' Serlo cried.

'He got away,' said Robin. 'He seized my knife when I tried to move him, cut his bindings and took my horse.'

'Which way did he go?' asked Lanfranc.

'I am not certain.'

Serlo scoffed.

'He pushed me away. Perhaps that direction?'

Robin nodded away from the route Much had taken.

'I will start after him,' said Lanfranc. 'See if I can track him. Lord Serlo, you said he had brown hair? Medium build?'

'More red than brown,' said Robin.

'It was brown,' said Serlo. 'He was young. I doubt he even knows how to ride a horse.'

Lanfranc nodded and rode away in the direction Robin had pointed. It was a piece of mercy that he had not brought his dogs with him. If they had caught a scent the boy would be done for. He had to hope that Much could hold on for long enough to outride any pursuers.

'How,' said Serlo, with hawk eyes on Robin, 'did he manage to cut through a leather leash so quickly that you did not notice?'

'How in Christ's name should I know? Do you think I wanted to give him my horse? That I'm so keen to wade through mud to get back home?'

Serlo gave Robin a look that said he did not know what Robin might want.

'I will have a spare horse brought for you,' he said, turning his own animal away from the clearing. 'But I may be some time.'

Serlo was true to his word. By the time a huntsman bounded through the forest with a horse Robin was pacing back and forth to keep warm. The sun was dipping below the treeline and the forest floor was cold.

'The sheriff told me to bring you to the castle,' the huntsman said.

'What for?'

'Something to do with the poachers, my lord. He has called for the lords of the county to meet with him.'

Had Much been caught in spite of Robin's efforts? Or, worse, Will? Robin knew he could not stand in judgement of his brother. Speaking against John Blunt and his men had been hard enough. Perhaps he ought to try to escape away to Will's home now, to warn him if he had not already been caught. But Robin's absence would be noted, and the way Serlo had looked at him before suggested he already suspected Robin's complicity in the poachers' escape. Better to find out what the Viponts wanted than to risk his situation needlessly.

In the private chamber of Nottingham Castle where the barons met, Robin found not only the Viponts and Sir Walter who had been out on the hunt earlier, but also their Norman friends, Lords de Caux and de la Guerche. Interesting, thought Robin, that the two barons whose interests were closest to the Viponts had attended this meeting when the remaining native lords had not. When Robin entered the chamber a hush fell. Not a good sign.

'We are glad you could join us, Lord Locksley,' said Eudo, wearing a crocodile smile. 'I trust you were not uncomfortable waiting in the forest?'

'No,' said Robin. He thought it best to be brief and show no opinion until he knew the cause of this meeting.

'You were saying?' Sir Walter prompted Eudo.

'The commons have become too defiant. It is the place of common-born men to obey their lords and the laws of their land. At present they are doing neither. We have had further proof of their disdain for law today, and it is some regret to me that not one of those found flouting our rights in the forest has been captured to face our justice.'

Serlo scowled at Robin. He tried not to smile. Thank Christ. Much, Will and their accomplice must still be safe.

'As I see it, the root of this problem is not only that these baseborn men have no respect for their lords, but also that they have the ability to move freely between their lands and those in the ownership of their betters. The forest rings a section of the county common land – men keep their flocks and crops there when they can find no other safe place for them. This patch of land allows these baseborn men to steal onto our manors and even into the royal forest, then flee back into their own homes without being caught. We have all seen how bold they have become at this game of cat and mouse. First they steal the fruits of the forest, then they move to poaching on their lord's estate, then they creep deeper into the woodland to attack the king's own bounty and then – well, we have all heard of their show of defiance when my family and our neighbours were out hawking. I believe that if we do not take a stand to end this lawlessness it will only worsen.'

Ranulf harrumphed himself upright in his seat. 'But what do you propose we do about it? We already have our men out watching the borders of our estates, but the forest is too large. We cannot police every part of it.'

'We do not need to. As I say, the root of this defiance is the common land at the edge of town, where it borders the forest. If we deny the people access to this land it will be considerably more difficult for them to creep between the lands of their lords and king. Let them see how it tastes to have their rights denied.'

'You will take their common land?' said Robin before he could stop himself. This was clear perversion of the ancient laws of England. The lords turned on him as one. He tried to moderate his tone as he continued, 'That land has been held in common since before the conquest. Surely the law prohibits its enclosure?'

'Many lands were held by other men a century ago,' said Sir Walter. He did not meet Robin's eye. 'The king himself has set a precedent. He has reclaimed what was once common scrubland as royal forest. The local religious have even done it. Have you seen the ditch around the Abbot of Rufford's forest? It would not surprise me if he built a palisade to keep his deer in.'

'The king may enclose whatever land he wishes,' said Robin, 'since all England is his by right. Surely if common land is to be enclosed, the matter should go to the royal courts to decide?'

'Nothing is being done in the royal courts,' said Serlo disdainfully. 'As long as the king is a German prisoner, the government of England is crippled. Even the justiciar he left to run the country has gone abroad. In their absence, it is for us to do as we think best for our lands.'

'I agree,' said Ranulf. 'The commons in Nottingham have shat all over our rights, why should we not deal the same with theirs?'

Robin moved to reply, but before he could do so Guy had spoken.

'But if you deny these men the land to pasture their flocks and grow their crops you will just drive them further into the forest to seek out food. These people act out of starvation, not rebellion.'

His relatives turned on him in surprise. Robin suspected that Viponts did not usually break rank. If his guess was right, those were Marian's opinions speaking through her betrothed.

'Whatever the cause of their insolence,' said Serlo, 'the effect is the same. I say we enclose that common land.'

'I agree,' said Lord de Caux.

There was a chorus of further agreement. Robin and Guy glanced at one another. Apparently they were the lone voices of dissent. Guy did not look overly pleased with his ally.

Although, thought Robin, they did not need to be lone voices. 'Surely,' he said, 'this is something for the entire county to decide. You should call all the local lords to a council before you decide anything. And legal precedents should be found if you do not wish to upset the commons still further.'

'Legal precedents?' cried Ranulf. 'We are their lords. It is the place of the base to obey, not to question.'

He shot a foul look at Guy. His son shrank into himself. Robin suspected that if the matter were allowed to rest now, Guy would be persuaded out of his opinion and into his father's. The argument would be lost.

'Lord D'Alselin would be very displeased to learn that he had been excluded from this discussion,' Robin said. 'His own lands border the town. He might see it as a move against his interests if we proceed without him.'

That gave them pause. Robin suspected that even the Viponts were a little afraid of Lord D'Alselin.

'There is no need for a council,' said Eudo. 'Sir Walter, you are our sheriff. If you think these lands represent a threat to the county's peace you can seize them now and make if official when the royal justices come to Nottinghamshire.'

'No,' said Sir Walter. 'No, Robin is right. We will decide this by a council of lords.'

Robin was the first out of the chamber when the meeting concluded. Sir Walter's cold shoulder gave him the perfect excuse to ignore his stepfather. If he was quick he could reach Will, offer his warning and be back at Locksley before Sir Walter had time for alarm. Just as Will had said, he was still living exactly where he had been four years before. Agnes Scarlette's croft was a mile inside the forest, on the outer edges of the Locksley manor, sheltered by trees on the path between Nottingham and Garsmount. When Robin arrived the croft was a single smoky pocket of light in the darkness. He knocked at the door with an eerie sense of having stepped back into another life. He could not count the number of times he had run to this place for shelter or kind words. He would arrive, soaked or bruised, and the door would open on the single chamber within, a hearth at the heart of it, a rough wooden bunk above, which he and Will had shared. Will's mother would greet him with an embrace and a drink, and smack his feet off her table and make him behave. Agnes had been more of a mother to him than his own.

The door opened. A none-too-thin woman with a face still handsome and hair still fairer than grey looked out. At sight of him she gasped and put her hand to her mouth. She could not draw her eyes from him, but she did not rush to embrace him or kiss his cheek. Instead, she did something that made Robin feel as despicable a man as had ever walked the earth. She knelt to him.

'My lord,' she said quietly.

There was a scraping sound and Will ran to the doorway. He met their guest with a cold glare.

'Get up, Mother. You've no need to bow to him like he was Christ.'

Agnes tutted at her son's blasphemy but did not rise. Robin could not bear it. Half of him wanted to leap back on his horse and ride away. Fortunately, that half did not overpower him. He knelt himself and took Agnes's hands.

'Please get up, Agnes,' he said. 'If anyone should kneel it's me to you.'

'Too right,' said Will.

Agnes looked up uncertainly, reading his face as she had whenever he had turned up at her door after fleeing Locksley Hall. Whatever she saw there pleased her. She pressed her hand to his cheek and embraced him. When she stood again there were tears on her cheeks. She ushered him into the croft, towards the table in the corner.

'Oh Robin,' she said, wiping away the tears. 'Can I call you Robin? It's good to see you again. Will said…' She did not tell him what Will had said. 'Sit with us, have a drink. I have some ale made up. Will, fetch the cups.'

Will did not move from the doorway. 'I want to know,' he said, 'why Lord Locksley is gracing us with his presence now when the thought of it seemed to disgust him a month ago?'

'You know why I'm here,' said Robin. 'I was in the forest earlier. I saw you.'

'Don't know what you mean.'

'Perhaps we should speak of it outside.' Robin glanced at Agnes.

Will shrugged. 'Might be best.'

'You can wait a moment,' said Agnes. 'He's only just got here, Will. Let him have a drink and then you can have your talk. Sit down, Robin.'

She pulled out a stool for him and bustled to fetch the ale and cups herself. With a dark look, Will sat too. Agnes set down the cups and sat herself, her chair pulled out in front of Robin's.

'Now let me look at you properly. Thank all the saints in heaven you're here. It was so hard to hear you were dead, Robin. I couldn't believe it. And having no grave to visit. I put flowers on your father's tomb instead. Have you been to it?'

'No.'

'Ah. Never mind that.' She lifted her cup of ale. 'Let us toast your continued life.'

'Even Will might drink to that,' said Robin.

Despite himself, Will smiled. 'Suppose it's better than the alternative.'

They clashed their cups against each other. Agnes still could not draw her eyes from Robin.

'You are so different,' she said.

'I'm not.'

'Yes, you are. And it's not this –' she gave the beard on his chin a tug '– or these.' She touched the patchwork of little scars on his hands and arms. 'You're a lord. Look how you sit.'

Robin looked down. He supposed he was sitting more upright than he used to.

'Seeing you stand at my door like that… If I hadn't known you so well before I wouldn't have recognised you.'

'War does that, I suppose.'

'War,' said Agnes, 'time, life. What do you think of the ale?'

'Best I've tasted in years. The stuff they have at the hall is nothing to it.'

Agnes smiled to herself. Will downed his cup, refilled it, topped up Robin's and got to his feet.

'Come on, Lord Locksley,' he said. 'Let's have this talk outside.'

He held the door open until Robin got up and walked through it. Will wandered a little way from the croft, out of the flickering shadows that surrounded it.

'So you saw me in the forest?' he said when they were far enough away not to be heard.

'Yes. Why do you think you got away?'

'My manly strength and swift limbs?'

'Much was caught.'

'But escaped I hear.'

'If Serlo de Vipont had had his way, Much would be a prisoner in Nottingham Castle waiting for a noose now.'

'And me too, I presume?' Will did not sound remotely concerned by the prospect.

'Surely you can see how dangerous this is? I'm guessing it wasn't the first time you've poached those lands. It's only good luck you haven't already been caught. Next time you might not be so lucky. And if you're hanged who will look after Agnes? Not to mention that your poaching has got the lords talking about enclosing the common land at the edge of town. It is not just you who is affected by your actions, Will.'

'Enclosing the common land? Then we've got no option but to poach. Otherwise how do you think we'll eat? Are we supposed to live on bark and shoes?'

'I could help you.'

Will shook his head, ignoring him. 'Heard you helped some of the kin of our hundred who got arrested.'

'Marian was the one who helped them. I just went with her.'

'Also heard you condemned John Blunt and his hundredmen to hang.'

Robin looked at Will in surprise. 'I was in the court that day,' he admitted.

'So you tried to stop it then?'

'No. No, I didn't.'

Will nodded. 'Thought not.' He took Robin's cup from his hand. 'Goodnight, Lord Locksley.'

'Will, please…'

'What do you think you're going to do, Robin? You can't keep coming to visit us. You can't just pretend the past five years haven't happened. You're a lord now.'

'I want to help you both.'

'Like our father did? Visit two, three times a year? Give us charity at New Year and Easter and invite us in for the harvest feast with the workers? Buy my mother cloth for a gown when you remember?'

'I'll give you whatever I can. If you don't want charity, I could give you a job in my household?'

'How? Way I heard it, Sir Walter's in charge of Locksley Hall and those vipers are running your estate. They won't let the likes of me work for you.'

'They might – if I ask…'

'They won't. I went to Sir Walter for help. A few months after our father died. People stopped buying Mother's ale all of a sudden, as if they'd been told. I lost my place in the castle armoury. We didn't have any money. So I asked Sir Walter if he'd take me on – didn't mind what job, scrubbing the kitchen, whatever he could give so we wouldn't starve. He'd already married your mother by then, moved into Locksley Hall.'

'So soon after my father's death?'

'Didn't they tell you that? Must have slipped their minds. Anyway, Sir Walter refused. Said he wouldn't take in strays and bastards. Then he had my mother whipped through the streets.'

Robin stood bolt upright. 'What?'

Will nodded, spat at his feet. 'It was one of the first things he did when he was made sheriff. He dragged my mother before a court and had the lords declare her a ribald. Their soldiers tore off her veil, pulled out her hair for everyone to see and clapped chain cuffs on her hands, then made her walk through the streets to the church to beg forgiveness for her sins.'

'What sins?'

'Letting your father have his way with her, once, twenty years ago. Letting me live.' Will's words hung wraith-misted in the air.

'I didn't know that.'

'No reason you should.' Will looked up at him. 'You didn't come to see us. No one at Locksley Hall would tell you about it. Maybe Marian I suppose. She brought us a bit of food now and then. Couldn't do it often or the sheriff would have made her stop.'

'I would never have agreed to let a court do that.'

'You agreed to hang John Blunt. You agreed to fine my neighbours out of their last chattels. You agreed to live with your mother and stuff your face with the vipers while your old friends starved. I don't know what you'd agree to now.'

'You're still my brother, Will.'

'Bastard brother.'

Will smiled. It was a twisted smile that got nowhere near humour. His eyes were dark as the forest's shadows. Robin was condemned by his own words, and worse, by his own actions. And he knew then that since he had returned to Nottinghamshire he had not done a single good act to outweigh the harm he had done to the people he once loved like family.

Robin returned to Locksley Hall with a shadow over him. He threw his horse's reins to the groom and marched to his chamber hoping to be left alone. Even Elaine's company would be more than he could bear. In his chamber the attendant Alan was setting the fire and preparing to roll out the servants' horsehair mattresses for the night. When his master arrived he awkwardly told him that Sir Walter had ordered him to the solar. Perhaps Robin should not have expected to escape company. He could hear his mother and stepfather muttering to each other from outside the door. He pushed it open.

'No need for it,' Sir Walter was saying, trying to soothe Lady Joan.

'No,' his wife insisted, shaking away his clasp and tweaking at the shoulders of his tunic in one movement. 'No, I wish to be here. He is my son.'

'Am I still?' said Robin. 'Well there's good news.'

Lady Joan turned on him. A battle was obviously taking place within her as to whether she would rage at him or let Sir Walter do the talking.

'I do not have words for you,' she said at length, battle won. She sat down and only then did Robin realise that Marian was in the chamber, uncomfortably perched on a stool. She widened her eyes at him in warning.

'Where did you disappear to?' asked Sir Walter, straight-backed, flint-eyed.

'I needed a drink to warm me after sitting all afternoon in that forest.'

'You could have asked for Lord Eudo's hospitality. There was no need to run away.'

'I wanted some time alone with my thoughts as well.'

'But as you just said, you had been sitting alone all afternoon.'

Robin bristled. Was he on trial, to be questioned like this by the sheriff? He set his teeth to keep himself from saying something he would regret.

'Our friends the Viponts are concerned. Serlo believes you allowed those poachers to escape earlier.'

'Why would I do that?'

'My question precisely.' Robin said nothing. 'Did you?'

'Of course he did not,' interrupted Marian. But her expression suggested that she too suspected he did.

'Quiet,' said Lady Joan, slapping Marian's hands. 'Your father is talking.'

'If you will not answer that question,' said Sir Walter, 'perhaps you will tell us why you have been frequenting the homes of criminals?'

Robin sensed a trap. Had he been followed to the Scarlettes' croft?

'What do you mean *criminals*?'

'As you should know, for a fortnight Lord Eudo's men have been watching the mob that attacked you in the forest –'

'You mean the men who asked for our help?'

'The men who you yourself told the court were carrying weapons.' Marian looked at Robin in surprise. 'You were seen visiting their homes only days ago, and today you allowed three poachers to outrun you, one on your own horse.'

Robin was losing patience. He could not speak, for he did not know what would fly from his mouth. Sir Walter took his silence for obstinacy.

'I do not understand this behaviour. You seek out the families of thieves and poachers to offer food from our own kitchens, you taunt the law. And as if you had not caused your family enough pain with your lawlessness, you drag my daughter into it.'

Robin and Marian both responded at once.

'I haven't dragged her into anything…'

'I told you it was me who took food for those families…'

'I have put,' cried Sir Walter over both of them, 'my own reputation in peril by supporting you among these lords. If you repay that kindness with scorn and defiance, I will not answer for my actions.'

'What will you do?' scoffed Robin. 'Seize my home? Take my lands? It's a little late for those threats.'

'You live with us on our charity…'

'No, you live in Locksley Hall because you married my mother. It was not Agnes Scarlette you should have punished for ribaldry. How long had my father been dead before you were in his bed?'

Sir Walter was too astonished to reply. Lady Joan's face flushed in horror. Robin could not look at them any longer. He turned on his heel. A chorus of shouts chased him across the hall and still echoed in his ears as he seized a horse from the stables. He took a cloak too, some groom's poor cloth, and with nothing else but the sword at his waist he galloped into the night.

He had ridden halfway to Nottingham before he thought about where he was going. The Viponts would not welcome him, and he would not seek their company now in any case. The Scarlettes' home was denied him. The prospect of begging for hospitality from the other lords of the county made him gag. And any welcome he might once have received from the families of John Blunt and his friends would now be cold indeed. There was only one place left he could think to go.

Lenton Priory was among the wealthiest religious houses in Nottinghamshire, and its prior could rival Eudo de Vipont in authority. But it was not towards the magnificent floortiles and painted archways that Robin wended his way. Beyond the priory, tucked behind the infirmary off the courtyard, close to the herb garden was a cell. The door was open, so Robin wandered in. A scratchy wool blanket on a rope-tied bed was all he found inside. The friar must not be there. Perhaps, since Ascension was dawning, he would be found amidst the worldly wealth of the church.

The church of the priory was in a state of excited activity. The oblates were stripping the altar of its Lenten cloth, washing it down with water and wine, standing ready with besoms to scrub it and re-cover it with sweet-scented herbs. The monks, meanwhile, were preparing linen towels and bowls of water to wash the feet of the poor. Already some eager souls were in the church, newly shaved and shorn to make confession before the celebration of Easter. Clappers and rattles stood ready to replace the silent bells, to call parishioners to mass that evening. Robin attracted some sidelong looks as he walked the aisle in his mud-smeared clothes and unkempt beard. He was on the point of asking for the man he sought when he saw a familiar form in an antechapel, kneeling before the

Virgin. Robin knelt beside him and leant his arms on the rail in seeming prayer.

'Brother, I wish to confess my sins.'

The cowled figure next to him seemed to smile in the shadows. He too was still bearded and wearing the plainest of unbleached robes.

'A friar is always willing to hear the sins of his fellow man.'

'I believe I have committed most of them.'

'Perhaps you have. Shall we see?'

'Sloth, for I was unwilling to take up arms in God's name.'

'Laziness is the bane of a lord's life.'

'Avarice and envy. I wish for lands that ought to be mine, for wealth that others possess.'

'Hm. You sound angry. Perhaps *ira* may be added to your list?'

'Anger has never been far from my heart.'

'So, that is four. Pope Gregory the First wrote that there are seven. Or perhaps you have all the sins of Solomon?'

'Lechery is another.'

'A common sin among soldiers, I understand. Have you merely contemplated lechery in your heart, or have you also committed carnal sins?'

'Both.'

'Ah.'

Robin hesitated before he spoke the last.

'Murder.'

'Again, my lord? It has become quite a habit.'

'I killed dozens of men in the Holy Land. At Acre I watched two thousand Saracens die.'

'The church would consider that no sin. You have elevated your soul in the eyes of God.'

'Even to take pleasure in killing?'

'Especially then. You do God's work.'

Robin was silent.

'But there is one question,' said the friar, 'that is most important of all. Are you penitent, brother, in body and soul?'

'Yes.'

The friar stood, smiled.

'Then allow this friar to get a man of God a drink.'

Friar Toki put his arm around Robin's shoulder, just as he had when he found a teenage murderer sheltering in a cave, and led him from the church. Before he left the Virgin he kissed the hem of her golden gown.

'I wish that I could have come with you,' said Toki as they sat together in the empty hall, two pots of sweet honey mead before them. Robin had talked for hours it seemed, of the Holy Land and Nottingham, of the Viponts and Elaine, of Will Scarlette and Marian's charity. But still the hall was dark as night, and no fast would be broken for some hours more.

'You could have come with me,' said Robin. 'I invited you to be my priest.'

Toki shook his head. 'And wear fine robes? Drink wine at the table of princes?

I think not.'

'You could have kept the robes you have.'

'I have been to war. That path is no longer mine. My path is winding and cold, and these poor feet are not intended to walk on foreign soil. Besides, I have God in my heart, what need have I to look him out in Golgotha?'

'It is just as well you are a friar,' said Robin, smiling. 'No bishop would have you.'

'I have found my place,' said Toki, gazing up into the shadows of the hall. 'The priory let me do my work and go where I like. They give me food and deny me money. I am happier now then when I lived in palaces. Yet here you are, Lord of Locksley, a victorious crusader and still discontented.'

'According to the law Lord Locksley is dead,' said Robin.

'Oh, we pity ourselves in our misery, do we not, my lord? There is your seventh sin.' Toki tapped Robin's chest, where the pilgrim's palms had been pinned to his tunic. 'But how can you be discontented when you have earned the badge of Jerusalem?

'That does not content you for long. Ever since I returned to Nottinghamshire I have felt like I did wrong. I try to be a good lord as my father wanted and all I seem to do is abuse the law and pervert justice, and for what? To have my hunting lands back? To sit in Locksley Hall without my mother there? So perhaps I should put aside lordly concerns and think only of being a good man, helping the weak. Still I do wrong and offend my family.'

'You think you must choose between being a good lord and a good man?'

'I have tried to be both and I cannot.'

He told Toki about the hundredmen, his old friends, who he had let face justice without once speaking up to support them. That decision sat heavy as a ball of lead in his stomach. He had not condemned them, but nor had he done anything to save them.

'Those men were almost certainly innocent,' he concluded. 'But I have allowed them to face death in order to win back an estate I never wanted before.'

Toki nodded his head contemplatively. 'A good lord needs his estate.'

'That is what I am saying. A good lord needs it, but a good man would not take it at the price of hanging innocent men.'

'Are they hanged already then?'

'Well – no. Not until Tuesday coming...'

'So a good lord – a man with the advantages of birth and rank – might be able to save them?'

'But the court has given its verdict. And I have nothing to pay one of their fines, never mind all of them. Even Marian could not buy them out now, with her father watching her like a hawk.'

'Now there is an example.'

'Of what?'

'Of how you could be. Look to the example of the Lady Marian. She appears a true noblewoman, yet she played the part of a friar, unrecognised by the world, giving alms to the poor. Surely you could also *seem* a good lord but *be* a good man?'

Robin squinted at his mead. 'Dissemble?'

'As long as your heart does not lie – and it is your heart that God sees – then it cannot be dissembling.'

Seem a good lord, Robin thought. Make more outward show. Perhaps that was where he had gone wrong. He had tried too hard to *be* a good lord, and all he needed was to appear one. What did it matter if he spent time with the lowly and criminal if the world did not know of it? He had seen with his own eyes, in his tricks with Will in their youth, that men were content to look only at the outer shell you showed the world. A nobleman was held to be noble as much for how he sat a horse and wore his fine clothes as for his acts. If a bastard brother could become a lord's son simply by putting on a different mantle, why could not Robin appear a true lord by doing the same? After all, he did nothing to help either his own cause or that of his old friends by exiling himself from the sources of power close to him. He could do more as part of the conclave of lords he was rejecting than he possibly could outside of them, and as long as they thought him one of them he might wear the cote of a lord to hide the skin of a good man. Even to hide the skin of a poacher.

In that moment Robin realised what he must do.

'There is a way to save those men,' he said, and now he stared not into his cup of drink but up into the warped glass of the hall windows. 'And to make things right with those I have wronged.'

Toki raised his cup in a toast. 'Squamae ceciderunt ab oculis eius,' he said. 'And lo, he could see again.'

There were several people who must help Robin for his scheme to succeed but not all needed to know it. As he rode back to Locksley Hall he turned the names over in his mind: Peter the clerk, a guard or two, Marian and the sheriff, Elaine, Thorfridh the hundredman, a man who could talk his way past any guard. He worked through the plan stage-by-stage so that when he dismounted the whole thing was formed – all that was left was to accomplish it. He crushed the pride in his heart as he re-entered his home. For this idea to work he must go begging to half a dozen people who would be all too happy to make him grovel. But they could shovel whatever muck they wanted for him to eat. As long as they believed the deceit that he was a penitential lord they would look no deeper into his intentions and his plan would succeed.

The hall was quiet in the dawn light. A few servants setting fires, the distant rattle of the kitchens. The door to his mother's chamber was closed, and within all was silence. He crept towards his own chamber, pausing as a chink of light fell over him. From the ladies' chamber, a figure appeared, stepping carefully over the sleeping form of a servant near the door.

'You are back then,' the figure said. She wrapped a cloak around herself. In the shadows she looked like an effigy. It was Marian.

'Were you worried?' smiled Robin.

'I was not.' Marian edged towards the hall stairs, inclining her head for Robin to do the same. 'Elaine spent half the night crying. I tried to tell her it was not unusual for you to disappear, but she only just fell asleep.'

'I will apologise when she wakes.'

In the half-light Robin could only make out the stark lines of Marian's face. Beneath her eyes were rims of shadow, as if a sculptor had smudged them with his thumb.

'Who told you about Agnes?' Marian asked. It was not the question Robin had expected.

'Will.'

'I would have told you myself,' she said, 'if I had thought any good would come of it. I hoped you might never hear of it. That you would have nothing more to forgive our parents for than marrying so quickly.' Robin gave a brusque laugh. Marian smiled ruefully. 'Yes, I suppose that was unlikely.'

In the hall a servant was sweeping the crumbs of last night's supper from the floor. Robin and Marian watched him for a while, unnoticed. A disc gleamed beneath his brush. He bent, inspected and pocketed the penny, looking furtively about the hall as he did so. Catching sight of the figures on the steps he started, seizing the brush to his chest as if it were a spear. Robin gestured for him to carry on. He could hardly begrudge the theft of a penny given what he was contemplating. He glanced at Marian. Now was probably as good a time as any.

'Have you heard about the enclosure?'

'No. What enclosure?'

'The common land between Nottingham and the forest. Eudo de Vipont wants to seize it to stop poachers.'

'To – to *stop* them? But without that land to farm people will starve. They barely have half the land they had a decade ago as it is, with the king claiming so much of it as royal forest…'

'I know,' nodded Robin. 'I tried to argue against it. It was agreed that we will gather the local lords to a council to decide. How do you think I can ensure the enclosure is defeated?'

Marian was surprised. 'You want my opinion?'

'Yes.'

She contemplated the floor, staring as if she could see the faces of the barons on the stones. 'I presume Serlo and Ranulf are in favour of the enclosure?'

'Yes, and Lord de Caux…'

'And Lord de la Guerche?' Robin nodded. 'All those two care about is squeezing as much money as possible from the land before they return to Normandy.'

'Guy spoke against it.'

Marian smiled to herself. 'That is good. But if Ranulf is in favour Guy might be persuaded out of that opinion. His father is…' She sought for a diplomatic description. 'Not the kindest of men.'

'Perhaps you could shore up his resolve?'

'I will try.' Marian clasped her hands together in thought. 'What about the religious lords?'

Robin had not even thought of them.

'I have only ever known them to attend the county courts when they had a vested interest in doing so, which is rarely enough. I presume they don't want their courts being interfered with, so they keep away from ours.'

'But they will have as much interest in those lands as anyone. The lay brothers of Lenton Priory use the common land, which could cause problems for the prior. And the Abbess of Newstead will argue against any enclosure – her lands border the Viponts' and she is always wrangling with them over who has greater authority.'

'Who is the abbess now?'

'Hawise de Ferrers. The late Earl of Derby's sister. She would probably listen to someone who fought beside her brother in the Holy Land. And my mother was related to her, should that be of use to you.' There was a stroke of luck. 'And Lord D'Alselin. Has he decided his opinion yet?'

'He was not there when it was discussed.'

'If you can persuade him to support you the Lords de Louvetot and Foliot will follow. My father has borne the brunt of that in the past. He says nothing is settled in this county unless Lord D'Alselin and Eudo de Vipont agree it.'

'So if one of them disagrees it gives us a better chance.'

She hesitated before asking her final question, 'What did my father say on the matter?'

'He was in favour of enclosing the land.'

'Do you think he could still be persuaded?'

'By you? You could persuade him that the sun was the moon.'

'I could before. Since he remarried…'

'I will speak to my mother if you speak to your father.'

'There's a sorry bargain. But I can try.'

'Thank you. You should go back to bed before this cold freezes you to the steps.'

Marian nodded and turned to leave.

'Actually, there is one other thing,' said Robin. 'I doubt your father will listen to me when it comes to this. I think alms should be given to the prisoners of Nottingham to celebrate Easter. An extra allowance of meat, perhaps some ale.'

'You mean the hundredmen who were arrested?' Marian did not say what Robin suspected she was thinking: *You mean the hundredmen you spoke against in the Viponts' court?* 'They are due to hang in five days.'

'All the more reason for a last scrap of charity.'

Marian drew her cloak closer around her shoulders.

'I will ask.'

She slunk back into the shadows beyond the stairs.

Everyone in Nottinghamshire had an angle you could file away at. Marian's had always been inclusion among the local lords. But despite his intention simply to use that angle to gain her assistance she had provided Robin with good counsel. Better, in fact, than most of the lords. Perhaps Friar Toki had been right, Robin thought. Perhaps he ought to follow Marian's example in more things.

Evidently her son's disappearance had not caused Lady Joan any loss of sleep.

She did not rise from her chamber until the servants had dined and the watery sun flooded the hall with light. As soon as she emerged Robin went to her to beg forgiveness. She made a pouting show of accepting it, and Sir Walter was likewise slow to hear Robin's plea. Nonetheless, both forgave him – or made an appearance of doing so, which was enough for the time-being. As Robin left them he saw Marian whisper something to her father. He followed her from the chamber. She wasted no time, that was certain. But regaining the approval of his parents and Marian was the easy task. There was one person whose agreement to participate in this plan would see it fail or succeed, and Robin feared that he would not so easily forgive and forget.

St Leonard, patron of prisoners, must have been watching over Robin, for when he sought out Will at the Scarlette croft on the eve of Good Friday, Agnes was out at church. Will was carrying sticks back from the forest for firewood and when he saw Robin on a stool outside his home he looked on the verge of throwing them at him.

'Unless you've brought a sack of food,' said Will, marching into the croft, 'we've nothing to say to each other.'

Regardless, Robin followed. 'I need your help,' he said.

'That's rich.' Will threw the sticks down at the edge of the warm ash pile of a hearth. 'Can't imagine what a bastard can do for a lord.'

'I'm going to free John Blunt and his men from the castle.'

Will paused halfway through taking a flint to the sticks. 'Persuaded the sheriff to release them, have you?'

'No, the barons still want to hang them. I said *free* them, help them escape.'

'How do you propose to do that?'

'Using a few old tricks. The Rufford switch. The Flambard bottle. Maybe the Alms Walk.'

Will struck the fire into life, tweaked the position of the twigs. 'So you can't do it without me then. What if I say no?'

'Then I'll try to find another way. Or I'll get caught, which is likelier.'

Will sat back on his heels. There was the slightest hint of a smile at the corner of his mouth. 'Got anyone else yet? You need more than two men to get past all the guards who watch the castle now, and even more to actually get the hundredmen away from Nottingham.'

'I have some idea who to ask. But there's no one I need – or want – at my side more than you. I had to come here first.'

Will could have asked any number of questions then. He could have demanded to know why Robin had suddenly changed his mind about the hundredmen, why his newly assumed noble froideur was slipping, exactly how the plan would work, when, where and with whom. But the one thing Robin had always been able to rely on in his brother – even more than fraternal affection or a sense of misplaced morality – was his capacity to ignore reason at the prospect of some excitement, and that capacity had not left him.

'I suppose I haven't anything better to do,' he said, offering his hand to Robin.

And the bargain was struck.

On his return to Locksley Hall that evening Robin found Waltheof awaiting him near the stables. The servant paused until the groom tending Robin's horse was out of earshot before speaking.

'Lady Marian has a message for you,' he said in a low voice. 'The sheriff has granted permission for alms to be dispensed to the prisoners.'

They walked together up the stairs into the hall, Robin taking his time removing his cloak and sword to provide cover for their conversation.

'She also suggests,' continued Waltheof as they reached the screens of the hallway, 'that it would be a simpler matter for you to arrange their delivery to the castle than for her to do so.'

He nodded towards a small table in the hall. The back of a veiled head was visible, the figure leaning over a board – Marian, playing at merills. Gytha was to one side of her, the attendant Edgar on the other. A little way distant was Sir Walter, warming himself by the fire. As he did so he glanced in Marian's direction. He watched as Edgar said something to her, noticed her smiling in response. As she replied the sheriff narrowed his eyes, his lips moving in mirror to hers, trying to make out her words.

'The sheriff has been keeping our lady closer ever since he learnt of her visits to his tenants,' said Waltheof. 'And since the Lords Vipont are spending Easter at the home of the Count of Mortain, she has less opportunity than normal to leave her father's side.'

'The Viponts will not be at the castle for Easter?' Robin tried to keep his voice even. That was a piece of almost divine good fortune.

'They tend to visit the count when he is in England for the Holy days. Not that the count observes them. I believe Lord Guy and his family leave for Clipstone Palace tomorrow.'

Clipstone. The royal hunting lodge was almost twenty miles from Nottingham. To go all that distance the Viponts must be intending a long visit.

'Did Lord Guy say when they will return?'

'Hocktide, probably the Tuesday after Easter. To see their prisoners hanged – forgive me, to see justice done.'

Four days, five at most. Long enough for Robin to accomplish what he had planned and the Viponts not to learn of it until it was too late.

'Thank you for that knowledge,' said Robin. 'Tell Marian that I will make sure the alms reach the castle before Easter morning.'

Robin made to leave but Waltheof stalled him. 'If you allow me, my lord,' he said, 'it was good of you to ask the sheriff for such a kindness to those condemned men.'

Robin caught the edge to Waltheof's words, and a passing keenness in his expression. The man was no fool. He must suspect that Lord Locksley's sudden altruism had more to it than seasonal benevolence. Robin considered. Waltheof had proven himself loyal and discreet when it came to his noble mistress. What was more, he had a personal interest in helping the hundredmen and spiting the Viponts, given the harm the lords' men had done his sister.

'I would do them a greater kindness if I had the opportunity,' Robin said. He retreated to the shadows of the screens passage, away from the eyes of Sir Walter. 'But I cannot say it would be within the bounds of the law.'

'I do not think it is lawful to hang those men,' said Waltheof gruffly, 'on the lies of a lord's servants. The law is abused every day by lords for land and money – why should it not be ignored to help innocent men?'

Well put, thought Robin. But there was still one more sticking point before Waltheof could be brought into the plan.

'Lady Marian cannot know anything of this. As her man, are you willing to lie to her?'

Waltheof contemplated his mistress. 'I will not lie to her,' he said at last. 'But that does not mean I will tell her more than she needs to know.'

'It will keep her safer if she knows nothing.'

Waltheof nodded. In the hall, Sir Walter still kept his grim watch over his daughter. You are looking the wrong way, Sheriff, Robin thought. And as long as Robin played his part well he would continue to do so until long after the hundredmen were free.

Easter

In the late hours of the Vigil of Easter two men approached Nottingham Castle. One wore the good wool and chain of a lord's steward. He had the look of an Englishman, but since many barons had taken native men into their household that was no cause for suspicion. At his side walked a hooded figure, leading a donkey laden with parcels in leather sacks and carrying a cask over his shoulder. This figure must surely be Norman, for his hair and eyes were dark and his beard stood stark against the tan of his face. Still, he was a lowly creature, that was plain enough. His clothes were patched and his linens sweat-stained. It was a cold night and the guards at the gatehouse had no desire to linger overlong for such a pair. They glanced at the sealed parchment in the steward's hand, saw the sign of the sheriff, something about a delivery of alms, and waved them into the yard.

'Christ be with you,' said the steward.

The pair unloaded their delivery in the yard. They gestured one of the castle servants over to help them, for whatever was in their parcels was heavy and had some distance still to be carried. Together they hobbled into the flickering light of the castle. Some passers-by still knelt at the altar halfway up the steps into the keep. No paschal candle had been placed there – perhaps the Viponts feared its theft from so open a location – but the altar was awash with smaller flames and the statues of the saints gleamed after their long Lenten concealment. Tomorrow would be a day of celebration, drunkenness and feasting, clamour and excitement. Only the hours of darkness separated that time from this last sober night. The anticipation of it hung in the air, tense as lightning.

In what had once been the ale cellar in the belly of the keep a dozen ragged men dozed and sat, the stink they had collected in that vaulted chamber scarcely bothering them after weeks of imprisonment. John Blunt counted prayers on his knuckles since he did not have a rosary. He heard a noise in the hall beyond the locked door. The guards greeting someone, or questioning. He could not tell. There was a scraping and he was blinded by a stream of light as a shuttered peephole in the door opened. The figures near him twitched and groaned as some were woken. A shadow crossing the light told them someone was looking down on them.

'We've brought a delivery for you from the sheriff,' said a voice John Blunt recognised. 'Don't get up or move suddenly. We come to bring Easter alms. Are you clear of the door?'

The men shuffled around to make room for the door to open. The lock on it was new and sprang out of place with an easy click, although the guard seemed to fumble with his keys. A figure appeared in the sudden light. John Blunt felt one of his fellow prisoners twitch to run through the open door, any opportunity to escape this hole. He seized the man's shoulder roughly. This was not the time for fool action. The figure in the doorway was hooded, but behind him John could see a man wearing richer clothes than he had any right to. Before anyone else could spy him, John himself shouted,

'What are the alms you bring?'

'Clothes,' hissed the hooded figure, throwing the parcels into the chamber. 'Get dressed fast as you can. Say nothing.'

'Meat,' called the steward behind him, loud enough for the guards to miss his accomplice's words. 'Quarters of cooked beef and mutton for you all. And something for your guards of course.'

The hooded man left the cell and the lock jolted back.

'That is good wine,' said one of the guards, downing his cup in one gulp. 'Not like the English stuff we have here. You have to drink that through gritted teeth.'

The steward's servant laughed. The other guard appointed to watch over the hundredmen of Nottingham pulled a face as the servant poured wine from the cask he had carried in.

'Doesn't seem right to drink now,' the guard said. 'Shouldn't we save this for tomorrow?'

The steward's servant took the cup from his hands.

'I'll have it if you don't want it,' he said, putting it to his lips.

'No, no,' said the guard and he seized his drink back. 'I didn't say I didn't want it. Have your own cup.'

'The sheriff wanted to reward you,' said the steward, 'for your good service. Let us have a toast to him.'

The steward refilled all their cups, raised them high and there was a silence punctuated only with slurps. His servant moved to fill the cups again the moment they were on the table. The guards did not look to see that theirs were the only empty cups.

'And a toast,' said the servant, 'with this good sir's permission, to Lord de Vipont, who put those men in a cell and gave us all a job to do when we could have been warm in our beds.'

They toasted again, drank again, the steward and his servant sipped their cups while the guards downed theirs, and again all were refilled. And so it went on. Toasts were drunk and cups refilled. The wine was strong, far stronger than the guards were used to, and the servant had forgotten the water, he said, to dilute the stuff. Never mind that, it still needed drinking. Soon not only was the wine drunk, but the guards were too. The cask was deceptively deep. The guards blinked and swayed, slumped on their stools, elbows missing the table as they leant forward to support themselves. The steward met his servant's eye, a message passing between them, and then drew out a roll of vellum.

'Now,' said the servant, 'we had better discuss our business. These men have been granted a special exemption to leave their cells for the dawn service in the town.'

The guards looked at him in confusion. One of them took up the document and unfurled it, eyes squinting to make out the words. He probably could not read it, in truth, but he knew the words for 'sheriff' and 'prisoner' and he could make them out among the muddle of penstrokes.

'This comes from the sheriff's chancery,' the servant continued. 'You can see his name and signature there.' He pointed.

'Is this a joke?' said the guard.

'No joke. The letter is clear enough. It's a dispensation for the prisoners to visit St Mary's Church. We have irons for them, and a guard is arriving at dawn to accompany us. Surely you are not questioning Sheriff Peverill?'

'No,' said the guard uncertainly. 'But prisoners are never allowed out of the keep.'

'And,' added his fellow, 'we had no word of this from Lord Vipont before he left.'

'The sheriff does not answer to Lord Vipont,' said the servant sternly. 'He answers to the king and no one else. It clearly states here that you are to release these prisoners, allow them to eat their penitential meal in peace and then permit them to leave with us before dawn.'

The guards were drunk enough to question their reason, but still they wavered. The servant stood, taking the document from their hands.

'Very well. Master Steward, I will have to go and wake the sheriff. He will not be happy to hear that these men have defied him but if that is what is takes –'

'No, wait.' The guards waved their hands, clawed at him to sit again. 'We will do as the sheriff commands. Bring the men out, give them their food and we will let you take them.'

'Good,' said the steward.

The guards stumbled to the door, fumbling their keys. The steward and servant watched closely.

'Will you have time to reach the priory?' the steward asked in a voice low enough not to be overheard.

Will Scarlette scratched his bearded chin. 'Should be fine.'

As John Blunt led the confused hundredmen from their cell Will winked. Good. They were all in their russet clothing, and all stood silent when they emerged. Will kept his hood low over his face, but the men knew him well enough. They knew the steward too: Thorfridh, the only man among them whose fine was paid, the only one to have escaped thanks to the good graces of Lady Marian. And here he was, welcoming them out of their cell, standing in fine clothes like a lord.

'Thank you, guards,' said Thorfridh with all the imperiousness he could muster. 'Hundredmen, you have been granted an Easter boon. I'll explain all, but first you –' he pointed at Will '– should ensure there are no further delays. We've wasted enough time. Guards, you've done your duty. You may enjoy your drink and rest. I'll watch the prisoners now.'

Will Scarlette bowed, grinned and bounded out of the cellar while the condemned men of Nottinghamshire gathered around the cellar table, the guards raising another cup of wine to Easter mercy.

Perhaps fittingly for a day of renewal, the Easter dawn service at Lenton Priory was accompanied by the shrieking of myriad infants. Families had come from all over the county to have their children baptised, some waiting months and risking their child's immortal soul to do so. Lady Joan heard the sound with all the grace of a woman who had been dragged from her bed in the darkness to worship at an altar miles from home.

'I simply do not understand why we must be here,' she muttered as the clergy took it in turns to creep to and kiss the crucifix on the altar steps, barefoot and on bent hand and knee. 'We have a perfectly serviceable chapel at Locksley.'

'Elaine wished it,' said Sir Walter, trying not to look displeased. 'And she is our guest.'

Elaine smiled at Robin conspiratorially. Any anger at his flight from Locksley Hall had been forgotten. She reached for his hand and entwined her fingers in his. He smiled back, then glanced up at the stained glass in the windows. The sun was beginning to filter through them. Already they had seen the sepulchre opened, the host carried around the priory beneath a velvet canopy. Soon men would join in creeping to the cross, and then the rite must surely be over. He had not expected it to go on this long. In the shadows by the antechapel he noticed Friar Toki. The friar met his eye, his hands pressed together in seeming prayer, then pointed two closed fingers in the direction of the curtained recess behind him. Robin nodded.

'Have you spoken to the prior yet?' Marian had leant closer to whisper the question.

It took Robin a moment to realise what she was talking about. The enclosure of the common land. That issue had fallen from his mind with the preparations for this morning. 'No,' he said.

'I could do it if you like?' Marian said. 'Prior Alexander has always been a friend to my father.'

'Thank you,' he said. He crossed himself. 'I did not want to think of temporal matters today.'

She raised an eyebrow but said nothing.

The moment the final prayer had been chanted and the mass was over, Robin turned to the group and made his excuses. He was going to pray with the friar for the rest of the morning, give thanks for his safe return, remember his father's soul. He should be back at Locksley in time for dinner. Alan the servant would attend him. His mother and Sir Walter only half-listened in their eagerness to escape the hordes of poor transporting their children and small gifts of food to the altar for blessing or offering. Elaine and Marian did not question him. He had pinned the crusader's palms back on his cloak that morning. It was entirely believable that his mind should be on nothing but their saviour on Easter day.

The friar held up the antechapel curtain for him to pass through. Alan waited for his lord at the altar. Within the antechapel closet Robin found Will, face scratched and in places bleeding. At Will's side was Waltheof, wearing a helmet that obscured most of his face and a tunic in the colours of the Vipont guard.

'Bloody hell, you took your time,' Will said when he saw Robin, and immediately pulled his clothes off. 'If I'd known how long you'd be I would have taken better care shaving.'

'Has everything gone to plan?' Robin asked, exchanging his rich clothes for Will's shabby poor ones.

'No problems. That wine would have rocked an elephant's wits and the document worked a treat. Your friend in the sheriff's chancery is good at his job.'

'Any problem getting those?' Robin asked Waltheof.

'Persuaded one of the Vipont's men to a game of dice. I never lose.'

'And the Viponts are still at Clipstone, visiting the Count of Mortain?'

'They left yesterday morning. Lord Guy told Lady Marian that they were stopping off at Newstead Abbey and won't return from Clipstone until tomorrow at the earliest.'

Will handed Robin the same document he had shown the guards in the castle cellar. 'You'll be needing this.' Robin passed his eye over it. 'It's all as it should be,' said Will. 'Get to the castle before those guards start asking questions.'

Robin pulled up his hood, nodded to Waltheof and both of them walked backwards out of the recess bowing.

'Lord Locksley,' Robin said, walking straight past his servant without raising so much as an eyebrow.

'Are you sure this is for all the prisoners?'

The guard at the gate of the inner bailey looked from the document in his hand to the bedraggled crowd before him.

'Of course,' said Thorfridh. 'Every prisoner in Nottingham Castle. The sheriff is thinking of their souls.'

The guard frowned at the shackled prisoners, at the steward and his servant, at the guard in a Vipont tunic at their rear. He looked tired. If Robin's guess was right he had been at his post all night. Even so, his instincts told him there was something awry here. Thorfridh looked at Robin anxiously. It was one thing sneaking two men and some packages into the castle, but brazenly leading a dozen condemned men out of it had unnerved him. Robin willed him not to lose his nerve.

The guard groaned. 'Go on then. But they'd best be back inside the walls before the bells stop ringing.'

Waltheof gave a shout to clear the way and pushed one of the prisoners forward. The pack of them marched purposefully out through the gateway. Robin glanced back over his shoulder. The guard was watching them, but had not run to investigate the cellars, thank God. The two guards reeking of wine and half-asleep would give the game away quick enough. He must have seen enough documents from the sheriff's office to know which were genuine. Thank Christ for Peter in the chancery. The clerk had not questioned the sudden charity of his master in allowing prisoners such liberty. After all, the sheriff himself had ordered him to allow a delivery of alms to the prisoners, why might he not also have allowed them to visit church on Easter morning? Peter did not seem to question much Robin told him. An admirable quality.

'You did well,' Robin said softly, pressing Thorfridh's shoulder. 'Not long now.'

They passed under the gates of the middle and outer baileys with little more than a waft of the dispensation. The castle yard was beginning to fill up with men and women celebrating Easter morning and the guards were distracted. With the hoods of their russet gowns over their heads the hundredmen were barely recognisable as the condemned prisoners of the castle's cell. As they passed out of the castle ward and into Nottingham the bells of St Mary's rang out, followed by those of St Peter's, then St Nicholas's. Distantly, even the bells of Lenton Priory could be heard echoing through the forest. Churchgoers spilled from Mass into the alehouses and then onto the streets, jugs of ale in hand.

Robin led the hundredmen into St Mary's against the tide. Priests were busy baptising whatever children had not found their way to Lenton. They scarcely glanced at the group in russet. There were others around the church wearing similar colours, the cheap cloth that lords handed out to the poor on Easter morning in return for the promise of prayers for their soul. The slight pallor and unkempt appearance of the hundredmen was concealed in the shadows of the church. Thorfridh led the men to kneel in one of the aisles, their clasped hands in front of them. Robin passed along the row of them unlocking their wrist irons and gathering them into a sack so they did not drop noisily to the floor. Waltheof kept a look-out. When all the chains were gathered together, Robin pushed them far under a bench. From above it looked like nothing more than a forgotten bundle.

'Cross yourselves,' said Robin, 'and we'll be away.'

'Wait,' said Waltheof. He held out his arm to bar them. Robin followed Waltheof's gaze to the entrance of the church. Two guards in the Vipont colours stood there, and between them was Lord Eudo's steward.

'What is Lanfranc doing here?' Robin breathed.

'A steward's place is in his lord's home,' Waltheof said. 'He'll have stayed behind to keep order while the Viponts are away.'

The hundredmen were looking now too. They all knew Lanfranc well enough – he had been the leader of the men arresting them and tearing up their homes.

Thurstan the blacksmith's son clenched his fists. 'I'll happily move him aside,' he growled.

'What should we do?' whispered Thorfridh.

Lanfranc was scanning the church's occupants. Had he heard about the hundredmen's outing? Robin played through solutions in his mind. They were inside the walls of the church, they could claim sanctuary there. But even as he thought it he foresaw Lanfranc's men, in swords and mail, dragging the hundredmen from the building. The moment they were on the steps those swords would be in their guts. The hundredmen were twitching, drawing attention to themselves as they bristled for a fight. People were starting to notice them. This was not what Robin had planned. They were supposed to be faceless, unnoticeable in their russets. If one of their number was recognised now Lanfranc would hear of it and that would be the end of them.

'Keep your heads down,' said Robin, 'and your hoods up. Do nothing to draw attention. Stick close to me, but separate from each other. Thorfridh, you'll need to talk.'

Thorfridh nodded but his face blanched. Robin's heart sank. He had chosen Thorfridh for this plan because he was strong and wanted to help his friends escape from prison. He had neither Will's fast wits nor his silver tongue. All he was supposed to do was look and walk like a steward. Robin tried not to let his concern show.

'Remember, you're the sheriff's steward,' he muttered to Thorfridh as they approached the door. 'You can go where you like. You don't have to answer to him.'

But even before they reached the door Robin felt Thorfridh swerving. He could not stop looking at Lanfranc. Lanfranc noticed. He held up his hand. When not only Thorfridh but a party of men in russets paused at his command Lanfranc frowned.

'I recognise you,' Lanfranc said to Thorfridh. 'Where have we met before?'

In the forest, thought Robin. In Lord Eudo's court. When Thorfridh came to you for justice and you beat him and threw him in a cell.

'I do not think we have,' said Thorfridh. 'Unless it was in the sheriff's office?'

'I know the men of the sheriff's office,' said Lanfranc. 'And I do not know you from there.'

'We are late, sir,' Robin said to Thorfridh, trying to keep his own face hidden within his hood so Lanfranc did not ask why Lord Locksley was wandering about in poor man's clothes. 'We'd best be on our way.'

'Stay one moment,' said Lanfranc. His hand fell on Thorfridh's arm. The touch looked light but Thorfridh froze as if in a vice. 'What is your position in the sheriff's household? You cannot be his steward for I know that man.'

'I – I am.'

Thorfridh froze. There was nothing for it, Robin thought. The longer they stood in the open the likelier it was that someone would recognise the hundredmen.

'He is Lord Locksley's steward,' Robin said. 'The old Lord Locksley, who's dead.'

'Yes,' said Thorfridh, nodding gratefully. 'We're dispensing alms in his memory.'

'A noble venture for a man with a dead master. And where are they?'

'Where are what?'

'The alms. You do not carry anything.'

Again Thorfridh looked to Robin. Lanfranc missed nothing. He could smell something rotten when a man in gentle clothes looked to one in rags for answers. Robin turned his head to keep Lanfranc's eyes from his, and as he did so he saw a cart at the edge of the market square. It was loaded with food and drink, a delivery to the alehouse no doubt.

'The alms are there,' Robin said. He pointed to the cart and raised his voice. 'Alms in Lord Locksley's memory. Food and drink for all who need them.' The milling crowd around the church door turned to look. Many of them wore rags or russets, were doubtless hungry for whatever free food they could get. 'We must get on with dispensing the alms, sir,' said Robin to Thorfridh. 'Now that we have said our prayers.' He turned his back on Lanfranc, addressed the crowd at large. 'Follow us. All true-hearted poor who remember Lord Locksley in their prayers. This way.'

Robin nudged Thorfridh onwards. Thorfridh gave Lanfranc a swift bow as he was pulled down the steps. If mingling into the crowd didn't work, thought Robin, then why not be at the head of it? Waltheof took his hint immediately, gestured for the hundredmen in their russets to join the swelling crowd across the square. Thanks be to St Leonard, no one was guarding the cart. Doubtless the deliveryman had been lured into the alehouse by the promise of a rewarding ale. I can always repay him, thought Robin. Once I am Lord Locksley again. Besides, desperate times demanded desperate measures, and if you could not help good men within the law, then you must do so outside it. Robin leapt onto the cart and pulled food from sacks. Thorfridh followed his lead, encouraging the crowd forward to accept the alms in return for prayers. John Blunt came up close to Robin's side and said,

'That bastard steward is still watching us.'

Robin nodded, pretended to be engrossed in unloading the cart.

'Tell the men,' he whispered, 'to get to the forest. You should be able to find the caves and abandoned crofts in there. Stay away from the roads and the boundaries of land. There is an area north of the common land – Waltheof can tell you – where you'll find shelter and a stream. We'll bring food and drink to you as soon as we can. In the meantime, make do with what you find there.'

John Blunt drew the eyes of his friends, and Robin watched as the message passed from one to the next. Under the cover of the screeching crowd, one by one they approached the cart, took a loaf of bread or piece of salted meat, nodded to Robin and left. Perhaps Lanfranc noticed, but in the confusion of comings and goings in the market square he would have been hard-pressed to make out which men were escaped prisoners and which innocent poor. Just as the supplies on the cart were running low, a man emerged from the alehouse in a blind panic.

'Get away from that!' he cried. 'Those are my deliveries.'

'Not today,' called Robin. 'Today they are alms.'

'This is theft,' cried the man. 'Stop! Stop before I call for help.'

He pushed against the crowd, and the crowd pushed back. They would not give up the chance of free food just on his say so. The man called for his friend, the crowd raised their fists. Just as the brawling started in earnest, Robin leapt from the cart, pulled Thorfridh after him and the pair of them fled the square unscathed. They were still running when they got to the King's Way. Between ragged breaths, Robin realised he was laughing. Laughing like a madman from sheer joy. Never mind that the Locksley name had been mentioned, that the Viponts' steward had seen them, that they had stolen from an alehouse to cover themselves – the hundredmen were free, and as far as any man could say, Robin of Locksley had spent the entire morning praying in Lenton Priory with a servant at his side.

Marian paced the hall, her skirts sweeping back and forth, the tapping of her shoes echoing off the empty chamber. Every time she turned she left a circular smear of rainwater on the flagstones. In her hands the parchment was damp from its journey through the wet Easter morning. The heavens had opened just as they left Lenton and soaked them through before they reached Locksley Hall. Marian took the rain as a blessing. As long as her family were distracted they would not see her with the parchment, or question her about its contents. She had a lie prepared just in case: she had written to the Abbess of Newstead because she was a distant relation and Marian had heard she was unwell. She wanted to inquire after the abbess's health to set her mind at ease, there was no need to trouble her father or stepmother until she knew if there was cause for concern, and now word had come with the good news that indeed, the abbess had fully recovered. As it happened, the lie had gone unspoken. Her family had scattered to change their clothes and prepare for the day's feasting. Elaine was beautifying herself, which Marian could only imagine meant washing and drying her face since there was little that could be done to improve on Nature's work. And Lady Joan and her father were clearly going to take their time dressing for supper if the jug of Gascon wine Marian had seen winging its way to their chamber was anything to go by.

Marian had not spoken to her father yet about the enclosure, and until she knew his mind she was resolved to keep the true reason for her correspondence with the abbess to herself. Every time she went to Sir Walter to discuss the common land, she found him with Lady Joan, and it was fruitless appealing to his compassion in her presence. If her father was still in favour of the enclosure, it would displease him to learn that his daughter was appealing to local lords to oppose it. If he was coming around to her opinion then learning that she had secretly discussed the matter with Robin might well send him reeling back to Ranulf de Vipont's way of thinking. Best to keep her own counsel until she knew her father's mind for certain. Now if only Lord Locksley would get back from his praying before the family finished their ablutions, she could deliver her intelligence and her father need never know what she had been up to. But she had been pacing the hall since the chapel bell rang for Vespers, and there was still no sign of him. As always, he was proving obdurate.

Just as she decided she could not stand being in her damp clothes any longer and would retire to her chamber to change she heard rapid steps on the stairwell and the next moment Robin appeared, shaking the rain from his cloak. He stopped short when he saw her. She glanced around quickly to ensure they were alone and gestured for him to join her by the fire. He looked suspicious, but joined her nonetheless.

'I was beginning to think you would be praying all day,' she said.

'Are you censuring my religious observance?' asked Robin. He might have been intending to reprimand, but he sounded amused.

She handed the parchment to him. He squinted to read the thin clerical hand, then turned the seal in his palm.

'From the Abbess of Newstead,' he said. 'Have you already read it?'

'Yes,' said Marian, her patience failing as he slowly took in the letter. 'I wrote her that you were willing to tell her about her brother's deeds in Acre, if in return she would listen to your concerns about the common land. She has accepted the proposal. You can visit her at any time.'

'I am not sure her brother's deeds will make good listening. He went to Acre, he got camp fever, he died.'

'Perhaps you could embellish that story a little,' Marian suggested. 'I spoke to Prior Alexander at Lenton this morning as well. He did not much like the thought of the common land being claimed by the Viponts when so many of the priory's lay brothers use it. If you could get him to the council of lords I think he will speak for you rather than them.'

'Thank you,' said Robin, making to leave with the letter.

'And,' Marian stepped into his path, 'I met with Guy before he left for Clipstone Palace. It was well I did. His father had almost twisted his thoughts completely. But he has turned them again. He will speak against the enclosure when the council meets. When I can find my father alone, I will appeal to him too.'

'You have been busy.'

'You asked me to help,' said Marian defensively. She thought she was being mocked. 'What has Lord D'Alselin said on the matter?'

He looked confused.

'You were going to speak to him?' Marian prompted.

'Ah. Yes.' He shook his head at his forgetfulness. 'I have not yet.'

'Oh.' Marian tried to hide her disappointment. She suspected she did not succeed. 'I thought you must have been meeting with him, since you have been away from the hall so much the last few days.'

'No,' he said. Then, sensing the need for an explanation, added, 'I have been riding. Making the most of this good weather. That is over now though, so I can write to D'Alselin today.'

He nodded farewell to her and hurried from the hall. She watched his wet footprints scuff the path of her circular pacing. The trail looked almost like water falling through an hourglass.

At the Easter feast in Locksley Hall, no one spoke of the hundredmen's escape. Robin thought the sheriff must know of it by then. A messenger had arrived from the castle not long before supper was served, and at the meal table Sir Walter's face was grim as thunder. Lady Joan clearly did not know the cause. She kept trying to meet his eye, but had the sense not to ask questions while they ate. Elaine and Marian, sensitive to the sheriff's mood, kept their conversation light and brief. It was not long before even their cheering efforts fell away and silence reigned in the hall.

Robin was glad of the quiet. He was thinking about the hundredmen in the forest. As long as they followed their instincts they should be able to keep ahead of any lawmen hunting for them. Lefchild had once told Robin how he had hidden in the top branches of a tree for three days to escape a woman's vengeful father. The men had food for today, and water in the streams, and together they knew the land better than any Vipont guard or Peverill man. The rain would be miserable, but if they could reach shelter in the sandstone caves they would have a happier time of it than their pursuers. The difficulty would be getting them more food and clothing in the days ahead. Who was best to carry it to them? Robin himself, since he must be considered innocent of any involvement? Or Will Scarlette, who could creep his way to the king's jewels in Westminster if set the challenge? He smiled to himself. His blood had raced through his veins that morning, as it had not done since he left the Holy Land. He had felt again that surge of energy, that concentration, which overtook him before a battle. On the long, tense army marches along the sea edge between Acre and Jaffa, waiting at every moment for an attack at their flank, he had felt as if every nerve in his body were singing at once while his mind was perfect silence. That singing silence had overtaken him as they ran from St Mary's to throw alms to the crowd.

His thoughts were interrupted as he heard, at the reaches of his thoughts, the sounds of men approaching. The crackle of the fire and patter of rain were overtaken by the cantering of horses, a dozen horses easily thought Robin, with dogs barking at their heels. The voices of men calling out to one another. As the sounds grew closer, the others at the table heard them too and tensed to listen. In an instant the noise was in the courtyard, flickers of light darting back and forth between the slats of the shutters at the windows. The horsemen halted – a watchman called out to them to know their business, was silenced by an order.

'Has the gate not been locked?' cried Lady Joan, her face white.

'The gate is not closed for another hour,' said Marian, still holding a piece of bread between her bowl and her mouth. She looked to her father.

'Ladies, you should retire,' said Sir Walter, standing. 'I wager I know who this is.'

The Viponts, thought Robin. And the next moment his guess was proved right. Crashing up the stairs and into the hall stormed a pack of Viponts, red-faced and glowering. Outside, it still rained and their faces and clothes all were streaked with trails of water. Behind them came their men, lances in hand and helms on their heads, glinting in the candlelight. Lady Joan cried out in alarm as Ranulf thundered all the way to Sir Walter's table without uncloaking himself or surrendering his weapon.

'How in Christ's name has this happened?' he was shouting. 'We have been gone barely two days and the castle is broken, criminals freed –'

'Control yourself, Father.' Guy ran after Ranulf and seized his arm. Ranulf looked on the brink of striking Guy for his insolence.

'You alarm the women,' his son said in a lower voice, quickly releasing his hold.

Robin glanced around. Elaine's hand was on his back, as if to shield herself from the onslaught of the Viponts. His mother had leapt to her feet and stood now, ashen at the sight of armed men – even armed lords – charging into her home. Marian had moved towards her father and her eyes were on him, not the Viponts, watching.

Eudo stepped forward, resting his own hand on his brother's arm for a moment. He nodded at Guy approvingly.

'Forgive us our choler,' he said silkily to the party at large. 'We returned to Nottingham Castle after receiving grievous intelligence from our steward. I presume you already know of it, Sheriff?'

'Yes.'

'Then perhaps we could speak with you,' Eudo's eyes flickered snake-like in Robin's direction, 'and Lord Locksley in private?'

'Grievous intelligence?' repeated Lady Joan in a whisper to her husband. 'What has happened?'

'Marian,' said Sir Walter, 'will you escort my lady to the solar?'

Marian did not move. She met Guy's eye. He nodded slowly. An acknowledgement, Robin thought, that he would talk to her later. On receiving that acknowledgement, Marian took Lady Joan by the arm and led her from the chamber. As they left Elaine whispered at Robin's shoulder, asking if he knew the cause of the Vipont rage. Robin said he did not, pressed her hand to comfort her, and she followed her cousin out of the hall. As soon as the ladies were gone, Sir Walter struck the table with the flat of his hand.

'It is not the custom of this county,' he said in a voice trembling with anger, 'for lords to bring weapons to the hall of their sheriff, nor to terrify his family.'

'We had no wish to alarm,' said Eudo before Ranulf could speak, 'but you must have expected our anger. We were in the company of the Count of Mortain when we received the news that the condemned men had escaped from his castle. Thank God, we did not have to reveal the full truth to him. The trust of our prince is the most precious thing to us, and to lose it through another's incompetence –'

'The castle is under your guardianship,' interrupted Sir Walter. 'If the men you appointed to watch it in your absence were not fit for the task, it is your mistake, not mine.'

'Our mistake?' Serlo cried contemptuously. 'Is it *our* mistake if our guards are handed documents signed by the sheriff's office? If men enter the castle bringing alms *you* have ordered? If a mob brawls before our steward in the name of *Lord Locksley*?'

The eyes of the chamber fell on Robin. He forced an expression of surprise.

'I caused no brawl,' he said. 'I was at Lenton Priory most of the day.'

'The mob started fighting,' said Guy, 'over alms dispensed in the name of your father.'

'A strange occurrence,' added Serlo. 'For a dead man to hand out alms.'

'Easter is a time of resurrection,' said Robin. Despite himself, he was smiling. 'But I did not order alms in my father's name. He had many servants and tenants who admired him when he was alive. Perhaps one of them doled out alms for his memory?'

There was some logic to what he said, as even the Viponts must admit. They knew that the late Lord of Locksley had been popular. Sir Walter nodded in agreement, unwilling for any blame to attach itself to his household.

'What of the alms you ordered, Sheriff?' asked Ranulf. 'Which of your servants delivered them to the castle? They should be brought before us to answer our questions.'

Sir Walter hesitated and Robin knew why. Marian had requested the alms for the hundredmen, and it had been to her that the alms were given. Perhaps the sheriff did not know that she had handed the responsibility for their delivery to Robin.

'I – I am not certain,' he said. He looked at Guy as he spoke. If he hoped his future son-in-law would realise the reason for his reticence he was not disappointed.

'The servants bearing alms might easily have been waylaid and had their goods stolen,' said Guy. 'Lanfranc said that the guards did not recognise the men as part of the sheriff's household.'

'What of the documents signed from the sheriff's chancery?' demanded Serlo. 'You cannot imagine those were stolen? There cannot be one man in a hundred who can write in this county.'

'Forgery is an easy enough skill to master,' said Robin. 'Any man who can write could have counterfeited such a document, and we are surrounded by religious houses with oblates, monks – lay brothers even – who might write. Did these documents which fooled your guards have the sheriff's seal attached?'

Serlo and Ranulf exchanged glances.

'Lanfranc did not mention it,' admitted Serlo.

'Then perhaps your men need to be trained to look for seals as well as signatures.'

'How dare you,' cried Ranulf. 'This youth defies us at every turn. We are trusted friends of a prince, but you scorn us, undermine our authority in this county.'

Eudo tried to calm him but he would not allow it.

'No, I have had enough. Since the day he returned he has been a thorn in our sides. Look to your family, Sheriff.'

'I will do as I think best,' said Sir Walter coolly. 'With my family, as with my county. Now as your sheriff, show me some respect.'

'How much longer do you imagine you will remain sheriff if the count learns of your ineptitude?' asked Eudo, matching Sir Walter's calm tone. 'If he was told that you put your family before this county's safety? The common lands harbour felons but you will not enclose them. Locksley allowed a poacher to escape but you did not so much as fine him.'

'Where would I get the money to pay a fine?' demanded Robin. 'You are still squatting on my lands.'

Eudo pointedly turned away from Robin.

'Remember, Sir Walter, who holds real power in Nottinghamshire. If you wish for us to keep the sorry state of affairs in your household from the count, you would be wise to show your loyalty to us. Do not defy us any further, and try to bring the men responsible for this outrage to justice as quickly as possible.'

He turned his back on the sheriff, an indignity that his brother and son repeated as they filed out of the hall. Guy bowed respectfully, but he too left without another word. Sir Walter stood in silence as the sounds of the Viponts mounting their horses and riding out of the courtyard echoed up from outside the walls. His face was red, his right hand twitching into a fist and out of it.

'Thank you for speaking in my defence,' he said at last. His voice was so low Robin could barely hear it. 'But I must ask you now that they are gone. Did you order alms for your father's soul?'

'No,' said Robin. It was true, after all.

'Do you know of any man who would have done it? Perhaps a man connected to the escaped prisoners?'

'No one. I was speaking the truth before – many men in my father's household were loyal to him, loved him even. But most of those men are not in your household, so I have not seen them since I returned.'

'What about…?' Sir Walter stopped himself.

Will, thought Robin, and in an instant any pity he felt for the sheriff's humiliation at the Viponts' hands dried up. He would not let his brother's safety be threatened to save Sir Walter from their suspicions.

'Will Scarlette has no part in this,' he said firmly. 'He does not have enough food to feed himself and Agnes, never mind handing bread out to every man in the market place.'

Sir Walter nodded briskly and walked away from Robin, to the fire. Robin could follow his stepfather's thoughts easily enough. The sheriff had noticed that Robin knew of Will's conditions, so he knew that the brothers had met since Robin's return. But any right Sir Walter had to chastise him for such a meeting had burnt away as soon as Robin knew of Agnes Scarlette's treatment at his hands. At least Sir Walter had the decency to look embarrassed. This did provide Robin with an opportunity, though. He had known that the Viponts would suspect someone connected to the sheriff as soon as they learnt of the document produced in his chancery. Admittedly, he had not expected for them to learn of it so soon. But that just meant Robin must act swiftly himself. If he was to protect his co-conspirators, it was essential that he was involved in the sheriff's hunt for the guilty parties.

'If I hear of any of my father's old servants being involved in this, I will tell you. Perhaps in return you would trust me to help find the men involved?' Sir Walter was uncertain. Robin leant closer. 'I could make sure that none of Marian's men are investigated?'

That caught him. 'I will take care of questioning my daughter's household,' Sir Walter said quickly. 'But I see no reason why you should not assist me. We are in this matter together, I think?' He gave a grim smile and added under his breath, 'Jesus help us.'

Hocktide

Through the mist-smeared dawn stole a cloaked figure on horseback. The earth was damp and moisture clung to the cobwebs strung between the trees. Robin ducked beneath one such glistening trap as the forest pressed in tight around him. Despite the early hour it could have been dusk for all the daylight piercing the thick canopy of branches. A shaft of dust-moted light fell now and then across him and over the heavy saddlebags on his horse while they wound slowly through the trees. Ahead, at last, was the sandy cliff face with its patchwork of caves. The last sorry settlement of men he had passed was miles back, at the edge of the forest, but through the mist he could definitely see smoke issuing from one of the cave fissures. He halted his horse and listened. Distantly, a bird croaked in the treetops, but otherwise the forest was silent. He had listened and looked the whole way there and though he had seen nothing, heard nothing, he still could not be certain that he had not been followed. The Viponts' men could move as silently as him.

He pressed onwards, dismounting at the bottom of the cliffs and looping his horse's reins over a thorn bush. He whistled three times. From within the cave a whistle answered his. A face appeared at one of the crevices in the pitted sandstone. Robin recognised one of the hundredmen. The man nodded to him, then disappeared back into the cliff face. As Robin untied the saddlebags from his horse he heard a rustling at his side, then a soft thud and a figure appeared. Thurstan.

'Lord Locksley,' he said. His arms were folded and an axe was at his hip. Robin wondered where he had found it. Before he could ask, Thurstan turned and gestured for Robin to follow.

Concealed behind an expanse of twisted ivy, at the height of Robin's chest, was the entrance to the caves. Thurstan held the ivy screen aside as Robin threw the bags onto the ledge then lifted himself into the gap. Around the entrance water pooled and dripped, but a few steps within – and although stooped, Robin could easily move without needing to drop to his knees – the cave was dry.

'Straight ahead,' called Thurstan as he heaved himself after Robin. 'The ground slopes up. Watch your step.'

Robin followed the cave floor as it ascended, running his hand along the wall where darkness swallowed the tunnel. Every now and then a shaft of light would fall across the path and with it the slipperiness of mould over the floor, where the cave had crumbled away and formed a kind of window inside the rock. When the tunnel began to level out he smelt smoke and saw flickering shadows. A few steps further brought him to a cave chamber, large enough for a dozen men to sit and stand around a fire, with a chink in the wall above the level of their heads acting as a natural chimney, drawing smoke out of the space. The men lolling around the fire stood to welcome him, taking the bags and dividing their contents.

'I hope there is enough food in those,' said Robin. 'It seemed safest to come alone, and this was all I could carry.'

'No ale,' said a morose voice. Lefchild stepped out of the shadows, his pale hair tinted red by the firelight. 'But I suppose meat is more important. Well met, Lord Locksley.'

He held out his arms and embraced Robin. He was the only one to greet Robin so warmly. The other men kept their distance once the food was received, retreating to their corners of the chamber. Some – those who had not known him before – glanced at him uncertainly, heads bowed, wondering whether they ought to kneel in the presence of a lord, thinking it odd to do so in such a place. Those he had known met his eye, challenging him. They would remember how he chastised John Blunt for addressing him as 'Master Robin'. He understood their wariness. He had denied their plea for intervention in the forest and condemned them in the court – but he had also sprung them from imprisonment, saved them from death and brought them food in their exile. Yes, he understood their mistrust, and he knew that he must address it.

'I wanted to bring you this parcel of food,' he said, loud enough that his voice echoed off the close walls of the cave, 'so that I could speak to you all. I know I've wronged you in the past – some of you worse than can be forgiven.'

He glanced at Thurstan. The blacksmith met his eye coldly.

'Could you forgive Will's killer?' he asked, his voice a low rumble against the stone.

It was a question Robin had asked himself, often, in the past four years. If the knife had slipped another way, been in another man's hands, he could well have been asking it in truth. His response was always the same.

'Not easily.'

'Then you understand. I won't resent you being here, not after you saved us all from the noose. But I can't call you a friend.'

Robin nodded. It was more than he had thought Geraint's brother would give him. He turned back to the rest of the chamber. There was no need to raise his voice now, every eye and ear was on him.

'I won't offer the rest of you excuses for my wrongs these last few weeks, except to say that I thought I was doing right. I was a fool to think that. Will has told me a dozen times that I'm an idiot. You can tell me too.'

'You're an idiot,' called Lefchild, then laughed. It broke the silent wall of men around Robin. Some of them laughed too, nervously. They stopped watching him quite so closely, so coldly.

'I'm sorry for all the harm I have done you. That harm can't be undone, but I will do everything I can now to make amends. It doesn't bleach out my mistakes, and I don't expect you to think it does. But if you let me, I'll help you and your kin however you ask.'

John Blunt stepped forward.

'My lord –' John began.

'Robin,' he interrupted. 'Please. I'm not your lord here.'

John smiled crookedly.

'Eat with us, Robin. Or at least sit by the fire and watch us eat.' He turned his back on the lord, a test perhaps of how truly he wished to be equal among them. Robin let him sit before joining the group. John noticed, nodded to himself and smiled again. 'You've enough to eat in your own home, I think, that you won't begrudge us keeping this to ourselves.'

The men settled themselves around the fire again, some laughing quietly at John's words, others still watching for Robin's reaction. Most of these men knew no more of Lord Locksley than what they had heard from local gossips, and it would be some time before they were anywhere near comfortable in his presence. Robin was not fool enough to expect more than that. No man forgot a wrong done against him and his kin just because he once sat round a fire with the wrongdoer. But at least they had not turned him away once their supplies were delivered. He waited for them to eat their fill before speaking again.

'Have you had any trouble since you reached the forest?' he asked.

'Not yet,' replied John. 'Sheriff's men came past once. Not seen anything of the Viponts.'

'They probably don't know about the caves.'

'We have someone on lookout all the time.'

'Good. And what about weapons? You may need them if you are found.'

John nodded to a dark corner, where the glint of metal was just visible. Robin went to look. There were a few sorry knives, some sticks, a short hunting bow next to a few arrows, things that Will had brought – even with Thurstan's axe it made for a pitiful arsenal.

'We gathered the sticks as we went,' said John. 'Some are sharpened, some can be used as clubs. If the sheriff's men get close enough for us to use them we'll probably be dead anyway.'

'Perhaps,' said Robin. 'I saw a group of pilgrims with nothing but clubs and knives take down a mounted Saracen at Arsur.'

'We may as well be dead,' said a thickset man sitting in the shadows, perhaps twice Robin's age. 'We have our lives, but nothing else. We can't return to our homes or kin without being hanged.'

'Doleswif,' Lefchild called to the man, 'you've been talking like this since we left Nottingham. You could have stayed in that cell, and if you had you would already be dead. At least now you have a hope of helping your kin.'

'They would be better off if we were hanged, said Doleswif bitterly. 'When the county court meets it will call for us to come forward, we won't and we'll be declared outlaws. Everything that belonged to us will be seized, and as long as we're outlaws our children can't even inherit our lands or goods when we die.'

'That's true enough,' said another man. His hair and beard hung in a long blonde tangle like rope. Tosti was his name, John told Robin. 'How are we supposed to help our kin from inside a cave?'

'My family has one less mouth to feed now,' said a young man who had somehow managed to make himself more presentable than his fellows. His russets rested neatly on his folded arms. 'They're better off without me.'

'That would be true, Gilbert,' said Tosti, 'except they also have one less worker for their lands, one less man to bring in money. I daresay Lord Locksley won't be giving every one of our relatives dole?'

The men turned to Robin.

'No,' he admitted. 'I can't.'

Even if he and Marian went on another round of donations, giving clothing or fuel as well as stolen foodstuffs, they could hardly provide for the entire kin of a dozen men. And given how closely Sir Walter was watching his household since Easter Robin doubted whether they would even be able to steal such a quantity of supplies in the first place. Getting this parcel of food together had required some fast talking with the sheriff's clerk.

'Taxmen will arrive soon,' said Doleswif. 'How will our kin pay taxes if all our chattels are gone?'

'We could get money,' said Gilbert.

'You mean we could steal,' said Tosti. 'I was never a thief before. I'm not going to be one now. It's wrong.'

'You seem to have forgotten,' said John, 'that without the help of a thief we wouldn't be free now.'

'Will Scarlette could show us what to do,' said Lefchild. 'We can just take from the richer folk if that'll put your conscience at ease.'

Tosti did not agree. A group of men around him shouted out their own arguments against Lefchild and Gilbert.

'We could poach then,' cried Lefchild over them. 'There's no harm in that. Lords don't need all the deer in their parks. Eh, Robin?'

Robin had sat silently, listening to their arguments. He had already helped poachers to escape justice once, and stolen from the deliveryman in the market place. He could hardly argue against thieving now. All the same, the time might come when the hundredmen would be forgiven their crimes against the Viponts – if Robin could regain his lands and win the support of his fellow lords, another trial could take place, and without the Vipont influence the result would surely be different. When that day came, it would go easier with the men if they had not spent their time in the forest thieving from their neighbours.

'If you can keep from further lawbreaking perhaps you should.'

'That's easy enough for a lord to say,' cried Doleswif. 'Every law in England is made to help the lords and harm us.'

That argument received the loudest cheer of support so far.

'I won't deny that,' said Robin. 'But I agree with Gilbert here. As long as you're alive, your families have hope – hope for your return, hope for more food, because I am certain we can find a way to help them. If you're killed poaching, your families will suffer for it. We all need to be careful to keep you alive. And I promise you that as long as you are in the forest there will be one lord who is watching your families and using the law to protect them.'

The men shuffled as he fell silent. Perhaps some believed him, perhaps they just wanted to end the quarrel among them. Robin was speaking nothing less than the truth. He knew now that he would not desert these men, and nor would Will as long as he could keep out of trouble. As he poked another stick into the fire he caught John Blunt's eye. Blunt nodded, and smiled.

Robin rode back slowly through the brightening morning, the sun burning the mist from the fields. On those farms fortunate enough still to have livestock there was a flurry of activity. It was farrowing season, and the squeals of newborn piglets issued from straw-churned pens. It was strange to think of the rounds of the season continuing here, the swineherds shaking away their Easter hangovers, the women milking their cows and goats with full bellies for the first time in weeks. Soon it would be dry enough for roofs to be rethatched and sheep marked. From above this world, on horseback, Robin thought that of course these things must be done. These people would not care overmuch if the lords were fighting among themselves or that the sheriff might lose his position. They might not even care that a dozen condemned men were roaming the forest. What mattered to them was ensuring their animals lived and their grains were sowed. They watched the heavens and prayed to the saints, hoping the coming tax demands would not be too high and that their livelihood would thrive to support them. Life and death hung between a taxman's scales and the rain.

In the stables at Locksley Hall a groom was rubbing down a handsome palfrey, supervised critically by a squire in the Vipont colours. The squire nodded a greeting to Robin and told him he was accompanying Lord Guy. If Guy had left his attendant to harass the Peverill groom, perhaps he was discussing matters he did not wish to be reported back to his family. Robin remembered the nod he had given Marian yesterday. He must be telling her all about the escape of the condemned men – Robin's name could not help but be dragged into it. Would Marian presume his innocence and argue against Eudo's theory that he and the sheriff were purposefully trying to undermine the Viponts? For that matter, would Guy himself question his uncle's opinion? From what Robin had seen so far, for a grown man Guy was as much in thrall to his father as any of Ranulf's baseborn tenants. Those Viponts did not permit dissension from their own. Perhaps it was no surprise that the squire had been left outside.

Before Robin had even crossed the courtyard one of the ladies of Marian's household was at his elbow. She was a pale reed of a woman and her voice was low and mournful like a pipe. Estrild was her name, if Robin remembered right.

'My lady sent me to watch for your return, my lord,' she said, gaze fixed so firmly on the ground it was a wonder she did not walk into the wall. 'She is speaking with Lord Vipont in the solar. My lady asks you to join them.'

Robin hesitated. Guy might want to question him about his involvement in the events of yesterday.

'I will join them as soon as I have changed out of my riding clothes,' he said. That should give him time to consider how to answer Guy's queries. If he took long enough, Guy might even grow bored of waiting and leave.

'My lady asked that you go to the solar immediately on your return,' said

Estrild in a tone that brooked no refusal. 'It is urgent.'

Robin allowed himself to be led to the solar without delay. When they reached the door to the chamber Estrild knocked and then stood back. The door opened immediately, was held just open far enough to let him through, then shut again. Waltheof stood behind it. He gave Robin a nod but no other greeting. Anyone observing them would think they were as distant as any servant and lord could be. Marian and Guy were sitting by the fire, close enough to whisper. At the knock on the door they abruptly hushed.

'Good, Estrild found you,' Marian said, ushering Robin into the chamber with some relief.

Guy stood slowly to greet Robin. They met each other with curt formality.

'I do not wish to intrude,' Robin said. Marian gestured for him to sit, stayed standing herself. 'But your woman, Estrild was insistent. Do you choose all your attendants for their severity?'

'Gytha is not severe.'

Marian glanced at the old woman, who was inevitably acting chaperone. She regarded Robin with the cruel concentration that a spider gives a fly.

'No, you are quite right,' Robin said dryly. 'Gytha is sweet as cream.'

'You are not intruding in any case,' Marian went on. 'We need to discuss the enclosure of the common land. Guy has been telling me about his family's work to ensure it goes ahead, so we need to act quickly if we are to stop them.'

'I would have thought,' Robin said to Guy, 'that your family would be too busy searching for the escaped prisoners to concern themselves with this enclosure.'

'They are more concerned than ever,' said Guy bleakly. 'It was humiliating enough to be faced with armed men on a falconry expedition and poachers spoiling our hunt. But at least these trespasses were on lands that it is easy enough for common men to encroach. Now that even our castle has proven itself pregnable my family are worried that the count will lose his trust in us. The sheriff – forgive me, Marian – does not seem to take these matters as seriously as we do. My family will redouble all efforts to assert their authority over the county, and enclosing the common land is the first step to doing so.'

'You sound as if you agreed with them.'

Guy pursed his lips, paused, looked at Marian, seemed to consider the most diplomatic answer.

'I think the people of Nottinghamshire have become increasingly unruly in the last year or more, and I fear a harder hand is needed with them. However, I do not believe that the common land is so great a threat as my family perceive it. I admit that I am in a rather difficult position. I would not wish to side against my own family, nor against Marian's.'

He looked at Robin, with a keen expression that Robin did not trust.

'I am afraid we have caused trouble for Guy,' said Marian. 'The message that I sent to the Abbess of Newstead – remember, I had the reply on Easter morning? I had not realised that the abbess received my letter while the Lords Vipont were breaking their journey at the Abbey on the way to Clipstone.'

'The abbess rather unfortunately brought up the topic of enclosure in front of my family,' said Guy. 'They were far from pleased to learn that the two of you were eliciting the support of a religious lord against their interests.'

'They must have realised that we would gather our own supporters,' said Robin. 'I presume they have been doing the same thing.'

'But not with the religious lords,' said Guy. 'It has been generally understood until now that church matters remain the concern of the church, and that disputes over manorial land are settled by the lords.'

'But this is common land,' said Robin simply. 'It does not belong to a lord, so why should the temporal lords alone decide what happens to it? The commons cannot prevent the enclosure, so we must use whatever means we can to do so on their behalf.'

'I had heard you were a great friend of the common man,' said Guy. 'As for myself, I simply want to keep the peace. I will not support the enclosure when the barons meet to discuss the matter again, but I will also take no further steps to undermine my family. I would prefer that Marian followed my example.'

Now Robin understood.

'You want me to talk to the other lords, and leave you both out of it?'

'You know that I would do more,' said Marian quickly, 'but Guy has told me what happened between our families at Easter, of my father's quarrel with his family. His position as sheriff owes far more to the Viponts than to the king and if I am seen by Eudo and Ranulf to oppose their wishes, they may turn against my father even more.'

'How very politic,' said Robin coolly. He had expected Marian of all people to argue the side of the commons against the Viponts. Perhaps it was just as well she would not have a say in the council of barons, if Guy could so easily persuade her to give up her work against the enclosure because of one argument. Marian went red, but did not fall silent.

'I have tried to do as much as I can until now, with the religious lords. There is not much more that I could do. What is needed is for you to speak to Lord D'Alselin, today if you can. Already we have waited too long to appeal for his support. For all we know, Eudo has already been there and persuaded him to enclose the lands.'

'I will go now,' said Robin, making for the door.

'Wait,' called Marian. 'There is one other thing I wanted to discuss with you.' She looked at Guy. He frowned.

'I suppose you mean in private?'

'Just a family matter.'

Guy's frown deepened, but he nodded all the same.

'I presume,' said Robin as Guy was making his farewell to Marian, 'that your men have had no more luck in finding the escaped prisoners than the sheriff's?'

'We sent men out, but they found nothing. The rain had washed away any trail of men into the deeper forest, and there are so many people living or working at the edges of it that it would be futile to search there. All the locals he questioned claim to have seen nothing. Even the guards who watched the prisoners leave the castle have been useless. The descriptions they gave of the men with the sheriff's document and alms all conflicted. The criminals wore hoods so the guards could not even agree whether they were bearded or not. One says they had red hair, another brown… They are fortunate to escape with a beating.'

'I hope my nephew has not been upset,' said Robin, 'by the prisoners' escape, or this dispute between our families?'

'Jocelyn seems perfectly content. He considers himself a Vipont. Any arguments are beyond further understanding.'

Guy kissed Marian's hand, gave a curt bow to Robin and left. Those last words of his stung, and it was some moments before Robin noticed that Marian had moved over to the window and was waiting for him to join her there.

'Have you heard anything,' she asked, when he did so, and her low tone was eerily reminiscent of her father's, 'from the families of the hundredmen?'

'No,' Robin said carefully, 'why would I have?'

'Because I have. One of their wives came to me, almost as upset as if her husband had been hanged, crying that he was out in the forest with wolves, and he would starve to death or be eaten alive.'

'Why did she come to you?'

'She knew that I had paid for Waltheof's brother-in-law to be released. Thorfridh. She hoped I knew something. I could not help her, but I promised I would ask you.'

'There is no reason I would know more than you.'

Through the window, Robin watched Guy and his squire riding out of the courtyard. Marian glanced at them and then at her hands, spreading her long thin fingers out over the stone ledge.

'Some of the men who escaped were your friends,' she said quietly. 'I remember them from years ago. That pale one and the blacksmith's son. Even John – that is his name, is it not? The one who led them when we saw them all in the forest the day we were with the falcons. You have seen Will and Agnes Scarlette since you returned to Nottinghamshire. I thought perhaps you had seen others too?'

Robin glanced at Waltheof, wondering if he had confessed everything to his mistress after all. But his face was all innocence, barely hearing what they discussed. Perhaps Guy had shared his suspicions with Marian, had mentioned the alms given out in Lord Locksley's name. If Marian was willing to give up her concern for the enclosure because Guy had asked her to, it was equally possible that she was questioning Robin – and would report back his answers – at her future husband's request. He would not give them the satisfaction.

'Those men were my friends,' he said coldly, 'when I was a young fool. But they are not now. They are criminals.'

'What happened to those alms I gave you from my father?'

Now Robin was certain he was being interrogated.

'I had them sent to the castle.'

'By whom?'

'Why do you ask?'

'Why?' she cried with a sudden burst of anger. 'Because my father has been accused by Guy's family of helping those men escape, or at least of letting it happen through his incompetence. He has kept my name from the Viponts to protect me, but you and I both know that it is our fault, not his, that those alms were sent to the prisoners.'

'Have you told Guy I asked for the alms?'

'No. There is no need to worsen his opinion of you. Who took the alms to the castle?'

'Men I trust. That is all I will say.'

He bowed and stepped away from the window, but she moved to follow him.

'Men who were in your father's household?'

'I will not say any more. Your father has trusted me to question those I suspect of being involved, and I will.'

'So you have already questioned the men who made the delivery?'

Robin paused an instant before replying.

'You have not questioned them,' she cried. 'You are so certain they are innocent?'

'Yes, I am certain they did not help the prisoners escape. No, I have not questioned them yet.'

Marian shook her head in frustration.

'I know that you have no love for Guy or his family, or even for my father, but please, Robin, if you can end this dispute between them, please do it.'

'If you care so much about the Viponts, why do you not just let the enclosure go ahead? To hell with the common land, with the baseborn men and women who use it. Write to the abbess and tell her that you have changed your mind.'

'I…' Marian turned back to the window, again pressing her fingers firmly onto the stone, so firmly her knuckles shone white through her skin. 'I cannot…'

Across the room Gytha twitched. Robin glanced at the old woman, hesitating to rise and comfort her mistress, and was startled to see an expression of warm-hearted pity he had never known in her before. He looked back at Marian. She was staring out of the window with a hard intensity that almost concealed the tears at the corners of her eyes. It was a stare that he recognised from years ago, when they had been betrothed and he had been able to do seemingly nothing without causing her pain. Before, he had always stormed away from her hard stares, blamed her chastisement and his parents' censure for the way he behaved. He had thought of himself. Now, unbidden, he felt a surge of sympathy for her. He had been right to question Marian's divided loyalties when she asked him about the prisoners, but he had been wrong to consider those loyalties only as far as they affected him. To have your two families in dispute was hard, he knew that well enough, but to find yourself in opposition to both and never know where to place your loyalty was harder still. He wished he could offer her some sort of comfort. If she had been his sister or Elaine he would have embraced her. If she had been his mother he would have bowed before her. But since she was Marian he stood immobile.

'If I could help you,' he said at last, as softly as he was able, 'I would.'

It was not much, but he meant it. Perhaps she recognised the sincerity in his voice. She forced an awkward smile.

'The best way you can help is to speak to Lord D'Alselin.'

So that was what he did.

Garsmount nestled on a peak above a loop in the River Trent. Robin approached it from below, and the sight of it in the shade of the surrounding forest was enough to unnerve any man, let alone one going to beg a favour of its lord. The stone tower was dark and watchmen wandered the crenellations rising over it. They had not been there four years ago. Robin set his mind to his task and tried to ignore the shiver on his neck as the path he rode was swallowed by the tower's long shadow. Robin found Lord D'Alselin by the great fire in his hall, surrounded by his hunting dogs.

'I know why you are here,' he said the moment Robin walked into his sight. 'I have already had a visit from Eudo de Vipont. You wish to prevent the enclosure of the common land; he wishes to cause it.'

Robin stopped abruptly as Lord D'Alselin stood. He was a tall man, and swathed in furs as he was, there was something fearsomely beast-like in his movements. With a fleeting smile, Robin wondered how Elaine's troubadours would describe such a man: he might be a giant of the mountains or a scourging knight. The thought brought him a little cheer.

'I also hear from Lord Eudo,' D'Alselin continued, 'that it was you who insisted the lords wait to decide the matter until I could speak. Did you expect me to take your side?'

Robin's heart sank. If Lord D'Alselin supported Eudo de Vipont, there would be no way to stop the enclosure. Another tract of land stolen from the commons, more families condemned to starve. If he had the slimmest chance of persuading D'Alselin to his cause, he must choose his next words very carefully.

'I hoped you would agree with me,' he said. 'But I also did not think it right to decide such an important matter in your absence. I might not always have liked your judgements, but you are a local lord. The most important local lord after the sheriff – maybe even including him. You have more interest in this dispute than the Viponts.'

Lord D'Alselin shrugged. 'I have lands elsewhere, just like them.'

'But your family have been in Nottinghamshire for generations, just like mine. English and Norman landowners, both, intermarrying since the Conquest. You have always cared more about these lands than your others. Your home alone testifies to that. I hold no lands now, so perhaps you could say I have no right to speak on this matter, but I do not want to start trampling on the ancient laws of this county just because some locals ruined the Viponts' hunt.'

Lord D'Alselin rubbed one of his hunting dogs under its chin. Both dog and lord jutted their jaws forward and shook their heads. For a long time the master did not speak.

'You wanted to call me into this dispute because it suited your ends,' D'Alselin said at last, 'but at least you thought to include me. And you are right.

The D'Alselin family and the Garsides kept the law in these lands for generations. After I am gone I hope my sons and grandsons will continue to do so. You have not always agreed with the laws of our county, Lord Locksley, but I always have, and I have always observed them. I will not deprive the commons hereabouts of their rights on the request of half-a-dozen lords.' He looked Robin square in the eyes. 'When the lords come to council I will speak for your part, not theirs.'

D'Alselin did not smile, and Robin did not either, but as he bowed and thanked Lord D'Alselin he felt blood rush from his heart to his fingertips in relief. With D'Alselin's support and the religious lords in attendance, the Viponts could not defeat him. It may prove to be a small victory, but anything that lessened their grip on the barons of Nottinghamshire must be to his advantage. When he faced them again over the question of his inheritance, he could do so with some local influence at last. He left Garsmount's long shadow with the sun full on his face.

Farrowing

'I have taken your rook.'

Robin glanced up as he felt a light pressure on his hand. Elaine's fingers were on it, clasping a chess piece between them. She smiled.

'Wake up, Lord Locksley. You have been in a dream ever since we began this game.'

Robin took the rook and smiled in return.

'Forgive me, I was thinking…' About supplies, about the hundredmen's families, about how to keep ahead of the sheriff's guards, about making hunting bows and arrows from what they could gather in the forest.

'About the council of the lords?' said Elaine, completing his thoughts for herself. 'I know you have a lot on your mind. It is a shame you have to keep riding out to talk to barons all over the county about this common land. You have barely had a meal with us these last few days.'

Robin stifled a yawn. He had been riding out every day, that much was true, although only half of his time was spent pleading with the lords – the abbess, Lord Louvetot, the irascible Lord Foliot – and the other half squatting in a cave, handing over the small amount of food he could steal from the kitchens. He knew which activity he preferred. Gytha scowled at him from across the chamber and he removed his hand from Elaine's.

'I spoke to Peter the clerk yesterday,' Elaine continued, taking another of Robin's ill-placed pieces. 'While I was with Marian at the castle. He said that he expected a writ from Westminster any day about your lands. You know, I could very easily have spoken to Lady Idonea about the matter. She says that Serlo and Eudo are only being so obdurate in holding onto the Locksley estate because you do not pursue them more gently yourself.'

'You mean because I do not lick their boots?'

Elaine wrinkled her nose. 'You do not need to abase yourself.'

'When I regain my lands I want it to be because the law was rightly on my side, not because I had the Viponts plead to their friend the count.'

Now more than ever Robin wished to be free of any debt to that family. The hundredmen still had a hope of being pardoned by a county court, overriding the Viponts' decision, but only if he could be sure of the support of his fellow lords against them. And particularly only if the sheriff felt himself emboldened to do it. Until Robin was certain he would win such a trial he could not risk the hundredmen being found, but nor was he willing to make any overture to Lord Eudo's family.

'You could just be a little more obliging with them – if you paid one of these visits to their home rather than to every other lord's – or if you gave up this matter of the common land?'

Robin stood up suddenly. It was not Elaine's words that startled him – she had attempted this speech on him before – but a cry from Marian on the other side of the room. Waltheof had whispered something to her, and now both were on their feet, pale-faced. Marian called for Estrild to fetch her cloak, for Edgar to bring her horse.

'What is the matter?' Robin asked. He realised he addressed Waltheof, and turned instead to Marian. Elaine looked around at the flurry curiously.

'One – one of the tenants,' Marian said, but Estrild was pressing her cloak onto her shoulders and if she said more Robin did not hear it.

'It is raining,' said Elaine. 'Can your tenant not come to the hall? You will be soaked through if you go out.'

Marian bit her lip, frowned, did not reply, turned on the spot and hurried from the room. Elaine reached up to draw Robin back to their game, but he followed Waltheof after his mistress. The Englishman's face was grim.

'Thorfridh,' was all he said as Robin caught up to him. Marian was too close for him to say more. They hurried into the courtyard together, where Edgar was saddling Marian's horse. She pulled her gloves on, eager to be gone.

'Marian,' called Robin, 'what has happened?'

'Aelfeva's husband has been arrested. The one whose release I paid for.'

'On what charge?' Robin asked, but he knew before Marian spoke what the answer would be.

'For helping the hundredmen to escape. My father is already at the castle. Perhaps if I can speak to him –'

'Who has accused Thorfridh?'

'The Vipont steward. Lanfranc.'

Robin's stomach lurched. Lanfranc must finally have realised where he recognised Thorfridh from – must have wondered how the only hundredman to be released from prison ended up in rich robes at a church on the same morning the other prisoners escaped – must have considered how Thorfridh was at the very heart of the brawling crowd calling out for Lord Locksley's alms in the marketplace. He would call for the guards on duty that night to look at Thorfridh and that would be an end of it. They would recognise him, and even if their memories failed them doubtless a threat or coin from Lanfranc would persuade them. Thorfridh was as good as hanged. And then Robin had another grim realisation.

Marian stepped forward, her horse ready to leave. Just as she moved to mount the saddle Robin reached out and grasped her arm.

'Do not go to the castle,' he said.

Marian stared at him.

'I – I have to. Aelfeva has asked me to. She knows that Lanfranc is lying.'

'He is not.'

Marian looked between Robin and Waltheof in confusion. The servant's jaw was set tight and he watched Robin with a sudden glimmer of mistrust. Robin lowered his voice.

'Thorfridh was the one who delivered the sheriff's alms to the castle. Lanfranc must have seen him there. I do not doubt that he is innocent but if you go to him, you will only draw suspicion on yourself. And on the sheriff.' Marian was shaking her head, her hand still on the saddle of her horse. Robin continued, more urgently, 'you asked me before to tell you who had taken the alms. This is why I did not. Because you paid for Thorfridh's release from imprisonment, and you were the one who asked your father for alms to be taken to the other prisoners.'

'Surely you do not mean that I would be under any suspicion?'

'You have helped the hundredmen twice, and if the Viponts do not know it now they will eventually. Any assistance you give will be seen as assistance from the sheriff, against them. You should not help a third time. Let me go for you. I will take Waltheof, so you can be certain you will be told everything on our return. We can make sure the Viponts are not mistreating Thorfridh, and try to find a way to free him. A way to pay his fine, I mean, if that is what it will take.'

Robin looked to Waltheof for support. He nodded, following Robin's thoughts.

'Lord Locksley is right, my lady,' he said. 'Lord Eudo may not even allow you to visit Thorfridh, given your connection to him. When we return we can go together to Aelfeva and offer her comfort.'

Marian drew back uncertainly. But they were right – her interest in the accused man would only rouse the Viponts' suspicions against her father still further.

'Very well,' she said. 'But you should ask Guy for his help. Eudo and Ranulf may try to keep you away from Thorfridh. If you tell Guy you are doing this for me, he will assist you.'

Robin agreed and guided Marian back under the shelter of the hall's stairway. She watched as he and Waltheof prepared to leave. Waltheof bridled Robin's horse to speak to him away from Edgar's ears.

'I wondered why you were telling her Thorfridh made the delivery,' he said softly. 'I thought you were accusing him.'

'I need to find out if he has definitely been recognised by Lanfranc. If he has not, there is still a chance.'

'Perhaps there will be a way to free him?'

'Perhaps.'

Robin smiled confidently. But his stomach was like a ball of lead, pressing against his ribs. He feared he had tied himself a knot too tight to unravel. On the stairwell Marian's eyes were still on them. He waved to her as he and Waltheof set off to see if the last of the hundredmen could be freed.

As he passed into the middle bailey of Nottingham Castle the men at the gates watched Robin. A lot of men. The guard on the castle must have been doubled since Easter. Many of the men bowed their heads to him, recognising Lord Locksley. It might not be a good thing, he thought, that the guards were starting to know his face. He rode up the short incline to the inner bailey with lowering spirits. As his horse was stabled, Robin sent a page to find Guy. He waited in the antechamber next to the hall, hoping to God that none of the other lords were close by. Someone must have heard him, because before Eudo or even Lanfranc could pass him, Guy arrived with his squire. He could not conceal his surprise at a visit from Lord Locksley.

'You wanted to see me?' Guy asked.

'I am here for Marian,' said Robin. 'One of our tenants has been arrested, the brother-in-law of her man.' He gestured to Waltheof. 'She sent me to visit him so that she can tell his family how he is.'

'What is the man's name?'

'Thorfridh of Locksley.'

Guy raised his eyebrows.

'He was arrested for freeing the condemned men.'

'I heard.'

Guy scratched his chin, glanced towards the hall uneasily. He was considering how much trouble he would be in if his father found out. Robin would stake his life on it.

'For Marian?' Guy repeated.

'Yes.'

He flicked his hand towards his squire, telling him not to attend them.

'Follow me then. Quickly.'

He led Robin away from the great chambers of the castle, past the screens passage and into the buttery. Past the butts of wine and trestle tables they went, down a staircase that led to the service area of the keep and towards, Robin realised, the cellar in which the hundredmen had been imprisoned. At the passage leading to the cellar Guy paused and addressed Waltheof.

'Pick up a rush light,' he said. 'It is darker from here.'

Waltheof obeyed, stepping in front of Robin and holding the light high. Guy went down one more flight of stairs, behind a shelf containing rows of ale casks and through a doorway Robin had never seen before. Two guardsmen watched the group pass by, the rush flame glinting across their faces.

'Watch your step,' Guy called as he descended into the darkness.

Through the doorway the flagstone floor of the keep gave way to smooth sandstone. The walls were carved from the same yellow rock, chiselled out by men's hands, not built up by masons. They were descending into the rock face, Robin thought, deep into the cliff on which the castle was constructed.

Guy stopped at a bell-shaped chamber, before the ground sloped down again. A door had been forced into the sandstone, standing out unnaturally against the cliff wall. Two more guards stood on duty here. They recognised their Vipont lord, but they did not move an inch from the door until he told them his business there.

'Lord Locksley wishes to establish that the prisoner is being treated well,' said Guy. 'He will not take much of your time.'

The guards nodded and unbolted the door. A foul smell rose from within. Thorfridh must not be the first occupant it had held. Guy covered his nose with a square of silk against the stench.

'I can go in without you,' said Robin. 'I have smelt worse than that before.'

Guy nodded gratefully. 'I will wait here with your servant.'

He went to the other side of the passage, nodding to the guards to keep their watch. Reluctantly, Waltheof stayed with him. Robin stepped inside the cell and the door was closed behind him. A slim rectangle of light fell through a watching hatch in the door, but otherwise the cell was in darkness. A shadow fell across even that light as a guard stepped close enough to listen. Thorfridh blinked and twisted to see Robin. His hands and feet were shackled. His face was bruised, his lip cut, and around his wrists sores had already developed where the irons sat heavy against his skin.

'I'm here to see that you are not badly treated,' said Robin, loud enough for the guards outside. 'Lady Marian sent me.'

'God bless her,' Thorfridh said. His voice was a sore croak. 'And you, my lord.'

Robin moved away from the door, towards the back of the cell, then squatted over the muck of the floor.

'How is Aelfeva?' Thorfridh asked.

'Worried about you. She hopes you will be released.'

'That won't happen.' Thorfridh spoke low. 'That bastard steward knew my face – that's why they didn't hit me harder. So he could have the guards identify me. And this is what I deserve, my lord. I am guilty.'

'You haven't told them that?'

Thorfridh said nothing but his face showed the truth clear enough. Robin leant back against the wall in disbelief.

'Thorfridh, we were going to try to free you.'

'From here? You can't. I'm inside a rock inside a castle inside three sets of walls. I thought carefully before I did it, my lord, I swear. I told him that I was the one who came up with the whole plan, that I paid outlaws to help and now they won't be found because they've gone over the border. They want to know names, of course, but I won't give any. No matter what they do to me, I won't betray my friends.'

'I won't let them do anything to you. If you've already confessed there's not much more I can do, but stopping that is within my power.'

'Are the hundredmen still free?'

'Yes.'

'Good. I had no will to hang just for asking the Viponts for good lordship, but I'll be content to die if the hundredmen keep their lives.'

The guard thudded his fist against the door.

'That's long enough, my lord.'

'Please,' said Thorfridh, reaching his hands out to Robin as he stood. He caught at his sleeve. 'Please, Robin, will you protect Aelfeva and our child?'

'Do't doubt it.' He grasped Thorfridh's arm, wishing there was more he could do, wishing he had not involved Thorfridh in his scheme in the first place, wishing Lanfranc the steward had never been born. Useless thoughts. 'I'm sorry,' he said, and even that was not enough.

'Not your doing, my lord.' Thorfridh smiled. 'A man has free will.'

'God keep you.'

'And you.'

The door was opened, the guard stepping into the space it filled to prevent Thorfridh attempting any escape. Robin left the cell, looking back as the door was closed and bolted behind him. He lowered his voice and passed one of the guards a few coins.

'No man is to harm this prisoner. And if anyone tries, you are to send word to the sheriff immediately. Am I understood?'

The guard pocketed the coins.

'Yes, my lord.'

'If I find out you have deceived me – and I will find out – it will be the worse for you.'

He strode back the way he had come, feeling the pressure of Thorfridh's hand on his sleeve all the way up the stairs. Guy was silent behind him, relieved to have got away from the prisoner without being seen. Back on the lords' side of the castle they came to a halt, uncertain what to do next.

'Thank you for letting me see him,' said Robin. He could not force an appearance of gratitude, so the words sounded hollow.

'Certainly,' said Guy stiffly. 'Tell Marian that I am sorry if this saddens her, but she should prepare herself. That man will not be released.'

'I know it,' said Robin.

They took their leave of each other and Robin and Waltheof stepped back out into the fresh, cold air of the courtyard. The stink of the cell seemed to cling to him, even there.

'He cannot be freed,' said Waltheof. 'Can he?'

'No.'

Robin told Waltheof all that Thorfridh had said. His brother-in-law bowed his head.

'You should go to Aelfeva now. Tell her that I swore to Thorfridh to look after her, and I mean to keep that promise. Give her anything from Locksley Hall that she needs. I will answer to the sheriff.'

'Thank you, my lord.'

Waltheof wandered slowly towards the stable. Robin watched him go, those same useless thoughts crowding him again. As he looked down the hill his eye fell on a range of narrow windows beyond the walls of the inner bailey, candlelight flickering brightly even in the late afternoon. The chancery where Peter worked. Robin had heard nothing from the clerk in days. He hoped that silence was a good sign, but given the Viponts had already uncovered one of his accomplices, it was not impossible that they had recognised another. He walked as calmly as he could to the chancery. The sheriff's chancery was inside the castle walls, but outside the keep, away from the dangerous fires of the kitchens. Robin opened a smaller door within a great oak edifice to find a long, large chamber filled with desks, carefully positioned candles and strips of vellum to be cut to the necessary size. Next to the entrance sat a clerk sharpening his pen and yawning. On seeing Lord Locksley he stood up straight, and showed him immediately to Peter's desk. Peter looked up from his writ in surprise.

'My lord,' he said in a low tone – the chamber was silent but for the scratch of pens and suck of inkwells. 'I have had no reply from Westminster yet. I presume that is why you are here? To discuss the writs I sent about your estate?'

'Yes,' said Robin. 'I have a question about them.'

Peter gestured for Robin to follow him to the far end of the chamber, where a little closet had been set aside for conversation. Peter closed the door behind him and picked up a linen strip within to blot some of the ink from his fingers.

'I wanted to find out if all is well with you, since Easter?' Robin did not refer to the escape. Peter was as cunning as a knife. There was no need for explicitness.

'Yes, my lord. The sheriff's men questioned all the clerks, and then Lord Eudo's men repeated the task. A waste of resources, alas, for no man here has committed any crime.'

'You are certain you were believed?'

Peter smiled.

'You must remember, my lord, that I spend my life writing documents full of florid sincerity at the command of my betters. When I wrote to Westminster to gain your writs, my pen was filled with condemnation for the abominable injuries that have been done to you. You were Boethius suffering in his cell – I believe that was the metaphor I chose – and only these writs could provide the consolation that philosophy gave him. You cannot work in a chancery if you are overburdened with candour.'

'If that is the case,' said Robin coolly, 'you might have confessed everything to the sheriff's men and be lying now to me.'

'What could I tell them, my lord?' asked Peter, with complete unconcern. 'The only person I could name as involved in the escape is you. I know that you asked me to write a document offering Easter charity to some prisoners, but nothing more. If I had confessed this morsel of information, I think you would have been questioned yourself on the matter by now. And I also rather think I would have lost my position and been whipped.' He presented his shoulders to Robin. 'You are welcome to inspect my back, my lord if you do not believe my assurance that it is unharmed.'

'I believe you,' said Robin slowly. At the very least he believed that Peter had more to lose now than he had to gain if he chose to confess all to his master. 'But what of your brothers in chancery? Could any of them have given information to the sheriff or the Viponts that might endanger you?'

'I doubt it, my lord. We have all been so busy that no one has paid even fleeting attention to the activities of their brothers. Lady's Day is the peak of our activity and within a week we expect the arrival of the royal tax collectors. The Lords Vipont, I understand, desire their tenants to have paid their rents before then. Lord Ranulf has already sent men to his own estates for that purpose.'

Rent collection. Just what the hundredmen's families needed, thought Robin. There was a rap at the closet door. One of the clerks appeared at it, looking harassed.

'I beg forgiveness, my lord,' he said, then addressed Peter in Latin. Robin knew just enough of the language to follow his words. 'Brother, have you written the sheriff's response to the Yorkshire tax collectors?'

'I am finishing it now,' Peter replied.

'The sheriff's rider waits at the door.'

'Give him ale and it will be sealed when Lord Locksley leaves.'

The clerk scowled but closed the door. Peter rolled his eyes.

'This Yorkshire matter has only added to our distraction,' he said.

'The clerk spoke of tax collectors?'

'Yes. We had word from the royal tax collectors in the north this afternoon. One of their wagons was attacked on the road and all its silver taken.'

'All of it?'

'I daresay a penny or two fell through the cracks.'

'Do they know who took the money?'

'Ghosts, apparently, of starved men. Or so the guards on the wagon reported. Our sheriff has promised to send men to meet the collectors at the border between our counties to provide a larger escort. They have chosen to travel separately from the wagons for the time being, so the sheriff must provide men enough to protect both. I should close the message before Brother Matthew tries to do it for me. Nothing is more unprofessional than two clerks' hands in one message.'

Robin led Peter out of the closet and back to his desk. A thought was prickling at the back of his mind, and it was not relief at Peter's escape from the sheriff's suspicions.

'If you have time,' he said in a low voice while Peter bent back to his work, 'can you make a copy of the message describing the Yorkshiremen's attack on that tax wagon? I would be interested to read it.'

With Peter's assurance that he would do so, Robin left the sheriff's chancery.

Robin rode hard through the forest to bring the hundredmen news of Thorfridh's arrest. He feared what would happen if anyone else told them of it. The men had few enough weapons but after days confined inside a cave they would be bristling for action. There might be little thought for the odds ranged against them, and certainly little knowledge of the increased security at the castle. But as fast as Robin travelled, word travelled faster. When he pulled himself inside the cave he found it alive with twisting shadows and shuffling noise, the men readying themselves to leave. He ran along the pathway into the cave chamber. John Blunt greeted him grimly.

'Thank Jesus you are here,' he said in a low voice. 'Have you heard about Thorfridh?'

'I've just been to visit him. Tell me you're not planning to free him.'

'I say it is a fool's errand but they won't listen.'

John looked over his shoulder and Robin followed his eye to Will Scarlette, who was squatting over the measly arsenal the men had gathered. It was exactly as Robin had feared. He moved towards the fire at the heart of the room and raised his voice to get the men's attention. It was grudgingly given, above the bustle of arming.

'Put down your weapons.'

'We're going to get Thorfridh.' Thurstan raised his axe. It glittered red in the firelight. 'If you want to help us, lord, you'll bring us more weapons.'

'I won't. I've just come from the castle. The guard has doubled and everyone is on watch for both you and any attempt to free Thorfridh. You won't get past the barbican.'

Thurstan spat into the fire.

'You managed to get all of us out,' Lefchild said. 'We only want one man.'

'I got you out against half the guard and with the Viponts twenty miles away. Even then, we were almost stopped by the steward. And they've put Thorfridh even further away from the rest of the castle. He's in a cell underneath the keep, within Castle Rock itself.'

'I said we couldn't do it,' muttered Doleswif, putting down the sharpened stick he had been turning in his hands. 'Every one of us is a marked man. They'll know us in an instant.'

'Thorfridh did not abandon us,' Thurstan said doggedly. 'He was free, he could have left us to rot but he risked himself for us. We can't just leave him to hang now.'

'We could wear different clothes again,' said Will.

'Where will you get them?' asked Robin. 'Even if you steal a dozen monks' habits those guards will still stop you. And when you're recognised you'll hang. There won't be a chance to save you.'

'Coward,' hissed men around the fire. John Blunt stepped forward.

'It helps no one,' he said, 'if we get ourselves killed trying to free a man who cannot be freed. Will, you said something about the hanging.'

'He's to hang on market day,' said Will bitterly. 'From the middle gatehouse, I heard.'

'The gatehouse,' John repeated. 'You know what that means. From now until his last breath, they're keeping Thorfridh inside that castle. We couldn't even make a charge at him to save him on a scaffold.' He turned to Robin. 'If you could, would you save Thorfridh?'

'Yes.'

'Can we save him and live?'

'No.'

'When you spoke to him today did he ask you to organise an escape?'

'He was content to die if all of you lived.'

John raised his arms, palms up, to the group. He said nothing. The men looked into the fire, at the cave walls, up to the ceiling. They knew it was true, but they did not want to admit it. Will met Robin's eye bitterly. For once, his crooked mouth was not smiling.

'We can't help Thorfridh,' said Robin in a low voice, 'but if we're alive and free, we can help his wife and child. We can help all of your kin.'

'From in here?' Lefchild gestured at the cave walls.

'Here and the forest. Especially the forest.'

'How?'

'We reclaim the money that is taken from your kin in rent and tax.'

'Reclaim it?' Thurstan repeated, brow furrowed.

'Men in Yorkshire have done it. Anything they can do, I say we can do better.'

'You mean steal,' said Tosti.

'That is what I mean. But I can't tell you any more now. This week the lords are coming together in a council to decide whether the common land north of Nottingham should be enclosed. I think I've got enough support now to save the land, but I can't risk doing anything foolish before I'm sure of it. Once that matter is settled I will tell you how we can retake your money and help your kin. Can you wait?'

Every eye in the cave was on him.

'That common land has saved my tithing through more than one winter when the harvest failed,' said John.

Thurstan looked around the cave, at the faces of his friends. He dropped his axe into the corner of the cave and nodded. 'We'll wait.'

The barons met on the feast of St Pelagius to finally settle the matter of the common land. Robin had been to the Abbey of Newstead to persuade the abbess to attend, he had once more visited the prior of Lenton to ensure his support, he had been told by Marian that the sheriff might well support their cause over the Viponts, given the indignity he had suffered from the Norman lords at Easter. He had done everything he possibly could to ensure that the decision went his way. Since he could not save Thorfridh he was determined to do everything in his power to help the other common men of Nottinghamshire.

The great hall of Nottingham Castle was fuller than Robin had ever seen it. The battle lines were drawn clearly enough. The religious lords sat on one side of the columns dividing the hall, Lord D'Alselin at their side, Guy close enough but not quite willing to remove himself from the cluster of Viponts facing them. Serlo, Eudo, Ranulf and the Lords de Caux and de la Guerche regarded their colleagues with affected indifference. The enigmatic Lords Louvetot and Foliot stood about watching their fellows. Neither had attended the Hundred Court – perhaps because their lands sat further to the west of the county, or perhaps through sheer disinterest – but both came now, and exchanged pleasantries with Lord D'Alselin as if they were old friends. D'Alselin nodded a greeting to Robin as he sat next to him. The sheriff took a seat on the hall dais and called for silence. He started to remind everyone why they were meeting, but was interrupted by Lord Ranulf.

'We all know why we are here,' he said gruffly. 'Let's get to the meat of it.'

Sir Walter nodded stiffly and invited Robin to make his case against the enclosure.

'This land has been held to common use for centuries,' he said, as calmly and slowly as he had heard his father speak in public. 'At the writing of the great book of King William it was listed as such. The last king, Henry, did not enclose it, nor has his son. The people of Nottinghamshire depend on that land to feed them when their harvests fail, when flooding washes out their soil, when summer heat brings sickness to their livestock. If we expect to gather rent from our tenants and tax for the king and count –' remembering what Peter had told him, he looked straight at Ranulf as he said this '– we must maintain this land for the use of the commons.'

He sat, and Sir Walter asked Lord Eudo to reply. Eudo stood slowly and spoke in a voice almost of indifference.

'I can only repeat arguments I have already made. The commons of this county take their lords and the offices we represent for fools. This has been shown once more since Easter in the escape from justice of a dozen condemned men. The men have not been found, so their kin and neighbours must be aiding them. Thank God one of their number has been dealt with. Any right these people once had to enjoy their privileges must now be held forfeit.'

Eudo sat and was silent. Robin frowned. Was that all he was going to say?

The lords debated the matter – or, rather, the lords opposing the enclosure had their say, while the Norman lords offered little in the way of counter argument. It was as if they knew they were defeated and refused to spend energy in a lost cause. Sir Walter evidently felt the same as Robin. Before even an hour had passed he called for the lords to decide what should happen to the lands. It fell out just as Robin had hoped. The abbess and the prior sided with him and Guy to maintain the common land, while the Norman lords wanted it enclosed. Just as Marian had said, Louvetot and Foliot waited for D'Alselin to choose a side then followed his lead. The majority of lords thus appealed against the enclosure, and the sheriff did not even need to state his own opinion for the matter to be settled.

'The common land,' said Sir Walter, shooting a smile at the defeated Viponts, 'will not be enclosed. Thank Christ that matter is resolved.'

He stood up in relief and the hall exhaled as one. The Viponts leant back in their seats exchanging glances, the religious lords started making their farewells, Louvetot and Foliot – pleased to have chosen the winning side – congratulated themselves loudly, and D'Alselin slapped Robin on the back without a word, wearing what almost amounted to a smile. In the midst of the celebration and commiseration in the hall the arrival of a knight into their midst went unnoticed. Emblazoned on his tabard was a lion, claws raised and jaws open. Robin saw him just as the knight shouted for silence. He stepped aside. Through the doorway came a lord Robin had never seen before, followed by such a press of attendants that most had to loiter in the courtyard outside. He was dressed in delicate purple samite, the warmest of fur linings to his lilac cloak. His hair and beard were neatly trimmed, both tinged with red. The room fell to its knees. Robin did not need to be told that this was the king's brother John, Count of Mortain, come to Nottingham at last.

'You may rise,' the count said, in a voice soft and lilting as a woman's. Eudo and Ranulf moved forward on their bent knees to kiss the ring on the count's finger.

'It is an honour to see you once again within the walls of your castle, Lord Count,' said Eudo.

The count's eyes roved about the hall, taking in all its details with the stealthy swiftness of a hawk. 'What a fine little council you have assembled,' he said. 'The Lord of Lenton, the Lady of Newstead – have you been praying for your prince?'

He laughed to himself quietly. The prior forced a smile, the abbess did not. Everyone knew that the count was not a godly man. He mocked the church. His father might have been the slayer of blessed St Thomas Becket, but Count John scorned the church as only a man with no mind for his soul could. Once, it was said, he had promised to convert to Islam if only he could have Saladin's soldiers at his disposal. The count's eyes counted off everyone in the hall. He knew them all; they were of little interest to him. Serlo and Guy he embraced absently, Lord de Caux he kissed on the cheek, de la Guerche he patted on the head as if he were a dog. His eye fell on Robin. He paused.

'I do not know you.'

'This is the Lord of Locksley,' said Eudo de Vipont. 'He has been for some years in the Holy Land.'

At mention of the Crusades the count blanched, then his cheeks flushed fierce red. He turned on the spot to face Sir Walter and refused to look at Robin again.

'I am here on important business, Sheriff. I wish to enclose the common land that borders our estate.'

The whole hall followed the count's gaze to Sir Walter.

'Enclose it, my lord?' the sheriff repeated. 'That is a matter we have been debating even now. It has been decided among the lords here that that land will not be…'

'I am going to enclose it,' said the count firmly. 'My friend Eudo has told me all about the state of lawlessness in this county and I will not permit such disregard for order within my own lands. I have just been inspecting the scrub of land now, and I do not think it will be any loss to the people. I brought my own clerk with me to draw up the necessary papers. The land is going to be declared forest.'

'Is that – forgive me,' stammered Sir Walter, looking around at the barons in confusion. 'I understood only the king could afforest land.'

Again the colour in the count's face drained and refilled, like a cup of white wine tainted with red. He did not refer to his brother by name.

'His own lands, certainly. But these are mine. I paid him homage for them, and now I can do what I want with them. And I want to enclose them.'

He smiled, baring his teeth. The chamber stood silent. Robin looked at Guy, who stared at the floor in defeat, and then at Eudo. The lord returned his gaze triumphantly. Robin's fingers clutched the belt where his sword normally sat. The bastard must have been planning this for days. Perhaps even since they visited Clipstone. He had not bothered to argue the case put before him because he knew that he had already won it. What Doleswif had said was true, thought Robin: the law was made for lords, and every other man must just suffer it.

'I will have a feast in my castle tonight,' the count continued, looking around the chamber. 'In the hall, I think. You are all invited. Although it is a Friday.' He looked at the prior and abbess. 'Perhaps you will not like the meat I serve.' He grinned and turned towards the door. 'Until later, my lords. Crusader, come with me.'

The last words were thrown over the count's shoulder as he left the hall, and only when Sir Walter nudged him did Robin realise they were directed at him. He followed the count at a distance, his household closing rank behind him, shutting the hall door against the other lords. The count strode across the bailey yard, disregarding every bent knee and surprised cry. He paused, once, when he noticed one of the nuns who had attended the abbess from Newstead.

'A waste,' he said, but before Robin could reach his side he walked on.

They wove their way through the castle, to the inner bailey, into the keep and up the spiral staircase, into the royal chamber above the hall. A fire blazed and the floor had been sprinkled with rosewater and violet oil. Great beeswax candles burned around the chamber and the bed had what looked like new bolts of cloth around it. The Viponts had not been surprised by their guest's arrival, that was certain. The luxurious trappings of the chamber might as well have been ash to Robin. All he saw in them were the shattered fragments of his hopes – to retry the hundredmen, to protect their families and neighbours, to maintain their rights to the common land. All lay in ruins, not because of the law but because of one man's friendship with a prince.

The count dropped his cloak to the floor and threw himself onto the bed, feet up. One of his attendants moved quickly to remove his shoes and replace them with embroidered slippers. The count gestured for Robin to come closer and his attendants to retire. Only when Robin knelt at the count's side and the eyes of his servants were elsewhere did Count John let his easy smile slip.

'You have been fighting with my – brother.' He hesitated over that word. 'How was he when you last saw him?'

'He was well,' Robin replied. 'The king was ill for some time after his arrival in the East, but he recovered enough to lead us almost to Jerusalem.'

'Almost. I heard he refused to besiege it because he thought he would not win.'

'That is what I heard as well.'

The count giggled to himself nervously. 'The other lords were not pleased, I think? That is so like him. Senher Oc e Non. That is what his Occitan friends' men call him, is it not? My lord Yes and No. There is never a "perhaps" with him.'

Robin said nothing.

'Were you close to him?'

'No, my lord. I was not so fortunate.'

The count pulled a face. 'So you did not hear him speak of me?'

Robin wondered how best to answer. He had heard that the king left the Holy Land because word came that his brother had rebelled against him, that he was conspiring to steal the kingdom while the true king fought for his God. And he knew that this was at least partly true. The palisades and guards that had sprouted across Nottinghamshire were a testament to the unrest that the count had caused. But it was probably not politic to admit that.

'I never heard the king speak of you, my lord. But as I say, I was not close to him.'

The count nodded sagely, then leapt out of the bed and towards the fire. He reminded Robin of a teenager, the same unbounded energy, the same adolescent distraction – but the count had left adolescence a decade ago.

'I would be interested to hear what you know about sieges,' said the count, moving chess pieces on a board that looked halfway through a game. 'Do you play?'

'I know chess,' said Robin, 'but I do not play it well.'

'I am very good at it. That might surprise you.' He knocked over a bishop and removed it from the board. 'You will have seen many in the East, I suppose?'

'Chess games?'

'Sieges.'

'Yes, my lord. I fought at Acre and Jaffa. But surely you have experienced many yourself in Normandy?'

'More experience is always useful. My tutor used to tell me that. He died at Acre. Shouldn't have gone, the old fool.'

The count sat over his chessboard and contemplated it. They were alone, Robin thought. No Viponts here to twist Robin's words or argue against him. He had heard that the count was feckless, biddable, that he followed the last advice that he had heard. Just because the Viponts had their claws into him now, it did not mean they would keep them embedded there. If the count would only listen to another lord, hear another side of this story perhaps his mind could be changed. Robin would happily share his siege observations if it meant a chance of delaying the enclosure of the common land.

'I saw how the king raised the siege at Acre. I could tell you about that, if you wished?'

The count's eyes glittered. 'Yes,' he said eagerly, 'yes, that would be – helpful.'

'But I would ask you a favour in return, my lord.' The count hesitated, mistrustful. His fingers twitched against his thumb. 'I would ask you to reconsider the enclosure.'

'No.'

'But if you had heard the arguments we were putting before you arrived…'

'I said no.' The count smiled with all appearance of good humour, but there was a resolution beneath that brooked no argument. He knocked another piece from the board. 'You see, I can be like my brother when I wish.'

He waved a hand and an attendant stepped forward, gesturing Robin from the chamber. Robin bowed his head, feeling the breath pull from his lungs in one long, sick sigh. It had all been futile, he thought. All of the hours travelling, writing, talking, persuading, trying to draw together the lords temporal and religious in one cause, common with the common man. He would not attend the count's feast that evening, however much Elaine might plead. He could not stand to sit in the same hall, to share food and drink wine in the company of Lord Eudo and his pack of vipers. It was not the lords who had been made fools of, it was the law. Sir Walter might go if he wished – doubtless Lady Joan would preen and peacock herself in delight, to sit at the count's table – neither caring that whole families could die because of the obduracy of one man.

In the courtyard he seized his horse's reins from the Vipont groom who held them. Just as he mounted his saddle a shout from across the yard pulled him from his miserable thoughts. It was Peter, motioning for him to come closer. Robin rode over, instinct more than conscious caution making him look about to check who was watching.

'I have the copy for you, my lord,' said Peter when Robin was close enough to hear a whisper. 'The report by the tax collectors of Yorkshire of the attack on their tax wagon.' He placed a roll of parchment in Robin's hand. Inside was another, smaller document. 'I also thought it might be of interest to you to know how our own sheriff is protecting the taxes collected in Nottinghamshire. Six guards to a wagon, apparently.'

Peter bowed and hurried back into the chancery. Robin put the parchment inside his tunic, held firm by his belt. God bless the few good men left in this county. He rode out through the castle barbican. On the other side he turned and looked up at the remains of a poor man hanging there. He crossed himself. And God keep the good men whose lives this county had taken.

Floridus

They heard the wagon before they saw it. The heavy rolling of its wheels over crushed leaves, the slap of leather as the driver's reins lighted on his horses, the loops of mail on the guards' coats rubbing against one another. And just, at the very edge of hearing, the rustle of silver pennies as they shifted in their chests. Robin glanced at John, grinning as he rolled his knife back and forth in his fist. He knew Blunt must feel the same excitement, coiled in the pit of his stomach. There was a flash of helms through the trees. Two – four – six. Exactly as Peter had told him. The instant the wagon came into view, Thurstan stepped silently from the shadows into its path.

'Stand away, man,' called the driver. 'We are on the king's business.'

Thurstan said nothing.

The two guards riding ahead of the wagon spurred forward to circle Thurstan. He did not flinch.

'Stand away,' said one, 'or we will make you.'

Thurstan looked up at them.

'No.'

Two shapes dropped from the trees like over-ripe apples, colliding with the guards – one – two – both were unseated, winded as they fell to the ground. Their horses cantered away from them. The guards lurched to their feet, their fellows around the wagon already charging Thurstan. Before they reached him a line of rope tautened high across the path, caught two in the chest, brought both down. Two more apples fell from the tree, leapt onto the horses and rode away. The last two mounted guards reached Thurstan a moment too late. He leapt into the shrubs like a cat. One of them hacked and thrust at the undergrowth, the other rode to his companions. A shock of arrows hit them where they stood. Thud, thud, thud, thud. The bows were too small to drive the arrows through the guards' chainmail and into their flesh, but the force of the blows threw them off balance. As they reeled towards the verge, they were caught by strong hands, their helms turned on their heads, blinding them.

'Move,' cried the driver, slapping his reins for escape. Before the horses could respond there was a shower of shapes from the treetops, from the earth, from the shrubs lining the roads. A dozen men – it seemed like more – faces shrouded, clutching sharpened sticks and cudgels. Some dragged guards from their horses, some beat the others to the ground. A number seized the reins of the wagon and the horses themselves, pulled the driver from his perch and threw him amongst the guards. Before the guards could rouse themselves, ropes bound their wrists and ankles, their weapons were kicked away. From their helms came curses, but they could do nothing as the forestmen struck at them. The driver was blindfolded. Robin climbed down from his post.

'Leave them,' he said, his blood singing to strike them too. They were not the target. He nodded for Thurstan and Tosti and the other thick-armed hundredmen to seize the trunks. They smashed the locks open with an axe and pulled sack after sack of five-pound-weights of coin from within. The sacks were thrown to men at the road's edge, two each, then run deep into the forest.

That evening, a farmer walking geese to the market came across a shattered wagon, a dozen horses chewing the verge, and five blindfolded men sitting miserable in a puddle. Sherwood Forest had claimed its first victims.

Anyone passing the Leenside caves that evening might have wondered why shouts echoed seemingly from within the walls of rock, and looked twice at the red light gleaming through the chinks of fissures in the caveface. Inside, the hundredmen toasted their success. Will had provided some of Agnes's ale – not much, but even a cup was enough to get the men drunk after weeks of water – and Robin had brought as much food as he and Waltheof could safely carry from the kitchens of Locksley Hall. Robin and John tried to hush the men, but it was a fool's errand that night, and in truth they only did so half-heartedly. It had been a hard, miserable season for all of them, and with little else to celebrate until today but their continued existence, Robin could not deny them the chance to revel in this success.

'I have a toast,' called Lefchild, who could get drunk on a thimble of ale. He stumbled to his feet and raised his cup. 'To the tax collectors in Nottinghamshire. For employing England's most useless guards.'

The men cheered. Lefchild slumped down to eat.

'And I have one,' said John. 'To Thorfridh.'

There was no need for eulogies. The men raised their cups or their food-stained hands, and called out Thorfridh's name.

'I still wish the guards were dead,' said Kolbrand, one of the men unknown to Robin before. He was built like a bear and fought like a boar, and now his energies were bent on extracting every bit of nourishment from the small meal before him. 'I don't care if it would have brought more men into the forest to find us, I'd have liked to smash their heads into their helms.'

He pressed his hands together so hard his knuckles shone through his red skin.

'This is worse for them,' grinned Will. 'They'll have had plenty of time to feel foolish and sore-arsed on that roadside, and they'll feel even worse when the sheriff whips them for letting the money get stolen.'

'What about the horses?' said Doleswif. 'We could have sold them.'

'Or eaten them,' said Lefchild, snapping a bone to reach the marrow inside.

'It is too easy to track hooves,' said Gilbert loftily. 'Especially a dozen hoof prints that lead straight to our cave.'

Lefchild threw his drained bone at Gilbert's head.

'Pipe down, Magister.'

Gilbert could read, and this coupled with his lordly name brought mockery raining down on him. But then every man was mocked here. Some of them had even started jesting with Robin. He had not always taken a joke against himself well, but the more the men felt comfortable to mock him the more they accepted him as one of their number. It made him feel like a soldier again, like a man who had worth. For that he would take any number of nicknames.

'I'll pipe down completely,' said Gilbert, standing up. 'It's probably my watch now.'

'Don't break your neck climbing the tree,' called Lefchild as Gilbert went. 'Hands that hold pens are no use for real tasks.'

He cackled as Gilbert turned his back and left, loping in a half run down the passage and out of the caves.

'I hate to bring up practicalities,' said Thurstan, who had been drinking the same single cup of ale all evening, 'but how are we going to get this money to our kin?'

'We won't,' said John firmly. 'They will.'

He pointed to Will, to Waltheof, then to Robin.

'So we still can't see our kin,' said Thurstan. 'Even after this.'

'Especially after this,' said John.

Thurstan frowned into his cup.

'What were you expecting?' Kolbrand laughed. He was the only man in that cave confident enough to laugh in Thurstan's face when the smith was in one of his black moods. 'We've shamed the sheriff and his count friend twice now. We scorned his castle walls and now we've made fools of his tax collectors. They won't be happy until we're hanging from Nottingham gatehouse. We're never going home, son.' He tore one last string of meat from the bone in his hand. 'Still say we should've killed the guards, mind. Might as well hang for a pound as a penny.'

'We're hanging for five pounds apiece at the moment,' said Will. He raised one of the sacks high in the air with a holler. His fellows cheered him and hissed for him to be quiet in equal, raucous measure.

At least the noise distracted them from Kolbrand's words. It was true, thought Robin, as he looked around the cave. None of the hundredmen could return to their old lives now. But for Will, Robin and Waltheof it was a different matter. As long as they stayed beyond suspicion they could go on living two lives: the life of a respectable Nottinghamshire man, and the life of a fugitive in the forest.

'We'll make sure your kin get this money,' Robin said in a low voice to Thurstan, below the cries and crunching and slurps of the other men. 'And I can even let you see them take it.'

Thurstan opened his mouth to ask how, but before he could speak a thin streak of russet lightning bolted into the chamber, half falling as it leapt to kick out the fire. Lefchild shouted a protest as hot sparks and ash singed his legs.

'Hey, what are you doing – get off,' he cried.

Gilbert tumbled over the fire to push his hand over Lefchild's mouth. The boy was white-faced, sweat beading on his forehead.

'Lights,' he hissed, flapping his arms to silence the chamber. 'There are lights in the forest. Torches. Men are coming.'

The hundredmen leapt to their feet, joining in kicking out the fire, kicking their companions to alertness, kicking the bags of coins into a pile that would not rustle. The cave was engulfed in sudden silent darkness. Robin knelt, one hand futilely gripping his sword. He seized Gilbert's arm, pulled him close enough to whisper.

'Who are they?'

'Sheriff's men, I think,' Gilbert said, barely breathing. 'Christ, I swear they could hear you from half-a-mile off.'

Robin felt a grip on his collar. Above him John had made his way to the chink in the cave wall and was looking out on the woodland below. Robin stood to look with him. Distantly, weaving through the forest was a line of torches, swaying as if the men carrying them were on horseback. They were drawing closer. At the head of them was a man in mail, bearded and grey haired. It was the sheriff.

'Shit,' muttered Robin. 'Don't make a sound.'

The men tensed. One of them reached for a weapon, fumbled it, dropped it on the cave floor with a thud that seemed to boom in the echoing chamber. No one spoke to chastise him. The line of guards moved closer, closer. They were riding directly towards the caves. Had they heard the noises before, seen the firelight? Had they heard that echo? Robin kept his eye to the cave fissure, his face in the shadows. Sir Walter was at the foot of the caves. He raised an arm, pointed for his men to search. They dismounted and spread out around the caves in silence. If they found the entrance behind the ivy, if they got inside the cave – what then? Could the hundredmen fight them? The passage was thin, only one or two men could come through it at a time. In a castle stairwell they would be sitting ducks. But the hundredmen's arrows were gone, they had no crossbows to pick off one guard after another. And sharpened sticks and rabbit bones would hardly bring down armoured fighters. If they found the cave the sheriff's men did not even need to enter it. They could pile up dry leaves and throw in their torches, burning the men in the chamber without risking a single one of their own lives. Robin swallowed.

One of the guards approached the screen of ivy. He looked up and down it, pressed through the leaves to the cave wall. His hands were low, lower than the level of the opening into the passage. He swore suddenly. He had pricked his hand on a sharp edge in the rock face. He shook his hand with gritted teeth and walked away from the ivy, shaking his head. All the guards were returning to Sir Walter. None had found a way into the caves. The sheriff sighed, looked up at the sandstone cliffs. Robin pulled his head away from the fissure, so fast he knocked the back of it. He balled his hand into a fist to stop himself swearing. When he braved looking out of the fissure again the sheriff had turned his horse and the other men were mounting theirs. Raising their torches once more, they set off back into the forest.

Robin exhaled and slumped back against the cave wall. As his eyes adjusted to the darkness inside he saw the other men doing the same, shaking their heads and sitting back around the ashes of the fire. Lefchild put his arm around Gilbert's shoulders and kissed him on top of his head.

'Good work, Magister,' he breathed as the lad shrugged him away. 'Those eyes of yours are good for something after all.'

'They know about the wagon then,' said Will. When he sat there was a rustle of coins.

'We need to get rid of that money fast,' said John. 'If we're found before it's been passed to our kin we might as well never have taken it.'

'And you need to find somewhere else to hide,' added Robin. 'Gilbert, you can read. Can you write as well?'

'Yes, my lord. My father was a priest. My hand isn't handsome, but it's clear enough to be understood.'

'How many of the rest of your kin read?'

The men answered in a jumble.

'Not many,' Robin concluded. 'But your kin can be trusted to pass a message from one to another I think. Will and Waltheof and I can see to that. You all need to move on.'

'To another cave?' asked Doleswif.

'Deeper into the forest. Stay on high ground.'

John nodded. He knew the forest well enough, he would lead them right.

'Waltheof, Will. Take your share now and let's go.'

'Aren't you taking a share?' Gilbert asked.

Lefchild smacked the back of his head. 'He's a lord, Magister. Use your mind. He doesn't need our coin.'

Robin forced a smile. 'Not as long as I can avoid the sheriff on the way back.'

Robin led the way out of the caves. Waltheof and Will filled their purses with as much as they could carry and followed him. At the base of the cave passage, Robin dropped out into the forest and breathed deeply. The air smelt of damp leaves and earth. And for the first time since he had returned to Nottinghamshire he felt glad to be Lord Locksley.

Twelve people went into Sherwood Forest on the feast day of St Anselm. They came from all over the same hundred in Nottinghamshire, but each from a different trade and a different family: the blacksmith's wife, the thatcher's brother, the brewer, the carpenter, the priest's sister. All of them, at the chiming of an hour throughout the day, walked cautiously into the woodland, along the King's Way. At the same point – give or take a few confused steps – they turned off the road into the unmarked forest, following a brook that skirted the old common lands, up a rise near a cluster of caves, towards a clearing where there stood a tall tree with a thick trunk. The tree had been struck by lightning, or perhaps set on fire during the Anarchy – the story varied from village to village. Either way, it had been split down the middle and now stood, totally dead, with its stick-like branches outstretched and its centre billowing out like a skin full of ale. Every one of these individuals followed instructions – some reading them off scraps of vellum, others remembering the words told them by a friend – to arrive at the tree, and then reached inside it to remove three sacks, each of which they hid about their person. And then every one of them returned the way they had come, smiling to themselves and the world in general.

They did not realise it but as they walked through the forest that day these people were watched. Above them in the trees, in the caves, on hillocks and on the opposite side of the brook. At every point of their journey a figure in ragged russets hid within the forest to watch them pass. The figures did not move from their vantage points, did not call out, but they too smiled when they saw the sack-laden visitors to the forest returning from the tree.

Robin watched the last of the visitors turn back onto the King's Road with a contented sigh. He waited until he was certain he was alone to stretch out his spine, stand up tall from his hiding place and go to fetch his horse. At his side had rested a hunting bow and arrows, even the body of a rabbit he had shot during his wait. Had anyone recognised him squatting all day by the road he had wanted to ensure he had an excuse for his odd behaviour. Now he mounted his horse. He rode the same route as the forest's visitors. At every point where they had been watched he whistled. He got a whistle in response and then heard movement: the hundredmen leaving their perches and returning to their hideout. Their day's work was done. They had all seen their kin receiving the rewards from the tax wagon, they had kept their promise not to speak to their family as they passed, and now they could retire content in the knowledge that even from their exile in the forest they had helped their loved ones.

At the tree Robin found Will, picking up a penny or two that had fallen into the hollow inside. Lefchild idly sat in the branches above, swinging his legs.

'Any trouble?' Robin asked.

'None.' Will slipped the coins into his purse. 'But I think my spine's crooked now. Next time let's use a mule.'

He rubbed his back. Will had ferried the sacks of coin from a cave nearby to the tree trunk, replacing three bags every time three were taken. Robin felt cruel for giving his brother the most arduous task, but since Will was the only man who had not fled justice it was safe for him to be seen moving through the forest. And what was more, it was always wise to give Will something physical to do to distract him, otherwise he would get bored and make mischief. Robin pulled Lefchild's leg like a church bell and he leapt down from the tree like a lark landing.

'John and I found something that could be useful,' he said, 'when we cleared out of the caves. Have you time to see it now? It's a fair walk.'

Robin did. Lefchild led them deeper into the forest, through the thick tree cover, over patches of earth that had not been churned by foot or hoof for years. The forest pressed close around them, enveloping them in a deep quiet, birdcall echoing suddenly through the trees like a child's cry in a church. Every now and then there would be a rustle at their feet then the sudden flash of colour – silver hares, blazing fox fur, pheasant feathers – as animals unused to man's presence fled from their approach. Watching where he led his horse to avoid stumbling roots, Robin did not see Lefchild stop until his boot hit Will's shoulder. Murmuring an apology – it seemed wrong to disturb the stillness of that forest with his own voice – Robin looked up. And only then did he see the clearing. Once it had held a croft, a range of buildings perhaps, large enough for two families and all their animals. Now the forest had reclaimed most of the dwellings, stones caught half-tumbling by ivy and shrub. The thatch on the roof was almost rotten away, and beneath the balding straw Robin could see the bones of the building. The beams were green where the rain had fallen on them, but the trees around the clearing had created enough shelter to keep the worst of Nature's efforts from the croft. Against the wall of one building was a sage bush, the remnants no doubt of a herb kitchen.

There was a whistle from the opposite side of the clearing. Lefchild whistled in response, and John appeared, leading the rest of the hundredmen.

'Haven't seen a soul coming this way,' he called. 'I doubt anyone's been back here in a decade or more.'

The men spread out across the clearing, investigating the ruined buildings. John headed for the croft. Robin followed him, a number of others at his heels.

'We found it last night while hunting,' John explained. They had to duck to get through the croft doorway. Inside it was dark, darker than Robin had expected, and drier too. 'There's a bakehouse round the back. The roof's fallen in worse there but we could get the oven going again easily enough.'

'This could be easily fixed,' said one of the men, patting the roof beams with an experienced hand. 'At least enough to keep out the weather. If we can't get to reeds we can daub it.'

'What was your job before?' asked Robin. He knew no more of the man than his name: Grimm.

'Thatcher. Worked with Tosti's father now and then – he's a carpenter.'

A face appeared in the roof. Lefchild clambered over the wall and landed cat-like in the croft.

'This will do well,' he said, looking around with the same contentment as if the mouldering ruin was a cathedral.

'We could do with some women in it,' said Madalgrim the baker.

Lefchild laughed.

'I meant to cook,' Madalgrim protested, 'and tidy it up a bit. We had a fire in our home once and my wife and our girls had everything back to best before the next day dawned.'

Robin met John's eye. The older man regarded the croft more distantly than his fellows.

'A word,' Robin said, inclining his head towards the door. John followed him outside. Kolbrand and Tosti were having a heated debate about which was the best animal to keep in a croft like this. Goats seemed to be winning the day. Robin walked far enough from them not to be overhead.

'Women, John?' he said. 'And animals and baking?'

'I know, they're getting carried away with it all. But you should leave them be for now. Jesus knows we've been downhearted enough since Thorfridh was taken. Anything that stops us being at each other's throats and starts making us work together is to the good.'

'I can see this is a good place to live, but I'm not sure it's a good place to hide. You need to remember that you're all fugitives, one step away from outlawry. If you keep moving there's less chance that the sheriff and the Viponts will follow a trail. If you stay here – especially if you invite others to join you –'

'Then we might be found. Or perhaps it'll make us safer.' John gestured to the forest beyond them. 'We're miles from the nearest road or home. No one has been this way since Henry was king. There are any number of men hiding in this forest, some have been here for years, and they just get forgotten about.'

'The Viponts aren't going to forget you. We made fools of them and every day that you draw breath is another affront to them.'

'So we don't bring anyone else here. You know as well as I do that eventually these men will try to meet their kin. As long as we all agree that no one else – no one – comes here, it's as good a hiding place as any.'

Robin looked at the men as they moved around the clearing, into and out of buildings, gesturing towards roofs that would be built and pens that would hold all the animals they could catch. Doleswif and Gilbert were collecting fallen stones and piling them up to reuse in the walls. They already saw a future for themselves here. Robin could not blame them for preferring this to a cave. And as long as he was sleeping in a bed with clean linens and a herb-scented fireplace he could hardly argue against their enjoying the minimal luxury of a bakehouse.

'No one?' Robin repeated.

'I'll make sure of it.'

'Then you had better tell me what supplies you'll need. I'll see what I can take from the hall.'

When Robin and Will left the clearing the hundredmen were still in good spirits. They would hunt out their own supplies where they could, but axes were needed, and lathes if possible. Robin donated his hunting arrows to their cause but they would need more of those, and more rope or twine, spades even, to trap animals to feed them. Everything would be easier, Robin thought, if he was Lord Locksley in more than name. If he could donate supplies and food and drink to the men, send his own trusted servants into the forest to deliver them instead of sneaking constantly around the sheriff and his mother. Even around Marian and Elaine. Elaine had viewed his charitable venture with Marian as Christian, but ultimately futile. He suspected that even Marian would baulk at providing aid to wanted criminals.

Days passed swiftly. The sheriff's men continued to search the forest, but Robin made sure now that he was in their party when they did so. He would not be caught offguard again after such a close miss in the caves. If Sir Walter's searches came within a mile of the abandoned croft he was ready to divert them with false signs of fugitives in another direction. Fortunately, even that level of subterfuge had so far been unnecessary. The sheriff and his men always returned to their homes without success, and eventually it became so embarrassing to Sir Walter to pursue these fruitless quests that he gave them up. The Viponts were not so easily downcast. Their men, led by the untiring Lanfranc, circled the villages and homes of Nottinghamshire, always keeping a special watch on the kin of the escaped men. More than once Robin had seen men in the Vipont colours tracking the thatcher Grimm's family from task to task. Sir Walter grumbled to Robin that he was not pleased to see so many Vipont men on his roads. But as long as the Count of Mortain remained in Nottinghamshire there was little he could do to oppose them.

One morning, as April gave way to May, Robin went to the kitchens on a pretence of inquiring with the steward about the Ascension feast for his mother and found Will Scarlette warming himself over a copper. One of the spitboys was laughing uproariously while the cook raised a wooden ladle threateningly behind them. Will noticed Robin and called out to him.

'What are you doing in the kitchens, Lord Locksley?'

'I might ask you the same question.'

At mention of Robin's name the whole kitchen had fallen silent. He gestured for them to return to their work.

'Visiting my beloved brother, of course.'

'Forgive me, my lord,' said the cook, almost prostrating himself before Robin, 'but I could not make him leave.'

'No harm done,' said Robin. 'Have that boy bring my brother something to eat and we won't mention this to Lady Joan or Sir Walter.'

The cook waved the ladle at the spitboy and blessed Robin in equal measure. As soon as they had gathered ale, bread and cheese Robin led Will out of the kitchen – checking that none of his family were close enough to see them – and into the kennels. Wulfstan gave them an unconcerned wave of greeting and carried on with his work. Will settled on a pile of dog blankets and took the food from Robin.

'A man could be insulted,' said Will, 'when his brother makes him eat with the hounds rather than the men.'

'Dogs are more discreet than servants.'

'Aren't you eating?' smiled Will, biting into a chunk of cheese. 'You know, you shouldn't feed me too well. I'll hang around you like a stray cat. Your mother might poison the milk to get rid of me.'

Robin smiled despite himself. 'How did you get past the porter?'

'Didn't. I jumped the wall. The north side needs repairing.'

'I'll be sure to tell the sheriff.' Robin sat beside him. He noticed that for all Will's jokes there was something of the stray about him. He looked half-starved. Whatever he had spent his tax wagon pennies on, it was clearly not food.

'The men have been asking,' said Will between slurps of ale, 'when the next one's going to be?'

'The next one?'

'The next raid. The sheriff must have sent for more taxmen. The crown hasn't got the amount it wanted from us, so the taxmen will come back for more. Your man in the chancery should be able to get the details.'

'There won't be another raid,' said Robin. 'We attacked that wagon to provide for the families of the hundredmen, and now they're provided for.'

'They can't live on a few pounds forever.'

'Compared with what most of them usually earn, a few pounds is a fortune.'

'A fortune divided stops being a fortune, starts just looking like pennies again.' Will paused as Wulfstan came in to fetch one of the hounds then disappeared into the yard again. He lowered his voice. 'Every family split the money, gave some to friends, or neighbours who had greater need. They didn't hoard it for themselves. And I can barely go into Nottingham without people coming begging to me. Not because they know about the hundredmen, before you start, but because of you. They think the sheriff has got vast sums hidden away in here just waiting to be handed out. There isn't a family in the county who isn't in need.'

'I know there are a lot of hungry families,' said Robin. Marian had not been out on another of her charitable missions since the sheriff had learnt of them, and all of Robin's thefts from Locksley Hall had gone to feed and clothe the hundredmen. 'But it's only spring. It's expected to be a warm summer, the harvest should be good. Then everyone will be better off. We shouldn't risk all our necks in another raid while the count and his royal guard are in Nottinghamshire.'

'Didn't think you'd mind risking your neck.'

'I'm not just thinking of myself. You must have seen the Vipont guard all over the county, watching the men's families for the slightest sign that will connect them to the escape. If there is another theft of taxes those families will be under more suspicion, and we both know how the Viponts' steward expresses his suspicion.'

'We can make sure the money's divided even further this time. Then there won't be anything to connect the hundredmen to the raid.'

It was a good idea. But ensuring a dozen men's families received their cut of the raided taxes without anyone finding out had been dangerous. Adding most of their neighbours into the mix only increased the chances of someone reporting back to the sheriff. It would only take one loose word to arrest Will or Waltheof. And Robin had already seen the swiftness of the Viponts' justice after Thorfridh was taken.

'The men are safe in the croft for now,' said Robin. 'I think we should leave it that way.'

Will sighed and wiped crumbs from his front. 'I suppose the repairs will keep them occupied for the time-being. If you can steal them, John told me which supplies they need.'

'We can look in the outhouses now,' said Robin, getting to his feet, 'if you've finished your food.'

Just as Will was standing to join him the door to the kennels flew open. Robin spun around as Elaine and Marian stepped into the gloom. At sight of them Will dropped to his knees, hiding his face. Elaine looked from him to Robin in confusion.

'I have been looking for you,' she said. 'When Estrild said she saw you going into the kennels with a pauper I did not believe her. Obviously I was wrong.'

'Get up, Will,' said Marian in a low voice, looking over her shoulder to check the courtyard. Will had remained kneeling all the time that Elaine spoke, in the humble manner of any servant, hoping not to be recognised. It was a false hope.

'*Will*?' repeated Elaine, frowning at Will's dirt-smeared and torn clothing. 'You are very familiar with this – man. Is he one of the tenants you gave charity to?'

Marian said nothing, looking to Robin to answer the question. It was his choice, clearly, to lie or reveal the truth. Since Marian had already recognised Will, there seemed little point in deception.

'This is my brother,' Robin said. 'Will, this is Elaine Peverill, Marian's cousin. You remember Marian I expect.'

'Of course.' Will grinned at Marian, gave her a low bow. 'Lady Peverill.'

Elaine looked at him with the same expression a laundress gives a grease stain. 'Why are you talking to your father's bastard here?'

Will's smile instantly dropped. 'Because we're talking about things,' he said sharply, 'that don't concern anyone in Locksley Hall. Except maybe Marian. Marian's good at keeping secrets as I recall.'

'What secrets?' Elaine turned to Robin. 'Why should Marian know them?'

'Marian does not know them,' Robin said quickly. 'Will is joking. We just wanted a private conversation.'

'Then why are you hiding here? Why not speak in the solar?'

'I'm not allowed inside,' said Will. 'Better I stay out here with the dogs.'

'My father and stepmother do not much like Will,' said Marian. 'They are wrong to think as they do, of course.'

Will laughed. 'You're an idiot, brother. You should've married this good woman when you had the chance. Now I'll have to.'

'Marian is already betrothed,' said Elaine icily. 'And so is Robin.'

'Is he?' Will swivelled between Elaine and his brother. 'Are you?'

'I hope that Agnes is well,' Marian interrupted. 'Perhaps I can fetch some food for you to take back to her?' She held her arm out towards the door. 'Come to the hall with me.'

'Lady Joan won't like that,' said Will, following her all the same.

'Good,' said Marian, almost quiet enough for only Will to hear. As Will passed her, Elaine's eyes widened. She glanced quickly from him to Robin and back again.

'I heard that you had a brother,' she said when he was gone. Her voice was soft, but no gentler. 'Since you never mentioned him to me I presumed you did not see him. I hear he is renowned throughout the county as a drunkard.'

'Did my mother tell you that?'

'No, I heard it at Nottingham Castle when I was visiting Lord Eudo.'

'I do not think it is any concern of his what my brother drinks.' Despite himself, Robin felt a stab of jealousy. 'Why were you visiting Eudo de Vipont?'

'It seemed politic for one of us to do so, after you offended them over that common land dispute. Lord Eudo's family are so close to the Count of Mortain it would be idiocy not to remain on good terms with them.'

Robin ignored that aspersion. 'I have no great desire to bow and scrape to the count, let alone his pets.'

'Even greater idiocy,' Elaine muttered. She picked up a leash and wrapped it around her fingers, watching her skin flush and then blanche as she wound and unwound it. 'If the king does not have a child soon the count will be our next king, and he will remember the lords who supported him now. When that day comes, it will help your appeal for the Locksley estate if you were one of those lords rather than the stubborn fools who argue against him.'

'I will wait for the true king to come home,' said Robin, 'rather than appealing to his little brother. Courting the count would make no difference to my suit against the Viponts in any case. You know as well as I do that they have their claws deep into him. If it came down to a decision between their interests and mine he would choose theirs every time.'

'All the more reason to appeal to him now. He has always been good to his English subjects. Better even than King Richard.'

Robin said nothing.

'Of course, you could try being more accommodating to the Viponts as well.'

'I will not listen to this again…'

Elaine threw the leash on the ground.

'I do not understand you,' she cried. 'You behave as if you did not care about regaining Locksley. You know that until you have that estate we cannot marry, my parents will not allow it.'

'I know. I have sent for writs from Westminster.'

'Yes, and none have appeared. Even when they do, they will only get you so far. Influence is what matters, not lawyers and letters, but you are too proud to admit that. I had heard that you preferred the company of baseborn men to your own rank when you were young, but I thought you had changed your habits. Clearly I was mistaken. When you should be visiting the count and courting the Viponts you prefer to sit watching bastards eat cheese in a kennel.'

'Do not call Will a bastard.' Robin bent to pick up the leash, struggling to keep his temper. 'He is my brother.'

'Your half-blood brother. Why is he here anyway? Is it because of your inheritance?'

'No, why should it be?'

'Perhaps he has heard you are trying to reclaim your rightful estate and he wants to claim it for himself.'

'That is not why he was here. But he has a right to some of that estate.'

'No,' Elaine said firmly, 'he does not.'

Robin hung the leash back on the wall, saying nothing. Wulfstan returned with the dog he had been exercising. Seeing the two of them there, he hesitated. Elaine waved a hand to dismiss him. They stood in silence, looking at the earth, at the walls, at the roof. Anything but each other.

'I do not want to quarrel,' Elaine said at last.

'Then let us stop discussing this.'

'Please understand me first. I do not speak against your brother purposely to vex you. I only say this because I want you to have everything you deserve. I have known other families have their estates stolen from them by bast–' she stopped herself, corrected her words. 'By illegitimate children through lawsuits and flattery.'

'Will has nothing to pay for a lawsuit,' said Robin. Since she made an effort to be civil, he would do the same. 'And he is not exactly inclined to flattery, as you might have noticed.'

'He flattered Marian.'

'Did he?'

She nodded. There was something almost childlike in her sincerity. If he did not know better, he might have thought her jealous.

'You noticed the resemblance between us?' He changed the subject.

'Yes. I had heard that you looked alike, not that you were mirrors of each other.'

If Elaine had not heard of it, then Lord Eudo and his family must also be ignorant of Will's similarity to Robin. It would be best if that remained the case. Robin was not eager for the Viponts to discover that through Will he had a means of being in two places at once.

'Please do not tell anyone of Will's being here.'

She smiled conspiratorially. 'I will not mention it to your mother if that is what you are afraid of.'

'Or to the Viponts.' Her smile faltered. 'I do not want them to know any more about my family than is absolutely necessary. Because of Jocelyn,' he lied swiftly. 'My nephew is only of interest to them because of his right to the Locksley estate. If Lord Eudo thinks that Will could challenge his inheritance, he might not be so kind to the boy.'

Elaine seemed on the verge of disputing Robin's low opinion of Eudo de Vipont, but bit the remark back. She looked up at him and all trace of discord was gone.

'Jocelyn may not have the opportunity to inherit,' she said, holding out her hand to him. 'We will have sons enough of our own to claim the estate.'

Robin took her hand and kissed it. She laced her arm through his as they left the kennel and returned to the warm spring freshness of the courtyard.

Rogation

At the outer reaches of the Locksley manor, where the green lane curved towards the King's Way was the blacksmith's forge. Smoke often spewed from the forge, and at first as Robin approached it from the forest he thought that was all he saw. He was thinking over what Will had said to him in the kennels, of how to divide money between so many people that the sheriff and the Viponts could not suspect one family over another. Along the lane's edge a farmer was struggling to plough his strip of land with oxen too stubborn to move. The farmer noticed the smoke around the forge and paused over his plough. Robin followed his eye. There was something unnatural in that smoke, something more than the bellowed steam off the smith's fire. Half of the roof was wreathed in it now. He pressed his horse forward. As he rounded a bend in the lane he saw the cause of it. The forge was on fire, and the house next to it was crackling with smoke as well. Half a dozen men stood around the building in red and gold. One held a horse for their master: Lanfranc. Thorold the smith was an old man, half blind from years of hovering over smoking metal, but the father of Geraint and Thurstan was no weakling. One of Lanfranc's men cradled his jaw, and Thorold himself sprawled on the ground, clutching his head in his hands. Next to him a woman dabbed at his bleeding scalp with a scrap of linen. It was Aedith, Thurstan's wife. With her other hand she was holding tight to an infant.

'What is happening here?' Robin called.

The guards turned to look at him. Aedith struggled to her feet, the child still clinging on.

'A spark from the forge has set the building alight,' said Lanfranc, giving Lord Locksley the shortest of reverences.

A fortunate coincidence, thought Robin, watching one of the Vipont guards pat ash from his hands.

'Did the forge strike Thorold in the head as well?'

'My guard did that. We were trying to arrest the smith and he resisted.'

'On what charge?'

'We found a stash of money in their roof. Either this family are minting coins illegally or they have received stolen goods.'

'What were you doing in their roof in the first place?'

'No right,' Aedith called in faltering French. 'No right. Stop this.'

'This woman's husband,' Lanfranc said, ignoring her, 'was one of those felons who escaped the castle. It seems likely that this money comes from the tax wagon that was attacked two weeks ago.'

'Why is that likely?' Robin asked.

Lanfranc looked up at him with a sneer. 'These people could not get such sums from honest means.'

Robin moved closer to the steward. 'These people can and have made good money from their work,' he said in a low voice. 'That was always the way before your masters came to this county.'

Lanfranc's response was forestalled by a scream. The flames had reached the thatch on top of the roof. The child cried out and covered its eyes with Aedith's skirt.

'They have seen enough,' said Lanfranc. 'Arrest them.'

The guards roughly lifted the smith and tried to seize Aedith.

'We have done nothing…' she cried.

She moved towards Lanfranc, her arms out, imploring. One of his men stepped in front of her and shoved her back. The child holding her skirts fell over with a shriek. Robin drew his sword and pushed his horse right up to the guard, striking him across the back with the flat of his blade. The guard stumbled forward, into Lanfranc, who pushed him roughly away. Robin pointed his sword at the guards holding Thorold by the arms. One of them let go. The other looked to Lanfranc.

'You have no right to arrest these people,' said Robin. 'And absolutely none to mistreat them as you do.'

'I have the right to keep law in the lands of Lord de Vipont,' said Lanfranc. 'And I suspect this family of breaking those laws.'

'These are the Locksley lands.'

'Which belong to Lord de Vipont.'

'Not as long as I breathe.'

Lanfranc's hand was on his sword. Robin's eye did not slip from his. He barely blinked. In that moment he meant what he said. If he had to die to protect this one family, he would do it. Lanfranc let go of his sword.

'Take them. My master will expect to see them tried in the sheriff's court. If they are not he will know whose fault it is.'

Lanfranc turned his back on Robin without any further deference. He mounted his horse and rode off at the head of his guard without looking back. Only when they were out of sight did Aedith look to Robin, apprehensive.

'Are – are you going to take us to the sheriff, my lord?'

'No,' said Robin, dismounting. 'But you can't stay here. Can you walk?'

'Yes… Are we going far?'

'A few miles.'

Aedith looked from the flaming ruins of her home to the road where Robin's horse stood. She nodded. 'My father will need help.'

Robin and Aedith assisted the old man onto his horse, and the child up in front of him.

'Are there any tools kept in your outbuildings?'

Aedith said there were.

'Then fetch them quickly.'

Aedith ran to do so, returning with a sack only slightly weighted down: a pair of singed bellows, a mallet and tongs could be seen sticking out the top.

'Most of our things were inside.'

She bit her lip to keep from crying.

'This will be enough. Hold onto the bridle if you get tired.'

Robin took the sack of tools and pulled his horse to follow him. Aedith took hold of the bridle on the other side of him, whispering soothing words to her child. They headed for the King's Way, following it until Robin saw a party in brightly coloured tunics ahead. He directed them off the road and into the thickets alongside the verge.

'Are we going to the blasted tree again?' Aedith asked quietly.

'No. Further.'

They continued in silence. They passed no one else on their journey, and Aedith did not ask again where they were heading. Robin could not have explained if she had. All he knew was that he wanted to protect this family and there was only one place in Nottinghamshire he could think of which would do that.

When they neared the croft clearing Tosti dropped from a tree watch point to see them pass. He tugged at his tangled beard in confusion and called for Thurstan. He was helping Grimm replace the roof on the largest croft. Thurstan stared at the sight of Aedith, walking into the forest with Robin and his family as if he doubted his own eyes. Then he leapt from the roof and ran to meet her. Word passed around the men quickly, and from all their tasks in the clearing – even from their watches – they gathered to meet the new arrivals. Thurstan's child shrieked with laughter at being bundled from one set of arms to another. Doleswif asked the question that many of the men must have wondered:

'Why is Thurstan's wife allowed here?'

'Because their home has been destroyed.' Robin told them of how he had found Lanfranc burning down the smithy, and of the incriminating stash of coins that had been discovered.

'Can we feed three more mouths?' asked Tosti.

'We'll have to,' said Madalgrim the baker, wiping a tear from his eye as he passed the child to John. Like most of the men he had children of his own beyond the forest. 'This is a blessing. If we can gather some hops Aedith can brew for us, eh, Aedith?'

'And I can smith more easily with these,' said Thurstan quickly, drawing the tools Aedith had brought from the sack. 'Not to mention with my father here. We need more arrow heads.'

'All our kin could help,' said Doleswif. 'But I didn't think we were allowed them here.' He looked coldly at Robin.

'Your kin are all still safe,' said Robin.

'Are you sure?' Tosti asked. 'If that bastard steward searched Thurstan's home he must have searched ours too.'

'Mine are probably better at hiding things,' muttered Kolbrand. 'More fool them.'

'Most of your kin gave away more money,' said Aedith. 'I was trying to keep ours – we will have another mouth to feed in a few months. I didn't want to lose it before then, but we've lost it anyway…'

Her voice trailed away. Thurstan embraced her.

'We can get more money,' said Lefchild. 'If we wait for the next tax collection.'

'Lord Robin said we should not do another raid so soon,' interrupted Gilbert. 'Will told us that.'

'That is what I said,' Robin muttered, watching Thorold being helped onto a battered stool. 'But the idea of making an ass of the Viponts' men is certainly appealing at this moment.'

'We could do it,' Lefchild said eagerly. 'Will and me thought of a way. All it would take is one fine set of clothes.'

'The next tax wagon will be guarded even more heavily,' said John sternly. He had clearly heard this scheme before. 'The sheriff is no fool. We used up the few arrows we had in the last raid and whatever we can make now should be used for hunting.'

'It's safest just to carry on as we are,' Tosti agreed, 'rather than wasting our time and stocks on plans that could get us killed. We should keep improving the croft, hunt for animals more often. We could even start growing crops.'

'And wait for our kin to starve or hang?' interrupted Kolbrand. 'I'm bored off my arse of wattling and thatching. I want to wring that bastard Lanfranc's neck. I want revenge for Thorfridh.'

Many of the men cheered his words.

'But think of what might happen to our kin,' Doleswif called over them, 'if we're caught.'

John looked to Robin to pacify them, but he was in no mood to do so. Lanfranc had proven once again that day how little regard he had for the people of Nottinghamshire. In the name of 'law-keeping' he was willing to burn down homes and attack women and old men. As long as he and his masters held sway over the county that would be the only law the poor would know. But perhaps if the Viponts were shown to have lost control of their lands, if their so-called laws kept being flouted and their coin stolen, the Count of Mortain would lose faith in them and they in turn would lose their authority.

'There is a way,' he said, thinking aloud, 'that we could take those taxes and make sure your kin are not suspected of being involved. We could even make the Viponts seem as culpable as anyone.'

'Then we should do it,' said Kolbrand. Now more voices joined his to call for action.

'But first,' said Robin, quieting them with a raised hand, 'I want to hear Lefchild's plan.'

The responsibility for collecting Nottinghamshire's taxes lay with the local men – bailiffs of the township, trusted men of the hundred – but responsibility for delivering the money to the Exchequer belonged wholly to the royal tax collectors and their clerk. Once all the funds had been assessed, assembled and checked by the sheriff, the tax collectors took possession of them. Given the indignities the collectors had suffered at the hands of Nottinghamshire's inhabitants a few weeks before, Sir Walter was making every effort to ensure that their second attempt to deliver the taxes went smoothly, and left no bitter memories to be reported back to Westminster. Part of this effort included making an elaborate display of county amity by inviting neighbouring lords to join Sir Walter's family for a May feast before the collectors headed south. Robin had no doubt that this banquet was as much his mother's scheme as the sheriff's. The ladies in his household were all determined to reconcile their family to the Viponts, and pastries and meat seemed as good a first step towards that as any.

Robin had promised Elaine that he would be civil to the Viponts, but no more than that. His continued displeasure with Lord Eudo's family gave him the perfect excuse to position himself at a distance from them at the supper table, conveniently closer to the tax collectors. From this vantage point he would be able to question the taxmen about their preparations to convey the taxes from Locksley Hall without too much interference from the other lords. The position of the hall on the outer limits of Sherwood Forest ensured that the collectors could not avoid passing through the forest for at least part of their journey, and Robin meant to learn exactly how much.

Since it was the season of Maying, garlands of hawthorn and wreaths of woodbine decked the hall. Lady Joan had spent vast sums on the meal: subtleties of sugar in the form of monsters terminated each course and meats of every variety were served boiled, roasted and encased in pastry. Robin wished he could carry one of the great sugar creatures into the forest for the men – one alone would keep them fed for a day. However, he suspected its loss would not go unnoticed. Polite, if strained, conversation carried the company through one course before Serlo de Vipont punctured the bubble of civility by calling to Robin from the opposite end of the table.

'Lord Locksley. The sheriff has just told me about your misfortune with the prisoners Lanfranc put into your charge. He tells me they escaped from you into the forest?'

'Yes,' said Robin. 'Unfortunately.'

'Oh I quite understand. It must have been difficult to keep hold of them. Lanfranc said the group was made up of a blind old man, a woman *and* an infant. Quite a challenge for a lord who has marched against the Saracen.'

The room had fallen silent. Elaine put her hand on Robin's and squeezed it, bidding him not to lose his temper.

'It is remarkable,' Serlo continued, 'how many criminals in your charge seem to escape.'

'I might say the same of your castle's prisoners.'

Robin smiled at the scowl that fell over Serlo's face. The tax collectors collectively averted their gaze. Their leader addressed the sheriff in the hope of changing the topic.

'Has there been any progress in finding the devils who attacked the last tax wagon?'

'No,' replied Ranulf gruffly. He threw his wine down his throat and slammed his cup onto the table so sharply Guy flinched.

'It – it was the same in Yorkshire,' the collector said, making an effort to maintain his joviality. 'These baseborn men know their own countryside too well.'

Lady Joan turned the conversation towards wine and slowly the upper end of the hall returned to a low rumble of conversation.

The collector sitting closest to Robin, a chinless creature called Ralph de Waltham, turned to Marian and Elaine.

'I hope you have not been overly alarmed by the reports of these thieves in the forest,' he said self-importantly. 'There will not be a repeat of the last – eh – misfortune to befall the taxes.'

'How can you be certain?' Marian asked.

'We will be significantly better guarded.'

'More than half-a-dozen men?' Robin prompted.

'There will be eight guards riding with us,' said Ralph, counting on his fingers, 'and eight with the wagon, then a further eight divided so that four ride ahead of us and four in the rear, to guard against any assaults.'

'With all of those guards, you still travel separately?'

'Certainly,' he said firmly. 'In Derby a group of London lawyers were mistaken for us and pelted with stones. We will take every precaution to ensure that both we and the money return to Westminster unscathed. We will not move within half-a-mile of the wagon.'

'Very wise,' said Robin, committing the details of the location and numbers of guards to memory. There would be no need to gather information from Peter the clerk on this occasion.

'We hope,' Ralph continued, 'to be out of Nottinghamshire before the Rogation days. The prospect of great crowds of local men with sticks is not an appealing one.'

'That is wise,' said Guy, who had heard the end of the conversation. 'The locals hereabouts seem to celebrate every religious festival with drunkenness. Given their recent unruliness it would not surprise me if the processions and boundary beating turned into a riot. Look at what happened on Easter morning in Nottingham.'

He very definitely trained his gaze on Robin, then turned to Marian and Elaine.

'You should join us on the Vipont lands. The bounds of our estate are being walked in combination with some of those of the count. We will ride, of course. One of the canons of Southwell is coming to bless the earth.'

'I hope the canon will not be overtired,' said Marian. 'He will have a long journey this year, now the common lands have been added to the count's estate.'

'I do not think he will tire,' said Guy, either not detecting or choosing to ignore the tone of Marian's words. 'He will be drawn in a litter.'

'Lord Locksley and I will watch the Rogation processions together,' said Elaine, sounding disappointed. 'Otherwise I would have liked to meet the canon. Some old friar is leading the parishes near Locksley.'

'Friar Toki?' Marian asked, surprised.

'Yes,' said Robin, spearing a ball of mincemeat. 'I encouraged the hundredmen of Locksley to follow a more humble man so they would remember the real meaning of the season. Too often Rogationtide is overtaken by pride and pomp, competing with neighbours as to whose church holds the best relic, who has the wealthier cross.'

'I suppose there would be little use in your tenants competing with their neighbours,' said Guy coolly, 'given who your neighbours are.'

Fortunately, at that point further discussion was halted as the second course concluded and a subtlety in the shape of a sea monster was paraded into the hall.

The trees did strange things to a man's imagination. The long slender birches seemed to shine in the darkness, the hawthorn's branches tapped against one another like a man rapping at a shutter. A dead man, thought Edric the guard as he heard that tap tap tapping for a second time. The wagon lurched through a puddle, spattering mud up his horse's legs and making Edric jump. He shook his head to calm himself, wishing he had never heard a ghost story in his life. This forest must be full of spirits, just like the creatures that had attacked the wagon in Yorkshire. He had heard they wore rags and where eyes should be burnt red-hot coals. One report claimed the creatures had been skeletons or demons. None of the creatures sounded worse than another. Edric did not want to meet any of them. He wished that he was a tax collector and could sneak through the back roads in his fine robes, pretending to have nothing to do with the wagon of coins, rather than one of the saps who had agreed to guard it. An extra four pence had seemed such an enticing prospect when it was offered, especially for simply riding alongside a wagon, but now he would have paid twice that to be rid of the task.

Strange. He had thought for a moment that he could see a red man in the trees. A demon perhaps. He shuddered. When he looked again there was nothing there. He glanced over his shoulder at Algar, who was always half asleep during long journeys. Edric did not know how he had ever been appointed to this position. He scooped up an acorn and threw it at Algar's head. He started upright. Edric laughed.

Just as he turned back to the road there was a flash of red again and out of the black forest tore a shrieking demon. Edric tugged on his reins, so hard that his horse almost stumbled beneath him.

'Help,' the demon cried. It lowered its hood. Underneath it had a man's face. 'We have been attacked.'

Edric looked more closely as the wagon rumbled to a halt before them. It was no demon but a man in crimson, his face bloodied.

'Who are you?' called Hamo, who led the guards. A sensible question, Edric thought.

'Ralph de Waltham,' the demon replied. 'One of the royal tax collectors, man, you must recognise me.'

Edric could barely remember the tax collectors. They had been so eager to keep themselves apart from the wagon and its guards, going about hooded and cloaked to avoid being recognised. Edric would not have known them from

Adam.

'We have been attacked,' de Waltham repeated. 'A pack of forestmen leapt from the woods and chased us. I managed to escape but the other collectors have been injured. You must come and help us. God knows there might be more of them.'

'We have to stay with the wagon,' said Hamo. 'What happened to your own guards?'

'Dead, I think. One fled the moment the forestmen appeared, another fell from his horse, there were arrows shot at us… Please, we are wasting time. You must come with me.'

Hamo looked about. Eight was more guard than one wagon really needed, and if the forestmen were attacking the tax collectors perhaps the taxes themselves were safe for now. His eye fell on Edric. No, Edric thought, not me. Please.

'Algar, Odo, Edric – go with de Waltham.'

Edric cursed inwardly. De Waltham spurred his horse ahead.

'Bless you, master. You three, this way.'

Edric bustled and tugged at his horse to follow. De Waltham sped ahead so fast he could barely keep up. Odo and Algar raced alongside, back down the road and into the forest. Edric leant close to his horse's neck to keep the scratching twigs away from his helm. It would be just his luck if a thorn pierced his eyes.

'Where were you attacked?' called Odo.

They seemed to be riding a long way from the road.

'This way,' de Waltham called. He leapt a fallen tree and turned to his left. The guards pursued as fast as they could. Edric was not a strong horseman, and this desperate charge through shrub was setting his nerves on edge. He heard a squawk from behind him. Algar had been unseated by a low branch, and tumbled into the undergrowth.

'Wait!' Edric called.

'No time,' shouted de Waltham. Edric looked from his retreating figure to Algar. The forest creaked tight around him. He had no idea where he was, and even less desire to be left in the woods with a wounded man. He charged onwards to catch up with Odo and de Waltham. Barely had he reached their side than de Waltham dropped back suddenly, his horse juddering into Edric's. Edric almost fell from the saddle.

'So sorry,' called de Waltham. But he did not look sorry, Edric thought.

'We must be almost there,' cried Odo.

'Oh yes,' said de Waltham.

He leapt away to their right, splashing through a brook. Edric could have sworn this was the opposite direction from where they had been heading before. They rode on, past caves and tree trunks, through thickets and around streams. Distantly, Edric thought he heard now and then a cry in the distance. Perhaps it was the other tax collectors, he thought, but they never seemed to grow any nearer. There was a shout, closer. Odo's horse stumbled over a tree root and threw him clear over its neck. He landed with a thump, his head barely missing a boulder.

'Wait now!' cried Edric.

'We cannot,' said de Waltham, still charging forward. He seemed to know where he was going. Odo pulled his helm off and stared at the earth, dazed. Again, Edric looked at the darkening forest, again at the disappearing figure of the tax collector. Again, he surged forward to follow. They passed a cave, a tree trunk, a stream. Edric was certain now that they were going in circles. They must have been riding for an hour or more.

'Here we are,' called de Waltham and Edric looked up in relief.

'What the –?'

They were nearing the road, and there, Edric saw through the twisted trees, was the wagon they had left an hour before.

'I thought you said we were finding your men.'

He looked more closely. The wagon's back end had been smashed to pieces. Silver pennies littered the path, as did arrows, sticks. The other guards were sprawled across the road, two tied to the wagon's wheels, another to a tree. Two lay unconscious – or dead – in the dirt. Edric had a sense of dread. He looked across at de Waltham. The horse was still riding on, but the tax collector had disappeared. Edric halted in confusion, turned about in his saddle looking for the man. Some distance further back in the undergrowth a red flash rustled and was gone.

'Demons,' said Edric as he approached the carnage of the raided tax wagon. 'Forest demons.'

'That is more money,' said Aedith, gazing with glittering eyes at the piles of pennies as they lay by the fireside, 'than I have seen in my entire life.'

'And more than we'll probably see again,' said Thurstan. Aedith was washing blood from his hand where his axe had slipped on the wagon's lock.

'Are you hurt badly?' asked Robin.

'A scratch,' said Thurstan. He smiled, more at his wife than Robin of course, but it was the warmest he had been towards him in years.

'Well I'm covered in bloody scratches,' said Lefchild, pulling splinters from his long white fingers. 'Don't know why I volunteered to be the idiot hauling the coins out.'

'Because you're no use with a bow,' said Madalgrim.

'Forgive me, Master Baker, I hadn't realised you were a master archer.'

'I'm better at shooting than you. Tell him, Magister.'

'Not at the moment,' said Gilbert, who was green.

'What happened to him?' Robin asked John.

'One of the guards got a bit close to him,' John said in a low voice. 'He nearly got his head split in two.'

Gilbert moaned at the memory.

'I'm sorry I wasn't there,' said Robin.

'I'm glad you weren't,' said John, who was also nursing some bruises. 'None of us could have ridden those guards halfway round the forest and back again.'

He licked his thumb and smudged it over Robin's brow. 'You've still got a bit of pig's blood there.'

Robin pulled his sleeve out and rubbed at his face. It had been a closer run thing, this second raid. Although only five guards had been left at the wagon, they had been prepared for an ambush. And whilst the hundredmen had strong arms from years of manual labour, they were not all used to wielding weapons. Swinging a scythe might not be so different from striking with a sword, but they had been fighting armoured men, some of them experienced guardsmen to the tax collectors. They were fortunate that splinters, cuts and sick stomachs were all they had suffered.

There was a whistle and a horn blast from the far side of the clearing, then the sound of a horse and hound trotting towards the croft. Husdent came running in as Will's unmistakable voice rang out.

'Our hero approaches,' he called as he ducked through the doorway. 'Your horse and bow is outside, Lord Locksley.'

'Where have I been?' Robin asked, taking his cloak and cote back from Will.

'You were shooting rabbits near Garsmount. You only got three.'

Will threw the rabbits towards Madalgrim. As a baker in his previous life he had taken on most of the cooking duties for the men.

'I see we did it then,' Will said, not sounding particularly pleased.

'I'm sorry you couldn't be a part of the ambush,' Robin said.

'That's the life of Lord Locksley's double. The money will be reward enough I suppose.' He eyed the pile of sacks. 'That's a lot of money to bury. I hope I left enough arrows.'

'Waltheof can bring more if need be. He and Toki will meet you at St Oswald's boundary after Nocturns.'

Will yawned, then spoke quickly in French. 'And you are certain you want to leave one sack for the snakes?'

Robin nodded. Aedith glanced between them, confused by what she thought she had heard.

'Then I will leave you for the night,' said Robin. Husdent reluctantly stood to join him. 'I will see you in the procession.'

'And I will see you,' Will said, 'from a distance.'

Rogation Monday dawned bright and clear, with the suspicious appearance from the edge of the woodland of several young couples, dew-dampened and hawthorn-haired. The church bells rang out from sunrise and in every village and church across the county youths ran to be the first to seize the clappers and bells, shouting as they ran down the lanes, whooping and pounding on the doors of their friends. Friar Toki was already waiting at St Oswald's church when the lads arrived. If he were not a humble man of God you might have suspected he had not seen his bed the night before. They waited, the friar, the leaping youths and the pile of birch twigs outside the church until a representative of almost every family on the Locksley manor had gathered and then they set off, a ringing, clapping, whooping, beating band carrying the cross from St Oswald's and a banner of the saint himself. They trekked first across the fields, to the very boundary of the manor. There, Toki paused them, raised his eyes and hands in prayer, begged for divine blessing on the crops that grew beneath them and gave a nod for the youths to beat the boundary. As they did so he stepped back from an arrow that had been buried flight-up in the earth, and over which he had been standing the whole time. One of the beaters dug into the earth with his bare hands and drew out a sack of coins.

'Petite et accipietis,' said Toki as the sack's contents were tipped into the pouches of the youths closest to the man who had dug it up. 'Ask and you shall receive.'

Then the friar made the sign of the cross over the earth and led the group on to the next boundary point. Again, a blessing, a litany, an arrow, a sack of coins beneath the earth. Such crops and their peculiar stalks could be found throughout the lands surrounding Locksley that day, for those who knew to look for them.

Robin, the sheriff and his family only arrived at the end of the procession. They paused at some distance from the crowd of bounds-beaters as it made its way back to its point of origin, where the staid or aged or female had gathered to greet its return and follow the friar all the way to church for a final mass. The sheriff rode out that day with most of his household in attendance. It made for a magnificent procession: Sir Walter and his wife in scarlet and silk, Elaine and Marian's long sleeves gleaming against the pale palfreys they rode, their servants wearing for the first time the colours Sir Walter had chosen for the Peverills, blue and yellow, banners in the same colours flying over their heads. With news of a second tax wagon ambushed in the forest, rumours milled throughout the county that the sheriff had lost control of the people. If even money bound for the royal treasury could not be kept safe how could the sheriff hope to make the commons observe his laws? Sir Walter responded to these mutterings with a show of defiance and of strength. Many of the household servants and grooms who flocked around him that morning were armed and all demonstrated the sheriff's wealth and thereby his power.

'They are very vigorous in their beatings this year,' said Sir Walter, squinting to watch the final boundary being struck. 'I can barely see the earth for all those sticks jumping up and down.'

'As long as they keep those twigs to themselves,' muttered Lady Joan, adjusting the brooch on her cloak.

Robin watched from behind them in the pack. The lads running about and beating almost completely obscured from view the man in the centre digging into the earth and dividing up the sack of coins within. There was a resounding 'amen' from the group then Friar Toki emerged from their midst, crossed himself and led them all back towards St Oswald's Church. As he passed the sheriff and his family Toki bowed his head. The youths stood about uncertainly as the sheriff and his retinue pressed in front of them to follow the friar to the church. Robin noticed that many of those in the pack of beaters wore pouches at their hip or purses around their necks. He hoped that they took to heart the words he knew Toki had told them when they found the coins: take this money, but do not spend it all at once and do not spend it too close to home. It was a risk including so many men in this donation, but none of them were told where the coins came from and hopefully none were foolish enough to risk losing them too quickly.

By mid-afternoon one of the boundary beaters lay blind drunk in a ditch. Having received his share of the silver crop that morning he had thrown a coin or two to his wife and children and taken the rest with him to the alehouse. A man could drink a lot of ale on the pouchful of pennies he grasped in his fist, and this man had certainly done so. The more he drank the louder he got and the less he noticed his company. Just before he ran out the door to be sick on himself and sprawl at the roadside three men had arrived, two in the red and gold of their master, one wearing a steward's fine cote. They inspected the pile of coins with which the man had paid for his ale and the poor leather pouch still stocked beyond its meagre capacity with money. They nodded to the hosteller in thanks and went outside to drag the man from his stupor to a cell in the castle.

Mass concluded, the Peverill party assembled to depart. With so many in attendance it took a long time for Sir Walter's constable to marshal them and longer still before the sheriff took up his position at their head to return to Locksley Hall. As they came along the Locksley Pass Sir Walter slowed. Robin peered around the sheriff's shoulder to see Lanfranc and two of his guards manhandling an inebriated farmer onto a mule. Sir Walter rode ahead to speak to them and Robin spurred his horse close behind.

'What is happening here?' Sir Walter asked Lanfranc, keeping his voice low enough for his family behind not to hear. The drunkard saw the sheriff and struggled to make a reverence from the mule's rump. He almost fell off and had to be shoved, by the buttocks, back onto the mule by a guard. 'Beyond the obvious,' Sir Walter added.

'This man was heard in the alehouse boasting of sudden riches,' said Lanfranc, trying to maintain a respectful composure in the face of the drunkard's fidgeting. 'He had a purse full of coin, despite the brewer telling us that this man has been in debt to all his neighbours for months.'

'You think this is the stolen money?' Sir Walter asked eagerly.

'It could be, my lord. We were taking him to the castle to question him. Once he is somewhat more sober.'

'I will come.'

So far the only information that had been gleaned about the theft of the most recent taxes was one group of guards reporting that the thieves had been hooded with their faces covered – in number anything between half-a-dozen and fifty men – and one among them who insisted the deed had been committed by a devil. If this drunkard could offer more information, the sheriff would not miss the chance to learn it.

'May I join you?' asked Robin, turning his horse without waiting for a reply. He knew exactly where this man's sudden riches had come from, and he wanted to ensure that he knew as much of the man's explanation for them as the sheriff and the Viponts did. Sir Walter explained their departure to Lady Joan – who harrumphed bitterly at how it would affect their supper plans – and, accompanied by a dozen of his liveried servants he and Robin set off for the castle with Lanfranc and his prisoner.

By the time they reached the castle walls the drunkard had been sick again, fallen off the mule twice and started singing a song to which he only knew half the words, most of them anatomical. The sheriff had stopped Lanfranc's guard from striking the man repeatedly for fear he might be knocked out cold, delaying still further Sir Walter's supper and any revelation about the tax theft.

The drunkard was bundled off the mule and into a cell in the wine cellars with all possible haste. Lord Eudo and his family were still not returned from Rogation Mass but the sheriff insisted the man be questioned in their absence. Lanfranc did not wish to comply, but could hardly argue without the support of his masters behind him. The drunkard proved a difficult subject for interrogation. He knew no French and seemed barely capable of speaking English in his current condition. That would not, however, stop Lanfranc and Sir Walter from trying to question him. They set him on a stool and Lanfranc threw the drunkard's purse into his lap.

'Is this yours?'

The drunkard inspected it as if it was the first time he had ever seen a purse, then nodded.

'Where did you get these coins from?'

'Grud.'

'Speak clearly.'

'Grud. Came out of the grud.'

Ground, Robin thought. It was just as he had suspected. He sighed inwardly. It was for every man to choose how to spend his own coin, but he had not risked life and status for this fool to get drunk out of his eyeballs while others still starved.

'He is saying ground I think,' said Sir Walter.

'Yes, grund,' the drunkard repeated.

'How did it come out of the ground?' asked Lanfranc.

'We were beating the bounds and it was there.' He held out his arms before him for emphasis. 'There, in the grund. We dug it up.'

Lanfranc exchanged a glance with the sheriff.

'How did you know where to dig?' asked Lanfranc.

The man squinted, stared into the cell wall. His eyes crossed as he lost the trail of his own thoughts. He belched. Lanfranc struck him. It startled him into momentary sobriety.

'How did you know where to dig?'

'There were arrows in the earth.'

'Arrows?' asked Sir Walter. 'Is that what he said? There were arrows buried with the money?'

'No.' He shook his head. 'They were stuck in. Stuck in the earth.' He gestured. 'Like flowers.'

'And where did the money come from before it was in the ground?' Lanfranc asked.

The drunkard shrugged, looked bewildered.

'Grund,' he said again. 'Dunno. Just grund.'

Lanfranc leant closer. 'Who told you to dig up these arrows to find the money?'

Robin tensed.

'Tovild.'

'And Tovild is?'

'My wife. She heard it from Goda who heard it from Leofgyth. All of us heard it.'

'But *how* did you hear it?'

Again, the drunkard squinted at nothing, forcing his mind towards a memory that would not come.

'Priest?' he said uncertainly.

'The priest told you all?' Sir Walter asked eagerly.

A nod.

'Which priest?' Lanfranc asked.

'No,' the drunkard corrected himself. 'Not a priest.'

Lanfranc looked to be on the point of striking him again.

'You just told us that it was a priest.'

'No. Friar.'

Robin felt a prickling on the back of his neck. He refused to show any anxiety. There were dozens of friars in the county, perhaps scores of them. For a time, his unconcern seemed well-placed. Lanfranc and the drunkard went around in circles as he tried to remember the priest's name. It was Marcus, perhaps, or Wigot. It might have been Toroi. Was it Marchus? Eventually, he chose one letter and stuck to it. The name, he was sure, was Tork or Tuck or Thori…

'Toki?' suggested Sir Walter. He looked at Robin.

'Toki!' The drunkard pointed at the sheriff. 'That one.'

'You know this Friar Toki?' Lanfranc asked Sir Walter in French.

'I do,' said Robin. There was no point concealing a truth that Sir Walter would reveal in the end. 'He was a friend to me some years ago.'

'He is at Lenton Priory now,' said Sir Walter.

'I will go and question him,' said Lanfranc. 'I may get more sense from him than from this boil.'

'Will you free this man?' Robin asked. 'He does not seem to know where the money came from. Come to that, we do not know that the coins came from the stolen taxes.'

'It sounds like this man was not the only one who received such purses of money. I do not know where else such wealth of coin would appear from if not the taxes. Presuming this man is telling the truth and does not know the source of the money he still spent it. At the very least he can be a witness for us.'

'His family will not want him back in that state,' said Sir Walter. The drunkard had fallen asleep on his stool. He rocked teeteringly. 'Let us leave him and talk to Toki.'

'Please, my lord,' said Lanfranc, all charm. 'There is no need for you to join me. I can question this friar myself. You should go and enjoy your supper.'

Sir Walter hesitated. A meal with his family was more appealing than another interrogation, especially one that took him in the opposite direction from his home. Robin stepped in before he could be persuaded. He might need to speak on Toki's behalf. Although he knew the friar could take care of himself, he did not trust Lanfranc alone with him.

'I am certain it will not take long,' he said breezily. 'We can send one of your men back to Locksley Hall to tell my mother.'

So Sir Walter agreed to question Toki as well. They left the drunkard locked in the wine cellar and left the keep of Nottingham Castle. When they reached the stables in the middle bailey they found a bustle of grooms, unsaddling and unbridling the palfreys of Lord Eudo's family. Clearly the Viponts had returned from Mass. Lanfranc smiled.

'I must tell my master of all this,' he said. 'It will take more time, my lord sheriff…'

'We will come with you,' Robin interrupted. 'It may be that Lord de Vipont does not wish to make the journey to Lenton Priory when he is only just returned home again. If that is the case, myself and Sir Walter can go in your stead.'

He marched ahead of Lanfranc before the steward or the sheriff could make excuses to stall him. The Viponts were still divesting themselves of their mantles when they entered the chambers. A page was struggling to get Eudo's attention amidst the press of lords and servants.

'My lord,' he called, ducking as Eudo's mantle was flung over the chamberlain's shoulder, almost hitting him in the face.

But Eudo had noticed his visitors. He smiled with all outward show of joy to see his rival Sir Walter and the troublesome Lord Locksley in his home. He invited them to take some wine while his family changed their clothing.

'Before you leave, my lord,' the page began again, whispering at Lord Eudo's elbow.

Eudo turned to him with swift irritation and the page flinched.

'There – there is a letter for you.'

'Send it to my private chamber, I will read it there.'

'For all of you, my lord.'

Eudo's family paused.

'All of us?' Eudo repeated.

'All of the lords. And Master Steward. They all came at once. I – I think they may be important.'

Eudo frowned, remembered his guests, smiled widely at them.

'If they seem important,' he said, 'we had better read them now. Bring them here.'

The page hesitated, then ran down to an antechamber. He returned with another two pages, all carrying rolls of vellum with a small leather pouch tied around them.

'Who brought these?' Eudo asked.

'A man in our colours delivered them into this chamber. I do not know who brought them to the castle. Perhaps they are a Rogation gift?'

Eudo took the message held out to him. There was a chink of coin from the pouch. He looked to his son and brother suspiciously. He untied the pouch and handed it back to the page, unrolling the message it had bound. As he did so an arrow, crudely whittled from a stick of wood fell to the floor. Eudo stepped backwards as sharply as if the stick was a serpent.

'What does this mean?' Serlo asked, reaching for his own message. His too contained a wooden arrow. He tore open the pouch and tipped its contents onto the ground. There was a shower of silver pennies. Ranulf and Guy found their own deliveries contained the same. The chamber was filled with glistening coins. Eudo was reading the parchment.

'Show me your letter,' he said sharply, seizing Serlo's from his hands. Then Guy's. Then Ranulf's. Lanfranc held his out ready. He had already realised. 'All the same.'

The sheriff watched the proceedings in confusion.

'Arrows and a pouch of money,' he muttered to Robin. 'Just like the drunkard spoke of.'

Ranulf noticed his whispering. 'What is that you say?' he demanded.

'May we see the letter?' Robin asked.

The rest hesitated, but Eudo handed his message over. Robin held it between him and the sheriff and pretended to take in the words, the same words that he and Will and John had agreed to write, the words that Gilbert had penned for them.

'Lord of Nottingham. Ask and you shall receive. The wronged men of Sherwood.'

'You had better tell them about your drunkard, Lanfranc,' said the sheriff, taking the letter to reread for himself.

The Viponts turned expectantly to their steward, who explained as briefly as possible how he had encountered the drunk farmer with a suspiciously full purse then heard babblings about arrows and coin growing out of the earth.

'You suspect that his money came from the attack on the tax wagon,' said Eudo. It was not a question. 'Which means that these coins may as well.'

'Why have we been sent them?' Ranulf blustered. 'We had nothing to do with that attack. And what is the meaning of this arrow?'

'It might be a sigil,' said Serlo, turning to the sheriff. 'Do you recognise it?'

'It could be the symbol of a huntsman?' suggested Sir Walter. 'And the letter mentions the forest, where a huntsman might dwell.'

'The wronged men of Sherwood,' Guy said, looking into the message as if it would reveal an answer. 'Is it the prisoners who escaped the castle do you think? We believed they were concealed in the forest.'

'We have received the profits of theft,' said Eudo. 'Whoever sent this intended to make us as culpable as that drunken pig in the cell.'

He took all of the parchment scrolls and the arrows and threw them into the hearth at the heart of the hall.

'Gather the coin,' he ordered his family. 'Donate it to your servants or the altar. I will not keep money that could be tainted by sin. Lanfranc, you say that the drunkard named a friar leading him to the coin in the earth?'

'Friar Toki. Lord Locksley says he lives at Lenton Priory now.'

'Then we should pay this friar a visit.'

The bells were still chiming at Lenton Priory when the sheriff's party arrived. From the body of the church the voices of monks could be heard, singing through the Hours. Lord Eudo led the way around the great arches of the church towards the private quarters of the priory, where Prior Alexander could be found. They loitered in the cloisters while one of the lay brothers went to fetch his master. When the prior arrived, he was accompanied by Friar Toki.

'What is the meaning of this?' the prior asked, addressing the crowd of lords and servants coolly, his hands neatly tucked inside the sleeves of his vestment.

'We suspect your friar of being involved in handling stolen coins,' said Lord Eudo. 'Perhaps even of stealing them in the first place.'

'I find that rather hard to believe,' said the prior. 'Friar Toki, do you know what these lords speak of?'

Friar Toki looked all innocence. 'Alas, I do not.'

'There is your answer.'

'We did not ride all the way here,' cried Ranulf, 'to turn back without questioning the man.'

'Friar, do you wish to be questioned?'

'I can refuse very little of my Lord Locksley, but the bells will chime shortly for Terce and I wished to join the brothers. Perhaps if my lords ask their questions quickly?'

'Is it true,' said Eudo, 'that while you were blessing the fields this morning you found various stashes of coin buried?'

Toki looked amused. 'Who told you this peculiar story?'

'A farmer,' said Lanfranc.

'A drunk farmer,' added Robin.

The lords looked at him askance. He would do nothing to assist them at the priory. If his loyalties were questioned his old friendship with Toki gave him the perfect excuse for recalitrance.

'Did you find coins?' Lanfranc asked.

'There was the odd coin in the earth. There often are such to be found.'

'What about arrows?'

Toki made a show of thinking. The bells finished their jubilant chiming and started to toll the hour.

'I believe there may have been sticks. Perhaps feathers also. Might these be considered arrows?'

'You have answered enough,' the prior said. 'Go and join the brothers.' Toki bowed and left them.

'We have more questions,' Ranulf said.

'But I fear you will not be able to ask them.'

'We can return tomorrow,' said Serlo.

'No,' said the prior, with iron clarity. 'I do not wish Friar Toki to be questioned further. He has shown you the respect of answering your inquiries on this holy day, and I will not ask more of him. Even presuming that I believed he had committed any form of misdeed a friar, like all men of the cloth, can only be tried by the church. I could assemble an ecclesiastical court if I believed the case merited it, but given your only evidence lies in the words of a drunkard I am not so inclined.' The prior bowed. 'Good day, my lords.'

Ranulf snarled. 'Only tried by the church?' he repeated. 'You were happy enough to interfere in our affairs when the common land was debated.'

'And my interference made no difference at all. Perhaps you should learn from my mistake.'

The prior turned his back to them and went to join the chorus of voices singing within the Quire of his church.

Ascension

There were more men on the roads between Locksley Hall and the forest than Robin had expected. Perhaps he should not have been surprised. Two wagons loaded with money had been attacked in a month and the only clue to the culprits or their whereabouts was a drunkard's mumblings about arrows in the earth and a friar protected by church law. The patrolling men wore the colours of the sheriff, the Viponts, the grey and black of Garsmount Tower – Lord D'Alselin had never been one for conspicuous display – and everywhere were helms, lances, swords and mail coats. Many of the men greeted him, a curt nod or tipped lance. He returned their greetings, wanting to make no impression that would linger in their minds and certainly not rouse suspicion. We must all be careful, he thought, his brother at the forefront of his mind. We must be careful and keep ourselves hidden for a while.

He rode to the hundredmen's croft on a longer route that day, hoping to lose anyone considering following him to see what he was about. His path took him past a brewer's home, the ale-stake newly hung above the door to show a fresh batch of ale ready for tasting by the sheriff's men. To the rear of the building was a bakehouse, where a girl was raking out ash from the oven. Something about her was familiar to Robin, although he could not think where he would have met a brewer of her youth. Only when she smiled as she completed her task did he realise how he knew her. She had been one of those returning from the blasted tree with a sack full of coin. She must be kin to one of the hundredmen. He called out to her. Seeing a lord on horseback she dropped to her knee in alarm.

'There is no need for that,' he said, pausing under the ale-stake.

She looked up at him uncertainly. 'Are you a taster, my lord? I can fetch my mother for you. The ale is inside.'

'Your father is not home then?'

'No.'

'What occupation is your father?'

'He was a baker, my lord.'

There was only one baker among the hundredmen.

'Your father is Madalgrim.'

She nodded, very quickly, as if the speed made it less true. 'We have committed no crime, my lord.'

'I did not accuse you.'

'You are not one of Lord de Vipont's men?'

'That I am not. I know your father.'

She smiled again, and for a moment a shadow of Madalgrim's own look crossed her face. A woman's face appeared in an unshuttered window inside the croft, and then behind the door. She did not look pleased to see a lord speaking alone to her daughter.

'This man knows my father,' the girl said, going over to the woman and taking her hand. 'Perhaps he can help us?'

The woman did not take her eyes from Robin.

'We should not trouble Lord Locksley, Maud. I will argue my case in the Viponts' court when I am called to do so.'

'I would gladly help Madalgrim's kin,' said Robin. 'What case will you have to argue?'

The girl tapped her mother's arm and nodded up the road. Two men in Vipont colours were riding towards them. Seeing Lord Locksley with the family they bowed their heads and kept going.

'Perhaps,' said Robin when they were out of earshot, 'you have had trouble with Lord Vipont's steward?'

The girl urged her mother silently. The older brewer sighed and gave in.

'Master Lanfranc has accused us of allowing the townspeople of Nottingham to use my husband's bread oven rather than taking their bread to the castle to be baked and paying a fee. And he claims I sold my last batch of ale at too high a price per gallon – but I know I did not, for I always keep to the rules of the Assizes.'

'And for these actions you must speak in his master's court?'

'She'll speak,' the girl interrupted, 'but it won't make any difference. We'll be fined again, no matter what.'

'Again?'

'The steward has been visiting us every fortnight since my father was arrested – always just before the meeting of Lord Vipont's court – and finding something or other amiss. We won't have any coin left soon with all the fines we've had to pay.'

So Thurstan's family were not the only ones to have been persecuted by Lanfranc, simply his most visible victims. And by using his manorial court to try Madalgrim's family Eudo not only kept knowledge of his persecution from the sheriff, he also kept all the resultant fines for himself.

'It isn't just us either,' the girl continued. 'He's been looking for wrongdoing across all of our hundred since my father appealed against the taxes.'

'Why have you not complained against him?'

'My husband is missing and we have no other male kin,' said the brewer. 'It is difficult for us to argue against a lord's servant when my husband is virtually an outlaw.'

'But a lord could speak for us.' The girl fixed Robin with a smile.

'A lord could certainly try,' Robin replied. 'When is the next session of the Vipont court?'

'Tuesday after Ascension Sunday.'

Then, Robin resolved, before the court met he would do what he could to help them. He took from them the names of the other families who had been targeted by Lanfranc and went on his way. It was a subtler approach, he thought, for

Lanfranc to rob these families penny by penny rather than burning their homes or having his men beat them. So subtle that the other lords of Nottinghamshire had not noticed it happening. As soon as Robin returned from delivering supplies to the hundredmen in the forest he determined that he would speak with the sheriff on the matter. He suspected that Sir Walter might be glad of a reason to complain of the Viponts in his county court.

He was some distance into the forest when he first heard it. At the reaches of his hearing, a crack. A stick breaking beneath a footfall. A rustling. Then silence. It could have been an animal, thought Robin, but it could just as easily have been a man. Was he being followed? Immediately he thought of those two men in Vipont colours, of Lanfranc. He pressed his horse forward, turning his direction – very slightly, not enough to draw attention – away from the hundredmen's hideout. Follow me then, he thought, if that's what you're doing. He rode, slow and steady deeper into the forest. All the while, he watched at the edge of his vision, he listened. The further he went the more certain he was that he was being tracked. Was this the first time he had been followed, or was his pursuer just careless enough to be heard today? Either way, he needed to find out who it was. If they had trailed him before and discovered the croft they had to be silenced.

Robin nudged his horse into a trot and behind there was more rustling as his hunter sped up in turn, keeping to Robin's right hand side. Robin turned his horse suddenly to the right and dropped from the saddle, still holding the reins. The horse slowed but kept walking, its master crouching alongside then falling behind, keeping left, using the cover of the forest to watch the horse and the undergrowth around it. Sure enough, he saw a shadow creeping through the trees, still pursuing his riderless horse. He let the shadow get ahead of him – a hooded figure, not dressed showily or wearing the colours of any master; sensible for a tracker – and considered how much of a threat it was. It looked like a man, thin, wiry, seemingly unarmed. If it was indeed a Vipont guard they had not sent their best. Robin crept behind the figure, closer, silently, then pushed its hood down over its eyes, seized it by the arms and pushed it, face first, onto the ground. The tracker cried out and writhed, but his arms were caught and his legs thrashed helplessly. Robin whistled for his horse to halt.

'Get off me,' cried the squirming tracker. English.

'Who are you?' Robin said, not releasing his grip. 'Why are you following –?'

He was interrupted by a shower of stones and sticks from the undergrowth.

'Leave him alone!'

Another hooded figure launched itself towards him. He did not have power to draw his sword and keep his grip on his follower, and the next instant the creature was on his back, slapping and scratching at him. He ducked his head low and rolled sideways, taking the second attacker with him. Now his arm was free and he could reach for his sword while the scratching creature was briefly winded. He leapt to his feet an instant after the first tracker had done the same. The boy – that was all he was – raised his hands and called for his fellow to stop fighting. His voice was familiar. Robin looked again at the thin lad, his hair a matted crop darker than his eyebrows. It was Much.

'Sorry, my lord,' he said. His partner struggled to her feet as well: a girl, no older than him and glaring like a wolf. 'We didn't mean to hurt you.'

'You haven't,' said Robin, although the girl's scratches on his face and neck burnt. 'What are you doing following me? And who's this?'

'Edeva,' the girl said before Much had a chance. 'We're looking for my father.'

'He's Doleswif the hedger,' Much added.

'Then why are you tracking me like a dog? I don't know where your father is.'

'He was one of the prisoners who escaped Nottingham Castle,' Edeva said.

Robin said nothing. They looked at him expectantly – so expectantly he had a feeling of foreboding.

'We thought you might know where he is,' said Much.

'That is clear enough. Why?'

'You took Aedith and Thorold into the forest after the forge was burnt down, and they haven't come out again. So we thought you must have taken them to Thurstan. If you know where Thurstan is then perhaps you know where Doleswif is.'

Robin watched the boy carefully. If Much had seen him with the smith's family this could not have been the first time he had followed him.

'How long have you been tracking me?'

'Only since you got me away from that bastard – sorry, Lord Vipont. I was just – well – checking on you – now and then, not all the time. Seeing if you needed a servant. I think you do as well. You're always having to borrow Lady Marian's man, and he's not quiet like me.'

'Is that the blond one?' Edeva asked. 'Beard?'

Much nodded sagely. So the two of them had been spying on him together. Robin cast his mind back over the past weeks. He had thought himself so careful, had kept watch everywhere he went. Perhaps his mistake had been watching for soldiers when he should have been listening for teenage trackers. But if they had both been following him for that long, how had they not seen him with the hundredmen already?

'You have not followed me into the forest before.'

'No,' said Edeva. 'Not far into it. We thought we might get lost. And it's too noisy, as this fat-footed goat proved.'

She shoved Much playfully. He brushed her off.

'At first,' he said, 'we thought maybe you were visiting a woman in the forest because you kept going in with those saddlebags. Then I thought it couldn't be a woman because you went with the servant and I thought he would tell the Lady Marian about it. Edeva said it could be the hundredmen.'

'I live near John Blunt's cousin,' Edeva added. 'She was railing about how you used to be friends but you didn't help him when he was going to be hanged.' She held out both hands as if they were scales, tipping them from side to side. 'If you used to be his friend, I thought you might still be.'

'And who else have you told about this theory?'

'Only Much.'

'Only Edeva.'

Robin could not help but smile. If they were lying to him they were very good at it.

'Where was I,' he asked, testing them, 'on Easter morning?'

'Not sure,' said Much. 'I was at church.'

'The priory,' Edeva said. 'Then you left dressed differently.'

This pair were better than Lanfranc. He had better hope they spoke the truth when they said they had told no one else of his movements. Perhaps Robin had been wrong to reject Much's offer of service. Two such shrewd and silent spies could prove useful against the multiplying might of the Viponts.

'Will you take us to them then?' asked Edeva. 'I was right, wasn't I? You know where they are.'

'What will you do if I take you to the hundredmen?'

'Live with them,' said Edeva as if it was obvious. 'Even if my father wasn't here, I would still want to stay in the forest. It's safer here since the Viponts came. At least in the forest men don't come and smash your home to pieces because you look at them the wrong way.'

'Won't your kin miss you?'

'I don't have any kin but my father. My mother died last winter. My brothers were taken with the sweating sickness two summers back, my grandfather too.'

No wonder the girl had spent her time stalking after him, Robin thought. It sounded like a treat compared with staying in her empty home. Still, adolescents had a way of exaggerating their troubles – he should know – and he did not want to condemn a girl to isolation and possible starvation just because she was lonely.

'Can you hunt?' he asked. 'Fish? There's no easy food in the forest. No crops growing. You might be all right through summer but what will you do in winter?'

'There's still time to plant crops. Me and Much could make a little farm.'

'Me and Much?' Robin repeated, looking at the lad. He fidgeted under his gaze.

'Well – I can help,' Much said. 'Can't really leave my mother.'

'I won't need Much anyway if you tell me where my father is.'

She was certainly persistent.

'I'll take you to them,' Robin said, 'but I can't risk you seeing the route if you are lying to me.'

'We're not,' protested Much.

Edeva cut him off.

'Blindfold us then,' she said.

So Robin tore up the linen wrapping disguising a pot of wax in his saddlebag of supplies. He placed the pot in Much's left hand and put his right on the bridle of his horse. Edeva did the same as Robin tied the strips of linen over their eyes.

'Do not let go of the bridle,' he said, remounting the horse so he could keep a watch on them from above. 'If you try to look I will leave you here. Now watch your step.'

He nudged the horse slowly on, his two teenage hostages gingerly keeping pace at his side.

'Have you brought prisoners with you?' called John, laying down the slender branches of ash that he was peeling the bark from, and standing as he saw Robin and his attendants enter the clearing. 'Ah, I see you've got the wax I asked for.'

He took the pot from Much's hand and the boy pulled down his blindfold. Edeva waited until Robin gave her permission. She was a sensible child, he thought, as he dismounted. The youths stared at the scene before them: men who had escaped the castle and been hunted all over the county carrying on with daily tasks as if this clearing was just another village. Madalgrim was stirring a large pot in the open eaves of a disused animal pen; Grimm and Tosti were patching the roof over the croft, their work almost complete now; Ansculf the villein was coppicing a hazel to make a fence; Thurstan and Aedith were building a forge some distance away, making a ring of stones and shelter to keep the dangerous sparks from the rest of the buildings.

'Where is Doleswif?' Robin asked John.

'Fishing. Can we talk?'

'Look after my horse.' Robin gave the reins to Edeva. Much looked disappointed. 'I'm certainly not leaving it with you, lad. I haven't seen a hair of my last palfrey since you rode off with it.'

'It's probably still somewhere in the forest. Unless a wolf ate it.'

'I think that proves my point.'

Robin and John retreated a few steps from the pair. The other hundredmen paused in their tasks and came to greet the arrivals with no little confusion.

'When I found this croft,' said John in a low voice, 'you told me I must make sure that none of the men allowed their kin to come here, and yet it seems every time you visit you bring more of them with you.'

'Only one of those is kin. They've been following me, both of them, for weeks.'

'I presume they didn't find the croft before? Otherwise the blindfolds are not needed.'

Robin nodded.

'And will they be leaving with you?'

'Edeva wants to stay. I'd let her. She's no fool and I think she will work hard.'

John furrowed his brow.

'You stir up a wasp's nest every time you bring people. We all have kin we wish were here, but we have been keeping to our word and staying away from them. If some are allowed, the men think all should be.'

'Do you think that?'

John shrugged, sighed.

'My wife's been dead five years. I've got no children. But I've cousins and brothers and parents I can't help as long as I am here. If there's to be a rule we must all abide by it.'

He emphasised the word 'all'.

'You think I am being a lord again? One rule for me and one for you?'

'You are a lord, Robin. You were born to order; we were born to obey. But you should make your orders clear.'

Robin nodded slowly.

'Send Lefchild to fetch Doleswif and we can discuss this.'

Lefchild moved fast as a sighthound and Doleswif was back with him in a matter of moments. Robin had never seen the hedger smile before, but when he embraced his daughter Doleswif grinned so wide his face was in danger of cracking. The other hundredmen were not so glad to see the new faces.

'More mouths to feed?' said Kolbrand.

'I don't eat much,' said Edeva defensively. 'And Much isn't staying.'

'Aren't you Saegar the Miller's boy?' asked Tosti.

Much opened his mouth to reply but was cut off by Kolbrand.

'What do you mean he isn't staying? He's seen where we're hidden. He could tell the sheriff's men.'

'He won't,' said Tosti. 'He's a good lad this one.'

'I can help you,' said Much. 'I'm a good tracker. I've been following Lord Locksley for weeks and he didn't notice until today…'

'He's been *following* you?' Kolbrand advanced on Much with a knife. 'What have you seen?'

'I blindfolded him to bring him here,' said Robin, stepping between the two of them, 'and I will do the same when we leave. He doesn't know where we are and he won't tell anyone what he's seen. He owes me a silence.'

'I'm a good hunter,' Much said, with the same undeterred salesmanship he had exhibited the first time Robin met him. 'And a poacher. I can bring you meat if you let me see where to take it.'

'Bring it,' said Kolbrand, putting his knife back at his belt. 'But you won't get coin from us for it.'

'We haven't any left,' muttered Gilbert.

'I told you we should have kept some money back from the last raid,' said Tosti before he thought what he was saying.

'Raid?' Much was wide-eyed. 'You mean you were the ones who attacked the tax wagons? Who put those coins and arrows in the earth for the Rogation processions?'

'I'll have to kill him,' said Kolbrand. 'He knows too much.'

'I'll kill you first,' cried Edeva.

'There's no need to kill anyone,' said Robin, wishing he could retain some measure of calm in this clearing for more than a moment. 'Much, stop talking. I wanted you all here now so we could discuss this question of who can come to the clearing. John has told me that you still want your kin with you – that is understandable – so we should all decide together what to do about that.'

'All together?' said Lefchild, smiling. 'Is this the county court?'

'It's our court. Your court. Can I speak first?'

The men agreed.

'Here is the truth of it. While you are here, your kin are being punished for your crimes. The steward Lanfranc is using the law against them, fining them on all sorts of absurd charges, questioning them over and over about where you're hiding, searching for coins. Spreading money around the shire and sending it to the Viponts has only made them suspect more widely, not forget about your kin.'

'We should string that steward up,' growled Kolbrand.

'Perhaps,' agreed Robin. 'But before you hunt down the servant of the county's most powerful lords, let me try to stop him by appealing against him at law.'

'While you do that,' said Tosti, 'his men will still be chasing after our kin. You said when you brought Aedith and Thorold here that our kin were safe, but now you tell us they aren't.'

'They should all be brought here,' said Grimm. 'Let us protect them in the forest.'

Robin held up a hand to stem the tide of noisy agreement which met those words.

'Perhaps that is what we should do. But here is another truth for you. If your kin join you here they can't leave. If they have relatives in another village or hundred, they will not be able to see them for God knows how long. If they have trades that rely on visiting markets they will have to stop work – if they have any work at all that relies on something other than a stream or forest, they will have to stop work. They will have to live in isolation. Can you honestly say that you could support yourselves – find food and drink for everyone – under those conditions, and that your kin would wish to join you?'

'They should be given the choice,' said Thurstan. 'It is not for us to say.'

'And it is definitely not for you to do so,' said Kolbrand.

Some of the men raised their eyebrows at a free man talking to a lord in that way but Robin did not reprimand him. He had the right of it.

'Very well,' said Robin. 'You can decide this alone. Your necks are on the line if you are found and your kin are at risk while you wait. Take a tally among yourselves. I will be with Much and Edeva.' The teenagers leapt up to follow Robin as he walked away from the group.

'What do you think they'll decide?' Much asked keenly.

'I couldn't say.' Robin settled on a mossy stone outside the clearing, where the sound of a nearby brook could just be heard through the trees. It was swiftly stifled by the noise of the men arguing. 'They're as divided among themselves as they are united by their troubles. Even if they decide to give their kin the choice, I do not know how they will talk to them. The lords hereabouts are not stupid. If they see me and Will seeking out the relatives of every one of these men they will know we are up to something.'

Much suddenly stood up completely straight.

'I know how it could be done,' he said excitedly. 'What did you say before? Living in isolation. Which group of people are known to live away from the world, and not only allowed to hide themselves, but given supplies by their neighbours?'

'Is this a riddle?' said Edeva. 'I hate riddles.'

'Lepers.'

'You want the men to pretend to be lepers?' Robin smiled. 'Should I bring them walking sticks and clappers on my next visit?'

'They don't have to pretend to be anything. They can carry on as they are and just cover their faces if they leave the area around this clearing. You and me and all the rest of us who live outside the forest can let rumours go out that there are lepers in Sherwood. If we leave a bowl somewhere close to the road it can seem like it's just for the lepers, but the hundredmen's kin can use it – they can even meet the hundredmen to talk to them there.'

'You don't think the guardsmen all over this forest will find it strange that a leper hospital has suddenly sprouted up with lepers who loiter near the road?'

'Where could we leave a bowl?' Much asked Edeva, ignoring Robin. 'Usually it's a church, but the nearest church is too far from here.'

'The Saviour Oak,' said Edeva. 'That carved old stump north of the blasted tree. I've seen flowers left on it during the summer, and beads too.'

Robin knew the same tree, although he and Will had always called it the forest man. It was the remnants of a staghead tree, with the bearded face of a man carved into it, the mouth gaping open. When they were children Will had been fond of putting frogs in its mouth and daring Robin to put his hand inside.

'Perhaps,' he admitted, 'that could work. Can I trust you to tell their kin without being caught by Lord Vipont again?'

'That only happened once…'

'Once is enough to have you hanged or castrated. I'd rather avoid both.'

It seemed the hundredmen would be arguing their different views for some time, and Robin had other business to deal with. The longer he stayed in the forest the more opportunity Lanfranc had to send his men out harassing innocent families. He should leave them to their debate. He left Edeva to unpack the supplies he had brought and blindfolded Much until the boy was far enough away from the clearing for the men's voices to have faded from hearing. As soon as Much was able to see again he pressed Robin for information, questions about the escape from the castle, about the raids on the tax wagons, on their plans for the future, on how he was going to get back at Lanfranc. The only times he stopped asking questions were when he poured forth on plans for disguising the men as lepers and getting a message to their kin about meeting them. It was with some relief that Robin saw the King's Way up ahead and could tell Much to be quiet to avoid attracting attention. The lad put his head down.

Despite the late hour the King's Way was thronged with traffic. The rumble of wheels and whinnying of horses echoed through the forest even before the road itself came into view. When it did, the reason was immediately apparent. A lord's household was on the move. There were five wagons loaded with chests, each drawn by five horses. The lead wagon had already passed, and behind it, tied by its leash, trotted a hunting dog. More dogs followed each of the succeeding wagons. Servants walked alongside, each next to its household. The third wagon must contain chapel goods and chancery material, for a range of tonsured men surrounded it. One wagon looked to be loaded solely with butts of wine and ale. Behind these were packhorses, their packs bulging with plate and money, glinting through the chinks in the binding. On top of one of the wagons a gilded cage swayed, a collared monkey squatting in it.

Much stared as the household trundled past, taking up the whole width of the road. 'How much is all that worth?' he asked, eyeing the chests filled with silken clothing and tapestries, guarded by the keeper of the wardrobe. As it was dry one of the tapestries had been laid on top of the wagon, and one corner was flapping over the edge to reveal the horn of a unicorn.

'Hundreds of pounds,' said Robin.

'Imagine if you ambushed that.'

'Difficult, with a hundred men circling it. The lord will be at the rear. Keep your head down when we pass him.'

They rode along the edge of the road since there was no space to get onto the path. One pothole was causing the chamberlain particular difficulty. Wheels kept being sucked into the mud filling it, and one wagon was now mired in it, being both pushed and pulled by a score of men. Past the wagons and the packhorses were the senior servants, the men on horseback and the women in covered litters. Beyond them, finally, was the lord and his family. Robin recognised Lord Foliot, Lord D'Alselin's ally. Foliot saw Robin at the road's edge and rode over to him.

'Apologies for driving you off the path, Lord Locksley.'

'You are moving north?'

'Yes, to our estate in Yorkshire. I wanted to find a route that did not pass through the forest, the way that things have been recently, but avoiding the King's Way would have added days to our journey.'

'I am certain you will arrive safely.'

'You have more faith than I do. My wife insisted we bring crossbows with us. Even her ladies have them. Frightening thought.' He glanced towards the litter of women with a sigh. 'I just hope we will be beyond the forest in the open fields before dusk. I do not know what has happened to this county these last few years. In the time of the old king you could use this road alone at night without fear. Now I do not feel safe with guards. Tell your stepfather to take a firmer hand with the people here.'

'I think the firm hand is what has driven people to crime. And it is not the sheriff who holds the power in this county now. You know that as well as I do.'

'Hm. The Viponts are a touch overzealous, that is true.' There was a shout from further up the road. Foliot flinched. 'I am summoned. Best move quickly or I will find a bolt in my side.' He waved his farewell to Robin and rode back into the pack.

'Did he say something about the monkey?' Much asked, having squinted to try and understand all that passed between the lords while they spoke.

'No. But he gave a very good reason not to attack his wagon.' Robin nodded his head in the direction of the horsemen at the rear of the household, crossbows at their hips. They moved onto the packed gravel and fresh dung on the road.

'Are you certain he did not mention the monkey?'

***

Robin left Much at the crossroads and rode the last miles of his journey at a trot. As he made his way through the frenetic cleaning taking place in the great hall of Locksley Elaine appeared from the solar.

'What happened to your face?' she asked, reaching up to touch his cheek.

Edeva's scratches, he realised.

'I wasn't looking where I rode. Went straight into low-hanging twigs.'

'They look sore. You should ask Gytha for some balm.'

'I will live.' He kissed her hand. 'I had better change out of my travelling clothes before supper.' He paused on the verge of leaving. Much's voice was still chattering in his brain. He smiled to himself. 'I was distracted actually, when I was riding. I saw a pair of cloaked men wandering the forest with clappers and begging bowls.'

'And I thought the forest was just full of thieves and deer. It holds lepers too now, does it? What a bounty. Oh, and before you change – your mother said to make sure you put on something impressive for this evening. Your scarlet perhaps. We have guests.'

Robin's heart sank. Not the Viponts, he thought, and something of the thought must have crossed his face for Elaine frowned.

'The Prior of Lenton and Lords de Louvetot and D'Alselin are supping with us. I think my uncle is worried about his influence waning since he quarrelled with Lord Eudo. The May feast he held seems to have done little to reconcile them all, and now Lord de Caux and Lord de la Guerche have refused to attend the county court in person. They are sending their stewards.'

Perhaps, thought Robin, this would not be the best time to pass on Lord Foliot's reprimand about a firmer hand to his stepfather. However, it might be the perfect opportunity to appeal against Lanfranc, with two other lords who had little love for the man in attendance. Although he had no interest in the fine clothes his mother insisted he wear, he took some care dressing himself that evening, to ensure he looked the part of the discerning lord when he met their guests. Elaine was pleased to see it, although she repeated her advice about Gytha's balm.

They ate in the solar, away from the rest of the household, with one of Lady Joan's attendants playing the harp softly to accompany the meal. Lord D'Alselin, whose musical tastes Robin suspected inclined to the martial rather than the feminine, glowered when his seat was placed closest to the musician. He hunched over his plate with a grim countenance, only brightening when Elaine addressed him. Good fortune – or, rather, judicious seat grabbing – had put Robin next to the prior. He had thought of a way that Much's idea of disguising the hundredmen could be used not only to enable their families to meet with them, but also go some way to solving the problem of smuggling supplies into the forest.

'Prior, I wondered if I could prevail on your charity?'

'On the eve of Ascension, my lord, of course.'

'I believe a group of lepers have moved into the forest, between Newstead Abbey and the eastern King's Road. I am going to provide some sustenance for them, perhaps also building materials so they can make themselves a watertight dwelling – a hospital, if I can afford it. The Abbess of Newstead has already promised to offer me considerable support in the venture, and I hoped you might join her?'

The abbess and the prior had long been rivals. The prior was related to Lord de Lacy, whose extensive western lands bordered those of the abbess's nephew, the Earl of Derby. Family rivalries always ran deep, and since the abbess and the prior also shared the natural antagonism of two large religious foundations in the same county – competition over fishing rights in the River Leen, hunting rights to their surrounding forest, entitlement to gallows near the roadways – Robin knew that he could rely upon the prior's jealousy of any scheme which the abbess was funding to ensure he would likewise offer aid. He would not wish to be seen to be outdone, and nor would the abbess when Robin told her a similar lie the next time he visited her.

'It would give me joy to match any donation that the abbess has made,' said the prior. 'Have your clerk write out details of the materials and funds you require and I am certain I can find a way to deliver them to you.'

'I hope that the recent visit of our neighbours to your priory has not disturbed Friar Toki?'

'No, the friar is always in good spirits. He must be the most sanguine man I know.'

'There have been no difficulties arising from the disagreement, I hope?'

'Not as far as I am concerned. I had another visit from Lord Vipont's steward, delivering a message from his master. Odious man. He keeps a mistress, apparently, but he took great pleasure in lecturing me on the sanctity of my position.'

That would not have gone down well, Robin thought. But it served his ends perfectly.

'I cannot abide a man who does not know his station,' said Lady Joan. 'Whether you are a lord or a villein, you must behave as God has dictated, not seek to move above or below your natural order.'

She glanced at Robin. He wondered if Elaine had mentioned his meeting with Will in the kennels to her. Perhaps now was the time to prove his lordly credentials.

'How right you are, Mother. Which reminds me of a matter I wanted to raise at the next county court. A local servant has been persecuting families on the Locksley estate, as well as neighbouring lands of yours, Sir Walter. Fabricating stories of unfair trading and forcing fines onto those who can barely afford to pay them, simply to enrich his own master and perhaps because of some personal grievance. I have even heard stories of intimidation and damage to property.'

'I hope he is not one of my servants,' said Lord D'Alselin. 'I would have him hauled before my own manorial court.'

'He is not,' said Robin, 'but I am glad you would take such swift action. I believe that since the man's actions have affected a number of families across hundred boundaries the matter should be put before the county court, for the sheriff to settle.'

'Perhaps that is best,' said Sir Walter, not willing to commit to an opinion yet. 'What is the name of this servant?'

'Lanfranc, the steward of Lord Eudo de Vipont.'

A ringing silence followed his words. He expected the ladies to disapprove – they seemed to have taken it upon themselves to be the champions of the Viponts in every aspect of their lives – but was not prepared for the stony faces of the lords around him.

'Since this question concerns Lord de Vipont's servant,' Sir Walter said, 'it might be best that you make the complaint to him personally. I do not think there is a need to involve courts –'

'But our tenants are among the injured party,' interrupted Robin. 'The business should be decided in the county court.'

'It should not be decided at all,' said Lady Joan, laying down her knife with an angry clatter. 'It will only anger Lord Vipont and his relatives. Marian, you agree with me.'

It was not a question, and Marian did not answer.

'It is to be expected that a lady would wish to avoid conflict,' said the prior, smiling benevolently. 'And I think in this case we ought to heed her.'

That was not what Robin had expected.

'But Lanfranc has been preying on the weak and tormenting those who are innocent of any wrongdoing simply because they are unable to defend themselves.'

'Who are these people?' Elaine asked pointedly.

'Our tenants.'

'But why are they being *persecuted* by the steward? They must have done something wrong to deserve such attention.'

'They have not.' Her eyes were fixed on him, sharp as steel. 'I met Lord Foliot this afternoon on the King's Road, fleeing from his Nottinghamshire estates because of the lawlessness here these days. That lack of law applies as much to lord's servants as to baseborn men, and I believe Lanfranc is only fanning the flames of anger here with his actions. Clearly his masters permit it, for they benefit from any fines he can squeeze from these innocent –'

'They cannot be innocent if they are fined by the court,' said Elaine firmly. 'Only the guilty are punished.'

'From what I understand, those rules do not apply in these cases. Where no evidence exists of wrongdoing it is fabricated. However, when Lanfranc himself commits acts of arson…'

'Arson?' cried Lady Joan in disbelief.

'Yes, arson, on the forge at Green Lane Cross –'

'Did not the forge catch fire accidentally?' asked Lord de Louvetot.

'I was there. I saw it. It was no accident.'

'I remember,' said Sir Walter, 'that Lanfranc found evidence of criminal behaviour at that forge, that he entrusted the owners to your custody and that they escaped into the forest. I fear if you argue against Lanfranc over that point, it is not him who will come out worse. I cannot prevent you putting this case before the county court jury, but if you do so I will not offer you support. Nor, I think, will our neighbours.'

He looked at their guests. The prior shook his head. Lord de Louvetot was eyeing his plate with concentrated interest to avoid being drawn into an opinion. D'Alselin met his eye but his words were no comfort.

'I have no great love for the Viponts,' he said, 'but I have argued a hopeless case against them once. I do not like to repeat my mistakes. Lord Foliot probably has the best of it – stay away until this whole episode of disorder has blown over. No good comes of kicking a bee's nest.'

And with that the matter was resolved. Robin knew that the Viponts would not support his charge, nor their allies the Lords de Caux and de la Guerche. With Lord Foliot fleeing to avoid being involved in local disputes his steward was unlikely to argue the case for Robin in his absence. If the Prior of Lenton – who had been so quick to protect the friar against the Viponts and to complain of Lanfranc – would not offer Robin support, how could he expect it from the Abbeys of Newsted and Rufford? After all, the friar was a churchman and the religious lords protected their own, but in this case they had no vested interest. Even if Robin could persuade the town's representatives to support him, they would not stand long against the collected disapproval of all the county's lords. If he wanted to send Lanfranc the message that his persecution of the innocent would not be permitted to continue, he would have to find another way.

'How did your try with the law go?'

'It didn't.'

Over a cup of brackish water, Robin squatted miserably in the scant shelter of the Saviour Oak. It was raining, the driving rain of every spring as it gave way to summer, and he was already soaked through before he met Will and John to hear the hundredmen's decision. John wore an old hood that Robin had found and in his lap was a bell. The disguise of a leper made a change from that of a penitent.

'I'm not surprised that the sheriff refused to help you. As soon as a man takes control of the shire he loses his free will. He's always watching over his shoulder for the day his power's taken from him. He might as well be called the Morrisman of Nottingham. He leaps and suspects like he's playing a game of merrils.'

'Sir Walter wasn't the only one who refused to support me. The prior and Lord D'Alselin joined him for good measure. I have just been to Newstead Abbey and even the abbess – who I suspected was more of a man than any of them – refused to argue for me in the court. The case of the common land frightened them all. They fear that if they speak against Lord Vipont it'll be seen as a complaint against the Count of Mortain, and as long as he is in England and the king isn't, that could cause trouble in Nottinghamshire.'

'Every man wants to protect his own lands,' John said. 'Lord or common man, we all are born selfish.'

'But to let your own self-interest take precedence over doing what is right…'

Robin shook his head. 'They did say they would help the new leper hospital though.'

'The other lepers will be pleased.'

'And exactly how many lepers have you decided will be moving into your colony? How many hospital walls should I ask the abbess to pay for?'

'Not as many as you expected. Much has already managed to bring a couple of kin to this tree to meet their men. Madalgrim's women need their mash tuns and malt supplies to carry on their brewing, which is easier to do in their home than in the forest. Their case against Lanfranc will be heard in court this week but they seem resolved to keep brewing as long as they can afford to buy supplies. Ansculf and Siward's kin are tied to the land they plough. Tosti's parents, Gilbert's aunt and Kolbrand's sister – whose arms are bigger than his – want to join us, but there are still other kin to hear back from.'

'So the new wave joining the clearing will be elderly or female,' said Will. 'Not the most useful for raids.'

'Kolbrand's sister sounds like she might be,' said Robin. 'Besides, if the men have decided their kin are welcome, we must abide by that decision. What about your kin, John?'

'My cousins may come. They haven't much in the way of brain but they can both wield an axe or ploughshare well enough.'

Both Will and John spoke as if another attack of some sort was inevitable. Did that mean that the hundredmen were hoping for raids as well?

'You seem determined to keep the hundredmen outside the law.'

'You told us yourself. You tried appealing to the law, and it failed you.'

That much was certainly true. Robin had managed to unite lords against enclosing the common land, and the count had overturned his work. He had tried to stop Lanfranc at the courts and the lords had overturned that too. But even if the law had failed, surely there must be a way to punish Lanfranc for his abuses. Perhaps they were right, perhaps they would have to look beyond the normal channels of justice.

'We should give Lanfranc a taste of what he has doled out in this county. Try to stop him abusing the courts, even if only once. I want him to know that there are some people who can hold power over him. I want him humiliated or afraid, like he has humiliated and frightened the hundredmen's kin.'

'How are you going to do that?' John asked. 'He never leaves the castle without an armed guard.'

'I don't know yet. But I'm willing to work to find a way.'

'We should ask at the castle,' said Will. 'Every man has his weakness, and I'd bet a shilling his servants know about it.'

'Perhaps your friend in the chancery could help?' added John. 'He spends his life around private documents. There might be something in them that'll help bring Lanfranc to justice.'

And bringing Lanfranc to justice was exactly what Robin would do.

Robin and Will went to Nottingham Castle together, Robin dressed as a lord and Will in the slightly better clothing Robin had found for him to masquerade as his servant. At the stables they separated: Robin to the chancery and Will to sniff around the lower orders of the household, both to learn anything they could use against Lanfranc the steward. Robin had mixed fortunes with Peter the clerk. Lanfranc kept regular hours, did little but what he was commanded by his master and when he rode out he was always accompanied by men, particularly if he rode with the Viponts. Some of the servants whispered that he had a mistress somewhere in the town whose name might be Isabel, or possibly Elizabeth, but her home was not known to Peter. Perhaps that was not so surprising for a monk, thought Robin. He loitered in the chancery for as long as he could and then made his way back towards the stables to meet Will. His brother was some time in coming, and Robin was beginning to suspect his lingering would be noted when he finally appeared, pulling his hood over his face as he emerged into the light of the courtyard.

'We should go to the Iron Row,' Will said as he led Robin's horse through the outer bailey. 'Off the market in the French Borough.'

'Why?'

'Because the bastard has a mistress there. Petronella. She has red hair – that won't be the first thing we notice apparently – and she drinks Gascon wine.'

Robin grinned at his brother's powers of detection. Will had always been able to talk the birds from the trees, and among the lower orders of the household he would have far more gossip to learn than Robin could hear from a clerk.

'How did you come to know what wine she drinks?'

'One of the men in the buttery supplies Lanfranc with an extra jug every Monday before he rides to the Iron Row to meet her around dusk.'

'So he'll be there this coming Monday night.' That could be useful. The court Madalgrim's family were due to attend was meeting on Tuesday next. If there was a way to keep Lanfranc away from it, it would at least mean one less fine out of their pockets.

'He doesn't stay the night,' Will said, perhaps sharing some of Robin's train of thought. 'Him and the guard he takes are always back before the bells ring in the town for curfew.'

Robin rode through the town in silence. He was thinking of how to keep Lanfranc away from that court. If the steward rode alone they could ambush him on the journey back to the castle and hold him somewhere – by the docks perhaps, or in the cellar of an alehouse – until the court had met. But with even one guard that would be more difficult, and since it was now May the evenings were lengthening. It might still be just light enough in the town for them to be seen and taken. They could not bring the hundredmen from the forest to help them either. It was too great a risk to bring them into contact with Lanfranc, who could so easily recognise them and raise the hue and cry. He would have to rely on Will – and perhaps Much, if the lad could be trusted to do as he was told.

They had arrived at the market. As it was a Saturday the whole broad square milled with people – a convenient cover for a lord and his servant to be passing through, and particularly to be lingering. There was far more on offer here than in the daily market held in the older English borough of the town. A babble of accents from across the country and the continent filled their ears. Native cloth, wool and hides nestled alongside tin and lead from the south-west, spices from Spain, silks from Italy, metalware from the Low Countries, fine textiles and wine from southern France. In one corner of the square three ferrets ran around a merchant's body while a bear danced to the shrieks of excited children. No one looked twice at Robin and Will as they weaved towards Iron Row.

'If we could take some of this,' said Will, eyeing the stalls surrounding him, 'we could sell it on for quite a price. Or we could keep it. A tapestry would keep the draughts out of the croft.'

Robin nudged Will in the shoulder to direct his gaze. Not far up the street a young woman had emerged from one of the doors off Iron Row and was walking towards the market. Her girdle crossed under her breasts, which hardly needed the addition to draw the eye, wove behind her back and appeared again at her heavy hips, where it dangled almost to the ground. The veil on her head was edged back just enough to reveal red curls falling over her pale skin.

'For a deceitful thieving bastard,' said Will, 'he's not got poor taste.'

'Maybe one day, brother, if you keep stealing and lying you can have a ribald all of your own. Go and look at the door. I'll follow her.'

Will muttered away from Petronella and towards her home to inspect the lock holding it. It looked like she must live over one of the ironwork shops, perhaps with a brother – or a husband who could be relied on to be absent on Monday evenings. It would be best to know who else dwelled in that tenement before they risked taking Lanfranc there.

Robin followed her through the market, around the town and all the way back in a great loop without seeing her do more than exchange a greeting with other townsfolk. By the time she returned to Iron Row he knew he would have to take matters into his own hands. Her hands were reaching for the latch of her door when he called to her.

'Excuse me, my lady.'

She turned in surprise and smiled.

'I am not a lady, but you are kind to call me so. How may I help you, my lord?'

'You look to know this part of town well. Are you able to recommend a good ironmonger? My horse will need reshoeing before the month is out and the man I use in Sneinton charges a king's ransom these days.'

'Thulf is the cheapest. But I would not trust your horse to him. Esger charges more but his work is the finest.'

She gestured at the next door along. From the back of the building smoke issued, just as from most of those along this row. But not hers. He should have noticed that sooner.

'Your husband does not work iron? I took this to be a shop.'

'It was. My husband died a year ago. I should sell the shop, I know, but my mother-in-law is old and her husband owned it before Edric did. We are attached to the place.'

'You do not consider becoming an ironworker yourself?'

She laughed and held up her pale hands, remarkably unblemished for a widow. Presumably her mother-in-law had been the one doing most of the domestic work.

'I am too vain.'

'Thank you for your advice.'

He turned his horse. Will was waiting in the shadows of the washhouse on the opposite side of the square.

'She's watching you,' he said. 'Obviously favours your face.'

'Favours my clothes, more like. Her husband's been dead a year and her and her mother-in-law can still afford to hold a vacant shop. Maybe she thinks I could visit her on Tuesdays and fund a servant to keep them all. How was the latch?'

'Easy to shift. And I haven't seen anyone else coming in or out of the place. Must just be her and the mother-in-law.'

Robin was not listening. Over Will's shoulder his eye had been drawn by a stand with a mortar and pestle prominently displayed amidst a range of jars and phials.

'How would you feel,' he asked, 'about seeing Lanfranc bollock naked in the market place on Tuesday morning?'

'I'd rather see Petronella naked, but each to their own. I suppose watching children throw stones at a stripped steward would not be so bad. Hey, we could buy one of those ferrets and see what fun it had with him?'

'Maybe next time. You need to go back to the castle and make better friends with that servant in the buttery. I've got a draught to buy.'

Regular as a prior's tithe, Lanfranc and his man rode out of the castle bailey and into St Nicholas's parish the day after Ascension Sunday. On the other side of the river the bell for Vespers rang at Lenton Priory, and on the last chime a slender figure wandered the same route with apparent disinterest. When he arrived at Iron Row he found two shadows on opposite ends of the market place, one sweeping the path clear in front of a tenement, the other hooded and spooning the meat from a pie under the shelter of the washhouse roof. Will Scarlette looked around cautiously before joining the pie-eater.

'Where's the guard?' he asked. The shadows had already lengthened across the square and a star was blinking in the sky above them.

'Left straight away,' replied Robin, offering the pie to his brother. 'He's in the alehouse now.'

'That might make things easier.'

'Or harder. When he comes back and knocks for his master he's likely to run in if he gets no answer.'

'Just as well we've got all the might of a miller's boy with us then.' He glanced at Much, who was now moving the street's mess on to the next home's front path. 'How long will the draught take to work?'

'The apothecary said an hour at most.'

'You trust a man who sells pots of treacle next to a dancing bear?'

Robin left that question hanging. 'I presume you managed to get enough of the powder into the wine before your friend in the buttery took it?'

'Of course. How will we know when it's worked?'

'We'll wait another hour and go in.'

'Time for an ale then.'

Will cricked his spine and wandered towards the alehouse the guard had disappeared into. Robin waited outside Petronella's shop. When St Peter's church tower chimed he whistled for Much to stop sweeping. The lad threw down the brush and ran over. Moments later Will reappeared in the square and wandered over to Petronella's shop as if he owned it. He fiddled with the latch – Robin heard a clunk from across the square – and then went inside, holding the door open a crack for Robin and Much to follow.

'The guard is still drinking,' Will breathed when they were inside. A stairway that was little more than a ladder led straight ahead of them to the floor above the shop. 'I bought him a jug or two to keep him warm.'

'As long as it doesn't make him noisy.'

He let Will go up the stairway first, every creak making his shoulders tense. At the top of the stair, Will disappeared from view and then came back, not bothering to walk quietly.

'They're asleep,' he said. 'Although I'm not sure the lad should see them.'

Much virtually ran up the stairs while Will smirked at his brother. Robin made sure the latch on the door was replaced properly before following them.

'Where's the old woman?' he asked when he got into the chamber.

Lanfranc was sprawled on top of Petronella, both in their shifts on a straw mattress on the floorboards. Much looked disappointed. Will drew back a linen curtain over a closet space where the old woman snored, open-mouthed. In her hand was an empty wine cup.

'Probably a relief for the poor woman to be drugged,' said Will, sniffing the cup. 'Much, help my brother strip the steward.'

They wriggled Lanfranc's shift from him, trying to be careful not to jolt him about too much at first for fear of waking him. But whatever the apothecary put in his sleeping draught was effective. None of the trio even twitched in their sleep. Once the steward was laid out flat on the floor Robin took ash from the burnt out hearth and smeared it over Lanfranc's chest.

'What are you doing?'

Robin finished the daub and stood up to show his work. An ashen arrow covered Lanfranc's chest, just like the whittled sigils that had been rolled up with the Viponts' coin pouches at Rogation.

'Is that wise?' Will asked.

'Probably not. But I want him to know that there's someone else in the county who can hold a grudge and get away with it.'

He kicked Lanfranc in the leg for good measure. Suddenly a wooden thud echoed through the shop. The door. It must almost be the hour of curfew. The guard had returned to collect his master and escort him back to the castle.

'Get a blindfold and gag,' Robin hissed to Will. Not waiting to see his brother do so, he crept across the floorboards to the stair. The guard knocked again.

Robin descended the stairs as quietly as he could and when he was halfway down he gripped the steps with one hand and reached the other out to unhook the latch, then swung back up to the chamber above as quickly as he could.

The guard heard the noise.

'Master Steward?' he called. He tried the door and found it opening in his hands. Upstairs in the chamber, in creeping darkness Much, Will and Robin crouched in readiness. The coverlet had been thrown back over Petronella and the naked Lanfranc. Will handed Robin a strip of linen he had torn from the closet curtain and pushed his hand into the hollow of a ripped feather bolster, ready for the guard's head.

From the bottom of the stairs came a footfall, then the grating of metal over hardened leather. The guard had drawn his sword. A horse whinnied in the street, disguising the first of the guard's creaking steps on the stairway. There was no window in the chamber and the hearth fire had died. When the guard appeared at the top of the stair he paused a moment for his eyes to adjust to the darkness. He called out again. He's going to turn back, thought Robin. If he left the shop he might return with the town's watchmen. Will stood up, against the wall next to the doorway into the chamber, twitching to leap forward. Robin stood as well. There was a creak on the stair again. He was descending, back to the door. He could not be allowed to leave.

Will and Robin lunged at the same time, clumsily colliding with each other as they leapt out of the doorframe and towards the stair. Robin reached further, seizing the guard's collar and slamming the gag around his head – he missed the mouth and only succeeded in binding the gag under the guard's nose. Will shoved him aside, stumbling almost off the stair as he forced the bolster over him. The guard cried out. Too loud. He struggled, his sword crashing from side to side in the confinement of the stairway. He was making enough noise to bring the watchmen running, Robin thought. He put his hands around the man's throat and squeezed. It was enough to silence him. A shape leapt over Will and Robin's sprawling bodies and the guard's increasingly limp weight on the stair. Much jumped them with the grace of a cat, pushed the door shut, latched it, seized the guard around the waist to take his weight, pulled the gag over his mouth and forced Robin's hands from his throat. It would all have been immeasurably impressive if it had not ended with the guard falling in a dead faint onto Much and pinning him against the door with a squeal. Robin grinned at Will. His brother cackled and smacked him on the back.

'He's not a bad miller's lad this one.'

He rolled onto his knees and went to free Much. Once heaved back up the stairs, the guard's hands were bound behind him with one of Petronella's leather girdles and he was left on the mattress next to her. No reason he should not have a comfortable perch, Robin thought, given he would be there all night.

The guard had brought Lanfranc's horse to the door, but now it had wandered over to the washhouse. Much snuck out between circuits of the watchmen and tied it to a post there so it could drink without drawing too much attention. Meanwhile, Robin and Will waited for the bells of Matins.

When the gates were opened at dawn Constable Osbern found a small crowd already waiting. It was always the way. The gate at Cow Bar was closer to the English Borough market but it opened later and merchants would take any means necessary to ensure they snared the best position in the square. Rising slightly earlier and taking a longer route were the least of their efforts. He stepped aside as a flock of sheep pushed past him. The shepherd whistled and waved his crook to keep them in check.

'Looks like your alehouses stayed open late,' he laughed as he passed the constable.

Osbern followed the direction of his crook. A figure was lying prostrate in the middle of the square next to a horse. Surely he could not have been there all night? Osbern swore he could flog those night watchmen. Half of them were drunk on their circuits. He wouldn't be surprised if this drunkard in the square *was* a watchman. He marched with the crowd towards the figure. As he got closer his indignation increased. He was naked. This drunken idiot was nude as the day he was born, a smudge of dirt across his chest the only covering he had on.

'Hey! Wake up.'

The drunk's face was concealed by arms outstretched above his head.

'You there. I'll have you before the Assizes for this. Children live near here you know.'

He kicked at the man's legs, but he slumbered on. Somehow he seemed to have tangled his wrists in his horse's reins, which was how his arms stayed over his head all this time. Fine horse for a town drunk, Osbern thought. The saddle alone must be worth more than he earned in a month. The merchants and farmers were all laughing outright at the naked drunk. Osbern grabbed one of them by the arm.

'Lend him your mantle.'

'Use your own. I don't want my wool coated in ash.'

The merchant shook Osbern's grip off. The constable reluctantly knelt and removed his own mantle, pausing to brush some of the dirt from the drunk's chest. Odd, he thought. It looked like an arrow, pointing right at the man's head. The drunk's horse stepped away and tugged his arm away from his face. Osbern gasped. He threw his mantle over the man immediately, and started slapping at his face.

'Wake up,' he hissed. 'Wake up.'

The man groaned. Mumbled. His eyes fluttered open.

And so the first thing that Lanfranc the steward saw on the day of the Vipont Court was a score of merchants and one astonished constable laughing at his naked body.

The Viponts were furious. That was the first delicious piece of information Robin learned from the sheriff. They had chastised Lanfranc, the guard – once they had found him at Petronella's – the watchmen and constable of Nottingham, and they had demanded that Sir Walter hear the case of Lanfranc's attack and public mortification in the next county court session. This demand had swiftly been withdrawn once the sheriff reminded the lords that hearing the case would necessarily mean calling witnesses to Lanfranc's humiliation and keeping the affair in the mind of local men. No one had seen or heard anything to assist the arrest of any attackers. Perhaps, he suggested, it would be better simply to let the embarrassment quietly be forgotten? As Sir Walter told Robin that the Viponts had heeded this advice, the sheriff smiled to himself.

Robin did not expect any voices to come forward with information. No one had seen him, Will or Much and there would be few, even if they had, who had a reason to help the steward in Nottingham Castle. He had bullied and fined and now he must reap the enmity that he had sown in the hearts of his neighbours.

'I wish I'd seen it.'

That was the response of the hundredmen when Will and Much told the story. In their version of events the whole affair had been riddled with danger and the three of them were heroes. Will and Much's competitive embroidering of the truth would have had their listeners believe that each had been on the brink of death after a stabbing from the guardsman's sword. John Blunt rolled his eyes at Robin as Much began yet another rendition of the Ballad of Lanfranc's Balls and they left the hundredmen's fireside.

'Come up here,' said John, leading Robin onto the roof of what had been an animal pen. It was being restored to help accommodate new arrivals, and the bare slatted roof was now daubed, although patches were still covered only with sackcloth. From up there Robin was struck by how the clearing's inhabitants had expanded. In the caves they had seemed a small jumble of men, but now the group almost resembled a village: old and young, men and women, sharing a meal and planning their next day's repairwork, or smithing, or cooking, or visit to the Saviour Oak to pick up alms that had been left there, and perhaps also to meet a family member. It was all remarkably peaceful. It was easy to forget that across the county guards were hunting for the men sat blowing on their pottage at this fireside. John regarded the scene with a smile.

'Lefchild has come up with a name for this place. He says we've created a new hundred in the forest, one belonging to no one but ourselves, with the only tax our labour and the only rent our food – both of them going to our men and no one higher.'

'Fine words, although the Abbess of Newstead might not like them. I think we're legally in her hunting park. Fortunately she's not much of a sportswoman. What's the name Lefchild invented?'

'The Hundred of the Arrow.'

'You can tell he grew up in an alehouse. He's listened to too many travelling poets for his own good.'

John shrugged, smiled.

'I like it.'

'You're a fletcher. Of course you like it.'

'Speaking of which…'

John reached across Robin and pulled back a piece of sackcloth covering a hole in the roof. Beneath, resting warm and dry, were the feathered staves of scores of arrows.

'We are just waiting on Thurstan's forge for their heads. He thinks we have enough iron to melt down and make heads for these, but we will need more if we are to have a good supply for the future. A proper anvil wouldn't go amiss either.'

'What about bows?'

'Much easier. There's yew all over this forest and we've got sinew for the strings.' John hesitated and cracked his knuckles. It was an old habit of his that Robin knew presaged an important but not easy conversation.

'Thurstan had a question about the arrowheads, when he makes them. He wondered if they should be barbed for hunting small game or bodkin-pointed?'

'For larger game?'

'Much larger. The next royal tax collection will be at Michaelmas, but before then coin will keep moving around this shire. Tithes for the monks, rent and dues for our lords, taxes for our king and our count, shield money going from the knights to the exchequer. Not to mention the fines that are paid in the courts, which every man knows go into the pockets of the sheriff and his friends.'

'And you think we have a right to steal from every one of those? What have the monks ever done to you?'

'Perhaps we do not have a claim on that coin, but neither do the lords or the king. This king has barely been in the country since he was anointed. We've paid him money to take Jerusalem – he didn't – and now we're paying money to save him because he was fool enough to be kidnapped by a foreign prince. I don't know what we'll gain when he's free. He'll likely be in Aquitaine, not Nottingham.'

'Careful what you say, John.'

'All I'm saying is that whether the king is in power or his brother is, it ends the same way for us. There will always be an excuse to take our coin and our toil.'

'Perhaps it makes no difference. But if the king were free, his brother would not have the authority he has now, and if the count lacked authority, so would the Viponts. As long as Lord Eudo and his kin have their prince's favour they can keep browbeating poor and lord alike, I will stay Lord Locksley in name alone and you will have to live in this forest hoping not to be found.'

'So, since we cannot free the king, why should we not at least try to weaken the Viponts? Shame them and all the others who mistreat their vassals and villeins. Keep their pets from court like you kept Lanfranc from Madalgrim's kin so that no one is unfairly fined. Help not just our own people but all the men of Nottinghamshire by reminding these lords that their power comes with a responsibility to their vassals.'

'And help ourselves to coin in the meantime?'

'A happy by-blow.'

Robin pictured Lanfranc's outraged naked face in the marketplace that morning. Just the memory of it made him smile. And he knew as well as John that money was taken too often from those who could ill spare it, then stolen away even from its expressed purpose. While the king was gone, why not look to protect the weak and poor? Why not help the hundredmen whose whole lives had been held forfeit just because they tried to protect their neighbours from Lord Eudo's extortion? Robin looked again at the company around the fireside.

'What do the men think of this?'

'They want to do something more than build pens and poach. If you offer to lead them, they will start preparing for another raid tomorrow.'

They had men enough and the means of making weapons, of gaining supplies and money from this pretence of a hospital. Robin, Much and Will were still able to move freely, gathering information. Peter could tell them where and when money was being moved. And he must know other clerks, in the chanceries of the abbeys and priory, in the households of the lords temporal, writing up the cases presented before the courts, who could report on those cases that had been won unfairly.

'Then let's remind the Viponts what good lordship is.'

The golden summer of the Hundred of the Arrow had begun.

Harvest

The summer months were busy ones. As weeding and shearing gave way to rush-gathering and crop-reaping in Nottinghamshire the men of the forest did everything they could to make their new hundred successful. The 'leper hospital in the forest' that Lord Locksley so altruistically gathered money for was provided with hoes, rakes, seed, goats, pigs, chickens, even a cow, and all the abbess and prior wanted in response was for their benefactions to be known throughout the county. Lepers could be lucky, and association with them – even from a distance – reflected well on the religious lords. More in hope than experience, the hundredmen planted late crops in the hand-churned earth around animal pens at the edge of the clearing, but the summer was warm and just wet enough and the buds of barley and wheat appeared before May turned to June. The men's throats were wet with ale left by Agnes Scarlette and Madalgrim's kin at the Saviour Oak and rapidly run back to the clearing. Their bellies were never full but neither did they starve. And despite the guards who toured the forest, riding the King's Way daily to Nottingham, venturing towards the caves and past the blasted tree, despite even the huntsmen who rode south from Clipstone and west from Garsmount, no stranger was ever seen by the hundredmen as they kept their watch. Robin and John insisted that they keep lookouts posted, even if it drew the men away from their domestic chores. Better to have less food, Robin argued, than to hang.

The royal justices still did not come to Nottinghamshire. They seemed determined to stay south that year, and so the question of who rightfully owned the Locksley estate remained unresolved. Instead, news came to the county that King Richard had been put on trial by the German emperor for sowing dissent among his allies and plotting the death of the King of Jerusalem. Normandy looked likely to fall to the King of France, and there were whispers that King Richard himself might end a prisoner of King Philippe. Robin knew that that would be the end of all hopes of his return to England, and of the hundredmen's pardon.

He tried to keep his fears from them, and there were distractions enough for him to largely succeed. Fines from the manorial courts of the Viponts went missing every month in greater or lesser weight. Their neighbours suffered similar losses as they called in rents and dues, but Lord Eudo and his family could not help but notice that their own wagons were waylaid with greater frequency and determination. They doubled the guard and for a time the attacks subsided – Lords de la Guerche and de Caux found themselves suddenly the victims of financial raids. The money was divided as widely as possible, returning to the families who had been wrongfully deprived as well as the kin of the hundredmen. What food could be brought to the Saviour Oak in return was gratefully sucked into the slowly increasing stores of the Hundred of the Arrow.

Despite Robin's frustrated wait for the royal justices and king, there was cause for celebration and he gladly partook in it. In July the Hundred of the Arrow saw its first newborn: Aedith and Thurstan's second child was born and baptised by Agnes Scarlette who served as midwife. The child was named Tohyht and washed in the nearby stream, blessed by Friar Toki on one of his perambulations through the forest. The forestmen had started to fret for their souls as their good luck stretched, so chapel goods 'fell' from the wagon carrying parts of the Peverill estate to Locksley Hall at midsummer. A fingerbone of St Wulfstan, a crucifix and a cross were affixed to a rickety table in one corner of what had been a sty, and the friar paused in the clearing to say Mass with the men. The consecrated host was hidden in a box Gilbert whittled for the purpose, out of the reach of the mice that had started to visit the clearing.

The bonfires of St John's Eve dwindled to ash, and the ash to dust on the wind. The air filled with powdery straw as it was threshed, the harvest was gathered across England and for once there was reason to hope: food was plentiful, rain did not wash out the crops nor the sun parch them. In the forest the men and their kin who dared to join them had their own harvest feast, binding sheaths of thatch and birch and twig into crude arrow shapes and parading them around the clearing, attaching flower garlands over the lintel of the croft, the bakehouse, the forge, the animal pens, even the large building they were extending to form a communal longhouse in readiness for the winter months.

Across Nottinghamshire there were harvest festivities, and Nottingham Castle was no exception. There a great banquet was held with the promise of tumblers, acrobats, musicians, fools and singers, and every lord and lady in Nottinghamshire and Derbyshire was invited, to celebrate not only the turning of the seasons but also the confirmation of Marian and Guy's betrothal. After months of negotiations a contract had been signed by the couple's families and this would be the last celebration before their wedding took place at Martinmas. Despite the double cause for celebration and the expense lavished by the sheriff and the Lords Vipont – despite even the presence in the castle of the Count of Mortain and his vast entourage – the feast was a sombre occasion. For every vat of wine drunk and song sung there were whisperers in corners wearing anxious frowns. Ladies feared that the forestmen who attacked the knights and bailiffs carrying coin would steal away their possessions when they moved between their estates. Knights wondered how extra patrols of the sheriff's men and accompanying security for every sack of coin could yield so little result. Even normally peaceable barons believed stricter punishments were needed – hanging and mutilation must be inflicted on anyone found to be aiding the forestmen. They did not realise that many of those attending the banquet would by this ruling be hanged, for Lord Locksley's charitable venture had not been without support. Some of the lords wondered why they had not heard of architects or masons being employed for the scheme, but the fleeting glimpses of bell-wielding hooded figures in the forest were enough to make them glad Lord Locksley just got on with the matter alone.

One question that was on everyone's lips was how these forestmen – never seen, apparently lacking kin or neighbours – knew so much about the movements of the coin and goods they stole? Was someone, Lady de Louvetot whispered, in the sheriff's household feeding them information? Or perhaps, Lord de la Guerche wondered aloud, one of the local lords themselves was feeding a traitor? It was possible that every lord in the county had an untrustworthy servant whose ill treatment had led to vengeance. Which household might be next to have its goods stolen or court fines seized? Lady de Caux was so certain that one of her ladies must be in league with the forestmen that she was doing everything in her power to accommodate the woman and prevent her calling down an army of thieves on the household. Despite their high words of cruel punishments, Robin noted that since the hundredmen's attacks had increased in number, the lords in Nottinghamshire were all treating their attendants more warily – some might even say more kindly.

Robin watched the murmurings and fear weave around the great hall that evening. The Viponts were particularly close, constantly wheeling from one whispered conversation to another, casting dark looks around them then smiling broadly for their guests. They might smile less if they knew that even now the fines inflicted at their manorial court were being tailed through the forest by men with axes and arrows. That thought was a little comfort to Robin. He too was uneasy that evening. But it was not the forestmen's thefts that concerned him. He watched Marian move around the room with Guy, awkwardly making conversation with the local barons, her hand on his arm, her eyes directed shyly at the floor. He had never thought of Marian as weak but in the great hall of Lord Eudo and his kin she looked like a lamb among wolves. The only other woman in their clan was little recommendation for the life of a Lady Vipont. Lady Idonea was pale and sunken-cheeked and silent. Even as she talked to Marian over the heads of the boys – Roger and Jocelyn, clapping and jumping as they watched the tumbler – her smile was thin and apologetic. If she had ever had a spark of independence it was eaten up now.

When Guy was briefly distracted by Lady Foliot's good wishes Robin touched Marian's arm and gestured for her to join him in a window seat. She sat with some relief, allowing herself to abandon her straight-backed, downcast-eyed stance in his presence.

'I wish I could draw a tapestry over my head,' she said in a low voice. 'I do not like having everyone stare at me.'

'You may get your wish. I think Lady Louvetot is about to start singing. With that distraction no one will be looking at you.'

Marian smiled as she peered around the corner of the window, to where a startled pocket of guests were being treated to an Occitan song on the theme of slaying Saracens.

'Poor Lady Louvetot. She does love to sing.'

'Some say love is blind. In Lord Louvetot's case it must be deaf.'

Lord Louvetot looked on contentedly. The Count of Mortain doubled over laughing, his echoing giggles almost as high-pitched as her song. Lords Eudo and Ranulf glanced up from the cups they held close to their faces at the noise. Seeing their beloved count entertained they nodded in satisfaction and returned to their whispered conversation. Serlo was directing Lanfranc about something to do with one of the guests in another dark corner of the hall. Marian followed Robin's eye.

'Are you quite certain,' he asked quietly, 'that you want to marry into that family? I swear I have met assassins with more innocent countenances.'

'It is a little late for that question.' Marian's voice was light, but her honest face could not conceal a hint of anxiety. 'Besides, I am not marrying the whole family.'

'My mistake. I thought that must have been written into the contract.'

'Guy is better than the others. You have seen it yourself, how he helped us with the common land…'

'Which of course was a triumph.'

'He tried, that is what I mean. And once we have our own household we will be able to be more independent of the rest of the family.'

'Of course.' Robin did not believe it, and was convinced Marian did not either. The Viponts moved in packs.

'I hope to see you and Elaine at such a celebration soon.'

'That is in the lap of the royal justices.'

The writ of mort d'ancestor had finally arrived from Westminster, but without the royal justices making their circuit to Nottingham there was no point in the sheriff empanelling a local jury to decide the merits of the case. Everything waited on Westminster to send its judges north. Their continued absence had struck even Sir Walter as suspicious – one might almost imagine that they had been persuaded to stay away from Nottinghamshire.

'I know it is Eudo who holds the Locksley estate, not Guy, but if there is anything at all I can do to influence them...'

'Do not squander your influence in my cause.' Robin smiled. 'All will be well soon enough. The justices cannot stay away forever.'

Marian bit back the last words she would have spoken. Robin knew that, like Elaine, she was going to advise him to court the Viponts rather than waiting for the Royal Justices. But she took the gentle hint and said no more on the subject. She had changed, he thought. On the spur of the moment he leant forward and kissed her cheek. She blinked in surprise.

'Guy is a very fortunate man.'

He pressed her hand and left her to the attentions of the Abbess of Newstead, who had drunk one too many cups of wine and was ready to hold forth on the mysteries of matrimony. Eudo had detached himself from his muttering brother and wandered the hall now with the count, smiling and receiving reverence from every corner. The count found Guy sitting at a table with other young men and seized him playfully by the neck, forcing him to join their escort and pouring him a drink from the jug of wine carried by a servant only a step behind. Guy stayed with them until he caught Robin's eye. Then he made his excuses and came to join Lord Locksley with an awkward smile.

'I hope you are enjoying this evening?'

'Of course.'

'I am glad that any – uh, discord between us is now passed. I know that Marian is very – fond of you.'

That fact did not seem to give him any joy.

'Absence breeds fondness, I find.' And then, because Marian would want it, he added, 'But there was never any real discord between us.'

'Hm, yes.' Guy drank his wine to smooth over that wrinkle. 'I meant the discord between our families. I am glad you have come to terms with my uncle.'

'Terms?'

'He told me about your agreement. I think it is an excellent one. And believe me, I hold no ill will that Peverill Tower will be removed from Marian's marriage portion. It is right that her father returns there.'

Robin did not understand. 'I am not aware of any agreement with Lord Eudo.'

'Forgive me, perhaps I have misunderstood. My uncle seemed very certain about it. He is granting you Locksley Hall to live in until your inheritance is settled by the justices. Sir Walter and Lady Joan are removing to Peverill Tower as soon as Marian is married so that you and Elaine can occupy Locksley.'

'And what am I doing to reward Lord Eudo's generosity?'

Guy blustered, realising he had made a mistake in mentioning the agreement, eager not to displease his family by saying more. Perhaps Robin should go and speak to Sir Walter about it? But Robin would not so easily be swayed. Reluctantly, and looking about to ensure his words would not be overheard by anyone, Guy leant closer.

'As I understand it, you are to allow Jocelyn to remain with my uncle – at least until you have sons of your own to assure their inheritance – and you have agreed not to speak against my family in any cases put before the local courts.'

Losing Jocelyn's wardship, and potentially leaving open a rival claim to the Locksley estate. Supporting the Viponts in all their legal endeavours, right or wrong, and becoming as much their pet as Lords de Caux and de la Guerche. Presumably standing ready to do the Count of Mortain's bidding as well. Those certainly were advantageous terms for the Viponts. But not ones that Robin himself would ever have agreed to, which meant that someone else had been his mouthpiece. Someone who had been trusted as such by Lord Eudo, who was no fool.

'And this was all settled as part of the final marriage negotiations?'

'So – so I believe.'

Robin excused himself before Guy could make any attempt to swear him to secrecy. Marian would not have made such promises on his behalf. Even Lady Joan and Sir Walter would have hesitated to do so without telling him. Which left only one likely culprit. Elaine was with Lord Eudo when Robin found her, fawning over his words and beaming up at him, her perfect pale face lightly flushed at the cheeks. Robin gave Eudo a curt nod. He seized Elaine's arm, demanded a word with her and pulled her away from the man before she could offer a word in argument. He led her all the way through the hall, up the stairs next to the well, past the armoury and into the chill air of the keep's stairwell. She cried out when he released his grip, rubbing her arm and staring at him in amazement. Robin watched her closely as he spoke, his voice harder even than he had expected.

'I hear I have made an agreement with your friend Lord Eudo. I am to give up my family, throw out my mother and surrender my scruples in return for gaining a home that is mine by right.'

Her face flushed, then set angrily – stubbornly – against his accusations.

'A wise agreement for a man who has lived only on the sufferance of his stepfather since Candlemas.'

'Wise or not, it is no agreement of mine. Which means that someone has played me for a fool. Someone has made promises on my behalf and against my interests to benefit the Viponts.'

'Against your interests? How can it be against your interests to restore an estate to you and gain influence with the most powerful lords in the county?'

'I heard of no estate being restored, only Locksley Hall.'

'Where the hall leads, the estate will follow.'

'Show me the document that swears to that.'

That gave her pause.

'Even if this agreement had been wholly to my benefit, I would still refuse to honour it. I cannot keep to a promise made for me by someone else.'

'I am not just anyone else. Your interests are mine –'

'If that was true you would not have gone to Lord Eudo and the others claiming to act on my behalf. They must have known you were not speaking with my consent, and if they did not they will have thought that I am incapable of acting on my own – that I have to hide behind a lady's skirts. You made me look like a weak fool.'

'No more of a fool than I appear. I have only your word and the promise of my parents that we will ever marry. There has been no contract signed.'

'How can I sign a contract when I have nothing to promise you?'

'Precisely.' She said it coldly. 'My mother will not agree to our marrying until you have your estate restored to you, and yet at every opportunity to gain Lord Vipont's trust, to win his influence for your cause, you have defied and ridiculed him. It seems that your enmity for Lord Eudo matters more to you than the restoration of your inheritance and certainly matters more than me.'

'That is not true. I wish to marry you, that has not changed…'

'But nor has anything else. What would we live on if we married? My dowry? That will be small indeed when I marry Lackland Locksley.'

Those words stung Robin worse than anything she had said. He struggled to suppress his anger, to be rational.

'I will regain my lands. The royal justices have to visit Nottinghamshire on their circuit, it is just a matter of time. Then my estate will be restored. With the sheriff supporting me and the local lords recognising me as my father's son, it will happen. And when it does I do not want to be bound by an alliance that is wholly against my conscience, never mind my interests. I will not take back my estate at the price of being the Viponts' lapdog.'

'You are impossible! How can friendship with the Viponts be against your conscience? What crimes have they committed?'

'They stole the common land.'

'The count did that.'

'They stole my land.'

'They believed you dead.'

'They have squeezed their tenants and my tenants and our neighbours' tenants until the pips squeaked out of them. They use the law only to help themselves, never to honour their responsibilities as lords.'

'Every lord's first responsibility is to his estate. They know that, Sir Walter knows it, every lord in Nottinghamshire knows it except you.'

Her words echoed from the roof of the stairwell, leaving a ringing silence in their wake. From the armoury came an awkward cough. Elaine lowered her voice.

'I pleaded with my mother to allow our betrothal. She did not want it for me. She has had other offers from lords who still hold their own estates, but I was certain.'

'Then perhaps you should pursue those other offers.'

Elaine's face flickered with uncertainty. 'You wish to end our betrothal?'

'No, I do not wish it. But I would not keep you from having what you want in a marriage. Nor can I easily forget that you went behind my back to make promises on my behalf – promises that you knew that I did not want to make. Marian and I had our differences, but she never would have deceived me in this way.'

Elaine's cheeks flushed fiercely. Without glancing in his direction she swept past him back into the keep. As she passed him, the trailing hem of her sleeve brushed against his side. The touch felt like a strike. He had spoken more calmly than he felt. In that moment he could have seized Lord Eudo and Elaine and dashed their heads together against a wall. A few months ago he might have felt powerless. Lackland Locksley Elaine had called him, and where land was power, he had absolutely none. But he had something else now. He had the Hundred of the Arrow at his back, and it was in his ability to knock Eudo from his horse in the hunt and leave him tied to a tree for days if he chose. Appealing as that prospect was, he would not act on it. He would strike Eudo where he would really be hurt – his influence, his allies. If he lost the trust of his fellow lords and precious count, it would be a crueller blow to him. The hundredmen had waited long enough. It was time now to take their revenge on Lord Eudo de Vipont.

A morning mist still veiled the dim light beyond the window and Marian was sleeping when Elaine stormed through their bedchamber. She shook her cousin and sat on her arm as she tried to wake her.

'He has gone out.'

Marian rubbed her eyes in confusion. 'Who? My father?'

'Of course not. Lord Locksley.' Something large and woollen landed on Marian's legs. Elaine leant close. 'Put your mantle on. We are going to follow him.'

'Why?'

'Because,' Elaine hissed, 'he must have a mistress.'

'He does not.'

'How would you know? His father did.'

'Yes, and everyone knew of it.'

Elaine tugged Marian and she let herself be pulled to her feet. Gytha had also been roused from her sleep and regarded the pair now with pursed lips and suspicion.

'Elaine wishes to have a morning ride,' said Marian. 'We will take attendants.'

Marian told Estrild to fetch Waltheof while Gytha dressed her. Elaine was already dressed and pacing the chamber. The instant Marian was decent she ran to meet the servants by their waiting horses.

'He went into the forest,' said Elaine, leaping into her saddle. 'Not towards his bastard brother's home, but north. We must be quick if we are to catch him.'

She set off at a gallop, her head turning this way and that to see signs of Robin's passing. Marian allowed her to get some way ahead before realising she was not going to slow her pace and increasing her own. She did not believe Robin had a mistress, but if cantering through the forest would do anything to calm Elaine she would go along with it. Marian did not know what had occurred between the two of them at the celebrations last night but both had returned in foul spirits. Perhaps once they found Robin Marian could try to reconcile them.

They were riding a long way, she noticed. The King's Way, which swung around from Nottingham, had risen up to meet them. Elaine crossed over the road and into the forest on the other side, passing an old carved tree with a begging bowl leaning against its roots. The sound of a bell echoed through the trees. Elaine drew up her horse and looked around in confusion.

'Have you lost the trail?' Marian asked.

'No,' said Elaine, refusing to admit defeat.

Waltheof was at Marian's side.

'I do not think it would be wise to go any further, my lady. You know that this forest is full of thieves and outlaws. If we are caught by a mob of felons I may not be able to hold them off for long enough to allow you ladies to escape.'

'Do not doubt yourself,' called Elaine. 'I have total faith in your ability to defend us.'

She spurred her horse on. Marian called after her to try to persuade her to follow Waltheof's advice but she would not heed. Just as Marian nudged her own horse to chase after Elaine she noticed a carving in one of the trees close by. It looked like the shape of an arrow had been scratched there. Odd. It was not the only such symbol in that stretch of the forest. The arrows pointed in different directions, some barb up, some feather. They did not seem to be showing a path through the forest, but the freshness of some of the carvings gave Marian pause.

Elaine slowed her pace now. The trees closed in more tightly around them and scrubby bushes threatened to stumble their horses.

'Perhaps Waltheof is right,' Marian said in a low voice. 'We can ask Robin what he has been up to when he arrives home.'

'He will lie. You told me yourself that he used to ride out into the forest alone, sometimes staying there all night. It *must* be a woman. That is the only reason he would –'

She broke off. Voices. Not much further ahead. The voices carried back to them through the forest. There was movement too, pale colours amidst the trees. Marian seized Elaine's bridle to halt her. They were only yards away from the figures in the trees – a number of them if Marian saw right, and all gathered close. Thieves, she thought.

'We should not go any closer.'

'But it is him.'

'It may not be. I do not wish to be robbed today…'

'Oh calm yourself.'

Elaine forced Marian's fingers from her bridle and surged into the press of figures between the trees. Swallowing a swelling tide of fear, Marian followed at a distance. She heard Elaine's voice crying out. Then another voice. It was Robin. She moved more swiftly to join them, overtaken by relief.

'Thank God. I was afraid we had ridden into a pack of outlaws…'

The smile died on her lips. Robin was there, with other men gathered about him, and Elaine still on horseback glowering. But something was not right. The men hurriedly pushed up their hoods – greying mantles of cheap, patched wool. One or two of them carried bells, one of them held a bucket filled with bread and dried meat. They looked to be lepers, but… Marian approached one of them and pushed back his hood. It was Tova's son, the one she had given charity to all those months ago. He smiled weakly. She had heard nothing to suggest he was sick. She reached for the hood of the next man and a hand came up to stop her. Dirty fingers gripped her wrist and a pair of dark eyes bored into her.

'Leave it.'

'Take your hand off her,' Elaine cried. She turned on Robin. 'Who are those men? Order them to unhand Marian.'

Robin murmured something. The hooded man released his grip, but did not reveal his face.

'Tenants,' said Robin. 'I have been offering them charity.'

They had been tenants, Marian knew that true enough as she peered into the hoods that they tried to conceal themselves with. But they were not any longer. She knew these men. Almost all of them, she knew. She had heard their names when their kin came to her pleading for mercy. She had heard their names again when her father cursed them after Easter. She had heard their names when the courts had declared them outlaws and their livelihoods forfeit because they had fled from justice. These were the hundredmen who had escaped Nottingham Castle.

She looked at Robin, and immediately wished she had not. She did not have a mummer's face. She could never mask her thoughts; they invaded her expression before she could even try to check them. Robin read her face – her expression – her thoughts. And he knew that she had recognised these men. He also knew that Elaine had not.

'Take your food and be on your way,' he said to the men. 'God keep you.'

They crossed themselves, bowed, nodded, scurried away as quickly as they could.

'*That* is why you rode out so early this morning?' cried Elaine. 'I did not even see you carrying food.'

'I was.' Robin was still watching Marian. 'And now I have delivered it, we should return to the hall. This forest is not a safe place for ladies.'

'I tried to tell them that,' said Waltheof. 'But my lady insisted.'

What was that? Marian thought. A glance between Waltheof and Robin. Only an instant's contact, but something had passed between them. Robin mounted his horse and moved alongside Elaine. Waltheof was beside Marian. She wanted to ask if he had recognised the men as well but something checked her. That glance made her suspect – she did not know what. But the man she had trusted so implicitly until a moment before now gave her cause for doubt. She followed Elaine and Robin in silence all the way back to the hall.

They, however, were not silent. Elaine muttered and whispered, complaining it seemed, although about what Marian did not hear. Perhaps her old complaint about Robin not seeking the influence of their neighbours. Whatever she said, it did not please Robin. He was silent and loudly vexed by turn. As soon as they reached Locksley Hall's stables Elaine leapt from the saddle and stormed inside. Marian made to follow her but was stalled by a hand on her arm.

'We should speak.'

Robin's hold was not firm but he had rarely touched her in the years that they had known each other, and his grip now, between her elbow and shoulder in the soft flesh of her arm, was peculiarly intimate. She allowed herself to be led away from the hall and towards the silent open space of the parkland that surrounded the building. Behind them Waltheof said something to Estrild to send her away and then followed at a distance. When they were beyond the hearing of the sheriff's servants Robin released Marian. Perhaps unconsciously, his hand went to the sword at his hip. He spoke in a low, serious tone that Marian had not heard in him before.

'It is very important that you do not lie to me. Did you know those men?'

'I…' There seemed nothing to gain from deceit. Not when her own face could betray her. 'Yes.'

'Are you going to tell your father you saw them?'

'I had not thought yet. How did you come to be offering them aid?'

'They are my friends.'

'They *are*? When I last asked you about them you told me they were the foolish friends of your childhood.'

'They were. They are still.'

Her head swam with questions. She hardly knew which to ask first. All this time, all these months since the men escaped, had he known they were disguised in the forest? Had he known that the leper's hospital whose cause he had so zealously pursued was nothing but a front for fugitives?

'The leper's hospital that you have been gathering funds for. Are any of those men truly sick?'

'Not with leprosy. But they are in need, and they will get no help if I do not give it to them.'

There was some truth in that. She was hardly able to cast stones when it came to methods of helping those in need, nor of exactly who to help. But if what she had heard was true, these men hardly deserved charity. They were thieves as well as fugitives. Of course, what she had heard came from the sheriff and the Viponts. It might not be the whole story.

'My father thinks that those men stole from the tax wagons. Do you know anything about that?'

'I think they are innocent.'

A fine way not to answer her question. Despite herself, she smiled. Robin sighed heavily.

'I would like to tell you everything, Marian. But I cannot. You will be married soon and your loyalty will be to them. His family. If I told you about this, you would end up telling them – perhaps you would not mean to, or want to, but you would do it in the end.'

'Women are as capable of keeping secrets as men.'

'I do not doubt that.'

'But you doubt me?'

He said nothing. Even as her lips parted to ask more she paused. He was right, about her loyalty at least. Robin had been almost a family member to her since their childhoods – albeit a family member of peculiar form, who had at times utterly infuriated her – but he would not remain so for long. A stepbrother could not take precedence over a husband, she was wise enough in the ways of marriage to know that. She did not begrudge those forestmen their freedom and if Robin claimed they were innocent she ought to believe his word. If her father or Guy asked her about the hundredmen she knew she could not dissemble, and if anything she told them led to those men being killed she did not think her conscience would stand it. Robin was right. There was sometimes danger in knowing too much.

'I will not ask you more questions.'

'Let me ask you one. Will you tell your father that you saw me helping them?'

And here was an example of the dangers of knowledge. She could not deceive her father. But what would be gained from telling him that Robin had given food to the hundredmen? He would demand to know the men's location, rail that Robin must stop helping them, order him to reveal what he knew about their crimes. He might be so angry that Robin would be turned out of the hall, and then where would he go? Guy would not let him stay with him and the only other kin he had lived in a leaking croft in the forest. Besides, it would make little difference. Robin would either continue to help his friends or he would not, and

Marian would not know of it.

'I saw you giving charity to men in need, as we have all heard that you do. It is not necessary for me to tell him anything more.'

His face beamed with relief.

'Thank you.'

'Tell me one thing in return though. My man, Waltheof. He has been helping you, hasn't he?'

'He – he knows the hundredmen through Thorfridh. He has offered a little assistance.'

'He did not tell me of it.'

'I asked him not to. He has broken no confidence of yours, believe me.'

Just as Marian suspected. The deceit in her trusted servant stung. She had believed that Waltheof was loyal to her above others – and he had been one of the few in her father's home whose loyalty she had so trusted.

'I do not want servants who keep secrets from me. Perhaps it would be better he becomes part of your household from now on. He can help you better that way.'

'Please do not give up your trust in him on my account.'

But that trust was already lost. Marian forced a smile. 'Make him your almoner. He has proven himself adept at giving charity.'

Michaelmas

The hundredmen of the Arrow were all in agreement that Lord Eudo de Vipont needed to be singled out for particular attention. Humiliating Lanfranc and depriving the Viponts of their court fines was satisfying, but what they really wanted was to cast a blow that wounded not only the Vipont pride but also their interests. The difficulty had been finding an opportunity. Since Lanfranc's public mortification Lord Eudo's household had kept itself close. The servants always travelled in pairs, visitors to the castle were watched closely and the forest avoided whenever possible. Even during the dry season when hunting was at its best the Viponts had eschewed their traditional sport for hawking and rides out in the open fields. But they could not avoid the forest forever and as Michaelmas approached Robin at last found his opportunity. The Count of Mortain was coming to Clipstone Park to hunt, and the Viponts had been invited to join him. They would not refuse the chance to meet their prince and they also could not reach Clipstone without passing through the forest. As if that were not clear enough evidence of divine sanction for the hundredmen, when the Viponts rode to meet their precious count they would be carrying half the furnishings of Nottingham's royal wardrobe with them.

A royal harbinger brought Lord Eudo the request. Most of the furnishings for Clipstone had been left in the wardrobe of Nottingham Castle and the count was not a man to do without his comforts. The harbinger asked that Lord Eudo arrange for the furnishings to accompany them when they came to Clipstone. Peter the clerk gave Robin a copy of the message the same day that the Viponts received it. When Robin read it he knew that this was the chance the hundredmen had waited for. Not only could they taunt the Viponts, but also lower them in the estimation of their precious Count of Mortain. A few fine furnishings would not go amiss in the Hundred either – with more kin arriving in the clearing they did not have enough mattresses to sleep on and Flemish tapestries would be more comfortable than earth and straw.

'We should throw the lot of it on a midden,' was Kolbrand's suggestion for what to do with the furnishings. He picked the dirt from his nails with a knife. 'See how he likes his lions and leopards caked in shit.'

'We should throw Lord Vipont on a midden,' said Lefchild.

'Throw the count…' called Much.

The men laughed. Robin had handed Peter's information from the harbinger to Gilbert, for the group to hear aloud. The prospect of this double blow against the Viponts and the count, whose residence at the castle last winter had robbed so many of their food, had cheered all their spirits.

'We can decide what to do with it all once we've got it,' said John Blunt.

'Robin, we need to know how many men are going to be with the Viponts. Can the clerk tell us?'

'Hopefully. He's keeping watch for any more messages in the chancery.'

'Will the Viponts ride with the wagons carrying the wardrobe?'

'I don't think so. I expect them to leave that to the count's steward. He's coming to Nottingham Castle the day before, then he will probably take the wagons at dawn. My guess would be that the Viponts follow them in the afternoon.'

'It should be easier if the lords are not there.'

'What if the guards have crossbows?' asked Much. 'We couldn't take the dues being carried to Lord de la Guerche because his men were too well-armed.'

'What a bloody waste of a day that was,' Kolbrand grumbled. 'Sat on our arses in trees.'

'We could take their strings?' Will suggested. 'As long as the armoury isn't too well-watched.'

'You'd still need to get into the keep in the first place,' said Robin, looking at the sky. It was a dull dagger grey. 'The simplest thing would be if it rained and their strings got too wet to use.'

'Ah, so prayer is the way forward. Who's the saint who intercedes for weather? Medard?'

'No, it's St Eurosia,' said Gilbert.

'It's not.'

'Pray to them both,' said Robin, 'and maybe one will listen.'

Perhaps the men's prayers were answered. Since the harvest was gathered the rain had held itself in check, but as Michaelmas approached the clouds burst. For three days there was drizzle, a mist that clung to the skin and drenched the clothes, enough that the roads grew slippery and the rivers lapped higher at their banks. Robin rode to the castle on a path whose potholes were deepening. It would not take much to trap a wagon's wheel or a horse's hoof in those, especially if nature was given a little help by spades. The only trouble might be if the royal steward decided to delay the movement of the furnishings until the roads had cleared. But if the count demanded his tapestries, the steward would have to provide them. Robin was hopeful that the count's steel will would show itself again.

His faith was rewarded when he arrived at the castle to meet Peter. The clerk came to speak to him in an antechamber of the keep, loudly discussing the planned circuits of the royal justices in the half-year to Lady's Day. The keep might belong to the Count of Mortain, but it was also a space over which the sheriff could claim precedence, so the Viponts could not ask Robin's business there. Once they were in the solitude of the antechamber Peter told Robin what he had heard and read.

'The Lords Vipont will not travel with the wagon. There is going to be a meeting of the county court the day before the count's arrival at Clipstone, which may overrun, so the steward will leave with the wagon at first light and the Viponts will follow when the court concludes.'

'How many men accompany it?'

'I have made a note of all the arrangements I have heard, and a few lines copied from messages between the steward and the lords. Here it is – oh, excuse me.'

He fumbled the document in passing it. Both Peter and Robin leant to pick it up. As they did so a shadow fell across them. Robin jolted back upright to find the door opened. Elaine and Marian stood there. Marian reached to pick up the scrap of vellum that had wafted towards them in the sudden draught from the door. Robin was next to her, seizing it back before her eyes had glanced at it. But Elaine was faster even than him. She frowned as Robin rolled it up.

'What are you doing in here? There is no marriage for you to arrange any more.'

'I still need to regain my estate,' said Robin, matching her coldness, 'with or without a wife.'

'Forgive us for intruding,' said Marian. She touched Elaine on the arm to encourage her to leave. Elaine turned on her heel but left the door open. Robin hurried to close it, lowering his voice.

'Could they have read what was written there?'

'I think not.'

Robin took the paper and pushed it inside his clothes so it was held in concealment under his belt.

'It is fortunate that was not the sheriff.'

'Yes,' said Robin. 'Best not to push our good fortune. I will leave. Thank you.'

Robin left the clerk to make his own way back to the chancery. He needed to get this information to the hundredmen as quickly as possible, before his good luck turned sour.

Since Elaine and Robin had ended their betrothal there had been little sign of the affection that had once existed between them. Marian wondered how long their feelings would have remained if they had married, once it was clear that a crusader-knight, even a lord of Locksley, did not have the estate a lady like Elaine required for her desired lifestyle. She loved her cousin as the only female companion of her own rank she had ever really known, but it was some relief to anticipate a future where they would not always be thrown together, when meetings at Peverill Tower between her father, stepmother and Lord and Lady Locksley would be inevitable. Managing Guy and Robin's antagonism would be enough of a burden. Then again, perhaps their relationship had changed. She had seen them speaking to each other equably enough at the betrothal feast. She had never given Guy any cause to be envious of Robin, and very much doubted he had ever done anything to inspire jealousy in Guy. It should be no concern of Guy's that, but for one mistake four years ago, Marian would have been Lady Locksley. But then at least such jealousy was a sign of Guy's fondness for her. She might almost have said love. For herself, she did not feel for him the great love that troubadours wrote and sang of, but she definitely felt affection, and that was enough to begin with. It was more than some felt in their whole marriage.

She realised she had walked ahead of Elaine. Her cousin was still loitering in the hall, watching the clerk Robin had been speaking with as he left the antechamber. There was nothing remarkable about the man but Elaine's eyes were eagle-fierce as she traced his passage across the hall and out down the stairwell. Marian rejoined her.

'Are you all right? I know it must be difficult to see Robin now…'

Elaine was not listening. 'I need to find Lord Eudo. Where do you think he will be?'

'I – Guy did not mention his being in the keep, so I suppose he may be in the middle bailey somewhere? Perhaps in his own chambers?'

Elaine nodded and set off in that direction. Marian told her attendants to have their riding clothes moved to the hall of the middle bailey and pursued her. If Waltheof had been there Marian would have talked to him about Elaine, sought his opinion on why she might be seeking Guy's uncle now. But Estrild and Edgar were too well-schooled in their duties to offer advice. They were good, reliable servants and they would not risk their positions as Waltheof had, helping the sheriff's daughter to follow her conscience against her father's wishes. As she went into the lodgings in the middle bailey she saw Waltheof ride out alongside Robin. She wondered if they were going to help the men in the forest again. Was that what the clerk's paper had been connected with? It must have contained something illicit for Robin to react so fiercely at its revelation. Elaine had stopped. She smiled at Marian sweetly.

'There is no need for you to come with me, my heart. It is just a little private matter. You should go ahead home.'

'My father said we must always travel with two attendants. I cannot leave without both my attendants, and I cannot leave you alone.'

'I am certain Lord Vipont will provide me with attendants if I request them.'

That was a presumption. Marian wondered at Elaine's sudden certainty in Lord Eudo's concern for her comfort. And why the urgent desire to speak with him now? Something in Elaine's behaviour made her uneasy.

'I will wait. I will not intrude on your privacy, of course – I can sit in the next chamber.'

That did not seem to please Elaine, but since Marian was now a month from being Lady Vipont and Elaine was an unmarried younger cousin she could not deny her. Lord Eudo looked surprised to see them, which at least suggested this was not a premeditated visit, and Marian quickly excused herself to the fireside in the antechamber with her attendants while Elaine conducted whatever business had brought her there. A tapestry hung halfway across the antechamber's entrance to keep its warmth in, but it did not fully muffle the sounds of conversation in the next chamber. Marian did not wish to eavesdrop, but it was hard not to. She gestured for Edgar and Estrild to carry on their work, laying out the still-damp mantles and riding boots from their journey to the castle, while she sat close to the tapestry.

Elaine and Lord Eudo stood at some distance in the chamber so some of their early conversation was lost, but when Marian heard her own name her ears pricked up. She moved her eye to the edge of the tapestry. If they have nothing to hide, she thought, then it does not matter that I listen. Eudo and Elaine were standing near the window, their forms silhouetted against the rivulets of rain that wound down the panes. They were close enough to embrace when Eudo spoke with a smile.

'It is always a delight to receive you, my lady. But I fear that Lord Locksley will be far from happy to hear we have spoken alone again.'

'What Lord Locksley feels is of no importance to me, since we are no longer betrothed.'

'My lady.' Eudo took Elaine's pale hand in both of his, holding it close against his heart. His face was all sudden sincerity and sympathy. 'I had heard whispers to that effect, but it grieves me to hear they are true. Will this deprive us all of your presence? Are you to leave Locksley Hall?'

'Not yet. I shall stay until Marian is married, so I may help her with her preparations, and then perhaps I shall return to my mother's home. Or Sir Walter may request that I join him and Lady Joan at Peverill Tower.'

'The latter would be more pleasing to everyone here at the castle. My daughter-in-law regards you as a true friend. And I would be sorry to see you leave also.'

Marian was on the brink of announcing herself. There was something so intimate in Lord Eudo's behaviour towards Elaine, and in Elaine's acquiescence to it, that she did not feel she could remain to witness it without breaching some confidence. However, the next moment her cousin spoke and all her resolve to leave was gone.

'If I do leave, there is something I feel I must tell you. I pray you will not be angry with me, but Marian and I heard a little of how those prisoners escaped at Easter. That somehow they had got hold of a document with the sheriff's seal. Have I understood correctly?'

'Yes. But this is not a suitable topic for me to discuss with a lady.'

'You are right of course. Only I did so wonder about that clerk hiding in the closet –'

'Which clerk?'

She had dropped the words like crumbs before a bird, and Lord Eudo of course leapt to follow them.

'One of the clerks in the chancery has been assisting Lord Locksley with his inheritance dispute. I introduced them, to tell the truth. Peter is his name. He came from Westminster.'

'What does this Peter have to do with the prisoners?'

'I just saw Peter giving Lord Locksley a document. I cannot be certain but it looked to have some marks of the sheriff's office upon it. They were exchanging the paper in ridiculous secrecy, in a closet in the keep, and although Lord Locksley claimed it was connected to his estate I am certain I saw reference to the Count of Mortain's household there, and the name of the count's steward. I do not know the reason for the secrecy or the deceit but clearly this clerk – whether alone or with his brothers in the chancery – is conveying information and papers out of the chancery, presumably for some fee. I do not think it impossible that one of those clerks was an accomplice to that man you hanged for releasing the prisoners.'

Eudo raised his hand and toyed with his beard. 'Did you see anything more that was written on this document?'

Elaine turned to face the window and her voice was lost as a log in the antechamber fire split in two, crackling and startling Marian out of her concentration. The rest of Elaine and Lord Eudo's conversation was lost to her. She fell into her own thoughts as she stared into the hearth. Thorfridh had taken the alms into the castle – Robin had admitted that – and he had somehow been able to show not only the legitimate documentation from the sheriff permitting him to do so, but also the falsified one allowing the prisoners to visit church, and thus escape. Was it possible that Robin himself had provided the second document? If so it was surely foolish to be known to do business with the clerk, Peter. Had Robin told Elaine something that might lead her to suspect Peter with such certainty that she now raised the matter with Eudo? If he had been so cautious of keeping information from Marian because of her connection to the Viponts, surely he would have been so with Elaine? But then, he might not know of Elaine's closeness to Eudo. Marian's head span. She ought to find Robin and demand to know the truth. But perhaps it was better to maintain her ignorance, for fear of what she might learn. Maybe, then, it was best to ask Elaine if Robin had told her anything. But then…

'I am ready to leave.'

Marian started as Elaine pulled back the tapestry to speak. Elaine laughed. A closing door and sound of departing footsteps told Marian that Eudo had left the chamber.

'I did not mean to startle you – you must have been thinking very deeply.'

'Yes.'

Marian smiled. As they put on their boots and mantles Elaine chattered away cheerfully, without any indication of the furtive conversation she had just been having. Marian half-listened, her mind still churning. Best to wait, she thought. Wait, listen. And make sure that Elaine did not make any future visits to the castle unaccompanied.

The last preparations were under way in the Hundred of the Arrow when Robin arrived. He could not take part in the raid. It was likely he would still be sitting in the county court in the morning, and as he did so he could watch the Viponts and alert the men if the lords made any last minute changes to their plan. Waltheof would be ready to ride out of the castle's stables at a moment's notice to follow the route of the count's wagons and warn the hundredmen if that happened. In his absence, leadership of the men was disputed between John Blunt and Will. Much and Kolbrand also loudly proclaimed their ability to lead this raid, but Robin trusted neither to do so. In truth, he would have been far happier to give the position to John, but Will was uncharacteristically dedicated to the task and refused to stand aside for him. The hundredmen would follow Robin's wishes in this – they might pay taxes to no one but themselves, but they still observed God's natural order of things when it came to their rank – and so it was he alone who must decide. Will grabbed him by the arm while John was distracted attaching flights to the arrows arranged in a pile at the fireside. Edeva silently copied him, taking little more time than the fletcher himself. Robin was glad that his faith in the girl had not been misplaced. Will walked him all the way to the stream before speaking.

'Have you made up your mind?'

'Not yet.'

'Why not? It's clear you should choose me. They follow your orders because you're a lord and they'll follow mine as much because I'm a lord's son as because you tell them to.'

Robin was not convinced of that. Will had not been raised as a lord. The men knew him as Agnes Scarlette's boy, quick-fingered and fast-talking, but the reason for his continued existence was held to be just as much good luck as good sense. Seeing Robin's doubt, Will changed tack.

'Please, brother. The men already trust John, he was their chief tithing-man before. But if you overlook me now when they know I wanted to lead, they'll lose respect for me.'

'You freed them from prison, Will. They will always respect you.'

'No, *you* freed them while I knelt at an altar – my knees still haven't recovered. They barely saw what I did for them.'

There was some truth in that. Will had not taken part in anywhere near the same number of raids and ambushes as the other men because he had so often been needed to provide Robin with an alibi. That was an important role – if Robin the forestman was recognised as Lord Locksley all the support and protection he provided for the men would be gone the instant he was arrested – but it was not one that earned Will much respect. And while John was the natural leader of these men in Robin's absence, if anything happened to him in the future, it would be wise to have another second-in-command the men would trust. Otherwise they might end up with Kolbrand as their leader through sheer force of willpower.

'All right. You lead this. But you keep your face covered and don't take any needless risks. If they carry dry crossbows, you let them pass.'

Will grinned, seized his brother on both cheeks and kissed his forehead. 'You won't be sorry for this.'

Robin wished that he had Will's certainty.

The day of the county court arrived, and sure enough there was so much to be settled at this busiest time of year that some cases were held over until the next morning. The rain held off, the sky lightened and when Robin arrived at the castle shortly after dawn it was to find the Count of Mortain's steward leading three wagons of royal furnishings out of the barbican and north, towards Clipstone. Robin sought Guy when he entered the hall and inquired if his family were still intending to follow the wagon that afternoon.

'Yes, as soon as our business here is concluded. Our horses are already saddled. I hope this court will not need to sit for more than another hour.'

Unfortunately for Guy, his wish was not to be fulfilled. Every hour that the court remained in session was another hour for the hundredmen to take on the count's men without the interference of the Vipont guard. Robin was acutely aware of this and took up considerable court time that morning querying witnesses on irrelevant details, asking for documents to be produced when they had long since been buried away in a lord's chancery, asking for clarification on a point of law that a royal justice would have been hard-pressed to answer. With every hour delayed the Viponts' faces grew darker and Robin's spirits rose. By now, he thought, the wagon will be nearing the thicker part of the forest, where the road is at its worst. By now the wheels of the first wagon will have caught in a mud-plugged dent in the path. By now half the guards will have been drawn away by thieves disappearing into the forest. By now the men will be cutting the horses' harness and diving back into the hedges at the roadside.

But eventually he could stall them no longer. The last case was heard before the bells chimed for Nones and Robin had to hope that the time he had given them would prove to be enough. An image presented itself of Kolbrand's fancy about the Count of Mortain's tapestries lying in a midden. There was a certain appeal to it now, he thought.

Robin accompanied Sir Walter on the road back to Locksley Hall. The sheriff was always in good humour after a court assize, when the thought of all the fines he had imposed flying towards his coffers combined with a more altruistic glow of appreciation for justice dispensed to the many.

'That fellow's going at a pace,' Sir Walter said as the town walls faded behind them. A lone rider was pounding the road coming south from the forest. 'Is he wearing the count's crest?'

A shudder slipped down Robin's spine. The Viponts had not even left for Clipstone yet. It was very early for word of the attack on the count's wagons to be returning to the castle. But when the sheriff waved the rider to a halt his fears were confirmed.

'The Count of Mortain's train has been attacked on the King's Way. My lord steward sent me to rally men to capture the thieves.'

'Thieves?' said Sir Walter. 'They try to steal from the count himself? Then we should not delay. We will follow you with our attendants and I will send one of my men to the castle for more.'

The sheriff's orders were quickly obeyed and the count's guard returned the way he had come to take them to the ambushed wagons.

It was strange to arrive at the aftermath of one of the hundredmen's raids. The three wagons had been gutted, axe wounds visible in their flanks, remnants of their contents scattered across the muddy ground. The guards were also spread far and wide, some clearly wounded, others tentatively exploring the forest for signs of the departed thieves. Arrows littered the road and were embedded into the wagon. The count's steward, sword still in hand, was directing his men for a search when the sheriff and Robin arrived. He started when he saw Robin, then shook his head as if dispelling a fantasy. There was blood pooling in the mud in places. The sight of it gave Robin pause. The hundredmen always intended to spill as little blood as possible. They had clearly made off with the goods as planned, but had there been injury to their own side during the skirmish?

'How much did they take?' Sir Walter asked.

The steward sheathed his sword and shook his head. 'Almost everything. They even took the saddlebag from my horse. They left the horse roaming the forest.'

'Are many of your men injured?'

'Half-a-dozen perhaps. The thieves were not mere opportunists. They had clearly planned this attack, drew half my men into the forest away from the wagons before attacking the rest, loosing the horses and stealing everything they could lay their hands on. They must have had accomplices waiting in the forest, for the stuff was gone before we could reach our crossbows.'

The crossbows had been jumbled into one wagon to keep dry and still lay there, although it looked like handfuls of bolts had been taken. Sir Walter noticed the odd angle of the first wagon, tilting into a pothole and blocking the passage of the rest.

'We think they dug that too.'

'Another planned attack,' Sir Walter sighed to Robin. 'How are these outlaws so well-informed? The count only requested his wardrobe be sent to him last week.'

'You are certain this was dug by men?' Robin asked of the hole.

He did not want the sheriff pursuing his line of thought. It could too easily lead to the castle chancery and thence to Peter the clerk. In fact, any means by which Robin could cast doubt on a planned attack, with inside information, would be to his benefit.

'The weather has been terrible these past few weeks, and this road is always sorely in need of repair.'

'It is possible.'

Behind the steward one of the guards rotated his sword arm in a stretch and Robin saw smears of blood there. He addressed the guard.

'Are you injured?'

'Not badly, my lord. I cut down one of theirs before he inflicted much damage.'

Cut down?

'Was he badly hurt?'

'One of them dragged him off, so I hope so.' He dipped a toe in one of the red pools. 'That's his.'

Robin wanted to ask more of this guard but before he could there was a commotion from the shrubs. A pair of the count's men dragged a hooded figure by the cloak around his neck. They threw him down before the sheriff and he landed up to his wrists in mud.

'We found this one running through the forest towards the road. Think he could be one of the thieves.'

The sheriff gestured and the figure's hood was drawn back. It was Much.

'That is not a thief,' said Robin quickly. 'He works for me, running messages.'

'What is he doing here?'

'Probably bringing me word of this attack. Is that so, boy?' he added in English.

Much nodded uncertainly. He seemed to want to say more but hesitated in front of the guards.

'Hmpf.' Sir Walter turned back to the steward to co-ordinate the search for the thieves before they could completely disappear to their hiding places. Much got to his feet quickly, but Robin led him away from the scene before letting him speak. Only then did he notice that the boy's hands were smeared all over – not just with mud but blood.

'Who's hurt?'

'Will. Badly.'

Robin did not wait to hear more before calling to Sir Walter.

'I am no use to you here, Sheriff. Let me ride back to Locksley Hall and I will call more men out for the search. They should be with you in an hour or two. That way you do not have to rely on Vipont men alone.'

Sir Walter agreed swiftly enough. He did not want the Viponts getting all the credit if they managed to find these thieves and restore the count's possessions. Waltheof pulled Much up onto the back of his horse and they followed Robin down the road at a reasonable pace until they were out of sight and sound of the sheriff's men.

'How badly hurt is he?' Robin asked.

'Bad. He's at the croft with Agnes now, but he needs a surgeon.'

Robin could not trust a physician from Sir Walter's household, nor could he rely on a townsman's silence, even if he was paid to keep it.

'I'll ride for the friar. Waltheof, go back to the hall and tell them about the attack. Send men back to the sheriff as quick as you can and gather linens, wine and honey to bring to the Scarlette croft.'

'If anyone asks I'll say Agnes is ill.'

'Good. Much, run back to the croft and tell them what we're doing. If the roads are kind we might even be back there before you.'

Much leapt from Waltheof's horse and the three of them set off in their different directions. Robin rode as if the devil was at his horse's tail. He passed a group of the Viponts' men riding in the opposite direction, eager to take up the hunt for the thieves. If Will had been injured, would the men have been able to return safely to the clearing? Would they have watched to ensure they were not followed, that their tracks were not easily traced? John must have taken command when he saw Will wounded, unless his blood had been among the other pools scattered across the road. For a moment Robin was overcome by anger. He should not have allowed his brother to lead the men. He had known that Will's eagerness would overcome caution, and yet he had allowed himself to be persuaded, and for what? Just so that Will did not lose face in front of the other men? He might lose a good deal more than that now, and in the absence of clear leadership the other men might well find themselves lugging tapestries in a circle that would swiftly be bisected by the sheriff's men. With these anxieties for company the ride to Lenton Priory seemed to take hours.

Some angel must have been watching over Will that day for Friar Toki had just returned from an extended perambulation of the local villages when Robin arrived at his cell. Despite his evident fatigue the friar hurried to the hospital and gathered together various supplies, which he bundled into a wooden case and a sack, attaching them to the back of the aged horse the priory had loaned him. The horse was too ancient for speed and Robin feared what they might arrive to find at the croft, delayed by its ambling pace. There was a line of guardsmen across the King's Way where it met the green lanes towards Locksley, warning all traffic to turn back as the Count of Mortain's steward had been attacked. They permitted Lord Locksley and the friar to pass freely, but the effort being expended by the sheriff, Viponts and count's steward made Robin uneasy. How long could the hundredmen conceal themselves and their rich spoils from such a combined force? Perhaps it had been folly to attack a prince's possessions.

At last they reached the Scarlette croft. Much was outside, keeping watch. When Robin saw him he threw the reins of his horse towards him and ran inside. There was a metallic tang overlaying the usual stale smell in the croft. A copper was bubbling over the hearth, blood-soaked linens being blanched in a pail of boiled water next to it. A lot of blood-soaked linens. Waltheof had reached the croft before him and was now mixing up a hot drink of red wine and herbs to restore the heat to Will's cooling body. Agnes knelt over a figure laid out on furs on the floor. When she leant back Robin saw Will, pale as ash, his shift torn open to reveal a long line of linen pressed tightly across his chest, steadily being reddened. He barely twitched, his eyes half-closed, looking up at the wall. Robin stood as if rooted. Friar Toki bustled past him, already unfolding his medicines.

'Have you tried to staunch the bleeding? Made up a poultice?'

'We waited for you. I've just been trying to stop the blood.'

The friar nodded and suggested Agnes had some wine to soothe her while he inspected Will. Agnes came over to Robin and embraced him tightly, kissing him on the cheek as she took a cup of wine from Waltheof with a trembling hand. Robin sat with her, waiting to be told what to do, watching Toki do his work. Much came inside and Waltheof silently took his place outside. Even Much was quiet, cowed by the sudden seriousness that had intruded into his adventures with the hundredmen.

'What happened?' Agnes asked. 'He said something about the count's tapestries. Thurstan carried him here with the lad, but both ran off for help the moment Will was inside.'

'Did Will tell you what we've been doing?' Robin asked while the friar peeled layers of bandage back and peered into the wound beneath.

'Of course.'

Of course, thought Robin. Agnes did not judge men for their actions, only their motives. If he had such a mother he would keep no secrets from her either.

'Will was leading them,' Agnes prompted. 'He told me the men were going to take something to shame the Viponts but he would tell me more after. Then he came back like this.'

Robin looked to Much to take up the story. He fidgeted uneasily.

'It – it all seemed to go well at first. The first wagon sank in a pothole we'd dug and Kolbrand drew away half the guard, further up the road and into the forest. I was with John Blunt and the rest, deeper in the woods, waiting to take the stuff the men brought and run off with it to hide. Will was waiting with archers and they definitely shot, because we heard them. But I think the guard who'd chased Kolbrand came back sooner than expected and there was fighting. I ran to see what was happening and there were drawn swords all over the place – Will was fighting one of the guards with a stick.'

'A stick?'

'He had a stick. The guard had a sword and he…' Much gestured a downward swipe with his arm, then traced it across his chest from his shoulder down to his lowest rib. 'John had come after me and he shot at the steward to stop him before he could strike Will again. It drove him back just long enough for Thurstan to grab Will and I ran with him to get back here. John must have taken over after that.'

The friar had come to join them.

'It's a deep wound,' he said softly. 'It will need stitching. Agnes, have you needle and thread? Something strong but not too thick. I will make up a plaster to cover the stitches, then he should lie still for as long as possible.' Agnes produced needle and thread from a sack of sewing. Toki dipped the needle into some of the hot water. 'Robin, I need a cup of wine. I'll give him a little henbane to drink, to help him to sleep and relieve the pain. You might want a drink too, I need your help.'

Robin filled a cup, drank it, refilled it then set it down on the floor. Toki poured a few drops of henbane into the cup and Agnes helped Will to drink it. The effort of leaning forward even slightly caused him to wince and grit his teeth. Agnes helped him settle flat again.

'When I say, Robin, draw back the linens here. I've cleaned the wound but I need you to hold the skin close while I stitch. And don't let him move.'

Robin did as he was told, but it was no easy task. At Acre he had watched as a fortress ditch was clogged with the corpses of soldiers and their horses, then at night seen the same bodies chopped up like firewood by their enemy to empty the channel. On the long hot march south along the Mediterranean he had seen a knight fighting with his helm lost, his face coated so deeply in blood that he could not see where his sword swung. He had seen heads cracked, throats split, spines broken, faces mutilated, limbs torn off. But none of those sights made him as sick as watching his brother being sewn up, while all the while his white fingers clawed into his arm in pain.

When it was done and the friar pressed a poultice over the wound Robin sat back on his heels, not feeling capable of standing. Mercifully, Will fell into a sleep while Toki completed his work but with his eyes closed and his skin pale and gleaming, Will might have been lying there dead. Robin built up the strength to stand simply to escape the sight. He drank another cup of wine, this one sweetened with honey.

'I've done what I can.'

Toki washed his hands while Agnes watched over Will.

'Will he – live?' Robin asked.

'Aries is in the ascendant in the heavens, so a wound to the chest like this can be safely treated.' Toki pressed Robin's arm with a reassuringly firm grip. 'And Saturn is dominant in the heavens, which is a good omen for healing.'

Robin was not certain he had faith in the stars. But for Agnes he forced a smile, tucked her under his arm to comfort her. Toki left a sack of medicines, with instructions that Robin only half-heard. Having done all he could he mounted his aged steed and set off back towards the priory, leaving the small gathering in the croft watching over Will.

Marian stared into the black circling water, swirling it around and around with one finger until her reflection had completely disappeared. She did not want to look at her face. It was never pleasing to her. Today she wished she could wear a veil all the way across it like women in the East.

'What do you see in there?'

Guy sat beside her on the pond's edge, looked into the pool.

'Water mostly,' Marian said. She drew her hand out and waved it in the air to dry. The rest of their party had wandered further into the walled garden. Elaine was leaning over a late blooming rose, her perfect neck the same colour as the flower bud. Marian sighed.

'Has there been any more word from the count about the attack on his train?' she asked, leaning back on her long arms in the pale afternoon sun.

'No.'

He glanced towards his family, turning the ring on his little finger around repeatedly. It was a nervous habit he had, which Marian noticed most often in relation to Lord Ranulf. She knew that the theft of the count's personal belongings must be an embarrassment for a family who considered themselves so closely trusted by the prince. Even worse, once the count had learnt of the theft he had insisted the Viponts stay south of the forest until they had something meaningful to report on either the apprehension of the thieves or the discovery of the stolen wardrobe goods.

'I am sorry your hunt was called off.'

'It is probably best. Riding all the way to Clipstone when the forest is stocked full of thieves and felons is not an appealing prospect. I am just glad we waited to follow the wagon, otherwise God knows what might have happened.'

The wagons might have been saved, Marian thought, but she kept it to herself.

Guy stood and offered her his hand to join him. They wandered towards the rest of his family in the castle's walled garden. Idonea was wafting a wasp away from her face while watching Jocelyn and Roger. The lords and Lanfranc were all clustered around Elaine like flies on – Marian smiled to herself, not finishing that thought. Like bees around a rose.

'The count's men gave the same description of the thieves as every other one we have heard since the tax wagons were attacked after Easter,' said Guy. 'They were hooded and their faces were covered. Oh! There was one strange thing one of the guards told us. You might find it amusing. During the attack one of the thieves was wounded, slashed right across the chest – forgive me if I speak of matters you do not wish to hear.'

'I will not swoon, do not fear. Why should it be strange that this man was wounded?'

'That was not the strange part. The strangeness was that as he was carried into the forest the thief's face was revealed to this guard. Apparently he looked the double of Lord Locksley.'

Marian's skin prickled. Guy looked at her, expecting a reaction. She forced herself to laugh.

'That is strange,' she said, 'as Lord Locksley was with you in the court.' There was, of course, just such a double living in a croft only a few miles from them, but she would not be the one to reveal that. 'I am sure the resemblance was very slight. The guard probably imagined it to be close because Lord Locksley was among the first faces he saw after the attack.'

'There might be another reason.' Elaine moved closer, her hand toying with the tendril vines of a wallflower. She wore a conspiratorial smile. Marian had not realised she was close enough to hear.

'No –' she said, no more than a breath. She shook her head sharply at her cousin, widening her eyes. Elaine ignored her, enjoying the inquiring attention of the lords as they turned to listen.

'What is that?' Eudo asked.

Elaine snapped one of the leaves from the vine. 'It might have been his brother.'

Marian reacted too slowly. 'It was more likely the man's imagination…' she said again, but no one was listening to her.

'The drunk?' Eudo asked. He glanced at his son. Marian watched the message pass between them all – Serlo to Ranulf, Ranulf to Guy. The missing link in a puzzling chain being revealed. 'Remind me of his name. It was some sort of cloth.'

'His brother does not look so similar,' said Marian more loudly. 'They are quite different. As I say, the man was probably –'

'Do not look similar?' Elaine cried. 'They might have been twins.'

'You have met him?' asked Serlo.

'Unfortunately. I thought him very coarse.'

'Where does he live, this coarse brother?' asked Eudo, smiling.

'Marian will know.' Eager eyes swiveled in her direction. 'She took his family alms. What was his mother's name, cousin?'

Marian felt like a lamb hemmed in by wolves. Thanks to Elaine, she could not now deny knowledge of Will, but nor was she willing to say anything that might see him put in jeopardy.

'I –' She swallowed. 'I really do not think that Will has any part in –'

'Will Scarlette,' Serlo cried. 'That was the name.'

'Is his mother the brewer Scarlette?' Lanfranc asked. 'She lives on the edge of the Locksley manor. Agnes, I think.'

'That is right,' said Elaine. 'Lord Locksley had some quarrel with the sheriff over her.'

'This is very useful information, dear Elaine,' said Eudo. 'Thank you.' He nodded to Lanfranc, who bowed and left them at a brisk walk. Eudo offered his arm to Elaine. 'Let us continue our walk.'

Guy took Marian's arm and she allowed herself to be drawn along with the rest of the group. But her eyes were on Lanfranc, moving ever closer to the castle. The closer he grew to it the more the breath caught in her chest. He was going to the Scarlettes' croft. He must be. Would he take armed men with him? Torches? She thought of Aelfeva after Thorfridh's first arrest, bruised and weeping amidst the broken shards of her home. What if Lanfranc's men harmed Agnes? What if – she could not deny the possibility, though it made her stomach turn – what if it *had* been Will who was wounded in that attack? He would be hanged. She could not stand idly by to let that happen. She drew her arm from Guy's.

'Excuse me,' she said. 'I feel ill.'

'You are pale,' Guy said, looking at her in alarm. He put his arm around her waist, as if she might faint at any moment. 'I should not have mentioned the wounded thief. I knew it was not right. Let me take you back indoors.'

She shook her head. Too slow, she thought. And she would be kept inside. She needed to find Robin, to go with him to warn Will. She could not argue against Lanfranc's word herself – she did not have the authority of Lord Locksley and she knew she could not rely on the support of her father. No, she must reach Robin quickly and then go to the Scarlettes' croft. Evening was not drawing in yet. Perhaps Will would still be out working.

The rest of the party had turned to see what was the matter.

'I will go home,' she said.

'You should not ride if you are unwell,' said Eudo.

'I will feel better as soon as I am back at Locksley Hall. I am certain.'

'Let me accompany you,' said Guy eagerly.

'I should come with you as well,' said Elaine, not eagerly at all.

'No.' She could not very well explain a diversion to the Scarlettes' croft with both of them watching her. 'I will go by myself. Edgar can ride with me. Thank you. Excuse me. I am sorry. Excuse me.' She broke away from Guy's grip and strode onwards before anyone could persuade her otherwise. Edgar was at her side immediately. 'Where is Lord Locksley?' she asked.

'At the hall, I think,' he said, surprised. 'He did not return until early this morning from whatever delayed him last night.'

'Run ahead and have my horse saddled. There is no time to waste.'

As Edgar broke into a run she squinted at the figure of Lanfranc, now barely visible in the archway leading to the castle. He would have to gather men, saddle his horse. Often he travelled with the Vipont guard accompanying on foot. She would have the advantage of him there. He should not see her leaving the castle though. She did not want to rouse his suspicion. As soon as she was out of sight of the Viponts and the garden she broke into a run.

Marian rode faster that day than she ever had in her life. She sat astride her horse not caring if her skirts hitched, not feeling the chafing of the horse's flanks against her legs. Her horse was so astonished at being pushed to such a sustained burst of speed that it sweated and trembled under her. They had escaped the castle unseen by Lanfranc at least, but she could not shake away the thought that every moment they were on the road he was catching up to them. She must stay ahead. She clung on to her horse, her own legs aching now. A loop in the path. And there. The gate of Locksley Hall. She shouted for the porter, drawing her horse to a juddering halt. He came out of his gatehouse and bowed to her.

'Is Lord Locksley here?' she called.

'No, my lady. He rode out not long after you did this afternoon. I thought he was joining you at the castle, perhaps?'

'No,' said Marian, grasping her reins tight enough to rub in frustration. 'He did not tell anyone where he was going then?'

'Not that I know, my lady.'

She glanced at the hall. She could not return and risk her father or Lady Joan engaging her in idle conversation, or – worse – asking questions of her. She turned to Edgar.

'Go to the hall, ask quickly if anyone knows where Lord Locksley has gone. I will ride towards the Scarlette croft.'

'I will go, my lady, but you should not ride alone on these roads. Dusk is coming on.'

Marian looked back up the road. The sun was starting to dip in the sky. The idea of riding through the green lanes and forest in creeping darkness made her shudder. She should not waste time out of fear, but neither would it be wise to put herself into unnecessary – time wasting – danger.

'Go to the hall,' she said at last, 'and have one of the other servants inquire about Lord Locksley for you – only ones I trust. Gytha, Estrild or Waltheof, Alan if you can find him. They can ride out to us if they learn anything. Quickly.'

Edgar nodded and galloped on towards the hall. Marian exhaled deeply and loosened her grip on the reins. A breath of wind caught her skirt, blowing it close against her leg. It was wick with the horse's sweat. She patted his neck and waited.

After the briefest of visits to Locksley Hall to change his clothes and assure the sheriff that he had spent last night searching for the thieves rather than sheltering with one of them, Robin rode out again. No sign had been found of the men who attacked the count's train by Sir Walter's men but he needed to be certain that they were safe in the clearing and no one else had been injured during the attack. Thankfully, he arrived to a full Hundred. Though some had been wounded, none were as seriously hurt as Will and all who went out on the raid had returned. They had been very fortunate, John said, and Robin entirely agreed with him. Best not to push such good fortune. They should tend to their wounded and put all thought of further raids aside for the time-being.

Dusk was drawing in by the time Waltheof and Robin turned back onto the

Locksley road, riding side by side, making no haste after a day and night of anxiety. Robin thought of his bed, wishing he had been able to provide Will with a more comfortable place to convalesce. He would be glad of it himself that night. He had scarcely slept at the croft the night before, every noise outside making him imagine the sheriff's men and every heavy breath and murmur from Will jolting him awake to check he was still alive. As the forest receded and their path rose, Robin heard a shout then pounding hooves. He sat up in his saddle to see two figures racing along the path. As one grew closer he recognised Marian, her face flushed. She was calling out to him. At first he could not understand her.

'Will,' she repeated. 'Lanfranc is on his way to arrest him. He thinks he attacked the count's wagons…'

Robin heard no more. He turned his horse in the lane and virtually kicked it in the direction of the Scarlette croft. When they were almost there Marian called his name again. Her voice trembled. She pointed to the sky. With a sickening stab he saw orange painted across the darkening dusk, twisting smoke – flames. He felt like he was running on quicksand, his heart pounding so hard in his chest he thought it would burst. He had never known fear like the last yards of that ride to his brother's home. When they arrived he thought he was too late. Lanfranc's men were already there and had dragged Will and Agnes from the croft. Will was sprawled on the earth, his hands clasping his chest beneath the fur covering him but his body still. Agnes sobbed over him, held back from touching him by one of Lanfranc's men. Much was cradling his stomach, his face bloodied, only a matter of yards from the croft. He looked like he had been stopped as he tried to run into the building. Fire was licking at the thatched roof now and in the darkness the twisting flames cast hellish shadows over the scene.

Robin leapt from his horse towards Will, seizing him in his arms. Will twitched slightly, opened one eye, then the other. Groaned. His hand fluttered to his chest again. A shadow fell over them. Robin looked up into Lanfranc's gleaming red face.

'This man,' he said quietly, 'has a wound that matches one inflicted by one of the Count of Mortain's guards during the attack on his wardrobe.'

He reached down, batted away Will's hands and tugged at his shift. Beneath, the poultice had been torn away and Will's wound was bleeding again. He gritted his teeth in pain. Marian, who had run to check on Much, put her hands over her mouth in shock at sight of the wound.

'He received that wound while hunting with me,' said Robin.

'No antler cuts as clean as that.'

'His spear slipped in his hand when he fell from his horse.'

'And yet he is remarkably uninjured elsewhere.' Lanfranc gestured to his men. 'Whatever the reason, you will have your opportunity to speak it in court. For now we are arresting this man. If he lives long enough, he will be tried by the sheriff for leading all of the thefts in the forest that have taken place this year.'

Robin gently lowered Will to the ground, drawing his shift over the wound. He stood toe to toe with Lanfranc. The steward did not falter.

'This man is my brother,' Robin said, as steadily as his pounding heart would let him. 'I should be the one to arrest him.'

'Without wishing to offend, my lord, the last time you were left responsible for a felon they escaped in less than a day. The time before that it was under an hour. I do not believe you are capable of taking this man to prison.'

Robin felt cold pressure on his hand and realised it was gripping his sword. Marian rushed forward before he could unsheathe it.

'Master Steward, since this man is injured, I believe he should have the attention of a physician before he is imprisoned. If he has committed these crimes, you do not wish him to die from his wounds before he can be tried, surely?'

'My wishes are not important, my lady. I follow the commands of my lord Vipont. As should you.'

Marian blanched with anger. Agnes had been released by the guards and now knelt over Will, kissing his forehead. Robin stood over the pair of them to prevent any of Lanfranc's men separating them. Marian stepped back from Lanfranc, into the circle of Robin and the Scarlettes. Robin looked around, his fingers tensing on his sword. There were more than a dozen guards here as well as Lanfranc. Even with Waltheof and Edgar – presuming Edgar was willing to fight for him – Robin could not hope to bring them all down. He felt his stomach contract like a fist. He would have to let them take Will. Either that or be killed by these men, and probably kill Agnes and harm Marian as well. He removed his hand from his sword and called to Lanfranc.

'When I return to Locksley Hall,' he said, 'I will tell the sheriff that at your order these men have attacked an innocent woman –'

'Who was harbouring a felon,' Lanfranc interrupted.

'– that they burnt down her home –'

'Where the felon was hidden.'

'– and that they committed violence on a child.'

He gestured to Much, who Marian had helped to his feet.

'Or did you have evidence against the boy as well?'

'We found him eating at the felon's table.'

Robin barked a laugh.

'Hospitality is against your master's law, then?' Robin stepped towards Lanfranc, lowering his voice. 'I will also be certain to tell the sheriff that you treated his daughter with the same discourtesy you speak about me.'

Lanfranc smiled icily.

'And your sheriff will do absolutely nothing to me as long as I am the trusted servant of Lord Vipont. As you well know.' He addressed the Vipont guard. 'Get the felon into the cart we found. Leave the woman and boy, we've got their names. Lord Locksley can always attempt to arrest them. He might last two days before they escape.'

The men laughed as they followed his instructions. Lanfranc mounted his horse with a cold bow to Marian. Robin knelt beside Will.

'I will free you,' he whispered, clasping his brother's icy hands. 'I will not let you hang.'

'Good,' Will muttered, smiling between gritted teeth. 'I'm very attached to my neck.'

He was hauled up and pushed into a two-wheeled cart for one of the men to push in front of him as the guard closed ranks against Robin. Then they left, leaving a dribbling trail of blood and a crackling croft in their wake.

'I'm sorry,' cried Much, twitching with anger and frustration. 'I tried to stop them. I tried.'

'I know,' said Robin.

He walked around the croft, seeing if anything could be saved for Agnes's trade. But the tuns and paddles she used were all inside the building, along with all her supplies. When he reached the front of the croft again Agnes was weeping in Marian's arms. Much had sat down and was staring at the earth helplessly while Waltheof and Edgar watched the flames. Robin took Agnes from Marian's awkward embrace and held her until her tears subsided. He would not let anything happen to Will. He thought it, he knew it, he repeated it like a credo in his head. If he had to bribe every man in the county court or burn down the castle to get him out, he would save his brother. And he would not let harm come to Agnes. Which meant there was only one place she could go.

'Waltheof, go with Marian back to the hall. Much, come with me and Agnes. I'll take you somewhere safe. Lanfranc knows you now, it would be best you don't return to your home.'

'Where are you taking them?' Marian asked, then realised he must mean wherever the hundredmen were concealed. 'Are you certain that it is safe, this place in the forest? I know Will would not tell the Viponts anything, but they might find out some other way.'

'Perhaps.'

'I can ask my father if Agnes can take refuge with us.'

'My mother will not allow it.'

Marian started to argue, then checked herself. He was right. Lady Joan would care little that Agnes's home had been destroyed and her son wounded, perhaps mortally. In her eyes Agnes reaped the rewards of her own sin. Robin helped Agnes onto his horse and Marian was on the point of returning to her own when she remembered Guy's words earlier that day.

'There is something else you should know as well.'

She gestured Robin away from the others. It felt like breaking a bond of trust between her and Guy to reveal such information but in her heart she knew that her loyalties still lay as much with Robin's family as with Guy's. She spoke quietly enough so that Robin could barely hear her words, never mind the others in the clearing.

'The guard Lanfranc spoke of – the one who wounded Will – saw his face. If he is called as a witness in court his word and that wound will be enough to…' She could not bring herself to say aloud what would happen then. 'You should try to find the guard.'

Robin nodded. Marian went to join Waltheof and Edgar on the other side of the clearing before he could say more.

'I might not return to the hall tonight,' Robin called. 'Will you make my excuses?'

'Of course. Shall I tell them you are with Agnes?'

'Tell them – tell them I am out searching for thieves.'

'I will.'

'Marian.' She looked back at Robin in surprise. 'Thank you.'

She turned herself to the road without another word.

Ploughing

When the men saw Robin leading Agnes and an injured Much to their Hundred in darkness they ran to learn what had happened. The news that Will had been taken was received with shouts of anger and defiance, and assurances to Agnes that they would get him back. She said nothing, her arms tightly folded across her chest, her face still pale from the shock of Lanfranc's attack, but she forced a smile for them. Aedith led her to the fire in the half-built longhouse to sit on the count's stolen cushions and eat from a gilded bowl. Edeva and Doleswif took Much away to tend to his injuries and Robin was left in the midst of the men's fury. John Blunt fanned their shouts down to a lower pitch and put his hand on Robin's back.

'Have you eaten today? We've plenty to share.'

Gilbert was suddenly at Robin's elbow. 'Robin, can I show you something?'

'Leave it for another time, lad,' said John.

'But I think Robin needs to know about this as soon as possible.'

'What is it, Gilbert?'

Robin slumped onto one of the count's silken bolsters at the fire's edge. He felt like he had not eaten or slept in days. Gilbert ran into the croft and emerged a moment later clutching a roll of vellum. He laid it out before Robin. Rubbing his eyes roughly he bent over to read it in the firelight. Before he had read two lines of the carefully scrawling writing there Robin had seized the parchment and held it up in front of his disbelieving eyes.

'Where did you find this?'

'It was in one of the saddlebags of the count's horses – the steward's I think. In all the confusion yesterday I didn't have time to read it. I was right to show you, wasn't I?'

'Yes, you were.' Robin gestured Gilbert closer and spoke in a low voice. 'Have you told anyone else what this says?'

'No.'

'Don't. Yet.' Robin gestured John close so that the two of them and Gilbert formed a small party out of hearing of the group at the fireside.

'I don't understand the language,' said Gilbert quietly. 'It isn't Latin – but I thought I knew this word.' He pointed at a single word, hidden in the midst of the dense text: Roi. 'That means king, doesn't it?'

'Yes. This is French. True French, I mean, I heard it in the East all the time, it's not so different from our lords' language when your ear tunes to it.'

'What does it say?' asked John.

'It is addressed to the count, but the usual platitudes aren't there, no list of titles.'

'I thought it was to John of Oxford?' said Gilbert.

'That is the count. He was born in Oxford. This message thanks him for the information he sent and says that everything points to the rumours being true. The king's ransom is almost gathered and soon the devil will be loose –'

'The devil?' asked Gilbert.

'The king,' said John.

'Then it suggests the count listen to the advice of his friend P.A. – that might be Philippe Auguste, the King of the French – to pay more to keep the devil snared, and if that fails the castle will stand ready to oppose anyone but its true lord. Presumably the true lord they mean is the count himself.' Robin turned the message over in his hands. 'There is no seal and no one named as the sender. Just this mark in the left corner.'

At the bottom of the page was a looped squiggle, like an 'S' on its side. It might have been a bridge, or a snake.

'This must be from the Viponts,' said John. 'Sir Walter Peverill wouldn't stand against the king.'

'Whoever it's from it means war. The count means to oppose his brother when he is freed. And Nottingham will be at the heart of it.' He rolled up the message. 'I should take this to the sheriff.'

'You can't. Where will you say you got it from?'

'I can say it was found during the search in the forest. He will easily believe thieves had little interest in documents they can't read. This could be a way to bring down the Viponts. We know now that they have been communicating with the count about preventing the king's return. If we found this message we could steal others too – more proof that they are plotting against the king – then the sheriff can bring them before a court.'

'And what if the king doesn't return – if they manage to keep him locked up in that German cell forever? Or what if he is freed and he goes back to Jerusalem or stays in Normandy, Aquitaine? The count won't look kindly on the lord who arrested his allies. It could be the end of Sir Walter, and while I don't love the man at least he keeps a check on Lord Eudo and his friends. Better we stay out of this.'

'We can't stay out of this, John. Just because no one has found this place yet doesn't mean they never will. If you've helped the king during his absence there's hope of a royal pardon for you all when he's free.'

John shook his head. He had no faith in the king's magnanimity.

'Besides, what will happen to these men's kin and neighbours if there is a war? Crops will get razed, women and children murdered, innocent men and prisoners killed. We might be able to prevent that war before it even begins.'

'Or you might just stir up a hornet's nest you can't run from. You haven't seen the worst of the Viponts, Robin, believe me. Your noble birth will only protect you from them for so long.'

'The only person at risk if I take this to the sheriff is myself, and that's a risk I'm happy to take.'

John sighed. 'As you like. But for now let's keep this between the three of us.

There's no need to rile up the men still further until we know what the sheriff will do. I suppose at least it might distract him from hunting us out for a while.'

The symbol on the message to the count niggled at Robin all night. If he could connect that symbol to the Viponts it would be a sure way to convince the sheriff of their complicity in this plot. But though he turned the image in his mind, and turned the message over and over before his eyes, he could not see a link. Before dawn he left the tapestry-strewn and crowded croft with some resolution. He would seek out Peter the clerk. A man who spent his whole life around documents must have more idea of the meaning of such symbols than anyone else in Nottinghamshire. Robin had avoided visiting the chancery since Elaine and Marian had interrupted his last meeting with Peter. He would have preferred to have known another clerk now who he could ask, but there was no way to show the symbol without also revealing the message next to it, and Peter was the only clerk whose discretion he could rely on.

His faith was not misplaced. Inside the chancery's antechamber Peter raised an eyebrow at the message when Robin presented it to him but said nothing about its contents.

'Have you ever seen that symbol before?'

'No. It does not resemble any seals I know either.' He turned the message around in his hands. 'It could be a bridge. The Viponts are connected to the Vieuxpont family. Their name means –'

'The old bridge.' Robin competed his sentence for him. Of course. A bridge. Robin could see it more clearly now. Peter handed the message back to him.

'Is that at all helpful?'

'Very.' Robin replaced the document inside his tunic. 'Do you know anything about the men who were guarding the count's wardrobe when it was attacked?'

Peter's eyebrows raised, the only sign of surprise he ever exhibited.

'I believe some of them were hired locally. I might be able to learn more from records of their pay. Is it important?'

'It could save a man's life.'

'Then I will look.'

'You are a good man. Thank you.'

Robin led the way out of the closet and back to the chancery. To his surprise Eudo was loitering over the desk of one of the other clerks. He met Robin's eye with a flash of triumph swiftly stifled by a smile.

'How strange to find you here, Lord Locksley. Are you on the sheriff's business?'

'In a manner of speaking.'

Eudo watched Peter leave the closet and return to his desk, then turned back to Robin.

'You look tired, my lord. I hope that the events of last night did not overly distress you?'

'If my brother's mistreatment did not affect me it would be a poor reflection on our family.'

'Fraternal affection is an underrepresented virtue in these times.'

The words in the message to the count about his brother flashed through Robin's mind: keep the devil snared. Lord Eudo was not wrong.

'I had hoped that while I was here I might visit my brother?'

'I do not think that would be wise. The count is very anxious to ensure we learn the truth about the attack on his wardrobe and –'

'You think Will might tell me something that will prevent that happening?'

'You have already admitted your great affection for your brother. To want to help him is natural, but I cannot permit you to do so at present. You can appeal to the constable if you wish, but he will say the same as me I think.'

Robin left Lord Eudo with an almost insuperable urge to hit someone. That would not be his final word on visiting Will, but in that moment he needed to put other interests ahead of his concern for his brother. He needed to take word of the count's plot to Sir Walter. He would need the sheriff's support against the Viponts if he was to bring them to heel, and the sooner he was assured of that support the more confident he could be in defying them.

At Locksley Hall dinner was still being prepared and whilst the servants had long been at their work, there was little sign of the family. Robin thought yearningly of the days of his father when no one in the hall would have stayed abed past morning Mass. Of course, in those days he would have loved the leisurely regime of his mother and Sir Walter. A man was never content with what he had.

He was on the point of sending a servant to ask for the sheriff to meet him in the solar when Marian appeared on the stairwell. She froze at sight of him and he looked away, inexplicably awkward. They had shared in the intimate horror of Will's capture and it was strange now to face each other across Locksley's great hall as trestle tables were erected for the servants' dinner. Marian recovered first.

'How is Agnes?' she asked, stepping out of the way of a bench as it was carried from the screens passage to the centre of the hall. She and Robin moved to the quiet of the windows overlooking the courtyard to talk.

'As you would imagine.'

'Were you – out there all night?'

'Not all night, I have just been at the castle.'

'To see Will?'

'The charming Lord Eudo would not let me.'

'I am going riding with Guy later. I could ask to visit him for you, at least until you are allowed?'

Robin longed for news of his brother, and the fear that in a cell such as Thorfridh had inhabited Will's wound would putrefy from lack of attention was constant. But he hesitated to accept her offer.

'It might not be a good idea. I would not want Eudo questioning your involvement with all this.'

'Lanfranc will have told him I brought you to the croft. I am already involved. I may as well try to take some benefit from it if I can. I will take preparations for a poultice and whatever else Gytha can spare, just in case I am able to visit him.'

Marian's will had always been strong, despite her ability to conceal that strength behind a mask of ladylike docility. Robin smiled. She was bolder than him in some ways, he thought.

'Thank you. If there is any way that the friar could bring medicine from the hospital to him, that would be appreciated as well. The Viponts do not trust Toki, so it may be difficult.'

'I will ask.'

'Thank you.'

'Is your father –?'

'He is still in bed but he is awake. He had a message from the count early this morning so he has been conducting business in his bedsheets. You can go in to him.'

Robin took her word on it and went to the great chamber. There he found Lady Joan yawning into a hand mirror while her lady plaited her hair and Sir Walter scowling over a pile of documents in his lap, settled against a mound of cushions, still in his nightshirt. His mother waved vaguely for him to go about his business. Robin hesitated to produce a letter revealing royal rebellion in such a domestic environment, particularly one in which his mother might overhear something. But she seemed absorbed in her ablutions, so he approached Sir Walter and settled in a chair at the side of the bed.

'What is it?' Sir Walter looked up. 'You are anxious. What is the matter?'

Robin handed over the letter.

'This was found in the forest. It must have come from the saddlebag of the count's steward.'

Sir Walter read the message with a sigh, then sat upright. He pulled at his beard and read it again. He looked Robin in the eye.

'Who has seen this?'

'Only us, and a clerk in your chancery who I trust. The steward must have known about it – he mentioned his saddlebag being taken when we first met him on the road – so Eudo will know it is missing.'

'You are certain this was sent by Lord Eudo?'

'If not him then his brother or son. I doubt Guy would be involved unless he was forced.'

He explained the connection between the Viponts and the bridge symbol at the edge of the page. Sir Walter rolled up the message with a heavy sigh.

'I had hoped when King Richard took the throne all the wars within that family would end. Was it not enough that their father died still at war with his sons? Now the sons continue the battle among themselves. If I could, I would avoid any involvement in this strife.'

'That will be difficult with the count as overlord of Nottinghamshire.'

'Impossible. And just when we have completed the arrangements for Marian's marriage. I do not want her marrying into a family who are about to be exiled or have their estates seized. I should talk to Lord Ranulf.'

He threw back the covers and called for water to wash. Robin rose to his feet in alarm.

'Surely it's not wise to go straight to the Viponts with this? If you do not give your support to them they will be angry.'

'I cannot support them in this, in betraying my king. Surely you would not counsel me to do so?'

'Of course not.' Robin followed Sir Walter to a washtable, keeping his voice as calm and quiet as he could to avoid attracting Lady Joan's attention. 'But you cannot simply confront them with this document and expect them to let it stand. You need the help of other lords, an alliance against the Viponts so that if they try to hold the castle for the count against the king you do not stand alone.'

'We already know that they will have the support of de la Guerche and de Caux. And if it came down to control of fortresses the seneschal of Tickhill Castle in the north. He is Lady Idonea's brother and will be loyal to the count.'

'But you can appeal to those who helped you before. D'Alselin, Louvetot, Foliot, the abbess, the prior. What about the lords who are in Normandy? Could they not be persuaded to return for this? The Earl of Derby's father died fighting with the king in the Holy Land, he will not now turn against him to support the count.'

'You want me to unite every lord in the county against my daughter's future family? I will not act in any way that harms Marian. The contract is signed now, it cannot be undone. As long as she is connected to the Viponts I will not work overtly against them.'

'Then do it secretly. As long as the Viponts know nothing of it, you can wait to see if war ever comes. It may be that the king is released before the count can act. Then the Viponts will never know that you tried to act against them. But you know that you cannot do nothing whilst they prepare for a war.'

Sir Walter was silent. He had heard Robin's argument but Robin was not certain he had really listened.

'I need to think on this,' he said at last as the jug of hot water arrived.

'This is treason, sheriff. Your duty is to the king.'

'My duty is and always has been to my family. I will have my men watch for any more messages between the count and the Viponts, but for now keep this letter between the two of us. When I have decided what further steps to take I will tell you.'

Robin bit back more words. He had given the sheriff the perfect opportunity to bring down the might of the Viponts, to weaken the count's influence in their county, and Sir Walter had chosen to equivocate. Perhaps he should not have expected more. He had no more desire to embroil Marian in a charge of treason than Sir Walter did, but to delay would surely only make her involvement more likely? Once she was Lady Vipont there would be no way to extricate her from a war.

It did not take much persuasion on Marian's part for Guy to permit her to visit Will. His father and uncle were away from the castle and he was always emboldened in their absence. He only promised her a few moments with Will, but that would be enough to give him some proper food and make sure his wounds were healing. Marian was surprised, though, when Guy led her not only down into the stores in the keep's cellar but even further, into the rock the castle was built on. Two guards yawned in the gaping darkness of hollowed sandstone, torches the only light beneath the earth.

'You are keeping him in a cave?' Marian said as the cell door was unlocked.

'It is the most secure cell in the castle. Given how easily his accomplices escaped it seemed a wise precaution.'

Marian certainly could not see how anyone would be able to free Will from this place. The door was opened and Will blinked and raised his shackled hands to shield himself from the light. He was lying on a bed chiselled from the walls with barely a blanket over him.

'Remove his shackles,' Marian told the guard.

'I do not think that is wise…' Guy began.

'Please. He is injured. He could not run four paces.'

Guy reluctantly nodded his agreement and the guard removed the shackles from Will's wrists and ankles. He sat up and smiled at Marian as he rotated his freed wrists.

'What an unlooked for pleasure,' he croaked. 'And Lord Vipont too. You look how I feel.'

Marian stepped inside the cell and pulled out the food and drink she had brought him. She had henbane too for pain, and clean linen and a poultice Gytha had helped her prepare. He ate the food greedily. Marian noticed that although his appetite had not suffered he sat with his arm cradled in front of him, as if protecting the wound across his chest. Every now and then he would stop moving suddenly, make a small noise like a gasp and his arm would twitch. He was still in pain. As he took the wine she had brought he spoke, low enough that Guy loitering outside could not hear.

'Is my mother safe?'

'Robin took her to the forest. She will be fine. He wanted to come here himself but Lord Eudo would not let him.'

They talked for some time. Marian insisted on seeing his wound and doing what she could to guard it from infection, despite his and Guy's protestations that she should not.

'Stubborn mare,' said Will with a smile as he gingerly patted the clean linens beneath his shift.

'Troublemaker,' Marian responded in kind. 'You need to be sewn up again. I cannot do that. I will have the friar sent to you tomorrow.'

Guy opened his mouth to disagree but Marian gave him a look that he knew would brook no refusal. He said nothing.

'We should leave you,' Marian said. 'But I will make sure you have enough food and drink. If I could I would move you to somewhere else in the castle.'

Guy looked outright alarmed at that suggestion.

'Beggars can't be choosers,' said Will, squeezing her hand in farewell. 'Thank you.'

Reluctantly, Marian left him to the darkness of his cell. She gave the guards outside a handsome purse of coins.

'Look after him,' she said. 'If his condition worsens I will know who to blame.'

She and Guy retreated a little further from the cell, but Guy took her arm and halted her before they ascended the stairs back to the keep.

'You are angry with me.'

'No. I simply do not understand why he must be treated so unkindly.'

'Because he is a criminal. I know you do not wish to believe it, Marian, but all the evidence we have suggests he has been leading felonies across the entire county. He has gathered enough money from his raids to build a castle of his own.'

'He has not been found guilty in a court yet. I will continue to believe he is innocent until the royal justices say otherwise.'

But Marian was not as certain as she sounded. She was not certain about Will's innocence, nor Robin's, nor Much's, nor even Waltheof's. The four of them and their hundredmen friends were mired too deep in secrecy for her to trust any of them. But that thought was not an easy one, so she suppressed it and spoke as if there was not a shadow of doubt in her mind.

'Let me try to cheer you a little,' said Guy. 'I could show you a secret?'

'I have had enough of secrets.'

'But this is not a bad one. And it is something only our family knows.'

Marian frowned. Guy was smiling at her like an eager child. He wanted to do something to prove himself to her, and she should not deny him the opportunity.

'All right. What is this secret?'

'Come this way.'

He took her hand in one of his, and in the other he placed a torch from one of the brackets in the wall. Then he pulled her after him down another tunnel in the sandstone. The ground beneath her feet sloped downwards and the tunnel grew thinner.

'Where are we going?' Marian asked, but Guy just grinned in response.

They walked for so long she had no idea how deep into the rock they had gone. She started when the firm sandy ground gave way to puddles and slippery moss. Guy held up his torch. They were at a door. Guy passed Marian the torch and knelt to unbolt and unlatch the many locks on the door. When he pulled it open the dark tunnel was filled with startling sunlight. Marian blinked and turned her head from it. When her eyes had recovered she stepped out, onto a sandy bank in empty marshland that stretched towards open countryside and river.

'Look behind you,' said Guy.

Marian turned and squinted up at the vast cliff of Castle Rock. The turrets and walls of the castle were far above her. She looked back to the marsh in confusion.

'How long has this been here?'

'It has only just been finished. It was the count's idea. He wanted a sally port that could not easily be seen by anyone besieging the castle.'

'He got his wish. Why would he be thinking about sieges?'

'Experience.' But Guy did not meet her eye. 'With all the troubles in Normandy the past few years, he wants to ensure his English holdings are as secure as possible.'

Marian stepped to the edge of the small sandy bank. It disappeared into deep marshes that seemed to encircle them, wide enough and reed-clogged that even reaching the river in the distance would be a challenge.

'What would he do once he was here though? A boat could stick in the reeds and there must be whirls that catch you.'

'Go north, skirting the edge of the rock. There is a surer pathway through the marsh. The water reaches up to your waist but you will not drown.'

'That is reassuring. And you say only your family know of this?'

'Them, Lanfranc and you. You must swear to keep this secret to yourself. Not even your father should know.'

'But my father is the sheriff.'

'Please, Marian. My uncle will be very angry if he knows I have told you and you did not promise silence.'

'Then – then I will not tell him.'

They stood at the marsh's edge a little while longer, watching crane wade past on their slender legs. Then they returned through the secret door, up the grave-dark tunnel and out to the keep at the top. In the great hall of the keep they found Sir Walter just arriving. He met Guy with some relief.

'I was hoping to talk to you,' he said in a low voice. 'It is rather urgent.'

'Of course,' said Guy.

'Marian, my heart,' said Sir Walter with a smile, 'why do you not go back to Locksley? I will meet you back there later.'

More secrets, Marian thought, but she agreed. She watched her father and Guy walk into one of the small chambers off the hall. Her father seemed to be holding tightly onto a roll of vellum in one hand, a message presumably. She pretended not to have seen it, nor be curious about its contents, and left the men to their secrecy.

Robin started awake. For a moment he did not know where he was or what had woken him. He lay diagonally across his bed, still wearing his riding boots and cloak, the fire in the hearth of his chamber recently banked and the shutters being closed with a clatter by a careless servant.

'Sorry, my lord,' the servant said. 'Supper is being served. In the solar.'

'How long have I been asleep?'

He cricked his neck. He remembered coming into his chamber and sitting on the bed, but nothing more. It had been three nights since he last really slept. No wonder he had passed out here.

'You have been in here since before dinner, my lord. A messenger arrived for you, but Lady Joan said we ought not to wake you.'

'Who was the messenger from?'

He had been going to change his clothes and ride out immediately for Garsmount. Appeal again to Lord D'Alselin for support. For all his words about Lanfranc and hopeless causes, he surely could not refuse to help Robin in a case of treason? Come to that, he had been going to visit half the lords of Nottinghamshire if he could. Now the whole day was wasted and he had achieved nothing but neck ache.

'From a clerk in the sheriff's chancery. He left the message. I can fetch it for you?'

'Yes, do.'

Robin pushed himself unwillingly out of bed and into a change of clothes. By the time he was half-dressed the servant had returned. The message had no great seal, just a small disc of unbroken wax holding it closed. Robin cracked it and unfurled the message. In the neat penstrokes of a clerical hand was written:

Locksley.

I have important information that will help your brother. Meet me alone at the Blasted Oak at dusk today.

Peter.

Robin looked with dismay at the darkening sky between the shutters. It was almost dusk now. Peter must have learnt more about the guards involved in the attack. And unless Robin rode like the wind, he would not be at the oak in time to hear it. He bundled the rest of his clothes on and ran for the stables.

When Robin turned off the King's Way towards the blasted oak the shadows were already lengthening into pools of night darkness. He hoped that Peter had not been waiting too long for him. It was not wise for a man who could not defend himself to wander the forest alone. Not for the first time he wondered at Peter's having chosen a meeting place so far from the castle to give him this information. But he had said that the guards were local men. Perhaps he could not trust the Vipont servants and his fellow clerks to report his investigations back to Lord Eudo or the count himself.

Through the trees he thought he saw Peter waiting by the oak, a still figure amidst the shivering autumn thickets. A blast of wind swirled leaves from the ground, momentarily blinding him in a whirl of reds and ambers. He swatted them away as he swung from his horse and towards the clearing on foot. He whistled a greeting to Peter so he would not be startled but the clerk did not look his way. Odd. Robin glanced around cautiously. It was hard to keep watch with the wind whooshing past the creaking trees and branches tapping against one another, striking leaves from one another's limbs. He looped his horse's reins over a stunted branch and crept closer alone. It certainly looked like Peter, his cowl over his tonsured head and his fingers blackened by ink. Dripping ink. Robin looked again. Liquid was running down the clerk's sleeve and along the length of his fingers, pooling at his feet. Robin drew his sword and looked around again. The forest revealed no signs of strangers. Under his foot a coin glinted, a survivor of the money left for the hundredmen's kin all those months ago. He stepped over it and rounded the oak to come face to face with Peter.

He met unblinking eyes, a mouth contorted and bloody, cheeks puffy with bruises. He was not leaning against the oak, he was pinned to it. Four arrows held his habit at the shoulders, driven so far into the wood even their fletchings were barely visible. Beneath one pair of arrows, where Peter's body slumped within his clothes, there was a large dark patch crusted with blood. This was not the work of an opportunistic thief. Someone had followed Peter here to commit murder. And there was only one family who Robin believed would have done it. He let out a furious cry and struck at the oak with his sword, scratching a long pale line into its withered trunk. He seized the ends of the arrows and tried to draw them out, to free Peter's body. The feathers and bark scratched at his hands, but he had barely removed one when a glinting beneath him drew his eye. In the dripping pool at Peter's feet lay a dagger. Robin picked it up, turning it in his hands for signs of who had done this. Had he seen this dagger in the belt of any of the Viponts, or their men? What about that bastard Lanfranc? His hands grew slick with blood from turning it.

There was a rustling behind him and he span around, just as the rustling echoed all around the clearing. Men emerged from the forest on every side of him, swords drawn, crossbows drawn. Men in crimson and gold.

'Stand there, my lord.'

Lanfranc walked towards the oak, through the closing ranks of men. He pointed his sword at Robin with a stone-hard face.

'Put down your weapons.'

'*My* weapons?' Robin sheathed his sword. The men did not lower theirs.

'The dagger as well.'

'This is not mine.'

'It is in your hands.'

Robin looked again at his hands. He was overtaken by a sudden, mad impulse to laugh. He had been caught red-handed. Very good, he thought. Very clever, Lord Eudo. How long had it taken him to arrange this? Robin threw the dagger to the ground and reached to his belt. The men stepped closer, tensed to strike. He drew out the message Peter had sent him and held it up for Lanfranc to see.

'Yours, I presume?'

Lanfranc took the message with a frown.

'I do not know what you mean, my lord. You had better come with us. If I have your assurance that you will not try to escape I will let you ride your horse, but I must bind your hands.'

Robin rubbed his hands on his mantle, trying to rid them of the blood.

'No.' Lanfranc stopped him. 'Leave that.'

One of the men had a rope at his hip. He bound Robin's hands tight away from each other so that he could not remove any more traces of blood. Other men cut Peter free of the arrows holding him in place. His body slumped to the earth like an overfull sack.

'Treat him with some respect,' Robin called out angrily.

The men exchanged glances but lifted Peter's body more carefully. Lanfranc led Robin to his horse, whose bridle two men had hold of, and offered a hand to assist him. He ignored it. He could run, he thought. Even with bound hands he was probably a better horseman than most of these. If he ducked low he might be able to avoid the crossbow bolts. Of course, if his horse was shot he could not outrun them. And to run suggested guilt. The sheriff would not believe him capable of this crime, but it was wise to give no cause for doubt. He allowed his horse to be pulled along in a line with the men. Lanfranc rode behind him, watching him the whole way. Robin could feel his eyes, his pig-like triumphant eyes, on him all the way to the castle.

Sowing

They put him in a cell. Not in one of the chambers of the middle bailey where guests were usually lodged but inside the keep, behind the wine butts. The same cell from which the hundredmen had escaped. There was irony, he thought darkly as the door was closed behind him and the latch jiggled shut. His hands were still bound so he squatted awkwardly on the cold stones. Lanfranc had taken his time getting Robin into the cell, making sure there were plenty of witnesses to Lord Locksley's blood-smeared arrival. The blood on his hands had dried now, sticky and caked, and he wanted to wash them, but he could barely reach to rub them against his clothes. After what felt like hours the door was opened and a guard held out a bowl of something grey, purporting to be edible.

'I can't eat with my hands bound.'

The guard glanced over his shoulder, to some figure behind him, hidden from view by the door. Robin did not doubt that it was Lanfranc. He must have received permission because the guard cautiously cut away the ropes and left a spoon in the stew. Before the door closed Robin shouted out, loud enough for his silent observer to hear.

'I want a priest.'

'You want to make a confession?' the guard asked.

'Why not? But I will only talk to the friar in Lenton Priory.'

'There's a priest in the castle. It would take less time.'

'Only the friar.'

The guard locked the door again. Robin ate some bites of the stew then pushed it away. He needed to warn the hundredmen that the Viponts knew of Peter's involvement with their thefts. That must be the reason they had killed Peter. And the rough treatment they had given him suggested they had been trying to extract information from him too – had he told them anything they could use to hunt down the hundredmen? He did not think Peter knew enough to do so, even if he had been willing, but it was best to be safe, and with the Prior of Lenton's protection Friar Toki was the only one who both knew the location of the Hundred and could reach it in safety. He should warn them to lay low for a while as well, at least until Robin was free. With Will wounded and captured, and now Robin taken too, the men should do everything in their power to keep themselves concealed from the forces of the Viponts.

There was no visit from the friar that night. Inside the cell it was hard to tell day from night, but the changeover of guards and noises from overhead of benches scraping for meals in the hall gave Robin some idea of the passing hours. The Viponts could keep Robin for days, weeks even, before bringing the case before a court. Perhaps they would not even admit to holding him in the keep, but hope everyone would think he was missing and let him slowly rot to death in secret? No, that was foolish. He had been seen by half the castle's inhabitants when he came in. Surely one of them must have told the sheriff? But if that was the case, why was Sir Walter not pressing for a trial? Why had no one visited Robin? Another day seemed to pass, another meal of grey slop and a bucket replaced his old one.

When finally a visitor came, it was not the friar he had asked for. It was the sheriff. In the sudden burst of light that blinded Robin when the door was thrown back, Sir Walter looked like some avenging angel, come from Heaven to seek him out. The next moment that impression was gone. Sir Walter seized him and dragged him out of the cell, amidst the guards' loud protests. Robin blinked and squinted in the candlelight. Lanfranc stood to bar Sir Walter's way out of the cellar, the many lords Vipont at his back. Waltheof was behind them, standing with Sir Walter's constable and servants. They all argued with each other, the noise crashing over Robin like a heaving wave. It was some moments before he could make out individual words.

'Outrage,' Sir Walter was crying. 'These conditions –'

He pulled himself away from the sheriff and stood up as tall as he could. The squalling voices fell away.

'Am I free?' he asked dryly. He already knew what the answer would be.

'No,' said Lord Eudo. 'You are going to stand trial for your crime.'

'An outrage,' Sir Walter cried again.

'You will go before the royal justices tomorrow,' said Eudo.

The royal justices, Robin thought. The men he had waited months for, and now finally they came at the bidding of the Viponts to condemn him. How convenient, that when he had needed them to restore his estates they had answered only with excuses, but when the Viponts called for a court of justice they came running. The count's influence again, no doubt.

'What crime am I charged with?'

'Murder.'

'Of which charge,' said Sir Walter firmly, 'you will be cleared. But until then you will not be kept in these conditions. You are a lord.'

'Not before the law,' said Eudo.

'I will not argue this again.'

Eudo stood resolute. 'The royal justices have still not recognised Lord Locksley's right to his inheritance, nor his title. We have treated him as a lord in the past out of respect for you, Sir Walter, but since this is a legal matter we must act within the law.'

'No, you must act as I command. I am the sheriff and it is my responsibility to imprison men according to their rank. If you will not let me bring Robin back to Locksley then I demand you move him to one of the bedchambers here.'

Ranulf stepped forward to argue, but Eudo halted him.

'Since you insist.' He spoke softly to Lanfranc, who nodded. 'Our steward will lead the way.'

Lanfranc and two guards encircled Robin to escort him out of the cellar. Sir

Walter walked alongside him, Waltheof taking the other flank, and a pack of the sheriff's servants followed behind.

'I was starting to think I had been forgotten,' said Robin as they weaved through the castle and into the biting cold fresh air beyond it.

'We were not told you were here,' said Sir Walter in a low growl. 'Lanfranc sent us on a merry chase to Lord de Caux's home before Marian learned from some servants of Guy's that you had been taken to the keep cellars. Are you hurt?'

'Nothing a bed won't mend.'

They said no more until they were within a small chamber inside the middle bailey. It was not richly furnished but to Robin the bed, chairs and fire within it were luxury enough.

'I will have my own men on guard outside,' said Sir Walter, dismissing Lanfranc. 'Lord Locksley will have the same food as the Lords Vipont – and as quickly as possible. Bring some hot water to wash as well.'

He entered the chamber and barred the door, listening for the retreating footsteps of the Vipont men. When he was satisfied he took a seat near the fire.

'You will have to stay here, for that I am sorry. Removing you to Locksley Hall would be a step too far.'

'Any improvement on that cell is welcome.'

Robin lay back on the bed, his spine twinging as it touched the bolster. Sir Walter watched him, his countenance grim. Robin felt a shudder of uncertainty. Was the sheriff really just treating him this way because it was how a lord should be kept? Did he suspect his stepson was guilty? He met Sir Walter's eye.

'I did not kill Peter.'

Sir Walter prodded the fire. 'I am glad to hear that. I would not wish my family's faith in you to be misplaced.'

His family, Robin thought, and he knew that Marian must be as much behind this insistence on his comfort as any sense of the sheriff's duty to a lord. He smiled ruefully. She always seemed to be at hand now when he needed help.

'The royal justices have arrived quickly. How long was I in that cell?'

'Three days. I suspect the justices were invited even before the clerk was found – not that there has been any evidence of that, of course.'

So he too believed that Peter's murder was a premeditated scheme to cast Robin as a killer. Robin felt a rush of relief. If the sheriff was suspicious of the Viponts, perhaps the royal justices would follow his example. He was, after all, the voice of authority in the county.

'Why have they done this to me now?'

'It – it is my doing, I fear. I went to Guy, after you brought me that letter to the count, and pleaded with him not to involve himself in a rebellion, should it occur. He will have told his family – that much I suspected he would do – but I thought if they knew we were watching them they might be more cautious, perhaps delay acting with the count at all.'

'So they did this to punish me for finding the letter?'

It seemed a great deal of trouble to go to on so meagre a cause for vengeance.

But then, Robin thought, they had other causes for resentment. He had drawn their neighbouring lords into an alliance against their plan for the common land, he had repeatedly refused to bend the knee to their authority, he had argued against their version of justice and he had even scorned a peaceful agreement once it had been made, thanks to Elaine's interference. More than that, his very existence harmed their interests – if he had never returned to Nottinghamshire they would be enjoying the Locksley estate free of his nagging influence. Robin remembered John Blunt's warning to him: *You haven't seen the worst of the Viponts. Your noble birth will only protect you from them for so long*. Perhaps their resentment towards him had been building ever since his return.

He saw again the flash of triumph on Eudo's face when he and Peter had emerged from the chancery antechamber together. A surge of remorse overtook him. He should never have involved Peter in these schemes.

'I showed Peter the letter. He was the one who told me what the symbol on it might be. No doubt that is why they chose him to be my victim. They not only silenced him, they tricked me to go into the woods by using someone I trusted.'

He told Sir Walter about the message that had arrived, asking Robin to meet Peter in the forest. That message, of course, had disappeared. There was nothing to suggest that Robin had not enticed the clerk into a trap, rather than the other way around.

There was a rap at the door. Sir Walter opened it. Waltheof stood there with a jug of hot water, soap, towels and bowl. Behind him another of the sheriff's servants held a tray of food and drink. Sir Walter gestured them in.

'I should leave you to rest. Robin, there is not much I can do tomorrow. If it was a county court I could have sway over the decision, but with the royal justices it is unlikely I will even be allowed to ask questions.' He stepped closer and gripped Robin's shoulder. 'But you should know that as far as I am concerned this is a family matter. You are part of my family and I will do whatever I can to protect you. The Viponts must not be permitted to pervert the law in this way. Guy has disappointed me, but I am glad of it. I now know that the only people we can trust are our own. If the Viponts are so desperate to band together, we will do the same. I will not bend the knee to them – or give them the benefit of my trust – again.'

That was something at least, thought Robin. One more ally against the Viponts.

Sir Walter forced a smile. 'I will have fresh clothes brought for you tomorrow morning.'

The servants followed Sir Walter from the chamber. Waltheof paused over his task and Sir Walter obviously took the hint that Robin might have some words to convey to his attendant. He closed the door and stood outside talking loudly to cover their conversation. Robin came over to the bowl of water and started to wash his hands, keeping his voice as low as possible, one eye on the door.

'I tried to get the friar to visit so I could find out what was happening outside that cell. Has Will been tried yet?'

'No.'

'Thank God. Can you take a message to the hundredmen? Are they still safe?'

'Safe but angry. They were trying to come up with a way to free you.'

'Tell them not to.'

'Me telling them might not be enough.'

'Persuade John. He'll talk them down. There is only one thing they can do which will help.'

'What?'

'They need to silence the guard who saw Will's face when they attacked the count's train. He's the same man who wounded him. If he is called as a witness at Will's trial there's no way Will can avoid the noose. The guards were mostly local men, it must be possible to trace them.'

'Silence him how?'

'Any way they can. He's a body for hire, so money might be enough. If it isn't – well, they have knives.'

Waltheof nodded, but said nothing. Robin sometimes forgot that his companions were not soldiers themselves, that they might baulk at shedding blood. He gazed into his own reflection in the washing bowl. In the lapping water he looked hooded, his dark hair and beard concealing half his features. All he could really see were his teeth, gleaming light like a wolf's maw in the shadows.

Before the next morning dawned Robin was awake. Even the welcome relief of a bed after days of straw on a cellar floor was not enough to entice him to sleep. He spent the night turning over in his mind the possible outcome of the court. If he was proclaimed guilty by the justices he could be hanged. At best, if the count or the king's chancellor in Westminster could be persuaded into it, he might get a pardon and be exiled again. The thought of leaving England once more, of being forced into another futile crusade or pressed into an army in Normandy, when he had come so close to regaining his father's lands, was almost worse than the noose.

The court of the royal justices was to be held in the great hall of the middle bailey and Robin heard the eager footfall and chatter of men flocking into the court for some time before he was himself sought to join them. Apparently his neighbours viewed this case as sufficiently interesting to warrant their personal attention. Even Lord Foliot had left his steward at home and come in person.

As he walked down to the hall along a thin passageway overlooking the courtyard he noticed Elaine, standing huddled with Serlo and Idonea Vipont. A blast of wind swirled her cloak tight around her body and Robin remembered the night they had quarrelled at the betrothal feast, her gown striking him as she left. Eudo came to join their party, wearing his finest robes and a gleeful expression. He kissed Elaine's hand and she fluttered over the attention like a bird. Her eye drifted beyond him to the window where Robin watched her. She met his eye with a sudden flush of shock and turned away. Clearly her adherence to the Vipont cause had only increased since Robin broke off their betrothal. Even the prospect of Robin being hanged because of that family could not dampen her ardour for the family. Once he was freed – he could not think 'if'

– he would personally ensure that Eudo de Vipont was dragged naked through the streets of Nottingham and dangled over the barbican in chains. The savage thought gave him a moment's respite from fears for the trial, but the next instant he was stepping through the door into the great hall and every eye in the chamber was trained on him. Faces he knew and those he barely recognised, all watching him walk towards the justices at their high table and stand to face their questioning. He stood straight backed and uncowed before them. The justice sitting in their centre called out to the lords gathered at the side of the room.

'Let us hear the appeal.'

Lord Eudo stepped forward and bowed to the justices. 'We appeal that Robin of Locksley has murdered Peter of Westminster, a clerk in the sheriff's chancery.'

Sitting near the edge of the high table Sir Walter shifted as if preparing to speak, but before he could stand Eudo continued.

'Furthermore, we appeal that Locksley did this to conceal from the world his more manifest crimes, in having led a band of armed thieves in the forest to attack wagons carrying taxes, fines and other fees rightfully belonging to the crown or his neighbouring lords.'

The last words were swallowed by a wave of exclamations. Robin met Sir Walter's eye in frozen astonishment. The sheriff looked as surprised as the rest of the chamber. He had obviously not been given warning of these additional charges. Robin felt a shiver run down his spine. It must have been for this that the Viponts kept him locked in a cell for days. They wanted to ensure he was unprepared for the charges laid against him, not only ignorant of anything he could use to defend himself but also weakened before this shock. Doubtless they hoped that in his fatigue he would condemn himself through some thoughtless word or action. He turned to Eudo, consciously training every part of himself to be calm, silent, unmoving. They would not force him into confession.

'And you claim both of these felonies must be presented before us at once?'

'Yes. One proves the other.'

'Very well. Let us hear from a witness, Brother Simon.'

Brother Simon, it transpired, was one of Peter's fellow clerks in chancery. He swore before the court that he had seen Peter and Robin repeatedly speak in private, had seen Peter copy documents that required no duplicate and had also seen Peter handing documents very similar to those copies to Robin. When Brother Simon retired from the court the chief justice addressed Robin.

'What were the documents Peter the clerk gave to you?'

'They related to my estate and my marriage. Writs, messages from Westminster.'

'Yet you discussed these matters in utmost secrecy. Why?'

'Neither of those matters concern others. What you call secrecy I call privacy.'

'In our experience only men with something to hide shield themselves from public gaze.'

'I have nothing to hide.'

'Then why did you not have one of the clerks in the sheriff's household deal with these affairs? Why seek out this clerk over all others, at some inconvenience to yourself?'

'He was recommended to me.'

'By Lady Elaine Peverill.'

Robin hesitated. How did the justices know that? 'Yes.'

'We have heard from another witness that your betrothal to the Lady Elaine was broken some weeks ago, yet still you sought the company of this clerk.'

'My estate has still not been settled. I needed advice from him on that matter. The royal justices kept delaying their circuit in Nottinghamshire.'

The justices did not like that comment. Robin bit his lip to try to prevent his anger getting the best of him.

'A witness who requested anonymity,' the chief justice continued, 'claims to have seen a document passed by the clerk to you which detailed the provisions put in place to protect the movement of furnishings from this castle to Clipstone Palace. Why did you require that document? It was not relevant to your estate.'

The net tightened. Only two people other than Robin and Peter had seen that document: Marian and Elaine. Could Marian have told Guy about it? Robin found it hard to believe that she would have done so when she had kept his confidence over the hundredmen in the forest. But he did not like the alternative. Was that the reason for Elaine and the Viponts' sudden affection? Had Elaine proven her loyalty to that family by sharing secrets that harmed Robin? Robin looked at Eudo as he replied, wishing he could strike the smug smile from his face.

'I think your witness is wrong. Perhaps they were paid to tell that lie, or perhaps they have a personal reason to speak against me.'

'Our witness spoke under oath. As do you. If you lie, you do so before God. Tell us why you needed that document.'

'No.'

Robin would reveal nothing that could harm the hundredmen, nothing that could link their actions to him and Peter.

Ranulf leapt to his feet and flung his finger towards Robin as if it was a sword. 'He will not tell us because he used that information to attack us. He has been leading those forestmen ever since he returned from the East. Why were there no attacks before he came here?'

The justices shouted for their attendants to restore order, for Ranulf to control himself or be escorted from the hall. With Eudo and Serlo whispering in his ear he calmed enough to sit down again, his face flushed with anger.

'There is another witness whose information on this point is relevant,' said the chief justice. 'Lanfranc the steward.'

Perfect, thought Robin. The Vipont dog, barking his accusations for the whole court. He wished he had slit his throat when he had him drugged and bound, rather than stopping at throwing him in the street naked.

'Peter the clerk came to me the day before his murder,' Lanfranc said when he stood before the court, 'and told me that Lord Locksley had threatened violence against him. He said he was afraid to go to the sheriff with his fears because of Lord Locksley's relationship to Sir Walter.'

The court turned to see how the sheriff took Lanfranc's claim. Sir Walter puffed out his cheeks in outrage at the aspersion against his biased justice, but did not stand and shout like Ranulf.

'Peter said he was in mortal fear of Lord Locksley because he had been seen giving documents to him and now Lord Locksley said he would have him killed before he could tell us what those documents contained.'

'Did he tell you what they contained?'

'He confessed that they were to enable thefts on local lords, particularly those that Lord Locksley wanted vengeance against. He had provided them to Lord Locksley because otherwise he feared he would be killed.'

Robin shook his head, almost smiling through gritted teeth. Liar, he thought. Liar.

Lanfranc sat down again, his voice a mask of innocence. The justice asked Robin whether he had threatened Peter, whether he knew that Peter had spoken to Lanfranc, whether he had gone to the blasted oak to argue with the clerk? No, Robin replied, over and over but the faces around the hall darkened with every question and the justices grew more severe. They had already decided, he thought. There was not a witness to say he had laid a hand on Peter, but the justices had already decided his guilt. Sir Walter suddenly stood up.

'I cannot sit silently any longer. I have judged hundreds of courts and never once seen the king's justice so misled. Baseless charges are being made against a lord by the servants of his accusers. A lord should not be spoken against by these commonborn men.'

'Perhaps this is the time,' called Eudo, 'to settle Lord Robin's claim on the Locksley estate once and for all. Any of these lords here could be called upon to do so.'

'We are already trying two cases at once,' said the chief justice wearily, 'must we really add a third?'

His colleagues muttered to one another again.

'Very well,' he said at length, 'it may be pertinent. I believe the writ of mort d'ancestor has already been addressed to our office?' A clerk rifled through a file and pulled out a writ for the justice to inspect. 'Call forth twelve compurgators.'

When Robin had imagined the restoration of his father's estate to its rightful owner he had never expected it to happen like this. In the midst of a trial that held his life in the balance, his enemies' lies still ringing in his ears, with the clerks of the royal justices chivvying lords and servants about the chamber. The compurgators were asked the same two questions over and over.

'Was the plaintiff's father, Robert, Lord Locksley, in peaceful possession of the estate in question when he died? Is the plaintiff Lord Locksley's heir?'

Twelve times the questions were asked, twelve times they were answered by the lords in that hall. The last to stand forward was Lord D'Alselin, who spoke with a clear voice that drowned out even the scurrying of the clerks and muttering of the justices. Having heard the twelve men recognise Robin before the court the justice rapped his knuckles on the table to draw the hall back to attention.

'Robin of Locksley is rightful heir to the Locksley estate and shall recover possession from the ward Jocelyn once this trial is over – if he is not hanged.'

A clerk hurried to write up a new writ of ownership. Eudo did not look remotely perturbed to have lost the Locksley estate. Obviously, thought Robin, the justice's last words were still singing in his ears.

'Before you sit down, Lord D'Alselin.' The chief justice took another document from one of his colleagues. 'Perhaps we could ask you a few more questions? It is related to the case against Lord Locksley.'

'As you wish.'

'You have recognised this man as Robin, son of Robert, Lord Locksley who died in the third year of the reign of King Richard?'

'Yes.'

'The same Robin, son of Robert, Lord Locksley who was convicted by a court in the last year of the reign of the late King Henry of having murdered Geraint, the blacksmith's son?'

Lord D'Alselin hesitated, glanced at Robin, spoke with less certainty. 'Yes.'

'He has done penance for that,' called out Sir Walter but the justice ignored him.

'The same Robin, son of Robert, Lord Locksley who in his youth was reprimanded before the county court for public drunkenness, for violence during a holy season, for disturbing the peace with his lowborn companions?'

'Yes.'

'And am I right in understanding that when Lord Locksley murdered this youth – as he confessed he did before the court – he did so with a knife?'

'Yes. But –'

'No need to expand on your answers,' said the chief justice. 'Yes is enough.'

He leant across to discuss something with his fellow justices, then again to murmur to his colleagues on the other side of the table. They all nodded. Not good, thought Robin. But the worst blow was yet to be struck.

'One final question, if you permit me?'

He did.

'Lord D'Alselin, is it true that sometimes Lord Robin's bastard brother attended your law courts pretending to be Lord Robin himself? That they so resemble each other as to be easily mistaken one for the other?'

There were murmurs in the hall, lords questioning how similar the men must be to be mistaken for one another, wondering aloud if the chief justice exaggerated the resemblance.

'They – there is a similarity,' began Lord D'Alselin.

The chief justice gestured towards Lord Eudo, who stood and addressed the hall himself.

'My family has harboured suspicions against Lord Locksley for some time, Lord Justices, but we hesitated to give voice to them. We could not understand how Lord Locksley could lead a band of thieves and yet always be elsewhere when felonies were committed. But the explanation for that is simple: thanks to his brother, Lord Locksley is able to appear to be in two places at once.'

With a nod towards the side of the hall a door flew open and there, standing in fine clothes, his hair brushed, his beard trimmed, was a second Lord Locksley in Will Scarlette. There were gasps around the chamber. The court stared from Robin to Will and back to Robin, scarcely believing the truth of their eyes. Many of the lords knew Will Scarlette of old, but he and Robin had been careful to be seen together as little as possible since Robin's return, and time had dulled their memories. Now those memories rekindled. Of course, the pair had always been a mirror of each other. If Lord Locksley could achieve such a deceit with a simple change of clothes, was it not also possible he had deceived every lord in that chamber into thinking him an honest man? A man capable of standing in two sides of a hall at once was capable of anything, of any felony. Robin watched that thought ripple through the hall like stones cast in a river.

'May I speak?' he called over the noise.

'No you may not,' said the chief justice.

'Then I will,' said Sir Walter, rising again to address the hall. The voices bubbled away to a low murmur. 'All Lord Eudo has proven here is that Lord Locksley has a brother who looks like him. This does not prove that either of these men was present when any of the crimes you mentioned took place.'

'But our witness does,' said Eudo.

Oh no, thought Robin. The chief justice called for the hall to settle while a witness was brought forward. Just as he had feared, the man crossing the tiles in his best wool was the same armed guard who had been smeared with Will's blood at the roadside. That was the end of it, surely. Even if his own noble birth saved him from the noose, Will would hang for their crimes. If Lord Eudo de Vipont had any say in the matter both of them would take their identical faces to the gallows. He sought Will's eye and knew that his brother was thinking the same thing. Robin forced himself to suppress any signs of guilt or anxiety as the guard swore to speak the truth.

'Master Henry of Nottingham,' said the chief justice, 'you were among the men paid to protect the Count of Mortain's possessions as they were transported to Clipstone?'

'I was. I get hired for rough work fairly often. Usually just moving barrels of ale, not a prince's things.'

'Yes would have been enough, thank you. And when the count's wagons were attacked you wounded one of the thieves, across the chest?'

'Yes.'

'I will remind my fellow justices that Master William Scarlette has a wound across his own chest, which he claims he received while hunting. Master Henry, please look carefully at Robin of Locksley and Master Scarlette. Did the thief that you wounded look like either of these two men?'

The guard squinted at Will on the other side of the hall, then at Robin, then smiled.

'No.'

'I beg your pardon?'

'No. Neither of them. The thief I saw was shorter, lighter haired.'

The chief justice shot a confused look at Eudo.

'I understood that you had told Lanfranc the steward in Nottingham Castle that the man you injured looked like Lord Locksley?'

'Like him, yes. But he wasn't him. You see, Lord Locksley's was one of the first faces I saw after the attack and with the shock of fighting off that thief, I think I muddled their two faces in my mind. I've never actually wounded a man in a fight before, not as seriously as I hurt that thief. It took me a while to calm myself. I'm sure the lords gathered here felt the same when they first fought in a battle. And to be honest I don't believe that man there could have been the one I wounded. The thief I struck was bleeding so hard he must be dead, or very near it. This one just looks pale.'

Robin and Will grinned at each other in disbelief. Somehow, Waltheof had found a means not of silencing this guard, but of making him speak the words that helped their cause. If they were freed, Robin and Will would spend the rest of their lives ensuring Waltheof was very rich and very happy. If, he reminded himself. It was not certain yet. The guard was dismissed from court, the Viponts' glares following him all the way down the hall.

'I fear we have only two possible recourses,' said the chief justice. 'Either more witnesses can be called and we will hold another court afterwards, or if that is impossible this case must be decided by ordeal.'

'We would be happy to delay proceedings until more witnesses can be called,' said Eudo.

Of course he would, thought Robin. He had already proven his ability to stack a court full of 'witnesses' who by sheer coincidence all received their wages from his purse. Robin could not allow this case to go on any longer. To wait for witnesses would mean the certainty of defeat. He held up his hands and raised his voice above the clamour in the hall.

'I am innocent of what you claim,' he cried. 'And I swear that my brother is too. As a free man, I deny everything you have recounted here, word for word. I will clear myself by God's judgement. I will face the ordeal of the hot iron.'

The hall fell silent. The justices turned to him with the fascination of physicians inspecting a patient with a particularly rare disease.

'But he is clearly guilty,' shouted Ranulf. 'Both of them are. We can get witnesses –'

'There is no witness to the crime of Peter the clerk's murder,' called Sir Walter urgently. 'Those who arrested Robin arrived after Peter was already dead. And if there had been any other worthy witnesses to the attacks across this county, they would already have been called. Clearly, no man can stand as witness. God must do so.'

Sir Walter knew the law too well for the Viponts. He had judged and observed more courts in England than all of their family together, and they knew he was right, just as the royal justices did.

'Very well,' said the chief justice. 'Robin of Locksley and William Scarlette will both hold a hot iron and walk six paces. Their hands will be bound and inspected after three days. If their hands heal normally, God has made manifest their innocence. If there is any sign of infection it is clear the devil is being driven to the surface and we will know they are guilty.'

'Please allow us one kindness,' said Robin before the justices could pronounce the trial over. 'My brother's hunting injury still weakens him. Please let me take this ordeal for both of us.'

The justices conferred.

'The king's justice must always be even-handed. With that in mind, you may undertake this ordeal for both of you. Your right hand will bear witness to your own innocence, your left hand to that of your brother. Have Lord Locksley prepared for the ordeal.'

The justices' men led him to the chapel in the keep and pressed his knees to the ground. The sheriff insisted on accompanying him with his own attendants, but the Viponts were not far behind. The prospect of a hanged Lord Locksley was only slightly improved on by the prospect of a scalded and hanged Lord Locksley.

'My brother should be at my side,' Robin said as the Vipont guard made to press Will back down to his cell in the bowels of the keep. 'Since I take this ordeal for both of us.'

The representative of the justices agreed, and Robin and Will both knelt before the altar while the castle's priest was called to say Mass and an iron bar fetched. They bowed their heads and pressed their palms but when their lips moved it was not in prayer.

'Why did that guard lie?' Will whispered. 'He knew me, I could tell.'

'Waltheof must have paid him off. He didn't look to be rich, and we have half a palace's worth of metal and furnishings in the forest. How are you healing?'

'Not as badly as you might expect. The cell of theirs is a cave, but I like sandstone and I don't have to work. The friar came and stitched me up again.' Robin glanced at him. Will still looked ill. His face was pale and his eyes rimmed with shadows. He met his brother's eye for a moment. 'Are you sure this is a good idea?'

'It's the only idea I had. It was this or let them hang us.'

'They'll hang us anyway. We're both guilty.'

'I didn't kill Peter.'

'All right, you're innocent of that. Maybe only half your right hand will blister. Your left hand doesn't have a hope.' Robin smiled, but for once Will was serious. 'You should let me face my own ordeal.'

'No.'

'I'm not as bad as I was. Marian brought me some balm that Gytha made, and Friar Toki gave me a phial of henbane for the pain. Wish I had it now, we could share it.'

'I don't need it. And you are not going to the ordeal. It was my choice to have you lead the attack on the count's train, it was my failure that meant Lanfranc could take you. I need to make amends for those mistakes.'

'You're too noble for your own good. It's a serious failing.'

The priest had arrived, bearing holy water. A Vipont servant brought out two iron rods. The priest disappeared behind the rood screen to douse the irons in holy water and bless them, then they were placed on top of a brazier burning near the doorway. Robin felt a hand on his back and turned to see Sir Walter there.

'The irons will stay in the fire until Mass is over. I have a man watching it, to make sure Lord Eudo does not interfere.'

'How much interference could he give?' said Will. 'The fire will do the work for him.'

'I have also looked over the bindings for afterwards to make sure there is no dirt or anything else to cause infection. I have seen that trick played on a man before. You will go back to your chamber near the hall after this and your servant can attend you until your hands heal.'

'Let us just hope they do heal,' said Robin as the priest began intoning the Mass.

Sir Walter retired to the back of the chapel and the chamber was silent, but for the priest's voice. Robin tried to keep his mind clear, tried to put aside any doubt or guilty thoughts. But he could not stop himself glancing now and then towards the brazier, where the two irons steadily heated. He stared at the rood screen, where twelve apostles benevolently raised their hands in blessing, where the Gospels glistened, where the Virgin wept for her only son's death. Sir Walter had given him no message from his mother. Was she weeping now, fearing he might be hanged?

He realised with a start that the Mass was ending. The priest elevated the host, drank from his chalice, ate the communion bread and returned from behind the screen. There would be no further delay. The justices had arrived and watched now as tongs were brought to lift the irons from the fire. Robin held out his naked hands to them so they could ensure he had not used any remedies or preparations against the burns. One of the justices walked six paces up the aisle and laid a bucket of water at his feet.

'You must walk this far with your hands before you, clasping the irons tight, and only when you reach this point release them. If you open your hands before you reach this point it will be a sign of your guilt.'

A servant holding a stack of linens stood behind the bucket, glanced at the brazier, and took a step back. The chief justice gestured the priest forward. He raised his hands in prayer over the irons.

'Omnipotent, eternal God, we humbly beseech you to send your holy and true blessing on this iron, so that it should be a pleasing coolness to those who carry it with justice and fortitude but a burning fire to the wicked. Through Him whom hidden things do not escape let the righteousness of justice be manifested.'

The priest crossed himself. One of the justices lifted the glowing irons from the fire and held out the tongs before Robin. Even standing in front of them he could feel the heat rising from them. Every natural impulse in his body cried out against touching them. Only six steps, he thought. It did not look so far from here to the bucket of water. He let out one long, deep breath and put out his hands to seize the irons.

Instantly, pain seared through his body, not just his hands but up the length of his arms and into his chest. He almost jumped the first step, hurrying to rid himself of the blazing bars under his fingers. Those were the longest six steps of Robin's life. He felt his arms tremble, his legs almost giving way beneath him. He squeezed his eyes closed against the pain then opened them to find he had barely moved forwards. He gritted his teeth so tightly together he thought they would shatter. One more step. He lunged over the final flagstone and thrust his hands into the bucket of water. Steam boiled out of it, momentarily blinding him. The searing pain only intensified as he felt his arms drawn from the water and his trembling hands wrapped in linen. When he opened his eyes he could only see two throbbing linen-bound lumps where his hands had been.

'You have passed this first part,' said the chief justice. 'Do not touch the bindings or it will be a sign of your guilt. We will see you in three days.'

They filed from the chapel, the priest blessing them as they went. Sir Walter hurried to Robin's side and took his arm.

'You are white. Let's get you to your chamber quickly.'

Will must have been led away. Robin could not see him. With Waltheof on one side and the sheriff on the other he stumbled his way back to the middle bailey and into his chamber.

Three days had passed since the ordeal. Robin spent most of those days asleep, but unconscious hours offered no rest. The pain in his hands sent vivid nightmares through his mind as if he was still awake. He dreamt Lord Eudo's mouth belched fire and that he was fighting demons with leather wings and sulphur breath. He dreamt his hands were two lumps of wax that melted, pouring scalding liquid over the rest of his body. He fought sleep, wanting to avoid the terror of those visions and the certainty of guilt that they suggested, but he could not keep it away. In the few brief moments he was awake every drink he had sipped had been held in Waltheof's hands and every spoonful of food.

On the morning of the final day Waltheof helped him dress and dragged him into a semblance of alertness. He stood again in the court of the royal justices, surrounded by lords and their servants, the Viponts massed in one crimson corner while Sir Walter stood in another. There was a rippling through the crowd as of grass in a breeze and Marian appeared next to the sheriff. She sought and met Robin's gaze, forcing a smile. Her lips moved but he could not read what she said. The justices were entering the hall. They filed towards Robin. He held his hands out to them. One of them cut the bindings carefully, peeling away layers of linen. His fellows leant forward to smell for any sign of corruption. Satisfied, the last pieces of linen were unfurled. Beneath, Robin's hands each held a puckered white line down their centre and along the creases of his fingers, surrounded by a pink deep as a dyer's palm.

'The right is healing well.'

A moment's relief. Then fear.

'What about the left?'

They still peered at it. One raised his eyebrows. Another rubbed his nose uncertainly.

'It – is not suppurating,' said the nose-rubber. 'But…'

'Is that a blister?'

One of them prodded a pad of skin beneath his thumb. Robin could not completely suppress a wince. They noticed, shook their heads.

'It feels no different from the right,' he said quickly. 'Perhaps I held the iron for longer in my left hand.'

'That would impact on the result.'

'I told you we should have got the brother to do his own ordeal.'

'It is done now.' The chief justice stepped back. 'Your innocence is certain. Your brother's is not. But then, neither is his guilt. He will have to undertake his own ordeal.'

Robin started to interrupt but the justice overrode him.

'That can wait until he has recovered from this injury you spoke of. He will be tried again on our next circuit.'

'How long will that be?'

'We can keep him in the castle,' said Lord Eudo, who had been listening closely to every word. 'We are happy to do so.'

'That would be best.'

The justices filed back behind their table to give final judgement.

'William Scarlette will remain a prisoner in Nottingham Castle until royal justices next visit this county, when he will prove his innocence or guilt in an ordeal, unless more witnesses to his crimes have been found. Lord Locksley has proven his innocence before us. He will be released, although not to his home. It has become clear that your reputation, Lord Locksley, is not a high one in this county. Lords who are not trusted by their fellows are useless to their community. Your oaths cannot be used before the law, your justice must always be under question. As such, you cannot serve on local courts let alone lead them. In such cases in the past, where a man has proven his innocence but not restored his reputation, that man has always been exiled.'

There was a shout from the Viponts. Ranulf clapped his hands together with a barking laugh. The justice raised his palm for quiet.

'However, we choose a middle ground. You will be exiled from your estate – you must not spend another night under the roof of your manor – but you are permitted to remain within the county. Your family may offer you what support they wish, as long as you do not linger on their lands. Your estate will rest with your nephew, Jocelyn.'

Robin looked again at the Viponts. Their smiles were not so broad, but their victory was still clear. They had regained the Locksley estate, destroyed Robin's name and cast him out even of the scant comfort of his home with Sir Walter. The only home he had left was the forest. It was outlawry without the prospect of arrest. He was alive, he reminded himself, he was free. He looked at Will, defeated and pale, and knew he must consider himself fortunate.

'God keep you all,' concluded the justice.

The court was ended. Robin hurried over to Will, reaching out a hand without thinking. Will saw the burnt flesh there and shrank from it. The Vipont guards encircled him and marched him back towards his cell before he could speak a word.

'You should have said a proper goodbye.'

Robin turned to find Eudo de Vipont watching him, a cruel smile on his lips.

'Men often die in imprisonment, especially those recovering from injury.'

He dared to threaten Will now, when the royal justices were barely yards away?

'If you hurt him –'

'I said nothing about hurting him. I mentioned his death. So you had better tell your friends in the forest not to bother us again. If you want coin get it from your precious sheriff, or steal the king's ransom. If you do anything to hurt the interests of our family or the Count of Mortain it will be the worse for your brother.'

He stepped back with a forced smile over Robin's shoulder.

'Marian, dearheart. So good to see you. I presume you were here to support Guy through the rigours of this trial?'

Marian felt the coldness beneath his civil words.

'I came to see Robin freed, as I knew he would be.'

'How noble. Do be careful how much support you offer. It is so easy for a man to violate the conditions of his exile. I would hate to see Locksley sent out of the kingdom. Farewell, Lord Robin. I will remember you to Jocelyn.'

Marian and Robin watched Eudo leave. When Robin turned back to her, Marian's face was a mirror of his own, frustrated anger written all over it. Neither could give vent to it.

'My father would be so proud,' said Robin with an attempt at levity. 'I managed to regain our estates for all of three days before the Viponts clawed them back.'

'You will have them again. Once the king is released – and his ransom must be almost paid – you can receive a royal pardon and be a free man again.'

Robin clenched his fingers. A wave of hot pain coursed through them. He shook his hand as if he could rid it of the discomfort that way.

'Here.' Marian held a small clay jar out to him. 'It is aloe to cool the burns. Gytha gave it to me. You should put some on before we ride back to Locksley. You – you will need to gather your things there.'

Robin went to take the jar and almost dropped it as it brushed against the searing line in the centre of his hand. Marian caught it and poured some of the liquid inside onto her palm, holding it out flat for Robin to take. He tentatively spread it over his hands. It did give some relief.

'Gytha has more she can give you. Your hand could still get infected, especially if you do not have people to look after you.'

'Do not tell Lord Eudo that. I will be hanged from the nearest gatehouse.'

The ride back to Locksley was a silent one. Robin re-bound his hands with linen before putting his gloves on but despite the bindings and aloe he could still keep only the weakest of grips on his reins. Marian and Sir Walter were lost in their own thoughts too. It was a relief when they reached the hall. Sir Walter lingered in the courtyard after dismounting. Robin was not relishing telling his mother the outcome of the trial, and he imagined the sheriff imagined it with little more enthusiasm.

'Do you know where you will go when you leave us?' Sir Walter asked. 'I can write to our friends for support now if it will help. Lord D'Alselin will not refuse you hospitality. And the Abbess of Newstead is family.'

'Thank you, but I can see to it myself.'

'Very well. I will go and speak to your mother, prepare her a little. Marian, have some food sent to the solar. We should all eat together before Robin leaves us.'

He reluctantly led the way inside. Marian and Robin followed slowly.

'You are going to the forest, aren't you?' she said. 'To your *hospital*.'

'Yes.'

'Are you sure you will have enough food? I have heard lots of the tenants have been disappearing into the forest, your hospital must be overfilled.'

'There are more of us, but that means more to help hunt and gather.'

'With winter coming on there will not be much to gather. I will see if one of the salted pigs can be sent to you after Martinmas.'

'That would help.'

Marian stood in an awkward stillness. Suddenly she broke it, exhaling heavily as her fists clenched at her sides.

'I wish I could do more. It is not right to send you away, to keep Locksley from you, it is not.'

'I know,' said Robin with a bleak smile. 'But thank you. It is good to hear someone else say it.'

They found Lady Joan and Elaine in the solar. Robin's mother behaved just as he expected at the news of her only child's exile from her home. She was anxious for him, but all her anxieties were expressed in terms of her own discomfort and unhappiness. Robin was left wondering if she might have taken news of his execution better. Elaine watched him and his mother in silence. Every now and then she cast him a look halfway between pity and – if he was right – guilt, but whenever he caught her eye she set her face firmly against him and looked away. Marian stayed away from the solar until supper, and then promptly disappeared again.

Having eaten what he could with his aching hands and a cold feeling in the pit of his stomach, Robin prepared to leave Locksley Hall. Waltheof helped him gather his few belongings while Lady Joan fussed and fluttered. In the courtyard Marian was waiting by Robin's horse, two laden packhorses roped to its pommel. He looked at their baggage. There were smoked and salted meats, fish; loaves of hard bread; preserves of all kinds; apples and nuts; linens, clay jars filled no doubt with Gytha's mysterious balms. Attached to the side of one of the packs were two hunting bows and a stuffed quiver. Robin looked at Marian in surprise.

'I thought it would be sensible to give you some supplies now. Perhaps Waltheof can escort you into the forest and come back to my household when your hands are recovered – not that I think you need help.'

Waltheof had already prepared to follow his master, and although loath to admit it, Robin knew he would need assistance until his hands fully healed. Robin attached the last of his things to Waltheof's mount while Wulfstan brought his dog, Husdent to join them. The hound might not like its new home as much as its old, but Robin consoled himself with the thought that at least Husdent would not get fat in his old age.

He swiftly said his farewells. When he was in the saddle Marian stepped forward suddenly.

'Come back for the wedding,' she said.

'Your groom would not be pleased to see me there.'

'It is not his decision. And he cannot refuse you hospitality at Locksley Hall as long as my father lives here. I want you to be there.'

'I would be glad to. But perhaps you should speak to Guy first.' He gestured Marian closer. In a low voice he added, 'if you change your mind you can get a message to me if you leave it in the bowl under the Saviour Oak. Mark it with an arrow.'

'An arrow?'

'The men started using it as a symbol for our new hundred.'

'I suppose it is easier to draw than a leopard.'

Robin laughed. Elaine and Lady Joan looked at him as if he had gone mad. Sir Walter pressed a bag of coins into Waltheof's hands and put his arm around his daughter. Robin spurred his horse out of the courtyard and away from his old home. He had lived barely half a life, he thought, and already managed to be exiled twice. He should find a troubadour to write a song about himself. Just as he rode out through the gateway the snow started falling. Winter had arrived early in Locksley.

Martinmas

November was the month of bloodletting. Livestock too expensive to be kept through winter were slaughtered and salted down in preparation for the lean months ahead. Across Nottinghamshire the air was heavy with the tang of blood. Future hunger was always forgotten, though, in the last taste of fresh meat before winter really bit. Marian and Guy's wedding coincided with Martinmas, the last celebration until Christmas, and everyone was determined to enjoy it. Politics would be forgotten, neighbouring enmities put aside. The Viponts and the Peverills were uniting, and it was right that love should take the place of wrath.

Robin prepared for the wedding in the longhouse in the Hundred of the Arrow. Most of the clothes he had taken from Locksley were functional – hunting wools, thick leather boots – but today he took out one of the few fine cotes he had brought with him. It was dark blue with embroidery at the hem and cuffs, but like everything in the longhouse it was musty with damp and smoke. His mother would complain it was not fine enough. He smiled to himself. It had been weeks since he had thought about his mother. Strange, to imagine her concern for appearance while washing in silted brook water, half his mind on keeping watch and repairwork. He had the same sense of constant alertness in the forest that he had felt in the East, as if he were on campaign in enemy territory. But what exactly he was fighting for he did not know. He gave his hair the best brush he could with the horn-comb Agnes had lent him. Without a mirror he could not check his appearance, so he hoped for the best and went to ready his horse.

'Can you steal us some meat?' Much was at his elbow before he had even reached for his bridle. 'Or a jug of wine? Keep the cold off.'

'I'll see.'

Marian's promised delivery of salted pork had arrived at the Saviour Oak only the day before, but the storehouse was still far from full. The lords had been less generous in their donations to the 'leper hospital in the woods' since Robin's exile. Where exactly the hundredmen were going to find enough supplies to sustain them all through the winter was a pressing concern. Perhaps Robin could take some of the food from the kitchens before he left, if no one was watching. Although he did not want too many questions being asked of him, and anyone spying the onetime Lord of Locksley carrying a roasted goose into the woods was likely to ask questions. He put a saddlebag on the horse's rump just in case. There was always so much food produced for these occasions – if he had the chance to steal something away without being seen he must take it.

Much walked alongside him as he followed the line of the brook away from the clearing. A group of women were pounding their washing on the stones at the water's edge as they passed. Edeva looked up and whistled at Robin.

'You're looking very handsome,' she called.

There was a chorus of comment from the other women too. They had got used to seeing Lord Locksley dressed and working the same as the rest of them. One or two kept their eyes firmly lowered in embarrassment. They would not address a nobleman, and in his fine clothes that was what Robin had once again become.

'I could look that handsome,' grumbled Much, 'if I put on dyed wool.'

Agnes came over to them, her arms red from pounding against the cold water. 'You almost look like yourself again,' she said.

'It's just the clothes,' Robin said, made uneasy by the women's awkwardness.

'You wear them well.' Agnes kissed his hand with a smile.

She had grown thinner since Robin brought her to the Hundred. Older, too. She would always be beautiful in Robin's eyes but he could not help but see the deepening shadows under her eyes, the furrows in her brow. She worried about Will constantly, but kept her fears to herself and so they ate away at her. Even when she smiled he could see them, gnawing behind her eyes.

'I will ask Marian about Will,' he said. 'I told you about the message she left at the Saviour Oak, didn't I?'

'That she had visited him and he seemed to be improving. Yes. You told me.'

'She might have been to him again. There could be word on when his trial will be.'

Mention of the trial did not soothe her. She smiled again, but this time it looked forced.

'You'd best be leaving or you'll miss the bride.'

Much and Robin left her at the water's edge to her work and her worries. It was frustrating to be unable to visit Will or learn more of his welfare. Not for the first time Robin thought ruefully of the advantages there had been when he had been able to play the part of a lord all the time. At the Saviour Oak Much paused to check the collecting bowl – nothing had been left – and when they reached the King's Way they crossed over it, continuing through the forest. Halfway to Locksley they saw the arrow marking on the tree. To the east was a small cave with a sandy clearing in front of it. Robin whistled three times. John Blunt appeared at the cave mouth.

'All well?'

'The King's Way was deserted,' said Much, 'and the bowl was empty.'

'No change here either,' said John. 'We'll stay for the night watch and then head back in the morning.'

'Shall I call past on my way home?' asked Robin.

'Better take the main road. Have Waltheof go with you if you can. I don't trust the Viponts not to try something if you're alone.'

They had been watching for messages travelling between the Viponts and the count, or any other of their allies in the north, but so far had found no sign of them. Of course, it might be that Lord Eudo had become more cautious or had found other means of passing secret messages. Robin would be sure to ask the sheriff about that.

Lefchild dropped from a tree above Robin's head. Much gave a squawk of alarm.

'All's well closer to Locksley if you were wondering. Lots of coming and going now but nothing out of the ordinary for a wedding.'

'Good. Did you leave someone else to watch there?'

'Yes, yes. Doleswif is muttering away in a tree near the north wall. And Waltheof is inside, fetching and carrying. He'll pass a message if anything is amiss.'

One of the changes Robin had insisted on when he joined the men in the Hundred was that they set up watchposts across the forest to monitor the roads and keep a watch for any more parties of guards. There were too many lives at stake if the first warning they had of a body of the Viponts' men coming to the Hundred was a watch only yards away. So now there were men watching the sheriff's home and the castle for parties of men riding out to hunt for the forestmen. After the wedding Sir Walter would leave for Peverill Tower, and there would be another outpost to establish there. It meant drawing more men away from the Hundred and the work that needed to be done to maintain the buildings there, and also keeping men from hunting, but as winter bit and the cover of the forest receded it was more important to keep the Hundred protected. Besides, it was difficult to thatch in the snow.

Robin left John, Much and Lefchild to their watch and rode on. There were flurries of snow in the air as he neared the north wall of Locksley. Sure enough, Doleswif was keeping a grumbling lookout nearby. Some of the wall had fallen away, he noticed, and not been repaired.

At the hall all was busyness and excitement. Foliage hung across the stairwell up into the great hall and the route between there and the chapel of St Oswald was lined with small tinkling bells and ribbons. Even from the courtyard Robin could smell the meat roasting in the kitchen. His stomach groaned. He vowed that when he saw Waltheof he would ask him to spirit some food out of the kitchens to take back with them. The ladies were all in their chamber, from which the bubbling sounds of preparations issued. As Robin crossed the hall Elaine appeared from the chamber laughing with Estrild, her dark hair plaited with the same lilac silk that lined her gown. She stopped short at sight of him. Even when suspicious, he thought, she was still painfully beautiful. She called over her shoulder to his mother and walked back into the chamber without a word.

Lady Joan came out to greet her son in her accustomed fashion. He bowed and she held out her hand to be kissed. 'The day is ruined.' Rising, he asked why. 'It is snowing.'

'Locksley looks better in the snow.'

'I suppose it does glitter somewhat.' She touched the edge of his cote. 'Is this what you are wearing? It smells like tallow.'

Sir Walter arrived just in time to save Robin from irritation. He put his arm around his shoulder.

'Let us leave the ladies to their anxieties, Robin. Come to the solar with me. I have some wine.'

Lady Joan retreated to the ladies' chamber muttering that she would have liked to drink wine in the solar as well, if anyone had asked her. Sir Walter was clearly in too good a humour to let such maunderings disturb him. He poured Robin a cup of wine and they sat opposite one another. Robin suspected this was not his first drink of the day.

'You are in good spirits.'

Sir Walter and Marian had always been close. Robin had half expected the sheriff to be wet-eyed on the occasion of her leaving his home.

'I am resolved to have a peaceful day,' said Sir Walter. 'Hopefully this will be the beginning of a happier time for us all. Guy has made clear that he wishes our two families to be united from this day on, and I for one would welcome an end to the factionalism in this county.'

'Are you certain the rest of his family share that sentiment?'

'I think they do.' Sir Walter smiled. 'They have lost their advantage, Robin. The count of Mortain has still not forgiven them for losing half his wardrobe – he is not attending the wedding today, thank God, or your mother would be beside herself – and without his support they are no stronger than their neighbours. They have been making overtures to all the local lords for friendship, you know?'

'Why?'

'I think they have realised their error in relying too much on the count. There are rumours that the king will be free before the year is out, and if they prove true, the Viponts may find that their monarch is none too happy with how they have overstepped their authority in this county. The king can be very jealous of his possessions.'

'You are certain they are not just trying to raise support for the count? Remember the letter we found.'

'Believe me, I have not forgotten it. I have had my men watching the Viponts' envoys and their movements ever since you showed me that letter. Unless they are using extremely subtle means I do not believe that they have had any further contact with the count. Of course, should my trust prove to be misplaced we still have the original document you found. I keep it concealed in my chamber just in case I should ever feel the need to share its contents with the king.'

'Do they know that?'

'They know I have not destroyed it. They might surmise the rest. But since your exile I have found Lord Eudo and all his family to be considerably more obliging.'

Robin tensed his left hand around the cup. The right had healed well but the left still twinged.

'I am glad my exile has advantages for someone.'

He could not share Sir Walter's reawakened affection for the Viponts. He was not even certain that Sir Walter truly felt it in his heart. But he was a political man, and a pacific one. Robin could not begrudge him the latter sentiment, even if the former meant he cared little that Robin's brother still languished as a prisoner in Nottingham Castle because of the Viponts.

A few cups of wine more and Sir Walter was partway through a rambling anecdote about a pair of shoes Marian had owned as a child when the sound of horses signalled the arrival of the groom's party. Robin glanced out the window. There seemed a vast number of attendants among the horsemen in the courtyard. Perhaps the Viponts really were feeling vulnerable. Men who felt the need for such display often were.

When the Viponts entered the great hall to divest themselves of their arms and take up drinks Robin, Sir Walter and Lady Joan were waiting to meet them. Everyone had on their best crocodile smiles until they noticed Robin. Lord Eudo had too much self-control to react to the presence of the man he tried to hang at a family gathering, but Ranulf and Serlo were not willing to dissemble.

'What is that murderer doing here?' Ranulf demanded.

He took back his sword from the attendant who had only just received it and put it firmly back in his scabbard. Serlo glared. Guy fidgeted awkwardly.

'My stepson is here as our guest,' said Sir Walter. His jovial tone had noticeably slipped. 'As are you. Please, put yourselves at ease.'

He gestured towards the attendant, but Ranulf would not disarm. For once Eudo seemed unwilling to calm his choleric brother. Guy stepped between the two families apologetically.

'Please let us not begin the day with a quarrel.' His voice was low, as if half hoping not to be heard. 'He is part of the fam–'

'Did you know of this?'

Guy flinched.

'Yes, Father. Marian asked if I would mind and I said she should invite whoever she wished.'

'Whoever she wished,' said Serlo, 'should not include a murdering thief.'

Robin held up his palms, the scarred lines left by the irons still glistening there.

'These say I am neither of those things. But I am part of this family.'

'Thank Christ you are not a part of mine.'

Sir Walter's pacific intentions threatened to crumble before the wedding had even begun. He raised his hands for calm. 'In the eyes of the law, Robin has proven himself innocent of any felony…'

Ranulf and Serlo both interrupted at once. For Sir Walter, that was enough.

'I will not have this discord on my daughter's wedding day.' His voice was iron now. 'Perhaps you do not care about the process of law, my lords, but we do. Robin has proven his innocence before us all, and he is part of our family. This is my home, my county, and as both sheriff and host I say that either you will put down your arms and greet my guest or you will leave this hall.'

Ranulf's face glistened with rage. He raised a finger to Sir Walter, sharp as a knife.

'I will give up my sword, but I will not accept his presence here.' He turned the finger on Robin and poked him once in the chest. 'Stay out of my way or I will give you cause to regret it.'

He threw his sword onto the floor and stormed towards the fire. The white flecks of snow nestling on his clothes snuffed out one by one. Serlo went to join him. Idonea and Roger lingered near the doorway uncomfortably while Lady Joan attempted polite conversation. Guy took Sir Walter to one side and apologised. Eudo stood with his attendants, watching Robin with the cold concentration of a hawk. Undeterred, Robin greeted Jocelyn. He had hardly seen the boy since spring. He was taller, leaner. He would have freckles like his mother soon, Robin thought. He still had the seriousness of a far older child, but at least he did not look disappointed to find his uncle there.

It was not a comfortable day for Robin. The watchful eyes of the Viponts followed him when he walked to the chapel, during the ceremony, and as the bells chimed and the party returned to Locksley Hall their faces smiled but their eyes were still on him. At the supper in the hall he was offered a seat at the top table with his mother, but refused. He was a guest, but he did not need to be singled out for even further attention. He sat between their neighbouring lords and trusted servants, being ignored by both as far as possible. The Abbess of Newstead made an attempt at conversation, inquiring after the progress of his hospital, but he was suspicious of her attentions and answered briefly. In that hall and amidst that company he felt he could not let down his guard for a moment. When the abbess turned back to her other neighbours Robin ate in silence.

He had to sit and watch Eudo de Vipont fawning over Elaine – and, worse, her fawning over him in return, hands touching at the slightest excuse, furtive smiles passing between them, whispered conversations. Yet the instant he turned from Elaine a shadow passed over Eudo's face. He cast his eyes around the hall with such disdain Robin wondered why he had allowed this wedding to go ahead. It seemed a physical imposition to spend even the duration of the wedding feast in Locksley Hall. He easily found partners in his contempt. Serlo and Ranulf made little attempt to conceal their displeasure at Robin's continued presence. Serlo studiously avoided glancing at the corner of the hall where Robin sat, while Ranulf's furious gaze did not stray from it. He twisted his knife in his hands, around and around, the blade always pointing at Robin.

If Marian saw the discord among her guests she was studiously ignoring it. She sat on the dais beside Guy, her hair laced with flowers, talking contentedly to the family sitting either side of them. She looked happy, Robin thought, scarcely believing it. She reflected Guy's smiles and attentions. The thought of being forever snared in the clutches of his family did not seem to dampen her joy. Somehow that was worse than if she had sat weeping with despair.

He caught Waltheof's arm as he passed with a jug of wine. 'Gather what supplies you can. We should leave before the sun sets.'

He hoped to slip away unnoticed, but as he rose from the table Ranulf loudly raised his wine in the air. 'Thank Christ for that,' he cried, aiming his words towards his companions but his voice to the whole hall. 'The air is clearing in this place at last.'

He smashed his cup against his friend's and wine spilt across the table. Robin forced himself to ignore Ranulf, stepped over the bench and headed towards the screens. The other guests in the hall were likewise trying to ignore Ranulf, but he refused to let them. He got to his feet, unsteady with drink.

'A toast before Lackland Locksley leaves,' he shouted. The men around him stood in solidarity. 'To the Locksley estate. Let's hope that the taint of past lords will be washed away by the good lordship it is blessed with now.'

Robin could not stop himself.

'The only taint on my estate is the extortion and lawlessness your men have imposed on it.'

'Fine words,' said Serlo, 'from a murderer.'

Sir Walter stood now. 'There is no need for this discourtesy,' he called down the hall. 'My stepson has been a welcome guest and now he leaves, with our blessing.'

'He goes with the sheriff's blessing,' interrupted Ranulf. 'There lies the trouble, you see. Perhaps if the sheriff could control his own family he would be more capable of keeping the law in this county.'

Certain of the lords in the hall exchanged murmurs of agreement. Sir Walter could not fail to notice. He set his jaw in defiance, but his cheeks reddened. Would the Viponts not stop until they had humiliated him as well as Robin?

'I have already asked once today that you remember your respect for my rank,' he said.

Guy joined his own voice to those trying to soothe the situation. 'This is an occasion for joy,' he said. 'Reconciliation. Let us put aside –'

Ranulf would not hear him. 'I will put nothing aside. This murderer, this felon, this exile, should never have been allowed to enter this hall. He should not have been allowed to return. We have done nothing but offer kindness and he has thrown it back to us, spat on our generosity, shown us discourtesy and disrespect.'

'It is you who are showing disrespect,' cried Sir Walter.

Other voices were rising around the hall, some appealing for peace, others arguing one cause or the other. Robin tried to call over them, saying he was leaving, that they need not argue on his account any further, but no one listened. Even Eudo de Vipont had joined the quarrel. Sir Walter stood for it no longer. He threw back his seat at the high table, marched around it, off the dais and straight up to Eudo, his face inches from Lord Vipont's.

'I have had enough of your family's discourtesy,' he hissed. The hall hushed, shocked by the violence of the sheriff's anger. Everyone in the chamber could hear what he said. 'You ought to remember that I have information that could bring you all down. If you will not show me the respect due to a fellow lord, or to a sheriff, you will remember that one fact – if I wished, I could have you all hanged for treason. I have kept my silence this long for love of my daughter, but if you do not sit down and restrain your kin, I will break that silence. By God almighty, I swear I will.'

Eudo did not blink. His mind turned Sir Walter's words like cogs. His ears heard the silence of the hall, knew that every lord there was now wondering what the sheriff meant. Why did he threaten revelations of treason? What had the Viponts done? He smiled, slowly.

'Of course, my lord.' He sat, and with one hand called for the rest of his family and attendants to do the same. 'We are your honoured guests, and will respect your wishes.'

Even Ranulf, bristling with rage, was forced to join the humiliating submission that Eudo led them in. The hall fell silent. Sir Walter paced back to the high table, lifted his own cup of wine in a toast.

'To the happy union of our families.'

He threw back his drink and sat down. Around the hall pockets of whispered conversation gave way to chatter once more. Lords and servants alike glanced sideways at the Viponts as they sat, cowed and humiliated before their peers. Robin smiled, bowed towards the high table and left the hall, the image of mortified Lords Vipont held close in his mind.

While his horse was readied he stood under the eaves of the stables, watching snow drift between him and his old home, the windows glowing in the failing light. A pale figure appeared on the stairway and called his name. He waved to it, squinting through the snowflakes. Marian ran the distance between them.

'You are leaving early,' she said when she was next to him in the shelter.

'It is best to avoid the King's Way after dark. You should go back inside, it is cold.' His breath misted the frozen air. The snow had shrouded Locksley, muffling some of the sound from the hall opposite.

'I am sorry,' Marian said, 'that the meal ended like that.'

'It is not your doing.'

'Someone from their family ought to apologise, all the same.'

Their family, Robin thought. Her family now. It sorrowed him to think it.

'I have given you no wedding gift.'

'You have nothing to give, Robin.'

'Here.' He drew a ring from his little finger, a thick golden band inscribed with a cross. 'It was my sister's.'

He held it out to her. Marian looked at it in surprise but did not take it.

'I remember. She gave it to you when you left on crusade. I cannot take that from you.'

He drew Marian's hand from her side and pressed the ring into her palm. She looked at it and smiled, but when she met his eye there was sorrow mingled there too. Before she could speak another shadow ran through the snow calling for his horse. It was one of the Vipont servants. He started at sight of them.

'Did your master forget something?' said Robin coolly. 'His manners, perhaps.'

The servant gave an awkward smile and busied himself with his horse. Marian spoke more quietly.

'I do not know when we will see each other again. Guy defies his family in some things, but –'

'He will not do it in my cause.'

'I think not. And we will only stay in Nottinghamshire for a few months.

After that we will go to Normandy, to his lands there.'

The Vipont servant rode off into the mist with a bow.

'Until we meet again,' said Robin, 'that ring can remind you of a friend.'

'I will not forget you,' she said, almost laughing. 'You have been the bane of my life since we were six years old.'

'I know. I am sorry for that.'

'Sorry?' She smiled. 'That is a word I never thought I would hear you say.'

A gust of wind swirled snowflakes from the courtyard floor into the stable. Marian shivered.

'Go back to your guests and the fire,' said Robin. 'Waltheof is coming with the food.'

Marian put the ring on a finger of her right hand, nodded a goodbye and strode back to the hall, her pale dress catching in the churned snow, muddied and damp. Robin and Waltheof set off into the snowbound night. After the Viponts' shouts and threats, Robin thought it wise to heed John's earlier advice. He and Waltheof rode the long route back through the forest, taking the main roads. That way they could not be pursued without knowing of it. All the same, their ears listened constantly for movement at the road's edge, for the click of a drawn crossbow, the thrum of an arrow flying. It would be easy to kill a man in the November dark without being seen. That thought was at his heels all the way back. But if killers followed him on his route they never struck, and he arrived back at the Hundred without a scratch.

Sir Walter was dozing, his head leaning on his raised hand at the table. Marian put her arm around him gently. He sniffed awake. She smiled.

'You are tired, Father. You should go to bed.'

'A host cannot retire before his guests.'

'Guy and I are the hosts. You and your lady can leave us. Besides, most of the guests are gone. Even Lord Louvetot drew his wife away an hour ago. Only Guy's family and our servants are still drinking.'

Sir Walter looked around and saw she was right. The hall was a tangle of sprawling crimson and gold, blue and yellow. Despite the angry words exchanged earlier that evening, the Viponts had stubbornly remained to the last. Marian wondered at it.

'Joan will want to stay up a little longer,' said Sir Walter. 'But I will retire, if you permit me.'

She kissed his cheek. 'I insist.'

He stood wearily, kissed Lady Joan, whispered in her ear and turned to embrace Guy. 'May you have as much happiness in your marriage,' he said, 'as I have been blessed to have in both of mine, son. We will forget all these angry words, hm?'

He squeezed Marian's hand one final time and retired. Marian looked around the hall, suppressing a yawn. She would have liked to retire as well, but despite the moon being high in the sky her guests were still clearly not inclined to leave. Guy leant closer, kissing her hand. His dark eyes glittered in the candlelight. His cheeks were flushed. He had drunk too much, she thought. She wondered if, now they were married, she was allowed to tell him that. She smiled and looked away, slightly embarrassed by his attention. Lanfranc was circling the hall, going from one Vipont servant to another, speaking quietly to them. Across the chamber, Eudo hovered over a group of his men. He was watching her. Something in his gaze unsettled her. She had only ever known Eudo shower charming smiles on her, benevolent gazes. But now he looked at her with the cold disdain a peacock might give a fly. He glanced at Guy, said something to the men surrounding him and walked to the other end of the hall. She shuddered.

'What is the matter, my heart?' Guy pressed her hand between both of his. 'Are you cold?'

'Is your uncle angry with me?'

Guy looked at Eudo, who was now with his son's family, paternally ruffling Roger's hair. 'Not now that Locksley has left, surely.'

'I… No, it was nothing.'

'I will go and speak to him. If there is any bad blood we must let it before he leaves.'

He got to his feet, rather unsteadily, and stumbled his way towards his family. Marian tried not to watch, but she saw all of the men head for the screens passage. It was better, she thought, to resolve everything now. After all, tomorrow morning she would be leaving to live in the castle until Ranulf let them both go to their own home. She did not want to arrive to a frosty reception.

She felt a pressure on her shoulder. Gytha smiled down on her. 'Your father has retired, my lady. We should prepare you for bed.'

'Oh – but, the guests…'

'The last guests are leaving, child. Your servants do not count as company. Come now.'

She looped Marian's arm through her own and drew her from the table.

'You cannot.'

Guy looked at his family in disbelief.

'This is my wedding day. You cannot turn it into…'

'It is too late for your protests,' interrupted Eudo. 'Everything is already arranged. If you had wanted to prevent this misfortune you should have refused Locksley the hospitality of your wife's home.'

'That is why you are doing this? Because of Locksley? He is not even here.'

'Lords care more for their homes than for themselves,' said Serlo. 'He has already shown he is willing to endure personal injury with that fraud of an ordeal.'

'And the sheriff has had this coming for months,' growled Ranulf. 'Lording it over us, threatening us that he will tell the king about our message to the count. We have done nothing to deserve his censure. He needs to learn a lesson.'

Guy blanched. 'What do you mean? What will you do to him?'

'We,' said Eudo, 'will do nothing. But we will not warn him of what is to come. Since you are family, we are paying you the courtesy of a warning.'

'But I have done nothing wrong.'

'You have enabled your wife to support Locksley over our interests time and again. You spoke against us on the enclosure of the common land. You allowed Locksley to visit his accomplice Thorfridh in his cell. You yourself took your wife to see his bastard brother.'

'You knew of that?'

'Nothing escapes my notice, nephew. We let this marriage go ahead because you appealed for it, and because the Peverill estate is not inconsiderable. When Marian inherits it, you will be able to claim most of Northern Nottinghamshire in her right.'

'But she will not inherit for a while, surely?'

Guy started to plead again, but his uncle ignored him. Elaine had come to join them, wearing her riding mantle. Lady Joan was at her side.

'Elaine said she was going to come to the castle with you all this evening,' said Lady Joan. 'That hardly seems right.'

'My wife wishes her to pay us a visit,' said Serlo, so genially that Guy thought he must have imagined the madness of their conversation before.

'She is under my guardianship in Nottinghamshire. I feel I should accompany her with you. Marian has no more need of me. Can you not wait to visit until tomorrow, Elaine, so I can ride to the castle with you?'

'No, she cannot.' Eudo spoke harshly enough to puncture even Lady Joan's drunk contentment. One of Elaine's ladies looked at him apprehensively. He forced a smile.

'Lady Joan could ride with Elaine tonight,' said Guy quickly. 'And return first thing tomorrow.'

His family turned on him coldly. Elaine laughed at their displeasure. 'Yes,' she said to Eudo teasingly. 'Let my aunt stay with us all. Then she can avoid the noisy cleaning tomorrow morning. It will save her poor head.'

'Very well,' said Eudo. 'Have your mantle brought, my lady. We cannot delay our departure any longer.'

Elaine beamed at him. She could not know, thought Guy. She saw all this as a game. Eudo maintained his smile until Lady Joan and Elaine were walking out of the hall with Idonea. Then he gripped Guy's arm, his fingers holding so sharply Guy thought they might puncture his skin.

'We ride out now,' he said. 'Bring your wife to the stables before we leave, or you will stay here to face the consequences.'

Doleswif writhed uncomfortably in his perch. Lefchild had lent him a sling of leather to hold him more firmly in the tree – not everyone could be as comfortable as him sneaking through branches like a squirrel – but the strap tangled in his arm and pulled at his waist and every other conceivable way of wearing it discomforted him, no matter how he shifted. The cold was bitter too. The snow had stopped falling, but who knew how long that would last? A whistling wind tore through the treetops sending flurries of flakes down on his bald head every hour or so. He had only taken this watch because Kolbrand had noticed he was the last man to have offered to do it, and he could not stand the man's sniping any longer. It was hours since Lord Robin and Waltheof had left the hall. He yawned. Another splutter of snow tumbled from the branch above his head. As he wiped it angrily away he noticed the shadows.

Locksley Hall was surrounded by a low-lying haze from all the fires blazing inside it and the warm breath of its guests, so at first he thought he must be imagining them. Long, dark shapes stretching between the gatehouse and the hall, shuddering forwards when he blinked or looked away. But as he watched they grew more distinct, more real. The moon emerged from behind a cloud and he was certain. They were men. Strange. If they were late-arriving guests surely they would be on horseback? If they were poor men seeking alms, shouldn't the watchman at the gate have stopped them? They wore no colours and he could not make out their faces. They all moved steadily closer to the hall, dividing around its outer walls like water around a stone.

From within the hall came the sound of horses shifting noisily, and a dozen riders emerged, moving swifter than the occasion should have demanded. Perhaps there had been some disagreement at the feast. They were all well-dressed, their horses magnificently caparisoned, and behind them they drew more horses without riders or saddles. There were servants among them, he thought, but nowhere near as many as he would expect. Half their household must still be inside.

As soon as the riders were passed the waiting shadows surged into the courtyard. There were shouts of warning, the bark of dogs, the cries of horses, and then screams. Doleswif's eyes widened in fear. Figures ran back and forth in the yard, shadows crossed the windows wildly. Sparks leapt into the air and one of the outbuildings was alight, flames and smoke swirling into the night sky. Men were running from it, women too.

He sat in his perch, frozen with uncertainty. Should he wait, to see what happened? Should he run to John Blunt's outpost? If these men were attacking Locksley Hall they could surely not be hunting for the hundredmen? But what if they thought Robin was still inside, and he was their target? If they did not find him they would be likely to seek him in the forest next. A richly dressed man was fighting his way across the courtyard. He struck those who tried to impede his progress away with his sword and leapt onto a horse. It spurred from the horror of the flames and kicked down the shadow blocking its path, galloping across the smeared snow towards the gatehouse.

Doleswif looked away, struggling to unravel the leather sling. He had to warn the others. He knew it must be the right thing to do because he did not want to do it. That was always a sure sign. Free of the sling he started to climb down the tree, his icy hands scratching against the hard bark. When he reached the snowy ground he ran due north. That was easy. He just had to go the opposite direction from the wall. But it was not long before his certainty in his bearings wavered. He strode through the thick snow, his legs aching, looking at the trees for signs of his path. But even when he found the arrow markers the hundredmen had scratched into the forest they did not help him. He knew that not all of the arrows showed the route back to the Hundred. Every third arrow lied, he remembered. At least he thought it was the third. But then was this arrow in front of him the third or the fourth? It seemed a long time since he had passed the last one. Perhaps he had missed the lying arrow and this one led him back to the right path. He strode on, stumbling in the knee-deep furrows of snow, no longer knowing if he was going to the right way or wrong. The forest spread out all around him, snow muffling sound, trees shading vision. He wondered if he would ever make it back to the Hundred to warn them.

A shiver of cold ran down Marian's spine. She drew her shawl closer around herself, crossing her legs on the bed. If she had not been waiting for Guy she would have pulled her knees all the way up to her chin to hold the drifting warmth there. The fire was giving out more crackle and smoke than warmth. The wood must still be green. Her ladies had scattered scented herbs around the chamber and into the flames so at least the heavy smoke smelt sweet, and as she curled her stockinged toes into the rushes there was a release of rose-fresh vapour. Estrild brushed out her long hair, holding up strands as she caught knots to avoid the comb tugging at her mistress. The old palette at the foot of the bed having been removed, Gytha sat at Marian's feet on a footrest. The old woman felt her charge shiver and placed a soothing hand on her knee. Against the white of her silken shift Gytha's old lined hand looked burnt and calloused by age and work. Marian put her own hands on top. It would be strange to spend a night without the old woman's whistling snores puncturing the darkness. Stranger still to spend it with a man.

Noise still rose from the hall and would do half the night, Marian thought. Harps had long since given way to tambours and citterns, stamping feet and a discord of singing. Every now and then a man would start a raucous song and voices would join him, only to fall away as they forgot the words halfway through the second verse. The kitchens still seemed to be ablaze as well, although some guests must be leaving for she heard horses whinnying and fidgeting in the courtyard. Even with her shutters closed thuds and shouts echoed up to her chamber. Marian was pleased of the distraction. Better this than dark silence.

The door flew open. Guy ran in, almost falling over Gytha in his hurry to reach Marian. He seized her hand, reached under her arm to draw her to her feet.

'We need to leave.'

Marian half-smiled, confused by Guy's panicked expression. Gytha gave a little laugh.

'Of course you are eager to be alone with your bride, my lord. We will leave you.'

'Fine. Go. But we will go first.'

Guy seized Marian's mantle from a closet and threw it over her shoulders. He was wearing his own, she realised, as if he were about to go riding. From deep within the hall she heard a scream. Then shouts. Guy was directing Estrild to find shoes, any shoes. He shoved her in the direction of a chest. Marian took his hands – they were ice cold – and tried to make him look at her.

'What is wrong?'

'Do not ask questions now. We need to leave immediately.'

'Why?'

More shouts. A rumble of sound as of an unused door scraping open or benches being pushed back. The music had stopped, replaced by shouts. Estrild had found Marian's shoes. She knelt to tie them, but was not quick enough. Only one was on when Guy again grasped Marian's arm and tried to drag her from the chamber. She pulled away from him.

'I will not leave until you tell me what is happening.'

'This is not the time for questions. There are men inside the hall – can you not hear? They mean to kill us all unless we get away.'

Outside the window, there was a chorus of shouts: men, horses, dogs. From the hall the crashes and screams grew louder.

'Which men? Why are they here? Can't we reason with them?'

'No,' he said, his voice bitter as poison. 'No we cannot. We need to leave before –'

'Go,' said Marian, gesturing to her ladies. 'Gather your mantles and we will leave together.'

'Never mind about them,' said Guy. He seized her arm again, his grip stronger this time. 'We need to get out.'

He marched her from the chamber. On the stairs she saw her father's door opposite. Had he been warned? She pulled away from Guy, ran to the door. As her hand reached the latch he pulled it back.

'Let me go,' Marian said, twisting her arm to try to free it. 'I need to warn him.'

'You are wasting time.'

'We should help them.'

'I saw Elaine heading towards the stables with Eudo. Lady Joan was probably with them. Your father will be fine. Now come on.'

He held her wrist tight. Inside the chamber there were sounds of struggle. Marian would not be stopped. She wrestled against Guy's grip. He was stronger than her but he was also chivalrous. Marian's will did not allow for chivalry. She kicked him in the shin. In the brief moment that his hold on her wrists loosened she threw the door open. Sir Walter was in his nightclothes and shawl, a sword in his hand. Three men, hooded and plain-clothed, faced him across the chamber, all armed. One had lunged for a document that Sir Walter gripped firmly with his free hand. In the startled moment that they saw Marian in the doorway one of the attackers threw himself at her father and knocked him off balance. Marian cried out. She tried to run to him but Guy held her arms. There was a rush of blood and the attacker flew backwards, clutching his neck. Sir Walter's sword had done its work. Marian watched the man stagger and fall, the blood bubbling through his clothes, with a fascinated horror. She thought of the pigs slaughtered on their lands. She had never seen a man bleed like that.

Guy pressed her against the wall behind his own body as the two other attackers ran from the chamber.

'Stop them,' Marian said. But Guy did not move. He had no sword, she thought. Of course he had no sword. She listened to the retreating running steps of the armed men echo across the stairwell before they were swallowed by shouts.

Only then did she realise her father had not risen from the floor.

She pushed Guy away. He let her go this time. Sir Walter's feet were visible around the edge of the bed, hardly moving. And blood. Was it the other man's? She rounded the bedstead, the curtains drawn and hiding from view the rest of her father's body. His right hand still held his sword. His left was pressed against his chest, where the document was steadily turning red. She cried out, dropped to her knees beside him. Blood was pooling under his body. How was that possible? He had struck the attacker first, had killed him. Guy nudged a knife across the floor with his foot as he followed her. A bloody knife. The hooded man had struck when she came in. She had given that man the chance to kill her father.

Desperately, Marian pressed her hands over her father's heart, tried to lift him upright. His eyes, set in a face already ashen, flickered open. She pulled his head into her lap and he smiled. She tried to say his name and only a hiss of air came out, a strangled gasp. He might live, she thought. She pressed her hand close on the wound. He might live.

He moaned.

'We must go.' Guy touched her shoulder. Marian struck his hand away. 'Marian, we need to leave here now. Before our horses are taken.'

'No.'

Her voice was a whisper that even she could barely hear. Her eyes stung with tears she had not realised she was crying. Her father's hand was growing cold under hers. Cold, against the hot blood that would not stop flowing from his chest.

'If we do not leave soon we will both die. Your father – he would not want that.'

'I will not leave him.'

He might still live, she thought. His eyelids drooped and his pale lips murmured silent words. He might.

Guy crept to the window, opened the shutter. Strange flickers of light flashed across his face. The shrieks in the courtyard grew louder. 'They are loosing all the horses.' Guy's voice had a desperate, pleading edge. 'If we do not go they will kill us. Wait.' He looked again. 'They are firing the outhouses.' He strode back to her, sat on his haunches and touched her shoulder again. 'They will set fire to the hall, Marian. I know they will. We must get out before it is too late.'

'No, I will stay here. You go and help Gytha.'

'Gytha?'

'She is slow on the stairs. She will need help. Go and –'

'I am not going to wander about helping old women.' He sounded hysterical. 'We need to escape this place before they burn it down around us. If you will not come I will leave you.'

He stood up, but his voice still pleaded. 'I will.'

She looked at him in his fine wedding clothes, his dark eyes desperate, his pale hands held out to her as if in prayer. He looked like a child.

'No.'

She looked back at her father, took his right hand off his sword and held it tight on his chest. She felt Guy's eyes still on her, still pleading, still afraid. Then she heard him turn on his heels and run from the chamber. A wave of grief and fear surged through her. For a moment she thought it would drown her, the panic and horror. She felt it in her chest, her throat. She wanted to vomit it up or sob it out of her.

One of her father's trembling hands reached up to her face. She started.

'Father? Are you…'

He stroked her cheek and she felt a trail of something wet follow his touch. His lips moved again, his eyes struggled to stay open. She could not hear what he said. She bent closer, her ear almost touching his mouth before she could hear what he said.

'Get out.'

His hand fell back onto his chest. She sat up. His eyes were still half-open, his lips still parted. But she knew his life had gone. An icy breath of sorrow filled her lungs. She hugged his head close to hers and wished she could die as well. There was no use in trying to live. Guy had fled. The Viponts had fled. Her family had fled. Her father…

She smelt smoke. She listened. The cries had grown more desperate. Through the open shutter she saw dark swirling smoke and lurching fire. She needed to get out.

Gently, she pushed her father's body away, laying his head down onto the floor as softly as she could. Her white gown was red now, sodden. She felt like her legs would give way beneath her when she stood up. She tried anyway. Her mantle had fallen from her shoulders. She picked it up from the ground, and then also the knife. She looked at her father's body, so still, so pale. His hands still clasped that parchment. She carefully prised his fingers apart and took that too.

She crept to the door. Guy had pulled it behind him as he ran. She opened it a crack, pressed her face into the stairwell. There was no one there, but just as she was about to run towards her own chamber a hooded man appeared from within it. He shouted behind him, headed for the hall. Strange shadows danced on the walls. From the hall came more shouts. If she went down that stairwell she could not help but be seen – she would have to cross the length of the hall, go down the main steps and into the courtyard. She closed the door. There was another way. Her father's chamber had its own small stair that led to the kitchens. From there she could try to sneak around to the stables and find a horse, or just run across the empty grounds to escape.

She pulled back the tapestry that concealed the stair and ran down it, her one shoed foot tap-tapping. Too loud, she thought. She untied it and left it halfway down. There were no candles on the stair and surrounded by the black stone it felt like spiralling into the deepest of darknesses, of purgatory, of hopelessness, of hell. She squeezed her eyes shut, trying to force out thought. When she opened them there was a light ahead. She took the last few steps carefully, leaning over to look ahead to the corridor. The corridor led to a side entrance to the hall, where deliveries were made and could be monitored from above. Marian saw the door, only an empty hallway separating it from her. A way out. She ran towards it. She was within touching distance of it when the world span, her body whipped around by the force of a weight driving into her side. She smacked against the opposite wall, biting her lip, striking her nose. Whoever had ploughed into her pounded up the stairs she had just come down. Was it one of the hooded men, or one of her own servants? She hardly knew. She ran for the door, heaving at the latch. It did not move. It was locked.

She suppressed another wave of panic. The key must be somewhere close, in one of the offices of the kitchen. She crept through the passage connecting to it, looking in the steward's room, the stores, her naked feet slapping on the flagstones. The kitchen was ahead. A shadow lurched towards her. She screamed and held out her knife. Another scream replied. It was a woman. One of the laundresses. Marian saw her with relief.

'Are there any more servants that way?'

'The cook.' The laundress's teeth were chattering. 'The spitboy. They killed Morcar.' Marian did not know who Morcar was. 'Who are these devils?'

Unable to answer that question, Marian ran ahead of the laundress. In the kitchen the smell of roasted meats and spiced wine mingled with an acrid smoke. Marian covered her face with her sleeve, holding the small knife out in front of her in case any more hooded figures lunged at her. In one of the boiling houses a teenage boy cowered in the shadow of the copper. He gave a cry when Marian noticed him and pulled him out of the house. His shout brought the cook running, the largest knife in the kitchen clasped in his hand.

'I told you not to run that way, Emma,' he said to the laundress. 'I was about to chase after you.'

'The hall is on fire,' Marian said. 'We need to get out.'

She started towards a passage, but the cook stopped her.

'Not that way. I saw one of the bastards go up there just now. This way.'

He led the group through a small door that emerged into the sharp air of the service yard, shielded from view of the courtyard by the stables. Over the wall flames could be seen, leaping into the air from the hall. Marian saw them with a dismay that almost rooted her to the spot. Emma the laundress nudged her away from the sight. The service yard was the last walled section of the hall before it gave way to open grounds. Escape was in sight. Marian swapped the dagger into her other hand next to the parchment, stretched her fingers then passed it back. Only a few steps more. The moon was full above them. They could not help but cast great shadows all the way across the yard. The door to the grounds was in sight. The spitboy reached out his hands to it.

'What do we do?' Emma hissed.

The spitboy turned his back on her and unbolted the door. 'Do what I do,' he said as he flung the door open. 'Run.'

And he did. Emma and the cook raced after him, heading towards the gatehouse in the West. Marian looked from their disappearing silhouettes back towards the hall. The flames had crept to the roof of the kitchen now. The stables were little more than smouldering timbers. Through the smoke she saw men running from the hall, across the courtyard, back from the direction of the gatehouse. Some wore the colours of her father. Most looked the same as the attackers in her father's chamber. She recognised Edgar, wielding a club against a pack of hooded men near the kennels. A man raised what looked at first like a stick – it glinted in the firelight – brought it down on Edgar's back. He fell.

Marian waited no more. She ducked through the doorway and ran from the hall. As she ran the sounds of violence seemed to get louder, closer. She screwed up her eyes against them, balled her hands into fists around the knife and parchment, ran harder. Her feet pounded against the snow-packed earth, her breath came out in burning gasps until her body was almost numb with pain. She opened her eyes as the sounds finally receded. No. She stopped running. She had reached the limits of the estate. The boundary wall. No. She struck the stonework with her hand in frustration. She could not have run all this way only to be caught at the edge of Locksley's lands. She looked up. The wall towered above her head. She stepped back, looked side to side. Perhaps she imagined it, but the wall to her right looked lower. She crept closer. The closer she got, the more certain she was. Part of the masonry had come away near the top of the wall, and tumbled down onto the Locksley side. Without a thought she scrambled over the loose pile of fallen stones. The top was still almost beyond her reach. She threw the knife and parchment down, stretched her bloody fingers as far as she could, leapt, scrabbled her toes against the stone, felt her arms quiver as they pulled, and was up. She rolled so that her legs dropped down facing the wall on the other side and tried to let herself down gently. It was a longer drop on the other side. She winced as she landed on her naked scratched feet. And there it was: the forest, cold and snowbound. She panted its clean air into her lungs, pulled her mantle around her and ran to meet it.

Much saw it first. A gleaming shape like a moonbeam, flitting between the trees. He brought John to the cave mouth, low in the shadows, to watch it. Sometimes it huddled small and could have been a wandering animal; at others it was long and thin. Every now and then it turned and dark patches could be seen on it like a stretched calf's skin. It disappeared behind a tree and what might have been two arms reached up, tracing a marker.

'It's seen the arrow,' Much breathed.

Sure enough, the white figure set off determinedly in a straight line. It stumbled back into an animal form. As it dropped it made a sound. Not a cry or a moan or a gasp, but somewhere between the three.

'I'm going to take a closer look,' said John.

Much grasped at him. 'Don't, John. It's a ghost.'

'It can't do me much harm then.'

'Ghosts mean death. If it sees you it'll take your soul.'

'You've been listening to Lefchild.'

John pulled a hood down over his face, raised his bow and set off towards the shape. Much watched him creep towards the shape. He drew his own bow closer. And then, just in case, a knife as well. Who knew what a ghost might be capable of? The shape was man-like again. John approached it from behind the cover of a tree, placing his feet carefully so that his thin leather soles landed flat and silent on the forest floor. He was almost beside it. In one swift movement he lunged forward, bow drawn, shouting a warning as the shape turned to face him. It raised its arms, tried to back away from him, stumbled, fell into a huddle, moved crablike away from him. Why didn't John shoot? It was going to get away. Much heard him curse, lower his bow. He jumped as his own name was shouted.

'Much, get here now.'

He ran, almost stabbing himself with his arrow in his haste, throwing his bow into the air as he reached John to threaten the creature. John knocked his hands away, gave Much his bow to hold. He raised his own hands, palms outwards, and knelt before the creature. Only then did Much really look at it. The long white body was a nightgown, streaked with dirt, now bundled up around the creature's knees as she hugged them tight. Dark tendrils of hair fell over a face bloodied and bruised. The woman looked him in the eye. Oh, God. His hood. He had forgotten his hood. She stared at him, less afraid now than uncertain.

'M – Much?' she said.

And with a shudder she collapsed into the snow.

Sleep would not come to Robin. The longhouse in the Hundred was not an easy place to sleep in any case, with men lying all over its floor and the smoke of the hearth seeping into your lungs, forcing coughs as well as snores to issue from his companions' mouths. Still, Robin had slept in far worse conditions and he had the best position in the chamber, next to the warmth of the fire. Eventually he surrendered to wakefulness and got up, pulling his mantle from underneath him. In the flickering darkness he picked his way over the slumbering bodies to the door. The tasselled edge of one of the count's tapestries unfurled as he opened the door, rolling out like a tongue to reveal a sea monster. He stepped over it and closed the door.

The night air was ice cold. Through the canopy of trees overhead he could see the moon and stars, gleaming white in the blackness of sky. His breath misted his vision. He wandered between the Hundred's buildings, pausing at the altar in the old sty. Some kind intercessor must be watching over them. He sent men out to hunt far from the Hundred, insisted everyone took looping routes home after washing and working, had supplies carried by men rather than animal or cart because it was harder to follow their tracks. Even so it was miraculous that they had not been found.

A shout in the dark pierced his calm. He leapt into the shadows of the sty. He had no blade with him. The only heavy object to hand was the cross on the altar. He looked at it ruefully, hoping it did not come to that. A man almost fell into the clearing of the Hundred, a pale unmoving shape clasped in his arms. He righted himself and Robin recognised John Blunt. He emerged from the altar and ran to meet him as John kicked at the door of the croft where the women slept.

He was carrying a woman, Robin saw, her long hair hanging over a bloodied face, her body shrouded in a white gown stained with red. When John saw him he started, said nothing.

'What has happened?' Robin asked.

Agnes Scarlette had appeared at the door of the croft, rubbing her eyes in confusion. John moved past her and laid the woman down just inside, whispering something. When he came out he gripped Robin's arm with one hand and rubbed the other across his chin.

'Something has happened at Locksley Hall,' he said. 'I left Much at the outpost to keep watch.'

'Did Doleswif come to you?'

'No. She did.'

John's eyes were dark pools in the moonlight. Robin looked back towards the croft, a shudder of fear at his neck.

'Who was that?'

John cracked his knuckles, would not meet his eye. 'Lady Marian.'

'Is she –?' He could not even say the word.

'Most of the blood isn't hers. She has been hurt, but not as badly as it looks. We need to get some men to Locksley.'

Robin hesitated, his eyes still on the croft.

'She looked… I should see her, be sure she's all right.'

'Not now, Robin.'

John spoke in a low voice, looked Robin square in the eyes. His words finally pierced Robin's hearing. Locksley. Men.

'Yes. Yes, you're right.' He ran to the longhouse, kicked the closest men awake. 'Get up. Get armed.'

He circuited all the other buildings waking sleepers, called to Grimm who was on watch to the north. The Hundred's inhabitants came out into the moonlit clearing in swiftly sobered confusion. Robin was belting his sword to his hip, pulling weapons down from the roof where they were hidden.

'John will stay here with half the men. Everyone should arm themselves and be ready to fight. Waltheof, Kolbrand, Lefchild, Gilbert, come with me. Is that enough?'

Robin turned to John who shrugged uncertainly.

'Without word from Doleswif I don't know.'

'Better more of us are here to protect the Hundred.'

He hesitated again. This time John was ready for him. He took a firm grip on his arm and said in a low voice,

'I'll make sure she's all right.'

Robin nodded, threw the hood of his cloak over his head.

'You four, we're going to Locksley.'

The men glanced at each other uncertainly. They had arrived at the walls of Locksley Hall what felt like an hour ago – the stars had definitely turned in the sky – and yet Robin still sat silent. He glared at the flaming, broken hall. Every time a piece of timber fell his mouth twitched. But he said nothing. They all just stayed there, huddled on top of the frozen wall. Watching.

'Why is no one moving?' Gilbert plucked at his bowstring as if it was a harp.

'Because they're dead or fled,' said Kolbrand.

'No, I mean – why has no one come? The hue and cry must surely have been raised?'

'Half the lords of the county were still here when we left,' said Waltheof. 'They would have raised their own arms if they were attacked.'

Lefchild frowned. 'The men who did this must have waited until the guests were gone and everyone was in bed.'

'Everyone?' Gilbert chanced another glance at Robin. 'You mean – the sheriff? The ladies?'

They let the meaning of his words seep in.

'Who would have done this?' asked Waltheof, turning an axe in his hands.

'Who do you think?' growled Kolbrand. 'Bastard Viponts.'

'But wasn't it Lord Guy's wedding?' said Gilbert.

Robin turned suddenly and dropped to the earth. He strode towards the hall, sword in hand, clothes whipping in the wind. The men exchanged glances and followed his lead.

'What are we doing?' breathed Gilbert as they crept across the snow. 'If anyone sees us, we'll be arrested.'

'Then kill them,' said Kolbrand.

'I don't think you'll need to,' said Lefchild.

Between the gatehouse and the hall was a vast track of churned snow and the gate itself was open. But despite these signs of exodus, here and there were red smears and even bodies. The hundredmen crept around the burning outbuildings and into the remnants of the courtyard. The stone hall still belched smoke, its stained windows smashed or burnt.

'What are we looking for?' hissed Gilbert.

'Signs of who did this,' said Lefchild.

'We know who did this,' said Kolbrand. 'What do you expect, a bloody message in the snow?'

Gilbert pointed his bow towards the chapel on the stairwell. A linen standard had been roped over the cross and altar, part of it dangling and beating now and then as the wind swirled snow into spirals. As the air fell out of it, it collapsed to reveal the murderers' emblem. A painted arrow. Robin looked like he had been struck.

'Take that down,' he said. 'Take it down and burn it.'

'It might already have been seen,' argued Gilbert.

'Burn it.' His tone brooked no refusal.

Kolbrand took out a knife and started hacking the standard from its moorings. While the men stood by nervously Robin prowled the courtyard again. The stable was empty. Whether the horses had been loosed before the fire started or seized by those fleeing he could not tell. The kennel roof had collapsed. The thought of exploring inside made him sick, so he turned away from the building. He saw Edgar's body only yards away, a club still clutched in his fingers, his eyes staring unseeing into the sky. Robin wondered if he should close Edgar's eyes, but it seemed a deceit to suggest his end had been peaceful when all around was destruction. Poor Edgar, who had done nothing but serve his mistress faithfully every day of his service. This death should not have been his.

He watched as Kolbrand dragged the arrow banner to the burning outbuildings. The bodies of those who had attacked rather than defended the hall were easy to find. They wore no badge, no colours. Their faces were hooded and their clothing poor. They looked, he knew and it made the bile rise in his throat, like the forest thieves who had attacked the lords' coffers since April. He kicked one of the hooded corpses in its stomach. This was Eudo's doing. He knew it implicitly. No one else would be so cruelly clever, no one else would have the temerity to eat at a man's table then cut down his household like kindling, and no one else would have thought to point the finger of blame for this attack on the very men he knew Robin commanded.

The men spread out through the burnt-out buildings, and peered into those still burning, to seek signs of anyone still hiding. They found none. Robin sat in the midst of his burnt out home and waited for their return. He could not think. He would not let his mind wander until all the men were back before him. He felt like the bones in his chest had been drawn out one by one and he could not move from where he was sat, ash and snow combining in the air around him. Waltheof slumped to the ground next to him.

'I found the sheriff.' He threw his axe into the snow. 'But there is no sign of the ladies.'

'Could they –' his mind had started to roam, '– have been taken by the men who did this?'

Waltheof sighed, rubbing his hands over his red eyes. 'It is possible.'

Robin reached to offer Waltheof comfort. This was his home as much as Robin's, after all. But before a word fell from his mouth, across the empty sky came the shriek of a horse. Lefchild ran into the courtyard.

'There are men coming.'

Robin was on his feet already.

'Everyone to the wall. Now.'

The shout went up and the men started running. Robin ran and then lingered, ran and then lingered, counting their numbers as they sprinted towards the wall. Gilbert was among the last to reach them, having run due north rather than back the way they had come. Robin boosted Lefchild onto the wall as the horsemen rode through the gatehouse, then took Kolbrand's arm to be drawn up with them. He gestured the men to drop down to the safety of the forest while he ran, cat-like along the top of the wall to ensure Gilbert got over. Just as the horsemen came within sight of their stretch of wall Gilbert jumped and Robin dropped onto his belly, ready to drop if he was seen, but able to watch the horsemen while they explored the hall. If they were the Viponts he swore he would reach for a bow whether they were innocent or not.

'Who are they?' hissed Lefchild from below.

'Grey and black. Lord D'Alselin's men.'

'They must have seen the smoke from Garsmount,' said Waltheof.

'Took them long enough to get here,' muttered Kolbrand.

'Robin.' Gilbert reached up, panting, a crumpled roll of vellum in his hand. 'I found this near the wall. Recognise it?'

Robin took it, stared in surprise. It was the message to the count that proved the Viponts were plotting against the king. It was crushed from being held too tight and smeared all over with blood, but the words could still be read. They had done this, Robin thought as he watched Lord D'Alselin's men fan out around the building. The Viponts had destroyed Locksley Hall.

Advent

The sound of bells woke Friar Toki early on the morning after St Martin's feast. He was accustomed to bells tolling his hours and calling him to church, but this was the distant, desperate clamour of bells ringing to rouse men from their beds. He rose immediately. At the gates of Lenton Priory stood anxious figures, beating at the doors for sanctuary. The nightwatchman opened a small hatch within the great oak edifice and demanded to know the reason for their plea.

'A fire,' Toki heard, 'an attack on Locksley Hall.'

He hurried to welcome the men and women in. He knew many of them, servants of Sir Walter Peverill and his family. They were exhausted, frozen, shaking with shock and anger and fear. Toki and the brothers took them to the warm fires and spiced wines of the hospital. When they had calmed he asked one of them, a reed-like girl, what had happened. Between sucking sips of wine she told him. Locksley's servants had been almost all abed or drunk in the great hall with Lord Vipont's servants when hooded men broke in, smashing furniture and spreading fire. They seemed to know their way through the hall, ran in all directions, driving out the servants.

'Only the servants?' Toki asked. 'Where were the lords?'

'Lord Locksley left hours earlier. And the Lords Vipont were gone too, after most of the other guests. Lady Elaine and Lady Joan went with them. I – I could not find my mistress. I looked for her, but the fire was spreading. Edgar made me leave. I wanted to stay and search, truly.'

'I know you did, child.'

Toki went around the servants, asking each of them what had happened, and they all told the same story. Hooded men, shouting, fire, smashing, the lords nowhere to be seen. They had come from the forest, one man said, they must be the forest thieves who had been haunting the woods since spring. Toki smiled and thanked them, then took up his staff and sack and aged horse and left the priory. Nothing more would be learnt there. He thought of going to Locksley Hall himself, but on the road he met Lord D'Alselin's men heading towards Nottingham Castle. They had come from Locksley. In that direction the bells of St Oswald's church were still clanging in alarm. One of the men recognised him and volunteered more information, so Toki fell in with their party. They had arrived to find Locksley Hall unguarded, the gates open, horses missing, most of the household fled and none of the attackers lingering. Although the building was still burning they explored what they could, and believed they might have found the sheriff's body.

'His body?' Toki repeated.

D'Alselin's man nodded. 'It's being removed to St Oswald's but Lord

D'Alselin identified him.'

'Were any others killed?'

'A few of the attackers themselves, one or two servants who tried to fight them off.'

'And the family?'

'They all must have fled. If they did not come to the priory they are probably in the castle.'

Lady Elaine and Joan, with their attendants, were indeed under the protection of the Lords Vipont when Toki arrived, although both refused to come out into the public gaze. He wandered the castle, eyes and ears open to all, face blank and benevolent. It soon became clear that besides Robin and Sir Walter there were two noticeable absences from the Vipont party: the bride and groom. If they had not been hurt in the fire – and Toki hoped, as seemed the case, that they had not – then neither had sought sanctuary at the most obvious place to do so. Toki heard men say that Eudo had sent riders north, towards Peverill Tower, in case Marian and Guy had fled there. He had also sent men in their dozens into the forest in search of the thieves he believed to be responsible. Other lords were starting to assemble at the castle, or to send their servants with reports. No one had seen either bride or groom. Toki caught the eye of Lord D'Alselin as he nodded alongside Lord Eudo, listening to one of these reports. D'Alselin approached him in a quieter corner of the castle. The lord towered over him, even as he leant close enough for their words to be private.

'Have you seen Locksley?' D'Alselin asked.

'No. I hear he was at the hall last night but left before nightfall.'

'Will you see him?'

'Perhaps.'

'Tell him to keep away from Nottingham.'

'Keep away? I would expect him to be anxious for news of his family.'

'Lord Eudo believes he had something to do with this attack. He claims some of Sir Walter's servants found their way here in the night, that they believe Locksley was among the men who attacked the hall.'

Toki rubbed his thumb against the smoothed edge of his staff.

'That would be a strange thing for him to do.'

'It would. But Eudo insists Locksley is called here for questioning. If he is wise he will not answer that call.'

'Refuse to be questioned about a murder? That would rather invite suspicion.'

'All the same, I would advise him to keep away. Whether he comes or not Lord Eudo is likely to accuse him. Until there is a new sheriff the case cannot be heard. Locksley can come forward then.'

Toki nodded and ambled onwards. His apparent unconcern lasted all the way to the stables, and then he gathered his things once more and rode for the forest.

Marian stayed inside the croft for days. Sometimes Agnes Scarlette was there, sometimes a younger woman who seemed to be Agnes's assistant. She poured the drinks that Marian took, pressed poultices on her face and bound her hand, but never spoke. There were other women too, and they did not speak to Marian either. They whispered to each other and slept on the floor near her and ate their meals next to her, but their comings and goings confused Marian. She could never tell how many of them used the croft as they were all bound up in furs and wool, their hoods dripping with snow, their noses red. She thought perhaps there were more of them as time went on but she could not be certain.

On the morning that she left the croft all of the women – however many there might be – had gone. She forced herself up inch by inch: one elbow, then another, one wrist, then another gingerly touching the mattress, one knee up, then another. She rocked forwards onto her knees and pushed herself up slowly, her legs trembling at the effort after days of lying. She remembered her mother standing like this after one of her confinements when Marian was a child – she had had a son and was determined to be churched quickly so she could care for him. Marian had not thought of her mother in months. The memory was a little comfort to her as she raised her spinning head, blinked, pulled her mantle close and stepped awkwardly towards the doorway.

It was snowing. That was the first thing that struck her. The second was that there were a lot of buildings. She thought perhaps she was in a village, but it must be very close to the forest as there were trees pressing close all around. She could smell onions on the air. She inhaled the scent and for a moment memories threatened to overwhelm her. The feast at her wedding, cups being raised to her and Guy, the fire smoking in the centre of the hall, the shouts as her home was burnt around her, Guy leaving her, her father in her lap. She crushed her eyes shut and felt herself topple. A rough hand caught hers and she drew back in shock.

The man who went to catch her was familiar, but she could not place his name.

'Excuse me,' she said. 'I am sorry.'

She spoke French. He called out to another man, working on the rooftops, in English. It was a moment before she realised the name he had spoken.

'Robin is here?' she said, seizing the man's hand as she asked the question. His skin was tan but his hair was fair – or had been fair. Now it was streaked with brown and grey. He had wrinkles around his pale eyes that suggested laughter. John. John was his name.

'You are feeling more well, my lady?' he asked. His French was not very good.

'No,' she said.

'You have no shoes.'

She looked at her feet and realised he was right. Someone had put a pale blue woollen tunic on her and thick socks, but no shoes.

'I will –' he hesitated and then spoke in English. 'I'll find shoes for you and take you to the longhouse.'

She waited for him to do so and then struggled with the sturdy leather shoes and wooden pattens he found. She towered over him in them. He offered her his arm and she let herself be led away from the women's croft towards a larger building in the centre of the village. Or clearing perhaps, she thought. The forest seemed to stretch away in all directions from this small area of buildings and people. As she walked the people watched her pass. The younger woman who had helped Agnes ran over to her as she neared the longhouse.

'Does she speak English?' the girl asked John.

'I do,' said Marian.

'I'm Edeva. I'll come with you. Ladies are supposed to have women with them when they go to see men.'

Sensible child, Marian thought. More sensible than she was at that moment. 'Where am I, Edeva?'

'In the new hundred, my lady. The Hundred of the Arrow.'

Marian wanted to ask more questions but John was half-crouched in the doorway waiting for them to follow him, so she did. Inside, a small group sat around a fire eating from a communal pot, a few chickens and a goat keeping company with them. One of them leapt to his feet when she entered and ran to her. It was Much. He bounded over and dropped to his knees in front of her.

'My lady, we're so glad you're – here.'

Marian suspected his last word might have been 'alive' before he realised what he was saying. She reached to take his hand then saw her own were bound. The wall, she thought, with another judder of memory. She patted his shoulder instead.

'We don't have any chairs,' he said, gesturing for her to join them at the fireside. 'But you can sit on the stool.'

'Thank you.'

Agnes Scarlette was kneeling on the floor of the longhouse. When Marian sat she passed her a bowl of food without a word. The others around the fire smiled at her awkwardly while she spooned the stew in her hands back and forth. Much said he would go and find Robin. Marian did not feel much like eating but she stared into her food to avoid the curious eyes that surrounded her. Whether they stared because she was a noblewoman or simply because she was not dead she could not be certain. The longhouse's interest in a silent woman could only last so long, and the groups had fallen to talking among themselves when the door flew open and Robin lunged into the chamber, looking about urgently. He glanced over Marian once before he recognised her. His face, already flushed from running, darkened as it took in her split lip, the bruise around her eye, her bound hands. He did not say anything then, but stood in the doorway while everyone in the longhouse looked between him and Marian, waiting for one of them to speak. She did not know what to say, so she stared into her bowl again. Robin had never seen so much as a graze on her before. Young ladies were supposed to spend their childhoods being still and quiet, and when she had defied those strictures and fallen while running she had hidden her gashed knees rather than ask for help and admit to doing something wrong.

'Have you seen the Hundred?'

Marian looked up. Robin addressed her.

'No.'

He held out a hand to her, stepping over the bodies on the longhouse floor to reach her. Embarrassed, she got up by herself before he was at her side. The people in the longhouse still stared.

'We can talk properly outside,' Robin said in a low voice.

He let her lead the way out of the door and back into the clearing. Outside, despite the cold, there were people working everywhere. Without speaking, Robin directed her away from the activity of the Hundred, through the trees lining the limits of the clearing into the forest proper and up to the banks of a brook. There were no women beating their clothes in the ice-rimed water today. The snow drifted in fits from the sky. For a few moments they stood in awkward silence.

'Is it too cold?' Robin asked.

'No.' Marian held her mantle close and looked back towards the Hundred. 'How long has this been here?'

'A few months.'

'A few?'

'Half a year.'

Marian shook her head. It seemed impossible that all this time, all the months that lords had been sending men to search for thieves, they had not found the village growing in the depths of the forest. For the briefest of moments she had managed to turn her mind from Locksley Hall. Then she thought of lords' men, of thieves, of attack, and the hall once again pierced her thoughts. She had to ask the question she feared the answer to. For days it had drifted through her mind, tormenting her with hope and dread in equal measure.

'How many people escaped from Locksley?'

Robin did not turn his eye from her. A lesser man might have done.

'Most of the servants did, from what we have heard. Toki tells us that many of them got to Lenton, or the castle, seeking sanctuary. Waltheof left with me, so he is well. We have told Aelfeva.'

'Good.'

'Elaine and my mother were gone before any of it happened.' He hesitated. 'Your father –'

'I know about my father.'

'How –?'

'I was there. When he…' She swallowed. She still could not say that word. 'Do you know if Gytha is all right?'

'I think so. Wulfstan helped her to get away, apparently.'

'She would not have liked that.' Marian smiled, relief prickling behind her eyes. She blinked to keep back her tears. It was more than she had hoped. Thank God.

'You have not asked after Guy.'

'Have I not?' She contemplated a fraying edge on her sleeve.

'No one knows where he is. He was seen by the priest of St Oswald's riding south, but there has been no word from him. No one at the castle seems to know more than us. They sent men to Peverill Tower in case he was there, but found nothing.'

'But he is alive.'

Marian heard the words coming out of her mouth, dully. She hardly knew what she felt. She had not wanted him to be hurt, of course not, but she could not wholly say she was glad he was well. He had fled. That night and now. He had run from danger, abandoned her and her father to those men. She wondered if he would come back and a small part of her instantly hoped he did not. Robin was watching her, the anger and confusion playing across her face. She forced herself to be still.

'Do you know who did it?'

Now he turned away from her. 'I – I have some idea.'

'Do you think it was Eudo?'

'Yes.' He was surprised. 'Do you?'

'I have been thinking about it. All these images play in my mind. He spoke to Guy before they left. Their men were still all over the hall. Whoever attacked us was there quickly enough to be in my father's chamber moments after the Viponts rode out. Eudo could not have passed hooded thieves and not noticed, not tried to stop them. But the men wore no colours, so I cannot be certain.'

'Lord Eudo has accused me of leading the attack.'

'You? How could he think that? Why would you? That is your home.'

'Precisely. He has destroyed my name, my home. The only thing left is my life, which he can have if the courts decide I killed your father.'

'But he let you leave the hall that day. You all quarrelled but it seemed to be forgotten after you left. Why harm my father, just to blame you?'

'Your father knew too much.'

Robin held out a roll of vellum. The sight of it made Marian reel. It was the same document her father had been holding when the hooded men struck him. The same that she had carried all the way to the walls of Locksley. She could not take it. It was still smeared with blood, darker now and scratched. She looked at Robin in alarm.

'What is that? My father had it when…'

She did not finish that sentence but Robin knew what she meant and nodded. He told her about the message. How his men had found the message in the forest, how he had shown it to Sir Walter who told Guy who told Lord Eudo about its discovery. How this was the silence Sir Walter had spoken of at the wedding feast. Lastly, he read her its contents. She knew swiftly enough what they meant.

'Is that why they did it? To silence my father?'

'Perhaps. And to keep me quiet. And you. And Guy.'

She pressed her head into her hands, rubbing her forehead while trying to understand how such destruction and wrong could have come from one scrap of a message.

'Tell me one more thing. Honestly.'

Robin nodded.

'Was it these men who attacked the tax wagons, and the Count of Mortain's, and the lords' dues? All the crimes in the forest these past months. Was it them?'

He only hesitated for a moment.

'Yes.'

'Were you with them?'

'Sometimes.'

'And Will?'

'Yes.'

'Did you kill the clerk?'

'No. I have not spilt a drop of blood since I returned to Nottingham. I swear that.'

Marian bit her lip. This was why she had not asked more questions when she found Robin in the forest with the men disguised as lepers. Even then she had known. But she had wanted to pretend she did not.

'Perhaps that is why God let you prove your innocence in the ordeal.'

'Perhaps. Men say he is forgiving.'

'Obviously he must be. Do you have any other secrets? I should probably know before I leave.'

'Leave?'

'I cannot stay here. You must have hardly any food. I should not be taking it from you.'

'No one begrudges it.'

'Then they are very good. But I could eat at the expense of those who can afford it. My cousin in Newstead Abbey would take me in, and I would be safe there.'

'You want to become a nun? You were only married a few hours.'

Despite herself, Marian smiled. 'I think my cousin will let me stay without taking the veil.'

'You should do as you think best, Marian. But you are welcome here for as long as you want to stay.' He offered her his hand to return back to the longhouse.

'Can we sit here a little longer? I like the quiet, away from the Hundred. Or do you need to leave?'

'No. I can stay.'

They sat on the snowy banks of the brook and stared into the forest, at the woven sanctuary of trees that protected them.

Robin and Lefchild had taken night watch at the eastern outpost, halfway to Locksley. It was a quiet night, the only sounds the snow falling outside the caves and the crack of a fire inside. When they were relieved of their shelter the following morning the earth was blanketed by snow, ankle deep. They walked towards the Hundred slowly, pausing to check the Saviour Oak. When they reached it they found Madalgrim's wife leaving a large skin of ale. Lefchild called a greeting. She offered them a smile and a mouthful of ale to warm themselves.

'I'm glad to see you both. Aelfeva said you were safe, but with soldiers all over this forest I wanted to see for myself. Is Madalgrim well?'

'Hale as always,' said Lefchild.

'Tell him I asked after him. I miss him.'

'We will.'

'Any news from the castle?' asked Robin.

Her eyes widened. 'You haven't heard? The count's appointed a new sheriff.'

'The count has no right to do that.'

'Whether he has a right or not, he's done it.'

'Let me guess,' said Lefchild. 'Eudo de Vipont.'

She nodded. 'They've already held the first county court. You're under threat of outlawry, Lord Locksley. If you don't attend the next assizes…'

'What will they do? Seize my lands? Burn down my home?' Robin smiled. 'I don't need to go to their court for that to happen.'

'All the same…'

Lefchild held up a hand to silence her. From the direction of the King's Way they could hear horses.

'You'd better head on,' said Robin softly. 'Thank you for the ale. We'll pass your message to Madalgrim.'

He shouldered the ale and they parted ways. Robin and Lefchild had barely gone a few yards when voices joined the sound of whinnying horses. The men had followed them into the forest. One urged the other to silence and the voices fell away. In the deep snow hooves could not be heard but now and then the horses shuddered or snorted in the cold. And those sounds were drawing nearer. Robin looked around the forest floor that surrounded them. The snow was undisturbed further into the woodland, but where they had been there was a clear pathway of footfall.

'We're leaving tracks,' he whispered.

'One way not to.'

Lefchild looked to the trees.

'I haven't climbed a tree since I was a teenager.'

'Better hope you remember how to do it then.'

Lefchild held out his cupped hands, ready for Robin's foot. There was no use arguing – the horses were close now, any moment their pursuers would appear through the dense forest and it would be too late – so Robin stepped into Lefchild's grip and up, struggling onto a branch over their heads. The oaks in that stretch of forest were not high, but their limbs reached out wide and they had grown close enough together that if your balance was right, you could step from one branch to another and thus run along the trees for a mile. Lefchild leapt up after Robin, taking the ale from him.

'I'd better take that. You'll need your arms to balance.'

Lefchild led the way, clambering up the tree, ignoring the lower branches until he reached one that was thick enough to swing out onto. He padded along that branch almost to its end. Robin followed more cautiously, his frozen fingers hardly able to grip the branches, his feet sliding in the snow that covered the trees. Lefchild held out a hand to help him over the gap between two trees and he was on to the next one. Beneath them and some yards back, the men still searched, moving slow and silent along the footsteps that suddenly disappeared.

They looked around them in confusion, wondering if their prey had somehow retraced their own steps. They gesticulated to one another in a dumb show of disagreement about whether to go on or back.

Robin followed Lefchild along another branch, but as Lefchild bounded off it the whole thing shook, sending Robin to his hands and knees and releasing a shower of snow that tumbled to the earth below. They froze, hardly daring to look at their pursuers. Had they seen? No. They were still prowling for traces of footsteps. Lefchild gestured Robin to follow and he leapt over, pausing on the next tree to be sure he was not seen. The men below set off in the opposite direction, retracing the steps that led nowhere. When they were out of sight and sound, Lefchild and Robin climbed down from the tree and ran.

They arrived back at the Hundred just as Aedith was doling out food in the longhouse.

'Ale?' cried Kolbrand. 'At last.'

'From Madalgrim's wife,' said Lefchild, throwing it to him to pass around.

'She had news as well,' said Robin.

They told the men about Eudo's appointment as sheriff. That news was received angrily enough, and when they followed it with an account of how close they had come to being seen the faces around the fire were grim.

'How long ago was Eudo made sheriff?' asked Ansculf.

'Long enough for her to think we already knew.'

'This is useless,' said Thurstan, putting down his bowl with a clatter. 'We don't know anything that's going on beyond the forest. For all we know Eudo has an army of men ready to burn half the woods down to find us. We can't always be running. We need to be a step ahead of these men, to know when and where they're coming so we can be clear before they arrive.'

'What do you expect us to do, Thurstan?' said Lefchild. 'As long as we're lepers we can get around the forest without attracting too much attention, but lepers don't just wander into towns and castles asking to know what the sheriff's planning.'

'We need another clerk like Peter,' said Gilbert.

'Or another lord,' said Kolbrand, glancing at Robin.

'Never mind about the sheriff's men,' said Tosti, 'what are we going to do about food now? It sounds like Madalgrim's wife was nearly caught by those men at the Saviour Oak. Every time our kin go there to leave us what they can spare, they risk themselves. And since we can't go to the market to buy food – even if we had the money to do so – eventually what we have is going to run out.'

'It'll be a hungry Advent,' said Ansculf, gazing into his pottage morosely. There was already more water than stock to it.

'Could we try another raid?' suggested Much. 'Try to take a delivery of food while it's on its way to one of the lords.'

'After what happened to Will last time?' said Doleswif unenthusiastically. 'I don't want to be cut in half.'

'If we raid again the Viponts will kill Will,' said Robin.

'If he's still alive,' Kolbrand muttered.

'We wouldn't be able to anyway,' said Gilbert. 'We don't know when deliveries are being made or by which route or how well-protected they are. That's what we need a clerk to tell us.'

'Go get a job then,' said Lefchild. 'You'd make a good clerk.'

'Gladly. But while I'm asking for work, every man who knows my face could arrest me.'

'Ah. That.'

'We need someone in the castle,' said Much. 'Then they could find out about deliveries and watch the Viponts. What if I grew a beard?'

'I could do it.'

At first the hundredmen did not hear the voice in the shadows. Edeva shushed them. 'Say that again, my lady.'

Marian leant closer to the fire. 'I could go to the castle.'

The hundredmen looked among themselves, smiles spreading across their faces.

'Of course...'

'Why didn't we think before...?'

'A friend on the inside...'

'No,' said Robin. He stood up and passed his bowl back to Aedith, speaking French so only Marian heard him. 'You are not risking your life with that family.'

Marian responded in English. 'I can't stay here much longer. I'm well now. It isn't right that I steal the little you have when I could eat at a lord's table.'

'I'd rather eat at a lord's table too,' said Much. 'Do you need a servant?'

'Edeva could come with me, carry messages back to the Saviour Oak.' Marian turned to the girl. 'Do the Viponts know your face?'

'That bastard Lanfranc knew it once. But he hasn't seen me since spring. He can't remember every kinswoman he's ill-treated. There must be scores of us.'

Robin had not sat back down.

'Marian, we should talk outside.'

For a moment a stubborn look crossed her face and he thought she would refuse. But while that look remained, she did as he wished and followed him out of the door.

'I thought you and your men discussed these things together,' said Marian when they were in the clearing.

'Some things. You should not feel you have to do this. These men have helped you because it was right, not so that you would owe them anything.'

'But I do owe them, Robin. If John and Much had not found me I might have frozen to death in the forest. That is not why I offered to go to the castle though.'

'Then why?'

'Because I cannot just let Eudo carry on as if he has done nothing wrong. He murdered my father, he destroyed my home and now he sits in Nottingham Castle in the position my father should still hold. We both know he has plotted against the king. He is a traitor and a killer and I will not let him escape justice.'

'I understand,' said Robin more gently. 'But you do not have to hunt him down alone. We will think of another way.'

'No. Thurstan is right. As long as we are here we are all powerless. We know nothing, we can do nothing. But if I am in the castle I can watch Eudo, find evidence to prove what he has done. And I can make sure Will is all right, that your mother is safe.'

Robin looked away from her, wondering how to articulate what he was thinking. Of course he wanted his family to be protected, and there was no one else in the Hundred who could go to the castle without being arrested, never mind with any hope of gathering useful information. The arithmetic made sense. One woman in danger so dozens could be kept safe. But he could not stand for that one person to be Marian. He shook his head and met her eye again.

'If you are determined to do this we need to be certain that Eudo cannot suspect you. We need a reason that you are only coming back to the castle now, for where you have been all this time.'

'I have thought of that. I can say I was in Newstead Abbey. The abbess will go along with it, I am certain.'

'And to stop Eudo finding out that you are watching his messages?'

'I will do nothing for the first month or so. Just sit quietly and wait for them to trust me.'

'He might never trust you.'

'But he will eventually stop distrusting me.'

There was logic to that at least, perverse though it might be. Robin nodded, held out an arm to gesture her back inside. At the last moment he hesitated.

'Are you certain?'

She gave him a look, something between exasperated and amused. It was the sort of fond disrespect he had only ever received from the hundredmen and Will before. Seeing it on Marian's face made him laugh, despite all she was risking.

'All right,' he said. 'We will get you to the castle.'

Through the snow-bound hills, three figures approached Newstead Abbey. Two wore the hood and clapper of a leper, the other a poor man's mantle hiding a nobleman's cote. At the gates they were halted, words were exchanged then all proceeded, along the brushed flagstone pathway that led into the abbey's domestic buildings. The lepers were kept outside, in a fire-warmed chamber in the hospital, scented with frankincense and thyme. The man was led by the abbess's chamberlain to the very heart of the building, where the abbess's chamber divided the world of men from the cloistered dormitories of the nuns. There he waited under the chamberlain's watchful gaze until Abbess Hawise Ferrers returned from Mass. She sat behind her desk as a glass of wine was poured for them both, drank, looked over it and addressed her guest.

'As a justice in this county I ought to arrest you now, Lord Locksley.'

'I have already told your gatekeeper I am here for sanctuary. It would reflect poorly on your abbey if you violated that sacred bond.'

She pursed her lips and put her glass down.

'Very well, I grant you sanctuary. I can still send word to the sheriff so his men are waiting when you leave. You have forty days, should you wish to wait them out. The end result will be the same.'

'That would be the new sheriff, would it? The last one having been murdered.'

She crossed herself. 'Do not speak so freely of such felonies. Lord de Vipont claims that you were the one who killed my relatives, and I have little reason to believe otherwise.'

'Your relatives? More than one?'

'My cousin Marian still has not been found. We fear she died in the fire.'

So they did believe Marian dead. It was useful to know for certain.

'It would grieve me if she had.'

'Your grief is of little concern to me.'

'What evidence did Lord Vipont give to prove that I had committed this felony?'

'The men who attacked the hall appeared to be the same hooded thieves who repeatedly ambushed local lords' wagons in the forest.'

'That does not connect it to me. I underwent the ordeal to prove I was innocent of those charges.'

'A servant who escaped the fire claimed to have seen you there, even though you should have left several hours before.'

'But I thought the attackers were hooded? How did this servant recognise one as me?'

The abbess hesitated and for a moment a flicker of uncertainty crossed her face. 'Perhaps it was that they heard your voice.'

'I thought this evidence was presented to the jury in the county court where I was condemned. Did you not attend?'

'I did, but I cannot recall now the details of this witness's claim.'

'And what reason was given for my decision to destroy my home, to kill the stepfather and sister who supported me when no one else in the county would, to murder – cruelly murder – servants who had only ever shown me loyalty and kindness?'

'Lord Vipont said that you did it out of jealousy and vengeance for losing your estate after the ordeal. You have always been hot-headed. I think you yourself would admit to that.'

'Hot-headed enough to raise an army of murderers, command them to Locksley then patiently wait until every guest had left the hall before leading them in?'

'How do you know the guests had left when it happened?'

'I have my witnesses too.' Robin drank a little more wine. 'Or, it may be that Lord Vipont and his alleged witness lie. And if they lie, the same arguments against me could be applied to them. They also had a motive against Sir Walter, even more of one against me, and they were the last guests to leave the hall, seen by one witness – who I can produce – to leave most of their servants inside the hall, where they were joined by armed and hooded men.'

'What motive did they have against Sir Walter?'

'Sir Walter had proof of their treason. This.' He produced the message to the count. The bloody marks covering the outer edges gave the abbess pause, but she unrolled it all the same. 'I found this in the forest after the count's wardrobe was attacked. Sir Walter showed it to Lord Guy Vipont but kept it hidden in his own chamber until the king's return, just in case the Viponts continued their rebellion with the count. When Sir Walter died, he was holding this.'

'How did you come to have it?'

'I will tell you that, but first I want an assurance from you. I want you to extend your protection not only to me but to all those men and women who dwell on the lands neighbouring the abbey, whether they are tenants or not.'

'What interest do you have in my tenants?'

'None. I am only interested in the safety of the inhabitants of my hospital.'

'I am to do all that just so you tell me where you found this?'

'No, because if you give me that assurance I will give you a miracle.'

The abbess could not resist such an offer. She made a show of thinking, of inspecting the letter again, of tapping her fingers on the desk. But she agreed, just as he had known she would.

'Follow me.'

He strode from the chamber. He heard the abbess's chair scraping across the floor in her eagerness to follow. He did not look back, trusting to the sound of her footsteps to tell him she was there. He walked all the way to the hospital and once he and the abbess were inside, he closed the door.

'Here,' he said, walking over to one of the lepers, 'is your miracle.'

The leper stood, drew its hood back and raised its head. The abbess crossed herself, eyes wide with disbelief.

'Merciful mother of God. Marian?'

'Mother Abbess.' Marian knelt and kissed her cousin's hand. The abbess drew her into a fierce embrace.

'How –? You have been missing all this time, we had lost hope.'

She pulled out a chair for Marian at her table. The other leper had removed its hood – Marian said she was her servant. Robin sent an attendant for more wine and the four of them sat around the old table, where herbs were sliced and steeped, to explain to the abbess everything that had happened to Marian since her guests left on her wedding night. Almost everything. No mention was made of the hundredmen, the outposts keeping watch over the forest – it was all made to sound like Marian had been rescued by a passing worker from Lord Locksley's hospital and taken there to recover, at some remove from the lepers. The abbess listened, was prepared to believe, and eventually did believe what she was told.

'If you are certain that Lord Eudo was responsible for what happened at Locksley Hall, I will of course support you. But you should know that he is more influential now. The count appointed him sheriff.'

'We know,' said Marian.

'And he has taken control of the Peverill estate.'

'My father's lands? How?'

'After your father's death the lands should have descended to you, but you were missing, so the next of kin would have been Guy, who is also still missing, which left Guy's family as the successors to those lands. Eudo used the excuse of searching for you in order to move his men into the estate.'

'Is there any part of this county the Viponts do not have control of now?' said Robin darkly.

'Apparently my own lands, if your hospital is still thriving. And Lord D'Alselin's. He expressed his own doubts about your guilt, Robin, he did not believe you would have destroyed Locksley Hall.'

'That is one more supporter then.'

'I must say though,' continued the abbess, 'I have heard no other witnesses to the events of Locksley Hall speak out against Lord Eudo. If you wish to challenge this case in the courts you will have some difficulty.'

'No one else has spoken out because they are servants,' said Marian. 'Robin and I have seen firsthand how the Vipont men can mistreat those who challenge them. But we will not press this case yet. I want to gather more information first. If there is one letter that condemns Lord Eudo as a rebel against the king, there may be more.'

'How do you intend to do this?'

'I will ask to live at the castle with the rest of my family.'

The abbess sat back in her chair with a heavy sigh.

'Is that wise? If Lord Eudo is capable of burning down Locksley Hall to destroy evidence of his wrongdoing –'

'I have tried to persuade her against this,' said Robin. 'You will not succeed.'

'I am resolved to do this,' said Marian. 'We need justice.'

'That will also be difficult with Lord Eudo acting as judge in every county case.'

'Then we will wait for the king to be freed and plea directly to his courts. But I can learn more about that at the castle as well.'

'I can tell you something even now. I had word from my nephew this week, from Normandy. The first instalment of the king's ransom has finally been paid. The German emperor has agreed to release him after Epiphany.'

Marian and Robin met each other's eyes with wide smiles.

'That is good news,' said Marian.

'Hopefully there will be more of it soon. Now I have promised Lord Locksley that I will protect his hospital and those in it. Tell me what else I can do to help you.'

The winter months were hard for every poor hundred in England, but in the Hundred of the Arrow there was cause at least for hope. The abbess was true to her word. No sheriff's men came within the bounds of her estate and although watches were kept every hour of every day across the forest surrounding the Hundred there was never cause for fear. The men who still hunted for the fugitives and Lord Locksley did so in vain. Marian kept her promise too. Her arrival at the castle in the abbess's company, with tales of having claimed sanctuary at the abbey during her disappearance, was met with a mixture of wonder and suspicion by its lords. Elaine wept on her shoulder with joy, Lady

Joan smiled as much as sorrow allowed and the Viponts did their best to hide their alarm. For weeks Marian did nothing to raise their suspicions. She and Edeva sat, sewed and sang. The Viponts made every pretence of welcome and kept her in the comfort that a lady of their family ought to enjoy. They claimed to know nothing of Guy's location, and if they were lying they did it well enough that Marian could not inquire further. All the same, she was legally Lady Vipont and they would treat her as such. Marian suspected that the real reason for their benevolence was a desire to monitor her until they were certain she was no threat to them. As such, she made every effort not to appear interested in their business. She knew that the longer she remained in the castle being watched, the longer she could watch the Viponts in turn.

Edeva proved her worth early on. She was silent before the lords but talked easily with the servants. Her young face belied her years of hard experience, and all those who met her in the castle thought her the model of discretion. And so, one by one, they confided in her. She knew no French at first so Marian taught her the language. Soon she understood not only the English servants' talk, but also the senior household staff's. And every small stone of knowledge they gained she and Marian held close, slowly building the edifice of information that would condemn the Viponts before the king.

At New Year Marian sent, through the abbess, a delivery of alms to the Hundred. They celebrated the season of Epiphany with wine and meat, a relief after so many weeks of fasting. Word was sent too that the king's release had been delayed. There were rumours that the count had tried to pay his brother's captors to hold him in Germany for longer. That plan must have failed though, for by St Agnes's Eve Edeva brought news that the count had told all his castles in England to improve their defences. He was preparing for a war. The hundredmen prepared too. When – if – the king returned they would need to prove their loyalty if there was to be any hope of a royal pardon. Such proof was likely to be military. During the brief hours between watches and work, Robin taught the men their weapons. His own life seemed an endless round of hunting, watches, visits to the Savour Oak to collect messages from Marian, scrabbling for time to write replies of his own. He was astonished to pass the abbey one winter's day and hear Candlemas being celebrated within. And as spring finally thawed the icy dew on the forest floor and hardy snowdrops pushed through the crunching, compact earth the news that they had so long awaited arrived: the king had been released. He was on his way back to England. To Robin this news felt like having blood let. It provided no immediate relief, but like the release of bad humours from the body it promised relief to come.

In any case, it was cause for celebration. Robin gathered a group of the men together to hunt, and in honour of the king's imminent return they would not merely chase lowly hares and foxes and roe deer. That day they would pursue the great fallow deer of the forest. This meat was the best, but by the laws of England it was reserved for the king and his trusted friends. While the king was still abroad, Robin felt he could hardly argue against the hundredmen enjoying it in his absence. Not far from their northern outpost they saw the high grazed bark that told them a buck had passed that way. They tracked the beast through the forest, finding more grazes and droppings. Eventually they found the buck itself, scenting the air, tail raised. It knew it had been followed. Robin gestured silently and the men got to their knees, nocking arrows to their bows, drawing them to their chests. A pause as they made sure of their shot – to miss now would send the beast running, a wasted morning for them all – and then a thunk. The deer collapsed onto its side. Robin felt a shiver of disappointment that his had not been the fatal shot and looked to see which man was responsible. But the other men lowered their bows in confusion. Not one of them had loosed. A moment too late, Robin realised what had happened. He stepped back, waving for the men to follow, but a horse lunged alongside the deer and a young man leapt from it with a triumphant cry. He saw the men. He shouted again. There was a horn blast, the baying of dogs, the pounding of hooves and before Robin had been able to turn to run, they were surrounded.

There was no use trying to flee now. Men could never outrun hunting dogs. He told the men to lower their bows, to stand still, to give no cause for the hunters to harm them. He placed his own bow and arrow on the ground, raised his hands in submission and approached the pack of hunters. There was a surge from the rear of the group and a lord appeared. He was young, had a neatly trimmed beard and cheeks flushed from the hunt. A dog followed at his horse's hooves, sniffing at Robin and circling him. The lord looked down on him.

'You are hunting the king's deer.'

Robin replied in French. 'So are you, my lord.'

'I have permission.'

'From the Count of Mortain?'

'No,' said the lord suspiciously, 'from the true king.'

'How is that possible? The king is still in Europe.'

'I know, I was with his fleet on the coast of Flanders.' He studied Robin. 'You speak very finely for a poacher.'

He could pretend not to have been poaching, Robin thought, claim that they lost their way while searching for small game – with the abbess's permission, of course – and should now be released. But this lord would not believe that tale any more than Robin would once have. If he tried to deny their guilt they might all be arrested and hanged. As he was deciding how to respond a flash of red and yellow behind the lord caught his eye. The hunters all wore their greens, but one of them was fiddling with the clasp of a purse at his hip, which bore a heraldic symbol: red and yellow bell-like shapes criss-crossing one another. *Vaire or et gules.* A symbol Robin knew very well.

'Are you connected to the Earl of Derby?'

'I am the Earl of Derby.'

That explained how he came to be hunting on the abbess's estates. When last Robin had met him they had both been children, but the earl had spent many years on his Norman estates. Obviously he had been recently defending them in the name of the king. This was a piece of good fortune. The earl was the abbess's nephew and where she trusted he was likely to follow.

'I knew your father,' said Robin. 'I fought with him at Acre.'

The earl raised his eyebrows in surprise. Then realisation dawned.

'You are Robin of Locksley.'

'I am, my lord. Your aunt has given us the liberty of her lands.'

'And no doubt you were going to pay the king for any fallow deer you took at his expense.' His smile had something of Will's about it: a slyness behind his good humour. 'I had hoped to encounter you somewhere, Locksley. There is a matter I want to discuss with you. You have no horse?'

'Not here.'

He called for one of his attendants to dismount.

'Take this one. My men will be some time unmaking the animal in any case. It will give us time to talk at the abbey.'

Robin hesitated, glancing towards his companions.

'Your men may go free.'

With a whispered warning to follow a longer route back to the Hundred in case they were pursued, Robin left the hundredmen and followed the earl back to the abbey. To his surprise Newstead teemed with men in Derby's vair badge, running back and forth with the trappings of war, even among the cloisters of the abbey itself.

'You have brought an army with you.'

'No, just a handful of soldiers from Normandy. The bulk of my force waits to be assembled in Derbyshire. I had hoped they might not be needed but it seems inevitable now.'

Derby led him to a chamber in the outer walls of Newstead, some distance from the nuns and priests of the abbey. He had wine poured and drank his thirstily. Robin thought on his words about the soldiers in Derbyshire.

'Is war certain?'

'I think so. The king sent me here to treat with the seneschal of Nottingham Castle. He refuses to surrender the fortress to anyone but the count.'

'That does not surprise me.'

'Nor me. The king's men should not have allowed the count to take Tickhill and Nottingham while the king was abroad. There has been nothing but trouble since.'

'Does Tickhill Castle also stand against the king?'

'Oh yes. The Bishop of Durham is treating with them, as I am here, but he has little hope of surrender either. He will have an easier time of it than we will at Nottingham if it comes to a siege.'

The earl poured himself another cup of wine.

'Who will lead such a siege? You?'

'No. The king himself.'

'The king is coming to Nottingham?' Robin was incredulous.

The earl frowned. 'Your doubt worries me. Every man I have passed on the road expressed the same disbelief. It will help the defenders' cause.'

'The king has been absent from this country so long.'

'And now he returns to put down a civil war. God is good.' He leant forward and rested his chin on the back of his hand. 'It is for this reason I brought you here. When I returned to Nottinghamshire yours was one of the first names I heard.'

'Oh?' Robin tried to conceal any suspicion. Derby noticed his tone.

'The whole county is talking of you. I have heard lords claim that you killed your family and burnt down your home in vengeance for losing it in the courts. The baseborn men say that you were hounded out of your estate and are now forced to starve in the forest. What I heard more than anything was that the people trust you, as they do not trust their other lords. Ordinarily, the opinion of the commons would matter little to me. But at this time such loyalty to lords could serve both our interests.'

'How?'

'Lord Eudo de Vipont currently holds your estates?'

'Yes.'

'Which means he can call on every man who owes him service to fight in his name. That is not an inconsiderable body of men. The Locksley hundred alone contains scores of potential soldiers, and your lands extend far beyond that.'

'Unfortunately they are no longer my lands.'

'But as I said, the Viponts can call on these men to fight for them – for the count – only through rights of tenure. Ties of birth and family loyalty go deeper than that. Your family has held power here for generations, your father – God rest him – was well-loved. And despite the whispers of lawlessness, of felony, of fraudulent ordeals and untrustworthy oaths that attach themselves to your name, still the men of this county are loyal to you before Lord Vipont. If you demanded it, they would all fight for your cause rather than his.'

'If I demanded it.'

Robin took a long drink of his wine to think. The earl did not demand such service, which meant that he was willing for a bargain to be struck. It was up to Robin to ensure that that bargain served his friends as much as it served the earl's.

'Many of the families on my estate have been driven from their homes through the Viponts' greed. They hide in the forest to escape hanging or punishment in their courts.'

The earl snorted. 'I had expected you to barter with me over the restoration of your estates, not the crimes of your tenants. What do you seek for them?'

'Pardons for every man and woman condemned in the Vipont courts since Lord Eudo took possession of my lands.'

The earl leant his head from side to side, as if balancing a scale.

'The king is not inclined to forgiveness. But I can appeal for it on your behalf. And what of yourself? I will confess, your experience will be useful if it comes to a siege of Nottingham Castle. You have fought in the sieges of the Holy Land – that is far from exceptional, many of the king's allies have done the same – and you have spent most of your life in and around that fortress – again, many local lords, myself included, have done so. But to combine both of those experiences with the knowledge of the Vipont family, and to hold the loyalty of the local men… That is valuable indeed. If you promise to fight for the king and bring your men to do the same, he would reward you. Those felonies I have heard you accused of would surely be forgotten?'

Robin dangled his wine in one hand. It would be good to be a free man, to enjoy the lands of his father's inheritance without always begging to another party. But he would not allow selfish desires to override his concern for the companions who had protected and fought alongside him for almost a year.

'I will bring what men and knowledge I can to the king's cause. But I must have assurance of a royal pardon not only for myself, but also for all my men.'

'I will ask.' The earl put down his glass, held out his hand. 'And in return, when the king commands, your men will come.'

Word went out from the Hundred of the Arrow. Across the county, the message went south. To St Oswald's Church, where the priest urged his congregation to be loyal to their true lord, who had fought for God and who now would put down the vipers of rebellion. To Lenton Priory, where Friar Toki carried word on his circuits, reminding tenant and villein alike that Robin of Locksley had proven himself innocent and penitent twice now, and if God marked him out for forgiveness, so should they. To the old meeting places of the Hundred of Locksley, where the chief tithing-man urged his hundredmen that justice could only be restored if the true lord was back in a position to dispense it. To the alestake of Madalgrim's home, where the brewsters reminded every customer to think of Lord Locksley as they downed their ale. To what had once been the commonland, around whose enclosures children throwing stones were told to tell their fathers to arm themselves to defend the lord who had tried to keep that land for the common men.

Whoever spread it and whatever the excuse given, the meaning was always the same: when Robin of Locksley called for arms, they must bring them. And as the words were repeated, as their tellers returned news to the Hundred, Robin received an answer that even he had not expected. They would come. When the king told Robin to show his loyalty, they would in turn prove theirs. The army of the arrow would assemble.

When Robin went to the Saviour Oak on the feast of St Fidelis two messages awaited him. One was squatting inside the tree yawning, and stood to meet him when he arrived.

'This'll be the last time I can come here,' Edeva said, passing him a roll of vellum. 'The castle will be sealed soon and if I'm outside it, I'll need a catapult to get back in.'

'You could stay outside. It would be safer.'

'No.' She looked offended. 'I'm not leaving my lady. Women have as much loyalty as men.'

He knew that well enough.

'I presume Marian still refuses to leave?'

'She says she'll be more use inside the castle than outside. The abbess offered to take us in again – Lady Joan as well – but your mother and Elaine think the castle is safer, and my lady doesn't want to leave them behind.'

'My mother does realise the castle is going to be besieged?'

'She says it's never been taken before so it won't be taken now. But I think the real reason is she's frightened to anger the Viponts. No wonder after what they did.'

Robin unrolled the message Marian had sent. It contained a record of all the deliveries of supplies – food, arms – that she had seen entering the castle, as well as an estimate of how many soldiers had joined the Viponts.

'They are certainly not preparing to treat for peace.'

Lords de Caux and de la Guerche had of course sent soldiers, but there were other names on Marian's list of those giving aid to the count's cause, names Robin was less familiar with: Murdac, Wenneval, Grendon, Russell. All had brought both knights and foot soldiers to the castle.

'Are all these men really willing to betray their king?'

'From what I've heard it's not that they want to betray the king, but that they want to prove their loyalty to the count. They don't believe the king will come.'

'The king is coming. Derby told me his ship has landed in Kent and he's expected to arrive in Nottinghamshire today or tomorrow.'

'Expected isn't the same as certain. We had word at the castle this morning that Tickhill is under siege. Obviously the negotiations broke down there too. They don't believe the king will fight them in person either.' She reached into her purse and pulled out a woven woollen band.

'Will you give this to Much? Just in case… You know. And tell my father I asked after him.'

Robin wrapped the band around Marian's message with a smile.

'Of course.'

'I'd better go back.'

'Will you have been missed?'

'In all the chaos at the castle? I doubt it.'

She pulled her hood over her head and reached for the bridle of the horse Marian had lent her.

'Shall I take a message back to my lady? Or your mother?'

Robin looked at the earth. He could not think how to say anything he thought or felt.

'Thank Marian for this. And… Tell them they're in my thoughts.'

Edeva smiled. 'They know that well enough.'

She nudged her horse back towards the road. Inside the mouth of the tree Robin found the second message. Two rolls of writing had been tied together and dangling from them was a wax seal. One was a letter of safe-conduct forbidding any man to harm the bearer on pain of punishment by the king himself. The second had the vair shield of Derby sketched on it in place of seal and name.

'The castle will not surrender,' it said. 'Time to pay your debt.'

1194

Lent

In the belly of Castle Rock Marian did not hear the army approaching. She was tending Will Scarlette in the guttering darkness of his cell when they felt a shudder deep in the earth.

'I've been here too long,' said Will dryly. 'We've reached the end of days.'

Marian left him his food and drink and hurried back into the keep. In the crammed stores of the basement men were running. She ignored them. She wanted to be up high, as high as it was possible to get, to see the vast vistas surrounding Nottingham. She ran up the spiral staircase, avoiding the anxious men running down. At the roof she burst through the door barely able to breathe and ran to the crenellations. Far beneath a vast shadow of men was steadily beating its way towards them, drums pounding, horns and trumpets blaring, standards fluttering. She had never seen such a vast stream of soldiers, nor heard such a cacophony of noise.

'Jesus.' A soldier further along the wall crossed himself, eyes wide as he stared down on the same sea of men. 'That *must* be the king. We're lost.'

She heard the same sentiment repeated all over the castle. Such noise and pomp would not be used for any army, surely. The king himself must be leading it. And if they defied the king they could expect no quarter when the castle fell, for castles always fell in the end. Any terms they were offered would surely involve punishment. Edeva found her in the gallery of the great hall, watching the weaving figures below as they muttered and bustled. Edeva had been listening around the castle, learning what the soldiers and servants were saying. She stood close to her mistress with a smile.

'Tickhill is going to surrender.'

'Already?'

'They only needed to hear that the king was in the army heading towards them and they decided to give up their castle.'

'Are you sure?'

'Lady Idonea's maid heard Serlo shouting at her. Her brother is the seneschal of Tickhill. They all expected him to stay loyal.'

'I am glad he did not.'

But, Marian wondered, if Tickhill, which was further north and strong as iron, surrendered before it had even seen how Nottingham withstood a siege, why was not Nottingham faltering?

The reason swiftly became clear. Eudo was no fool, and he had more interest even than Marian in learning the minds of his men. While the royal army were making camp beneath their walls he called his garrison together into the upper bailey beside the keep. The king was not leading the royal army himself, he said, and Tickhill had not surrendered. These were lies spread by the king's men to damage the trust that all men should have in their liegelord, the count. The enemy wished to draw them out of the safety of their fortress with trickery, but they would not succeed. Nottingham Castle had never been taken in a siege, he said, and never would be. They had food, they had water, they had arms and most importantly of all, they had men of courage defending. With these lies and flatteries the men were heartened and the meeting broke up in cheering as they ran to their posts on the walls.

Marian heard it all from the chapel overlooking the yard. It was with sinking spirits that she watched the preparations to withstand the siege. The barbican had already been sealed against any messengers or men escaping. Now Marian watched as the middle bailey's gatehouse was also closed up. She shuddered at that last possible way out being destroyed. Whether she had been right to stay or not, there was no going back now. There would be no escape now until the siege was broken.

War had come to Nottingham. Robin could hear it from miles away. The hammering of nails, sawing of wood, shouts of the harbingers, clanking of cooking pots, stamping of horses' hooves. What he could not hear he could picture long before he saw it: tents being pitched, the king's silken pavilion erected, swords and lances sharpened, armour rolled in barrels of sand to remove rust. All the noisy life that went into preparation for death.

Robin and Much came to the castle by the green lanes and forest paths, unwilling to chance a meeting with Vipont guards on the King's Way, even bearing the safe-conduct from the king. From the last hilltop before their route wound to the valley in which Nottingham nestled, they surveyed the armies. The castle looked secure on its rock, every wall patrolled by men, their armour glinting in the spring sunshine. They looked down onto the sprawling royal camp to the north, where the foundations of wooden towers and palisades were visible. Those towers were not bedded in the earth, thought Robin. He had seen just such towers before, surmounted on wheels and holding scores of crossbowmen as they thundered towards a castle just like this one. Much stared with wide eyes. For once, the lad was silent.

The king's safe-conduct eased their passage through the camp to the king's tent. Three lions bared their claws on a standard beating above. It whipped like a tail in the wind, as if longing to lunge towards its counterpart on the castle opposite: the lion snarling on its hind legs that was the symbol of the count. Outside the tent soldiers stood guard. They took Robin's sword and dagger and told Much to wait outside with his horse. Within, incense was burning and candles flickering. Highly-coloured rugs covered the far end of the tent, where a group of men stood around a table with a chessboard on it. A curtained-off area must hold the king's bed. One of the guards announced Lord Locksley, and Robin dropped to his knees, his hands raised in fealty.

'Get up.' Even with his eyes lowered, Robin could see the men parting to allow the king to look on him. 'And come closer.'

Robin did as commanded. The king sat in a chair, his arms resting: one on the carved body of a lion, the other on the winged back of a hawk. The king's own pale eyes gleamed more sharply than either of those predators. Even sitting he was clearly a tall man, well-built and muscled, if perhaps tending to fat around his middle. His hands and face had once been fair but now were red, doubtless burnt by the years of beating sun in the Holy Land and Aquitaine. He looked like his brother, Robin thought, as he noticed the same neat red beard and combed hair, but in every way writ large. He looked Robin up and down, appraising him.

'You have no armour?'

'I lost it on my return from the Holy Land, your grace.'

The Earl of Derby leant closer to the king and whispered something to him.

'Derby claims that my brother's seneschal here in Nottingham had you cast out of your home.'

'He also burnt it down, your grace. Lord Eudo de Vipont is his name.'

'I know him. His family holds fortresses on the borders of Normandy. I have heard men say that it was you who committed murder and destroyed your home. Locksheath, was it?'

'Locksley, your grace.'

He dismissed Robin's words with a raised hand.

'This is no time to concern ourselves with these matters. Once the siege is raised I will consider your case. In the meantime, you can demonstrate whether you are a lord worthy of my trust or not. Derby suggested your experience of warfare and these lands would be of use, and I am willing to put that to the test.'

'I hope to prove myself, your grace. I have gathered men for your cause.'

'Where are they?'

'They wait in the forest. They wanted some assurances from you before they came out of hiding.'

The king's face darkened. 'I do not barter with my subjects. They follow me or they pay the consequences.'

'Some of these men are outlaws, your grace. If they are seen by officers of the law without your protection, they may be harmed.'

'If they committed a crime they should pay for it.'

'They are innocent, your grace. They tried to reveal Lord Vipont's wrongdoing and were condemned in his court to keep them silent. They wish to prove their loyalty to you now, and thereby gain a pardon.'

'Talk is cheap, Lord Locksley. Since I was a child my mother taught me that it is what men do, not what they say, that shows their worth.'

The king thought, his jaw set, his body unmoving. It was like being in the presence of a statue. At last he nodded, sharply. 'Bring your men with my safe conduct. No soldier of mine will harm them.' A clerk stepped forward and placed a document in Robin's hands. The king then stood abruptly and the men dropped to their knees. 'Derby, have your servants arm Locksley. Give him a better horse if he needs it. I want to inspect the defences.'

He strode from the tent, his noblemen in swift pursuit. Derby smacked Robin in the arm as he passed.

'Don't get left behind, Locksley. He will want to talk to you.'
Robin leapt to his feet.

Outside, the entire camp was dropping to its knees as the king swept among them. He ignored them, focused solely on the castle walls and the words of his advisors. Robin looked around quickly. Much was staring after him, awestruck.

'W-was that the king?'

'Yes. Fetch the men. Tell them to bring all the arms they can. If any man tries to arrest you before you reach here, show them this.' He handed Much the letter of safe-conduct. 'They'll recognise the king's seal. Go.'

Much blinked as if dispelling an enchantment and stumbled as he jumped onto Robin's horse. Robin hoped he did not fall off on the journey. Derby was waiting a little behind the troop of earls following King Richard. They had ascended a mound at the limits of the camp, only a few hundred yards from the outer bailey. He smiled ruefully when Robin joined him.

'There is no directing a king, my lord. Did your years in the Holy Land not teach you that?'

'It did not, and nor did meeting his brother, although he was just as recalcitrant.'

'Yes, they are a family of stubborn asses – though I will call you a liar if you ever repeat it.'

He fell silent as they reached the inner circle of advisors. One of the earls was observing the safety of their camp and how close their men would need to be to be hit by the archers on the castle's walls.

'He is wrong,' Robin muttered to Derby. The earl looked at him in surprise. 'Those archers have longer bows than he thinks. They could hit us here if they wished.'

'Shoot at the king? They would live to regret that.'

'Locksley.' The king called Robin forward. 'You know these Viponts better than I do. Are they just making a show of defiance like their friends at Tickhill or do they mean to hold the castle for my brother indefinitely?'

'I do not believe they will surrender until the count gives them permission to do so.'

'That will not be soon in coming. Can we starve them out?'

'Eventually, but there are wells in the middle bailey and inside the keep. You cannot deny them access to water, and my friends have seen them taking in bulk loads of food against a siege. It might be wiser to concentrate your efforts on the garrison itself rather than its commanders. These men are faithful to their seneschal and the count, but their ultimate loyalty will be to the king.'

'Strange way to show such loyalty.' He watched a man on the barbican of the outer bailey pacing back and forth.

'I have heard that the garrison did not believe you were really returning. You have been gone many years, your grace.'

'That is entirely irrelevant. I am their king. If I say I am here I damned well am.'

'Lord Locksley has connections to the common men we do not,' said Derby cautiously. When the king did not reprimand him he continued, 'How do we convince the castle's defenders that this army truly is led by the king? Apparently our arrival with trumpets and heralds, flying the three lions was not enough.'

Robin looked at the king, standing in the same robes as his companions, no royal crest on his tunic, no vair on his robe.

'I remember, your grace, that at Acre you suffered from a terrible sickness.'

'I remember that too,' said the king gruffly. 'And?'

'Despite your illness you insisted on being carried out on a litter to shoot your crossbow at the city's defenders. The men took courage from seeing you fight among them.'

'We do not think it wise,' said one of the earls, 'for the king to fight in this quarrel. He has only just recovered from his incarceration, and with the fatigue of his long journey.'

'Quiet, Blondeville. You think I should fight, Locksley?'

'And be seen to be fighting. The Viponts have doubtless lied to their men to keep them firm in their defence. If those men see with their own eyes that they have been deceived their certainty in their commanders' word will be weakened and they may refuse to fight on.'

'*May* refuse.'

'It will encourage our own men as well.'

One of the earls stepped forward, gesturing to the works taking place at the edges of the camp. Where the work met the forest sawdust filled the air.

'You have noticed all this carpentry I expect?'

'The man is not blind, Huntingdon,' said the king.

The Earl of Huntingdon continued nonetheless.

'I was also honoured to serve King Richard in the Holy Land. We saw there the incredible feats that could be accomplished with counterweight trebuchets – their precision shooting had devastating effects.'

'I remember,' said Robin.

'We believe those engines of war can be used here just as successfully. Nottingham Castle is strong but it is still just a castle. Any stone can eventually be worn down.'

It was just a castle to him, but to Robin it was the fortress that held his brother, mother and friends. The notion of them being starved out was unpleasant; the idea of them being bombarded with stone and God knew what else was beyond imagining. However, one man's family would not persuade the king to abandon his most powerful weapons. Robin thought carefully before responding.

'A lengthy siege with engines will take more lives and damage more of the castle, making it useless to your grace in the future. If you permit me to advise, I would urge you to delay the use of the engines for now. Attack the outer and middle baileys instead, try to force them into submission and isolate the keep where the Viponts hide. The outer bailey is wooden – it will not take much more than manpower to bring that down. If fortune is on our side we might even be able to suppress the middle bailey too.'

The king squinted at the barbican, then turned back to Robin. 'I see the reasoning behind your words, Lord Locksley –'

But Robin heard no more. There was a shadow, hardly more than a speck of dirt in the sky at first, sailing through the air. As it grew closer – in the heartbeats that it flew – Robin watched it in stupid astonishment. And then, an instant before it struck, he leapt forward.

'Arrow!'

He pushed the king, making him stumble on the slick grassy slope. One of the earls had realised too, was lunging towards the king to shield him. None of them were armed or armoured. There was a flurry of movement and for one frozen instant it seemed the arrow had missed. Then Blondeville cried out and time unstuck.

'Get back!'

Huntingdon pressed the king low to the earth, striding backwards as quickly as he could while keeping him concealed. Derby and the other earls swerved between protecting their king and helping their companion. Robin ran to the stricken Blondeville, held him up as he collapsed. The arrow had struck his shoulder, above his heart Robin thought, but it was bedded deep. He looped Blondeville's other arm around his own shoulder to half-carry him back to the king's tent. Inside, the earls were speaking all at once, calling for physicians, for surgeons, for wine, urging the king to sit, urging him to move so they could inspect him for wounds. He swatted them away. When he saw Robin bring in Blondeville he drew back the curtains surrounding his bed so Blondeville could rest there until the doctor arrived. Then he seized Robin by the neck with one of his red hands.

'Proving your use already.' He addressed the tent at large. 'We follow Locksley's advice. Let that castle see what it is to defy their God-anointed king. Every man to armour. We will attack before noon.'

The day was warm and the mail cote sat heavy on Robin's shoulders. It had been over a year since he was armed, and many more since he was armed so heavily. At his side he noticed that the Earl of Huntingdon, like his king, wore a light cote of fewer links. It left more of the body susceptible to the piercing shot of arrows, but you could manoeuvre with less effort. And it wasn't so bloody hot. Robin leant his head, encased in padded linen and links of mail, to first the left side and then the right, stretching his neck. There was a tap at his foot.

'Here.'

Much held a great helm up to Robin. His arms trembled as Robin took his time in taking it. The Earl of Derby's destrier was a tall animal, far broader than the palfrey that Robin had been relying on all these months.

'Will I need to rescue you if you fall?'

'That's usually a squire's job. But given your horsemanship I wouldn't trust to it. I'll just try to get shot somewhere out of the way.'

Much laughed and went back to the clump of men behind the mounted lords. The sight of them gave Robin cheer. They were a ragged army, that was certain, with poor helms and hardly any harness. Instead of the bright stripes and fearsome beasts that gleamed on the standards of the other lords, their banner was of red wool, a white arrow daubed on it. Robin almost wished they could have delayed their coming longer, been late enough to avoid this assault on the castle. But if the king wished Robin's hundredmen to prove their loyalty with feats of arms, he supposed they must give them. The king's quartermasters were passing out broad shields, new-made, and the dented arms that could be gathered in the few short hours since the king called for this assault.

A trumpet blasted and the king emerged from his tent, mounted his horse, came to settle between Robin and Huntingdon. After the incident that morning the king was more cautious. The cavalry who would charge second – better protected by their armour and a more threatening sight to the castle's defenders – stood at the head of the army, some distance back from where the barbican's archer had struck that morning. Robin felt a shudder of anticipation. Despite all he knew of battle, of death, of the mortal danger that stalked men on the field of combat, there was still something exhilarating in the moments before the attack began.

He glanced at the keep and for a moment his focus slipped. His family lay within those walls. If the king's men overran the fortress they would give no quarter to guests of the rebel lords. Experience told him they could not reach all the way through the outer, the middle and the inner bailey in one assault but still his mind faltered. It was a strange thing, to wish for victory and yet be dwelling on a hope of defeat. A stillness settled over the army. Men silently prayed and crossed themselves. All eyes were set on the barbican before them. Robin touched his chest where the Jerusalem palms had once been pinned. Don't die now, he thought.

The king raised his sword and the lords turned their horses, letting the foot soldiers and their thick shields advance to the front. Robin rode past the men beneath the arrow standard, now hardly recognisable in their war gear. He shouted something, but barely knew what. Words of encouragement. Words of hope. On higher ground, the cavalry reassembled. Robin turned as quickly as he could, not wanting to miss the first moments of the battle.

A shout went up. A horn blast answered, a wall of cries and the foot soldiers advanced on the barbican. Arrows fell like rain on their helms. Crossbowmen leapt from behind the defences, shot their bolts and leapt back. From below, shields parted for an instant and bolts were sent up in response. They were at the gate. Already men toppled, from the wooden walls above and the melée beneath. A word was called, passing like a mantra back and back through the men until Robin heard it far behind them.

'Ram.'

A trundling triangle of hides and wood surged forwards, the great wooden bar inside scarcely visible. In the Holy Land he had seen such a frame burnt to cinders in an eye's blink after pots of Greek Fire exploded on top of it. But the defenders of Nottingham had no such weapons. Crossbow bolts and arrows were useless to stop the ram's advance. When it reached the barbican the soldiers lurched aside. Its first strike resounded like thunder.

'Ready yourselves.'

The king called for his shield and helm. Squires ran to bring the last heavy arms to their lords. Much ran forward with elbows out. He paused while Robin put on his helm then passed a lance into his outstretched right hand. Robin did a last check, a habit he had learnt years ago. Left elbow to sword pommel, right elbow to lance stave, left hand flexing on the strap of his shield, right hand flexing on the lance, head nudged to right and left to see that his helm was unmoving. All was well. And scarcely had he finished than another horn blared, another shout rose, another tide of men swept forward and Robin's heels were pressed to his horse's flanks. The ram had broken through. It was time for the cavalry to act.

Robin looked out unblinking through the narrow slit of vision his helm allowed. His breath reflected hot from the ventail of mail across his face. The barbican was ahead, the king's foot soldiers surging through it. Screams echoed now as much as warrior shouts. Robin heard the whistling and thunk of crossbow bolts and raised his shield as he passed under the shadows of the barbican. For an instant he was blind then a shock of sunlight greeted him. Ahead a pack of men in crimson-or advanced across the outer bailey. He took aim, set his lance firm under his arm, braced himself against the saddle and struck hard like a hammer into a soldier's chest. The shock pulsed through him and he loosed his grip, drew his sword, turned his horse and rode on. All around lances pierced and were abandoned, swords ripped from scabbards, swung hard against the men beneath. Robin was overtaken by the press and sweat of battle. His body struck and his instinct wheeled and his mind did not think at all. Blood roared in his ears and men roared at his heels. Bodies collapsed and blood showered and arrows whistled, but Robin pressed on. They had taken the outer bailey, that soon became clear. Most of the royal forces now were at the gate to the middle bailey.

Suddenly the king was ahead of him, surrounded by shield-wielding knights. He waved his sword aloft, towards a sortie of soldiers spilling out of the middle bailey from a sally port. They spurred towards the middle gatehouse, to cut down the attackers on their flank and force them back. Robin turned his horse and raced to stop their passage. Crossbowmen clustered tight over the stone walls of the middle bailey, shooting down on the king's force. Their shields offered protection but it would take only one stray bolt to bring down the king.

'Archers, here!' Robin shouted, waving to draw his force's attention. A contingent of them saw him, turned their bows.

And then the enemy knights were before him. He could not tell in that crush of steel and iron and wood whether the Viponts were among their number but he swung his sword as if they were. Other lords had ridden to protect the king and now their numbers outweighed the defenders'. As one the defenders turned their horses and fled. Back into the middle bailey, back behind their stone walls, their iron grill and a great oak door that could not be pressed open.

Robin lost all sense of the day passing, all sense of the men under the arrow banner that he had thought to find and protect. All he knew was that his arms ached and weakened but still the middle gatehouse could not be taken. A horn blew, a shout went up and the king's standard was retreating back through the barbican. His men followed suit. Robin started and turned in his saddle as he saw the waves of men running against him. He stood like a clod in a riverbed, unable to join the swell of retreat, scanning the field and the faces of the running soldiers for signs of his own men. He could not see them. As the last wave receded he turned himself and galloped in their wake.

In the safety of the royal camp he slid from his horse, exhausted. Much was at his side, drawing the shield from his arm, the helm from his head. He blinked and was surprised to see darkness creeping over the earth. The sun had set while they fought.

'Did we lose?' Much asked anxiously.

Robin held out his hands for the gauntlets to be drawn off, then tore at the leather strips tying his ventail across his face. His breath panted from him.

'No. The outer bailey is ours. We've taken one of their defences.'

He looked up at the castle. The open ground between the barbican and middle gatehouse was littered with corpses. Spent arrows, lances and bolts scattered, some still embedded in men or the earth. The whole field was trampled and bloodied.

'Are you hurt?'

Robin drew the mail coif from his head and unbuckled his sword belt.

'No. Have you seen the hundredmen coming back? Are they hurt?'

'John led them in not long before you. They're with the other foot soldiers. I can show you when you're out of your armour.'

The men fighting under the arrow standard were scattered throughout the camp, but Robin found his hundredmen huddled around a fire at the edge of it. Even as soldiers they sought the shelter of the forest. Thank God, all of them were there, and none seriously hurt. Gilbert's leg had been trampled but a surgeon had checked it was not broken. He sat now with it awkwardly thrust towards the fire, grimacing.

'Do you need anything for the pain?' Robin asked, sitting next to him.

'No.' Gilbert stretched his leg again and rubbed at his filthy hands.

'I just want to wash this blood off.'

'Much, have a bowl of hot water brought from the Earl of Derby's tent.'

'I'll get it now.'

Much ran to accomplish that task. Robin had insisted that he serve as squire on that day, in no small part in the hopes of keeping him alive and out of reach of the battle. The lad had not been happy to miss the excitement of battle but now he saw the men exhausted and bruised he seemed to make peace with his absence from it.

Jeering shouts echoed around the camp as a pocket of men were dragged by the necks and arms towards the security of the camp's palisades. They all wore the colours of the enemy.

'What's happening there?' asked Madalgrim.

'Those men were taken in the fight,' said Kolbrand. 'They're the king's prisoners now.'

The prisoners were forced to their knees inside the palisade, their hands bound.

'What will happen to them?' asked Gilbert.

'They refused to surrender,' said Lefchild. 'So the king can do what he wants with them. What do you think he'll do, Robin?'

Robin thought back to the king's words that morning. In every siege, the enemy's morale was as important as their physical wellbeing. It was too early for the defenders to worry about running out of food and soldiers. But it was not too early to give them a glimpse of the punishment awaiting them if they continued to defy the king.

'He'll kill them.' He looked towards the carpenters, still doing their work by tallow candles. 'He'll build a gallows large enough to be seen from the keep and then they'll hang before tomorrow's sun sets.'

The men fell silent, contemplated the cuts and bruises on their bodies.

A blast of light suddenly burst beneath the darkening sky. The barbican was on fire. A cheer went up around the camp.

'Did we do that?' asked Much, arriving with the water for Gilbert.

'It would be foolish for the defenders to do it,' said John.

The wood crackled and flared. Another source of fear, Robin thought. The king was no fool. The castle's defenders might be safe behind their stones for now, but with the barbican turning to ash there was one less wall between them and the king's vengeance.

The sound of hammers woke Marian before sunrise. She crept to her window and unshuttered it. In the royal camp, under the long shadow of Castle Rock a platform was being erected. She closed the shutter again and tried to go back to sleep. Only as she lay back in bed did she realise what the platform must be for. When she rose with the dawn and was dressed she tried not to look out the window, tried not to listen to the constant distant hammering. But when dawn had broken and the shadows rolled away Edeva gave a shout that brought her back to it. Sure enough, the platform now had a ladder leading up to it. From a horizontal beam above it ropes were hanging.

'They're going to kill those men,' said Edeva.

A line of soldiers in the colours of Vipont, de la Guerche, de Caux, Murdac, Wenneval, the count stood behind the nooses, their hands bound behind them. The king's army surrounded the gallows. In the midst of a group of lords stood one man taller than the others, red beard glinting in the morning sun. The lord next to him ascended the ladder and stood on the platform with his sword raised.

'All those who oppose the king,' he shouted, and his words resounded around the walls of the fortress, 'deserve death. Every rebel we capture will be hanged.'

The nooses were passed over the soldiers' heads.

'We should not watch,' murmured Marian but neither she nor Edeva moved from the window.

The lord swung his sword in a downward arc and the soldiers were pushed from the platform. Their bodies jerked as the noose caught their fall. The king's men cheered and hollered, threats mixing with victorious cries. Marian hoped that Robin's voice was not among them.

'Would they do that to us if we were captured?' Edeva asked in a low voice.

Marian did not answer. They would do it to everyone, she thought. We are all traitors inside this castle. She looked around her chamber, where the maids carried on their tasks while trying not to let their gaze creep towards the window. Marian looked down on the yard below, where soldiers prowled the walls and servants wandered back and forth, condemned to rebellion because their masters ordered it. She thought of Jocelyn and Roger, children in her eyes but lords before the law. Would they be pardoned if their guardians were not? She looked again at the bodies swinging from the gallows. She could not allow death to engulf this castle. She would not let the walls that her father had worked tirelessly to protect crumble like the smoke-shrouded remnants of the barbican. Her father would have enjoined peace, and she would too.

The king's siege engines had arrived. The carpenters and engineers had done their work and now, between the forest and the gallows, they were assembled. The army watched the towering structures with horrified fascination. They were glad to be fighting for the commander who owned such machines of death and not facing them inside the castle. One of the great stone-throwers towered over the others. The hundredmen stared at it, wide-eyed. They had never seen anything like it. Even the cranes and scaffolds that lifted stone to build cathedrals did not compare. The frame was wooden, riveted with metal, with one end of the central bar holding a vast weight of lead and stone, while the other end was high in the sky, a sling for stones that was wound back with spiralling ropes. In the Holy Lands Robin had seen just such a weapon aimed with incredible precision towards the very cornerstone of a wall, striking again and again at the same spot until the wall was reduced to dust. He looked from it to the stones of the castle. He had never imagined that the fortress could seem fragile.

'How do you stop a weapon like that?' Thurstan asked. His smith's mind turned over the trebuchet's construction with fascination.

'You build a bigger one for your own army,' said John.

'Or burn it,' said Robin. 'The Saracens sent parties of men out to destroy our weapons. That's why the king has armed soldiers watching every engine.'

He stepped aside to let another group of artillerists pass. They were led by the master engineer, waving people aside with a staff. A wagon followed him, the men surrounding it watching for every bump and pothole, reaching out to support their cargo. They were taking a lot of care over supplies of what looked like stones, Robin thought. Curious, he followed in their wake.

'Good day, my lord.'

The master engineer called out for a path to clear. When one soldier was too slow he bodily pushed him aside.

'More missiles?' Robin asked.

'Yes, my lord.' The master engineer glanced at him. There was something mistrusting in his look.

He halted the wagon some distance from the camp, where the carpenters were still building the last of the king's siege towers. The master engineer gave commands to the commander on guard there.

'When night falls, this area is to be watched by four guards, unilluminated.'

'No torches?'

'The enemy will see them. These supplies must not be found.'

While the master engineer was distracted Robin took the opportunity to peer inside the wagon. What he had taken for stones were not that at all. They were round clay jars, each carefully plugged and packed in sand. Robin crossed himself and stepped away from the wagon quickly. He knew what they were. He remembered in a searing flash a sound like thunder in heaven, a spear of fire that traced the sky, falling to his elbows and knees as the night's darkness was illuminated into unnatural day and flames burst all around him. Greek Fire. A fire that water only made burn harder, a fire that could not be beaten out. The king was going to use Greek Fire on the castle.

He ran for the Earl of Derby's tent, bursting in as the earl was sitting to his supper.

'Locksley,' he said, bemused by Robin's panicked expression. 'There is no need for such agitation. You are welcome to eat at my table.'

Robin did not sit, but blurted out his discovery of the wagon laden with pots of fire. To his astonishment the earl was not surprised. He laid down his knife and shook his head.

'I thought he might do something like this. You saw how angry the king was yesterday. If his brother were inside he would not consider it – he is strangely soft-hearted towards such a disloyal brother – but since he is not, the king feels emboldened to take whatever means necessary to regain that castle.'

'His brother may not be inside but mine is. My mother too.'

The earl paused with a glass of wine halfway to his lips.

'It grieves me to hear that.'

'Surely there is no need to use fire against the castle? We must be expecting more armies to join us here. Once they arrive we can launch another assault, take the building that way.'

'You know as well as I that such attacks are costly for our own men and achieve little. Even undermining the castle would take considerable time, and time is not something we have.' He leant forward and lowered his voice. 'This is not to be spread around the camp – we do not want to create a panic – but this morning we learnt from our scouts that the castle has somehow managed to get a message out. They have called for reinforcements from the north. We do not know where exactly, but if those reinforcements arrive and we have not weakened the forces in the castle we will be in a dangerous position.'

Dangerous was right. They would be crushed between two armies.

'Do not lose heart over this, Locksley. It has been known for the mere sight of siege engines being constructed to force a surrender. Admittedly, we have been building the engines all day in full sight of the castle and they have not wavered. But I am certain the king will try bombardment with stone before risking his own men using such –' the earl speared a piece of meat with his knife while he considered the right term '– volatile weapons.'

'Would the king listen to other means of forcing surrender?'

'He might hear them. Whether he listens is less certain.'

Robin drank his wine, his mind already trying to think of something – anything – that would stop the king unleashing his flame on the castle.

'When do you think stones will turn to fire?'

'Soon. I would say you have until the castle's reinforcements arrive to come up with an alternative. If you can conceive a better plan then perhaps the king will listen. Otherwise the best you can do is pray for your family's safe deliverance.'

Marian sat in silence at the supper table. No one was overly talkative. How could they be, when even through the shutters across the windows came the sounds of chopping, sawing, hammering, shouts? All the noise that men could make while assembling the machinery of death. Jocelyn and Roger sat silently, spooning food into their mouths without interest. The excitement of the siege had dissipated now and only weary anxiety was left. Idonea's large eyes were rimmed with shadows. She reached out a hand to Serlo over the table. He retreated from her touch and turned to his father.

'I had word just before I joined you,' he said in a low voice. 'My messenger has made it through the blockade. He should be at Tickhill before nightfall.'

'How did he manage that?' Elaine asked. She did not miss a thing. 'He must be a shadow to make it through the ranks of men outside.'

'We seek out shadows from their infancy,' said Eudo, whispering in her ear. 'We train them in the caves beneath the castle.'

Elaine giggled. Marian looked at her plate to hide her disdain. Lady Joan gave her hand a gentle squeeze. Her stepmother smiled weakly, conspiratorially. These were strange days, indeed, when she and Marian found themselves allies.

'What message are you sending to Tickhill?' Marian asked.

Serlo and Ranulf bristled. Eudo was briefly distracted from the fascination of Elaine's neck. He smiled silkily. 'We have just reminded them of where their loyalty ought to lie. We call for their garrison to come south to assist us.'

'But Tickhill has surrendered to the king.'

'No. It is simply negotiating with the lords he sent to besiege them. And while they talk, they are free to silently prepare themselves for the coming fight. When Tickhill hears that we still hold for the count it will shore up their resolve. They have means of sending local men to our aid. The count left them more than enough to hold the place.'

'And where is the count exactly? I notice he has not sent forces to help you.'

'You have so little faith, Marian. Your husband would not have doubted our lord.'

'The count would not raise arms against his own brother, not in the flesh.'

'How fortunate it is then the king is not outside the walls of our castle.'

Eudo's voice was soft as smoke, and like smoke his words were breathed in by every person in the chamber. He was wrong, Marian thought. He must know that he was wrong. It was blind faith that had kept the Vipont guard believing this fallacy. That could surely only last so long.

'And do you expect your reinforcements to arrive before or after those siege engines they are building have started their bombardment?'

'Do not speak of that,' Idonea said, laying down her knife. 'You will frighten the children.'

'After,' said Eudo, unperturbed, 'doubtless after. But there is no reason to fear, boys. This castle has never been taken in war. During the Anarchy, when Lady Marian's forefather might have seized the castle in the name of King Stephen, he turned away from it, knowing that it was a fool's venture to try to starve out so well-stocked a palace, and rank folly to try to knock it down stone by stone. Even if the king's men can break into the middle bailey our keep and inner bailey will hold. We have the upper ground, the stronger walls and the best protection. We can withstand a siege for as long as we wish.'

And how many more men will be hanged during that time? Marian wondered. Roger had edged closer to his mother and now curled his arm around her waist, leaning his pale face onto her breast. Serlo shook his head in his wife's direction and Idonea untangled his arm and put his hand back on the bench. Marian could not stand it. Would every man and woman in this castle have to die before Eudo and his family surrendered to the inevitable? Because it was inevitable. Every castle, even those built on rock, could be brought down by stone and fire and hunger in the end.

'Excuse me,' she said, standing up from the table. 'I have no appetite.'

She laid down her napkin and strode away from the chamber. Her absence would hardly be noticed, let alone concern them. She did not know where she was going at first, her legs guiding her upwards and outwards, climbing the spiralling staircases until she realised she was making for the roof. She was almost running by the time she reached it, her legs burning. The cold night air hit her with a shock. There were men all over the rooftop, up on the raised towers as well as gazing out from the crenellations. She climbed the wooden steps to the tower that overlooked the king's army beneath. As she leaned over the edge of the keep she felt her stomach lurch, and not just from the drop hundreds of feet to the earth. The sight beneath was awesome. The barbican still smoked and kindled in places and the many firelights of campfires cast a strange glow over the bodies of the hanged men, swaying limply in the breeze. There were tents, some little more than a hide strung over a tree branch, some gleaming pavilions. More engines had been constructed even since she had last looked out on the scene and they stood now like cranes or grasshoppers, one long arm raised into the sky, aching to be winched down to earth and loaded with stones. And around all this – these engines and fires and tents and death – stretching into the darkness, were men in numbers beyond counting.

We will lose, she thought. And probably we will die.

She shuddered. A hissing in the corner of her ear made her look to her side.

Two of the guards on the tower top were muttering to one another as they surveyed the same scene.

'They say it isn't the king…'

'But what if it is? I've never seen the man, I couldn't recognise him even out of armour. Jack told me it was one of the king's henchmen who was hit yesterday by that arrow.'

'It was the Earl of Chester's man. I saw his colours.'

'But what if it is the king?'

'Then we'll all be hanged if the castle falls.'

'Hanged at best. More likely tied to horses' tails and torn apart. I'm telling you, something about this feels wrong. I fought in Normandy and I never questioned our lords, but if we are shooting at God's anointed… We'll go to Hell, won't we?'

There was a long silence.

'I wouldn't let Hell worry you now. With all we've done already we're bound for it whether we kill a king or not.'

Hell, she thought. For some reason she was reminded of Eudo's words from the supper table: a messenger passing though the blockade, training shadows in the caves beneath the castle. And then another leap of memory. When Guy was still in Nottinghamshire, before he ran from Locksley Hall, and the two of them explored the castle, he revealing its secrets with little concern for how she might keep the information. The caves beneath the castle. And in that moment, Marian knew what she could do to end this.

In the bowels of Castle Rock the guards bowed to their visitor, exchanging a bemused glance. It was late for a lady to be visiting the prison cell. Marian produced a pot of salve from her pouch.

'He seemed to be worsening the last time I was here,' she said, holding out the pot for their inspection. 'I wanted to bring more medicine for him.'

One of the men removed the linen covering the pot and sniffed it. He handed it back.

'You are good to still think of him with an army at our gates. If the castle falls he will likely be killed with all the rest of us. Not you ladies of course,' he added as an afterthought. Perhaps Marian had looked alarmed.

'No,' she said and smiled.

She replaced the salve in the pouch at her belt and held out a purse in its place. Even in the guttering darkness of the cave it was clear the purse was filled with money.

'I need to speak to Scarlette alone.'

'We always let you see him alone,' said one of the guards suspiciously.

'No. I want you both to leave your posts, walk up to the keep and then return, slowly. I have business to discuss with Scarlette that is private. If you allow me to conduct that business, you can have this purse. And if you keep your silence for three days I will give you another.'

'What business can you need to discuss now? We are under siege.'

'And as you said, we may all die before the siege breaks. I need to clear my conscience. Do you want the money or not?'

One of the guard's hands twitched, eager to accept, but the other stayed him.

'There is no point taking money we will never get to spend.'

'That is not true,' said Marian. 'There are still numerous ways to spend coin inside the castle. I will not speculate, but I am certain you could imagine some if you tried.'

The guards glanced at one another.

'All we have to do is walk to the keep and back?'

'Then the purse is yours.'

One of them decided for both. He marched to Will's cell, unlocked the door and turned on his heel. The other hesitated, then followed him up the stairwell and out of sight. The instant their feet had disappeared from view Marian threw down the purse and rushed into Will's cell.

'Can you walk?' she asked, picking him up under one arm. 'Quickly?'

He had not been outside the cell in months. He had barely eaten or slept. His eyes were dark hollows in his face. But he was still Will Scarlette.

'Of course,' he said croakily. 'Been walking since I was a child. Where am I going?'

'The king leads an army against the castle. Robin is with him, part of the Earl of Derby's party if my guess is right. You need to reach Robin and tell him to give a message to the king.'

Will smiled at the absurdity of what she asked.

'I presume I'm flying there, am I? On the back of a pig?'

'There is a way out of these caves,' said Marian, pulling him out of his cell. He winced in the light of the chamber beyond. 'It leads all the way down to the river, and from there you can follow the water around to the king's camp in the north.' She watched the walls as she walked, Will stumbling and trembling in her wake. She put one hand out in front of her, feeling along the cold stone, the other holding Will's arm like a mother leading a naughty toddler. 'You don't need to pay any attention to this path until you reach the river. When you reach the camp you must find Robin and tell him this.'

She told him the message over and over, made him repeat it even while their feet fumbled along the cool pathways, descending into the bowels of Castle Rock. She did not know if he understood it, or if he even believed that the king was outside the walls. She only knew that if there was one person in the world whose luck she believed in – if there was one thief, one poacher, one outlaw who could make his way through a siege when every other person who tried would be caught or killed – then that person was Will Scarlette.

At the bottom of the cliff she heaved open the great oak door and immediately the hollow air of the caves was flooded with the smell of water, of fish, of mud. She pushed Will out ahead of her, his leather shoes slapping on the damp sand. Barely a dozen yards ahead of them two guards kept watch over the marsh, looking for anyone trying to break into the castle through that doorway. Will ducked to his knees. The guards had not heard him. Marian pulled the door almost closed, then at the last moment seized Will's hand.

'Deliver the message before dawn,' she whispered. She closed the door.

Back up the long winding pathway she went, the tang of the dockside swallowed up in moments. She felt that she had had a single breath and now was entombed. She was not afraid of being lost in these caves, or even of being caught by the Viponts. She was afraid that she had not freed Will quickly enough. At the cell the guards were staring between the purse on the floor and the empty cell.

'He is gone,' one of them cried.

'Of course he is gone,' said Marian, closing the cell door. 'What did you think I was going to do?'

'Where is he?'

'Outside the castle walls. You cannot get him back now.'

'Outside? How?'

'I used Lord Eudo's secret passage. Only those he most trusts can know of it.'

'And he let Scarlette out of it?'

'No, he did not,' said the second guard. 'Otherwise my lady would not have paid us and made us leave. He does not know of it. We should tell him. There may be a reward in it for us.'

Marian's heart thudded.

'All right, I admit,' she said quickly before they could leave. 'Lord Eudo does not know I freed Scarlette. But there is no reason for him to. This castle is going to fall. Whether it falls tomorrow by surrender or in three months' time when we are all starved and have eaten every last cat in the keep, it will fall. And when it does it will not matter that one prisoner escaped in the night.'

'Lord Vipont will punish us if we do not tell him.'

'He will punish you if you *do* tell him. You should not have left your post. You should not have taken a bribe. But at the moment there are far more important matters on Lord Vipont's mind than this prison cell. I will not tell him what you have done, if you do not tell him what I have done. If we all simply keep quiet, and you carry on guarding this cell as if nothing has changed, then when this siege ends no man will be able to say that you did not do your duty.'

They contemplated the empty cell, the purse of money, the stairs. Lord Eudo's punishment was not to be sought.

'You will keep silent too?'

'Yes,' said Marian, smiling with relief. 'Yes I will.'

The guards nodded and the bargain was struck.

The moon was still bright in the sky when Robin awoke. The Earl of Derby had given him a bed within his tent, despite Robin's protestations that he would be happy to sleep with the hundredmen. He had not expected to sleep at all, his mind refusing to turn from the image of Greek Fire smashing against the walls of Nottingham Castle. There must be a way to persuade the king against using it. There must, and yet he could not think of it. But perhaps the anxiety had wearied him, for when he retired that night he had slept instantly. Now he was awake those fears rushed in on him once more. He needed air. He always thought more clearly in the open air. He pulled on his clothes and left the tent.

The camp was littered with sleeping, snoring shapes and the dark figures of the men still keeping an unwearying watch over the trebuchets. There had been no sortie from the castle to damage the machines that night. Robin was glad of it. Any appeal to the king would go easier if the castle's defenders had not made another foolish strike against him. Robin circled the camp, nodding to the watchmen and being careful to announce himself before they saw him. The last thing he needed was a knife in the back from a jumpy guard. He reached the western limits of the royal army, near where the common land had once been. Now ditches and fence distorted the land. He leant against one of the clumps of fence and looked up at the vast bulk of the castle, glimmering in the moonlight.

There was a creak behind him. One of the fences being pressed. He glanced over his shoulder. Nothing there. He turned back to the castle, listening for more signs of movement. He got them quickly enough. A patter as the fence was released from whatever weight held it and a footstep. He did not turn this time, but kept listening, looking with the outer limits of his vision. It might just be an animal – one of the pigs that roamed the forest and town – but it might also be a party from the castle, come to seize hostages from among the sleeping soldiers or set fire to their siege engines. Another creak, another patter, another rustle of movement. Whatever it was, in a moment it would be alongside Robin. He wore no sword but at his belt was a knife. He took it in his hand and braced himself against any attempted strike. There was a footstep almost at his heel. He span with the knife raised, shouting a warning and met an echoing shout from a man behind him. They spoke at once. Robin did not hear what he said. But from the shadows he saw the last face he expected.

'Will?'

'Thank Christ it's you.' Will lunged to embrace him. 'I thought I was going to be stuck before I could speak.'

Robin stepped back, looked Will up and down. He looked like a sack of sticks and hair.

'How –?'

'I'll explain, but first I need to get a message to the king.'

Of course he did, Robin thought. That was of a piece with the madness of finding him outside a royal camp in the depths of night.

'I would have gotten here sooner but it's been a long time since I moved my legs. It took them a while to remember how to do it. Can you take me to him?'

'The king? No. But I can take you to a man who can.'

The Earl of Derby was not best pleased to be woken before dawn, and even less so to find a pale mess of a man sitting on one of his expensively painted chairs. But hearing that this man had escaped the castle with information that could help them defeat it instantly improved his spirits. He led both of them directly to the king's tent. When they were allowed to enter they found the king again in his carved seat, the lion and hawk's wooden eyes following them as they knelt before him. The Earl of Derby spoke for them.

'This man is Locksley's brother, held against his will inside the castle for several months. With the assistance of another ally he has escaped and brings information that will help us end this siege.'

The king took in Will's shabby clothes, pale complexion, matted beard and wet feet. 'How did you come to be held against your will?'

'I was a prisoner,' said Will.

The king did not like that. Robin swiftly added, 'Lord Eudo de Vipont accused him of various false crimes, just as he accused me, and even though I proved both our innocence at the ordeal he kept my brother prisoner.'

Robin held out his palms. The marks of the iron bars were still there, half a year later. Both had clearly healed without corruption. The king frowned.

'That is not how I expect the law to be kept. I will have my justices look into this case. And what was your means of escape?'

'Lady Marian – the old sheriff's daughter – learnt of a way out, through the rock. It leads to the river.'

'I have had men circling that cliff for days, and none saw signs of any other entrance.'

'It is difficult to reach,' said Will, gesturing to his damp shoes. 'To get to it from the western side you have to go through the marshes.'

'That must be how Eudo was able to send messengers north,' said Derby.

'Yes, that is part of what I need to tell you. Vipont has told Tickhill that they are holding the castle and called for their garrison to send reinforcements, in spite of any promises they have made for peace.'

The king's hands gripped the ends of his chair, blinding the lion and eagle.

'You say you know of a way to end this siege before the count's reinforcements arrive?'

'Marian had been gathering information from the soldiers as well as the lords inside the castle. The soldiers are only a step from surrender, she says, even against Lord Vipont's command, but they will do not do it until they are certain the king is here.'

'As you can clearly see,' said the king dryly, 'I am.'

'But the men inside still do not trust it. The Viponts have been lying to them since before you arrived. The advice I was to give is that you should let a delegation come out to meet you. Two knights – chosen by the garrison of men, not by Lord Eudo – should be allowed safe passage to treat with you. When they return to the castle they will tell everyone inside that they have seen with their own eyes that this army is led by the king and the garrison will surrender before the day is out. If they do not surrender, you can use that sally port to take down the castle from the inside.'

'Why should I treat with these defenders? Why not send soldiers through the sally port and end the siege immediately?'

'The tunnel is narrow. You will not get men in more than two abreast – maybe less with weapons – and as soon as the guards at the top of the tunnel see them, they will send for reinforcements. A pair of crossbowmen could pick your forces off one by one before you can take a step into the keep.'

'And once the Viponts know you have found that route,' added Robin swiftly, 'they will block it. Then Lord Eudo will find Will's cell empty and it will not take long to work out who is to blame. Marian is the one who gave us the information about supplies and soldiers before the siege began. It would be poor thanks to repay her with Eudo's vengeance.'

The king gave Robin a long, appraising look. 'Very well. We will try diplomacy first.'

'There is one other thing,' said Will, just as Robin felt confident again. 'Since these men have been fighting their king all this time they fear the punishment they might receive when the siege is broken. You should promise the delegation of knights a royal pardon for every man who surrenders.'

'A royal pardon for defying their God-anointed ruler.' He drummed his fingers on the hawk-head. 'When my vassals in Aquitaine rebelled against me I put them down with fire and iron. Every leader of every group of rebels had his eyes gouged out. And I love the people of Aquitaine, far more than I love the people of Nottinghamshire.'

'But perhaps,' said Robin, 'the people of Aquitaine do not love their duke as much as the people of Nottinghamshire love their king.'

The king sat back with a slow exhalation of breath that made the Earl of Derby wince. Robin did not look the king in the face but he felt his eyes boring into him all the same. Those eyes, so pale as to be serpentine in a face red as fire.

'Fine words, Locksley. You should become a troubadour. I can employ you for my mother. To ensure the castle garrison does not attempt to send out any more messengers we should send some of our forces to this sally port. Just enough to keep watch, some local archers would be best. Scarlette, you can show them the way?'

'I can. I think.'

'Derby, gather your men. They will know the area best. Locksley, you will join me to meet these knights.'

Robin never knew how the king managed to get a message to the garrison in the castle. He was made to wait in the royal tent all morning, long after Will and Derby returned from their work at the marshes. All he knew was that the king invited him to sit for dinner, and he had barely touched the food on his plate before the Earl of Huntingdon showed in two knights who had been sent from the fortress. They stood at the threshold of the tent, astonished to see the king cutting up trout and drinking wine only yards from the castle. King Richard hardly even looked at them.

'Well,' he said. 'What do you think? Am I here?'

The knights fell to their knees in response.

When they returned to the castle they bore a promise, signed under the royal seal, that every lowborn soldier would be allowed to leave freely, and that every knight would be pardoned on payment of a bond of good behaviour. Before the hour for supper came around, half the garrison had left the castle.

But it was not all that Robin had hoped. Half a garrison was not all. Half the men still waited inside, hoping for Tickhill's reinforcements, unwilling to betray one prince for another. The king was persuaded to allow a night to pass without further violence, but the next morning dawned and still there was no sign of surrender from the remaining defenders.

The king paced the limits of his camp, where the trebuchets were lined up, artillerists standing ready to shoot, engineers prepared for adjustments if needed to ensure maximum destruction. And the pots of Greek Fire still nestled in their sandboxes, close enough to be called for by the king. Robin looked from the pots to the king, to the castle. Will was at his side. He had shaved and washed and wore new clothes from Derby's wardrobe, but he still looked pale as a prince.

'I don't think they're going to surrender,' he muttered.

'They have to. Marian wouldn't have risked freeing you if she wasn't sure her message would work.'

'It did. Half of them are gone.'

'That's not enough.'

The king shook his head and drew his sword. 'I have waited long enough,' he called. 'Ready the engines.'

The artillerists heaved on the trebuchet handles, winching their long wooden necks down to the earth. The stones were pulled from the piles next to them, loaded into the slings. Robin turned from the sight of them, a bitter taste filling his mouth. After all that they had done to protect this place, he and Will and Marian and all the men of the Arrow, it would still be smashed to pieces before his eyes. He took one last look at the castle as it stood, undented in the sunlight. The middle bailey was strangely active. The men on top of it waved their arms, leapt about. The doors beneath swung open suddenly and a figure on horseback appeared. Robin ran to the king.

'Stop the engines.'

The king turned to see where he pointed.

'They are sending someone out. Stop them.'

The king shouted and the stones were pulled from the machines in an instant, the ropes unwound, the arms put back at rest. The horseman wore the fine clothes of a lord, his dark hair and beard neatly arranged. He raised one hand as he approached the royal camp, then the other. When he was close enough to see the king himself he pressed both hands together and dropped his head. He was offering his submission.

'Let him through,' said the king. 'Who is it? Eudo de Vipont?'

'No,' said Robin.

Eudo was playing the coward until the last. It was Serlo. Eudo had sent his son into the field of death that surrounded the castle rather than come out himself. But the meaning was the same. When Serlo dismounted before the king he knelt and offered his sword.

'The castle is yours,' he said. 'We surrender ourselves to the king's mercy.'

Resurrection

It was with a strange mixture of anxiety and eagerness that Robin rode through Nottingham Castle's stone gatehouse behind the king's men that morning. Even the thought of seeing Lord Eudo was like a hot stone in his gut, but he could not find his own family without also encountering the Viponts. The whole group of them came out to meet the king and the returning Serlo on the steps leading to the inner bailey. Robin was surprised at the sight of his mother: she looked older, thinner. But when she saw her son alongside the foremost earls of England she smiled, and Robin knew there was still plenty of the old Lady Joan there. Jocelyn stood next to Edeva, his hand clasped firmly in Marian's. She stood very tall and very still, but there was something defiant in her expression and when she found Robin among the press of lords her smile was triumphant. He mirrored it with his own.

The king did not dismount to address the castle's defenders. He told them that the last members of the garrison must leave, but the lords could stay at least until he had convened a council to settle the bonds they would pay to assure him of their future loyalty. His own soldiers would be taking over the castle until he appointed its new seneschal.

As the king's men fanned out through the castle to find lodgings and look to the defences, Robin went to greet his family. His mother offered her cheek to be kissed and held his hands in her own slightly longer than manners dictated. Jocelyn bowed solemnly. He stepped forward to meet Marian and paused, suddenly uncertain of himself. She offered neither cheek nor hand but spoke instead.

'Will reached you then.' Her voice was low and sober but her eyes danced.

'Safe and sound. If slightly damp. Did Eudo find out?'

'No. I do not think he even realises that his precious tunnel is no longer a secret.'

'So you are well then? All of you?' he added as an afterthought.

'Yes. But it will be a relief to leave this place.'

Robin was about to ask more, but the Earl of Derby was at his side.

'The king wishes to explore the forest. If you want to put any suits to him, Locksley you would be wise to join us.'

'Oh.' Robin glanced at Marian.

'Is this the late sheriff's daughter?' the earl asked.

'I am, my lord,' said Marian.

'Then I am glad to meet you, and to know we share a kinship. This castle owes you its gratitude. It was a brave thing you did, risking your safety to free Scarlette.'

'I was just saying that,' said Robin. 'Albeit not as well.'

The earl smiled at Marian.

'Ride with us if you wish, cousin. We are going on to Clipstone but we can accompany you as far as the turning to Newstead.'

'If my stepmother allows,' said Marian.

Lady Joan looked astonished that her permission would need to be sought. Accompanying the king anywhere was an honour that overrode every other concern. She would stay behind with Jocelyn and Edeva. As Marian's horse was brought to join the assembling royal retinue Robin looked around the courtyard. The Viponts stood in an anxious cluster, Idonea holding Roger close, Ranulf barking at servants to start gathering their belongings, Serlo striding back and forth between the king's supporters and his own men, trying to curry favour with both. Like two statues in their midst stood Elaine and Eudo, her hand on his arm. Eudo watched the activity of his family and everyone else in that yard as if they were scurrying ants, beneath his dignity. If his pride had been injured by defeat, he was not showing it. Elaine was more uncertain. She looked about her with an awkwardness Robin had never seen before. Her eye met his – Lackland Locksley now a knight in the company of the king – and she gave a weak smile, nodded her head to him.

'She is to marry Eudo,' said Lady Joan in a low voice.

'I thought as much.'

'Her mother has made all the arrangements. They will be wed after Easter and then she will go to Normandy with them.'

Robin returned Elaine's greeting then turned his gaze from her. Once he would have been jealous. Now he only felt pity. Marian was ready to leave, so they mounted their horses and joined the throng of lords and royal servants around the king. With the sounding of a horn, they rode out. Through the gatehouse with its gouged stones, across the outer bailey's churned earth and over the scorched timbers that had once been a barbican. At the edge of the royal camp, where it disappeared into forest, the hundredmen of the Arrow were gathering their things together and preparing to return to their hideout, the king's safe-conduct still firmly grasped in Much's hand. When he saw Robin and Marian in the rear of the king's retinue he shouted a cheer for them both. The hundredmen echoed his voice. The earls looked around in confusion, to see this ragged pack of men whooping and shouting for Locksley and a lady they had never seen before, treating them as the victors of Nottingham. Marian laughed and Robin shouted the men a loud greeting. Then they had left them behind and were on the King's Way, riding through glistening sunlight towards the shelter of the forest.

They talked as they rode, Marian and Robin. Of how the Hundred had passed the lean winter months and what had taken place inside Nottingham Castle. At the turning towards the Locksley hundred they found Lord D'Alselin waiting to join the pack. He had old ties to the king's family and now, like most of the local lords, he hoped those loyalties would win reward in the wake of other men's fall. He came alongside Robin and Marian and they were so deep in conversation his arrival startled them.

'Good to see you in finer company, Lord Locksley.'

'I doubt I will stay in it for long,' said Robin. 'The king will be heading south again soon. He will not want a poor lord like me in his company. Thank you, by the way, for the warning you gave the friar after Martinmas. It was many months ago but I have not forgotten it.'

'You know me, Locksley. I uphold the law above all else. I do not like to see it bent to a lord's will.'

'Then you have had a miserable few years.'

'Let us hope those days are behind us. I will leave you to your conversation. You looked thick as thieves when I arrived.'

'As thieves?' said Robin. 'What a strange thing to think of.'

With a gruff laugh D'Alselin left them. Not long after, their conversation was interrupted again. From further up the road, the Earl of Derby shouted Robin's name and gave an urgent gesture for him to join him.

'The king is discussing how to maintain his rule in Nottinghamshire once he leaves,' Derby said as soon as Robin was alongside. 'If you want to have any voice in this it would be best you are close.'

They edged themselves forwards through the pack of servants and lords surrounding the king.

'From what I hear law and order has broken down here in my absence,' the king was saying. 'The sheriffs must bear some responsibility, and the Lords Vipont. And my brother. Now those men are removed from their offices and influence we will have a clean slate. Lord Locksley, I owe you a debt. Derby mentioned something about a pardon?'

'Yes, your grace,' said Robin swiftly. 'Lord Vipont wrongfully condemned a dozen men of my hundred, and my brother, on the lies of his own servants. I would ask for those judgements to be overturned.'

'Your brother assisted me in this siege. He may be pardoned. But did not these hundredmen flee justice? I cannot be seen to allow men to flout my law.'

'They sought sanctuary,' said Robin, hoping the lie would be convincing enough. 'On the lands of the Abbey of Newstead. If your grace wishes to make a point of punishing them they could pay the fine originally demanded of them?'

'How do they have the money for that now if they did not before?'

Good question, thought Robin. 'God provides for his own, your grace. They are penitent men.'

'Very well.' The king pointed towards a servant close by, making notes on a wax tablet. 'Provide the courts with their names. If they pay the original fine, and an extra sixpence to God, they will be pardoned. If the abbess is content to let them stay on her lands, they may remain there.'

That might require more negotiation on Robin's part – and Marian's, since the abbess was more likely to grant her a request than Robin. It might finally be time to make use of the last remaining items from the Count of Mortain's wardrobe.

'May I ask,' Robin continued, thinking he might as well press his cause while he had the opportunity, 'what your grace is considering in relation to my estate and the Viponts?'

'For your good service at the siege I will have a pardon drawn up for you against any of the crimes you were accused of during my absence. The Lords Vipont will have to attend on me in Winchester after Easter. I am calling all those who opposed me to pay their bonds of good faith then. After that I expect they will return to their Norman estates. I will not allow them to remain in control of Nottingham Castle. They will be replaced by a seneschal of my own choosing.'

'So they are to go free?' Robin frowned.

'I cannot very well keep them prisoner. I need their family's support in Normandy if I am to have a hope of protecting my lands from King Philippe.'

'The Viponts hold a number of important castles on the boundaries between the king's lands and those of the French,' explained Derby.

'But what of the case against Lord Eudo for destroying Locksley Hall?' insisted Robin. 'For murdering Sir Walter?'

'Do you have witnesses to him committing these crimes?'

'Not exactly, but…'

'It may, I grant you, have been his men who did the work but I have heard men say that Lord Eudo himself was elsewhere. Since he has blamed you for the same crime and I have pardoned you of it I do not think you can argue against my pardoning him.'

'But I am innocent. Eudo killed Sir Walter to stop him revealing that the Viponts had been plotting with the Count of Mortain for months to hold this county against you.'

'And their family failed. My brother always gives up at the first show of any real resistance. The Viponts will be fined more heavily than some of my noblemen, they will lose their lands in this county. If you must, pursue your case through my courts, but I will ensure my justices know that it is against my wishes.'

In other words, thought Robin, it would be a hopeless case. The king regarded him coolly. 'You are making me question my decision to raise you, Lord Locksley.'

'Raise me?'

'To sheriff. Of Nottingham. Derby made a good case for you. Do not undo his work now.' The king was on the point of changing the subject when one of his servants murmured something in his ear. He nodded. 'My clerk reminds me that you will of course need to pay the customary fee for your position. Your lands were restored and then confiscated, is that right?'

'Yes.'

He addressed the clerk. 'Have the documents drawn up. Your estate is restored once more. Lord Locksley.'

And with that the matter was closed. The king's earls closed rank around him and Derby and Robin were edged towards their rear. He had regained his estate, been given an honour he had not expected, the hundredmen were free at last. But the Viponts would not face justice. That last fact left a bitter taste on the other joys.

'Cheer up, Locksley,' said the Earl of Derby. 'The king will think you ungrateful.'

'Thank you,' said Robin, 'for speaking to him in my cause.'

'If you remember that support when the Prior of Lenton or Lord de Lacy threaten my family's interests in this area I will consider my efforts worth taking. Since I cannot always be here I need allies looking out for my concerns in my absence.'

Robin nodded. He had known that Derby did not help him purely for his own sake, and if there had to be an alliance for him to regain his rights in Nottinghamshire – and with lords, there always had to be some sort of alliance – then this was the least of many evils.

'I will.'

He turned his horse and rode back down the road to Marian. She looked at him anxiously, reading his disappointment more clearly than his relief.

'Shall we find somewhere quieter?' he said, nodding into the forest.

'If you like.'

They rode through the woodland, hearing the distant calls of animals grow louder as they left the noise of men behind. Robin told Marian about the Viponts first. He thought it best to break the worst news rather than make her wait in uncertainty. She heard it quietly, her head bowed.

'I thought this might happen,' she said when she raised her eyes at last. 'The king is no different from the count when it comes to his own interests.'

By the time Robin had told her the rest they had reached a brook deep within the forest. Across the water a patch of early flowering bluebells shuddered in the breeze.

'This is not far from the Hundred,' Marian said, looking around. 'Unless I am lost?'

'No, you are right.'

They went to sit at the brook's edge, their horses' reins looped over the branch of a nearby tree. Marian said nothing. She picked up a thin fallen sapling branch and dangled it in the water, watching it being tugged by the brook's course.

'Are you thinking of your father?' Robin asked.

'No,' she said hesitantly. 'I have been thinking on something the abbess said, months ago. She was asking about my marriage, about whether I would want to maintain it if Guy was found again. At the time of course, I needed to get to Nottingham Castle and watch his family so it was simplest to be Lady Vipont. But now they have lost some of their influence no one could censure me for distancing myself from them.'

'No.' She volunteered no further information and Robin hesitated to request it but at last he could not restrain his curiosity. 'What was it the abbess said?'

'That the marriage was not legal.' Marian looked away. 'To have a true marriage there needs to be a wedding night, and half the hall's servants can bear witness to the fact there was not. Without that, I can appeal for the marriage to be dissolved. The abbess seemed to think it would be simple enough to accomplish. I would be Marian Peverill again, I could reclaim my father's lands.'

'If you need any advice on that, I have a little experience I could share.' Marian smiled at him. 'So would you go to live at Peverill Tower then?'

'I… Yes, I suppose I could.'

Again a sweeping change of emotion crossed her face. Something of disappointment, perhaps.

'It would be a shame though, after all your work to help the hundredmen of Locksley, not to mention the food you stole from the hall to feed the tenants, to sever that tie.' She nodded. 'Not that there is anything at the hall now, except burnt stones and timber.'

'Your hundredmen found an abandoned croft and turned it into a village. They could probably help rebuild a hall.'

'That is very true.'

Marian let go of the dangling branch and it swept downstream, gone in an instant. Her grey eyes still lingered over where it had been.

'I would prefer it,' said Robin, 'if you were not at Peverill Tower.'

'Oh?'

'It is too far.' She did not look up but the attention she seemed to pay to the water was deceiving. Her hands rested neatly in her lap, almost as if in prayer. Everything she appeared to be doing was cover for how intently she listened to what he was saying. Robin smiled. It was so entirely within character. 'It is strange, Marian, but since I returned to Nottingham everything has changed. My life has been unmade and rebuilt, I hope for the better.'

'I think so,' she said.

'Now for the first time since I returned I can think of a future here, in my own home, my father's lands. And I realise that in the midst of all of these changes, these uncertainties, there has always been one constant. The only thing that has not changed is you.'

She frowned, questioning that assessment of her character. He was not expressing himself right, he thought.

'I do not mean you are the same in every aspect, any more than I am. But you have always known best. That used to be infuriating, because you kept proving that what I thought best was wrong. And you have always worked harder and cared more and done more when it mattered – to help your family, to help whoever else needed it, even to help me, God help you. I did not see before that one of the shrewdest decisions my parents made was to arrange my marriage to you. They could see, just as Will could see, even John Blunt could see back then, that you were one of the best and wisest women in this county. And I did not see it then, but I do now. And if you would help me rebuild Locksley Hall, build it for both of us, it would be the surest step towards a good future I can imagine.'

'I do not think,' she said slowly, 'that I have ever heard you speak for that long.'

'It was the subject. I could go on?'

She smiled, shook her head. 'You are wrong.'

Robin wished she would look at him. 'About what?'

'About everything apart from the hall. And that Will was right. I will tell him you admitted that.'

'So?' He held out his hands to her. 'Will you take my ruined hall? My broken walls? My thieves and lepers?'

'I will take your hand.' She did. She looked up. She met his eye. She smiled. 'And we can work on the rest together.'

May

The king celebrated Easter at Winchester, in a hall laden with gold and banners, with all the nobles of his court cheering his name, and him in the centre of them, wearing his crown. The count was forgiven, but he still cowered in Normandy, too afraid to meet his brother face-to-face. By the month's end they would meet, the younger brother forgiven, their causes united against the King of France. Robin was not there. He spent his Easter morning travelling the lands that were his once more, from the Locksley Hundred in the south to the Hundred of the Arrow in the north, where the village had grown large enough for Thurstan to become chief tithing man. The fences enclosing the common land were torn down on the anniversary of the very day that the hundredmen should have hanged. They gathered together and wet the earth with ale as their animals were driven back through its boundaries. In honour of the occasion Robin made a considerable donation to Newstead Abbey for a new stained glass window.

A month had passed, and it did much to improve Locksley Hall. When Robin and Marian neared the gatehouse in the season of hawthorn and blossom they met a building that no longer showed scars, only a prospect for the future. Robin glanced at Marian as they approached, as had become his habit. This place had been the scene of loss and pain for her, and he always half-expected to see her recoil as they entered it. But he saw no signs of sadness behind her eyes. It was her home now as much as his and the memories they built were happy ones. She waved a greeting to Waltheof, who was supervising Grimm and Tosti's work on the gatehouse. He came to meet them.

'Gilbert wants you to look over the accounts again. I sent him to Nottingham so he will not be back before supper.'

'Good work,' said Marian. She smiled ruefully at Robin. 'I would never have advised you to employ him if I had realised how zealous he would be.'

'I think him and Much are in competition for who can pose me the most questions. Has my mother arrived?'

'She is in her old chamber. Agnes is in the solar.'

'She does realise they will have to speak to one another at the feast this evening?'

'Put Edeva between the two of them,' said Marian. 'She could have saved Abel from Cain.'

'Ah, the season of love.'

They passed under the shadow of the gate and found Will on a chair leaning against the outer wall, his face tilted to catch the sunlight. He opened his eyes and yawned at them when Robin's shadow fell over him.

'Aren't you supposed to be watching Jocelyn?' said Robin.

'I am. He's just over there.'

He waved his hand vaguely towards the butts Robin had built on the north-western wall. John was with the boy, fortunately, nudging his elbow higher as he drew his bowstring. His steward's duties were not supposed to extend to archery practice, but Robin trusted Jocelyn better to him than to Will's guardianship.

'He's not bad with that bow,' said Will. 'He'll be a good poacher one day.'

Robin and Marian exchanged a glance.

'I'm sure he meant hunter,' she said.

They entered the stable under the new lintel. It had been carved with a knotwork pattern, vine leaves and flowers studding it, and arrows crossed at its centre. That evening their family, their friends and their tenants would look up at it as they arrived for the May Day feast, ready to forget the hardships of winter and look forward to the promise of summer ahead. Robin helped Marian down from her horse. Together they walked hand-in-hand into Locksley Hall.

Addenda

Characters

Lords Temporal

King Richard: Eldest surviving son of Henry II and Eleanor of Aquitaine. King of the English, Duke of the Normans and Aquitainians, etc.
John, Count of Mortain: Youngest child of Henry II and last surviving brother of Richard I. Lord of Nottingham, Derby, Tickhill, etc.
Robin, Lord of Locksley: Son and heir of the Lord of Locksley. Presumed dead at the Siege of Acre (1189-91) during the Third Crusade.
Lady Marian Peverill: Daughter of the Sheriff of Nottingham, previously betrothed to Robin. Now betrothed to Guy de Vipont.
Sir Walter Peverill, Sheriff of Nottingham: Father of Marian. Lord of Peverill Tower, living in Locksley Hall.
Lady Joan Peverill: Mother of Robin. Widow of Lord Robert of Locksley. Now wife of Sir Walter Peverill.
Eudo de Vipont: *(pron. YEW-doh de VEE-pon)* Head of the Vipont family in England, with large estates in Normandy. Trusted ally of the Count of Mortain. Seneschal of Nottingham Castle and, as Jocelyn de Rodehode's guardian, custodian of the Locksley estate.
Serlo de Vipont: Eudo's son.
Ranulf de Vipont: Eudo's brother.
Guy de Vipont: Ranulf's son. Betrothed to Marian Peverill.
Idonea de Vipont: Serlo's wife, sister of the Seneschal of Tickhill Castle.
Roger de Vipont: Serlo and Idonea's son.
Jocelyn de Rodehode:*(pron. ROH-dode)* Robin's nephew, a ward of Eudo de Vipont.
Elaine Peverill: Niece of Sir Walter Peverill.
Geoffrey D'Alselin:*(pron. DAL-sell-in)* Lord of Garsmount Tower.
Richard de Louvetot: *(pron. LOOV-toh)* Lord in Nottinghamshire.
Gilbert Foliot:*(pron. FO-lee-oh)* Lord in Nottinghamshire and Yorkshire.
Roger de Caux:*(pron. KOH)* A Norman lord with lands in Nottinghamshire.
Aubrey de la Guerche:*(pron. GERSH)* A Norman lord with lands in Nottinghamshire.
William de Ferrers, Earl of Derby: Absent defending his Norman lands. Son of a hero of Acre.
Ranulf de Blondeville, Earl of Chester: Loyal lord of King Richard.
David of Scotland, Earl of Huntingdon: Brother of King Malcolm of Scotland. Went on crusade with King Richard.

Lords Religious

Alexander de Lacy, Prior of Lenton: Relative of the Lord of Pontefract.
Hawise de Ferrers, Abbess of Newstead: Aunt of the Earl of Derby, cousin of Marian Peverill's mother.
Edward, Abbot of Rufford

Common Born

Will Scarlette: Robin's bastard brother.
Agnes Scarlette: Will's mother. A brewer.
Friar Toki: Mendicant friar, currently lodging at Lenton Priory.
Lanfranc: Eudo de Vipont's steward.
Gytha: Marian's maid since childhood.
Waltheof: *(pron. WOL-thee-ov)* Marian's attendant. Brother of Aelfeva.
Edgar: Marian's attendant.
Estrild: Marian's maid.
Wulfstan: Huntsman at Locksley Hall.
Peter: Clerk in the Sheriff's Chancery.

The imprisoned Hundredmen of Locksley

John Blunt: A fletcher. Chief tithing man of the Hundred.
Thurstan:*(pron. TUR-stan)* A blacksmith. Elder brother of the late Geraint.
Lefchild: Son of an alehouse hosteller.
Doleswif: A hedger.
Madalgrim: A baker, married to a brewer.
Kolbrand: A builder.
Tosti: A carpenter.
Gilbert: A priest's son.
Grimm: A thatcher.
Ansculf: Villein (unfree).
Siward: Villein.
Thorfridh: *(pron. THOR-frith)* Waltheof's brother-in-law. Husband of Aelfeva.

Other

Murdoch, called Much: Son of Tova and Saegar, the late Miller of Locksley.
Edeva: Doleswif's daughter.
Thorold:*(pron. TOR-old)* Thurstan's father. Aged, half-blind blacksmith.
Aedith: *(pron. EE-dith)* Thurstan's wife.
Aelfeva: *(pron. EL-fev-er)*Sister of Waltheof, wife of Thorfridh. Tenant on the Locksley Estate.
Petronella: Lanfranc's mistress in Nottingham.

Historical Note

I am, by training and profession, a historian. But history is inherently about story-telling, and in this work – despite the research undertaken in its preparation – I tried to put the story first. That is perhaps more forgivable in a historical fiction about Robin Hood than any other topic because whether 'Robin' himself ever existed is at question. However, in this story the world Robin inhabits is real and based on known events during the reign of King Richard I. For the sake of transparency, I wanted to make clear a few liberties I have taken with the history of this period. The greatest liberty was with the gender of those at Newstead Abbey, which has become a convent under an abbess in this version of events rather than a monastery under an abbot. The Abbess of Newstead's political power is a reflection of a number of real religious women during the Middle Ages – the Abbesses of Fontevraud and Amesbury being two examples – but none were based in Nottinghamshire in the 1190s. Locksley Hall, Garsmount and Peverill Tower are fictional. However, there were local connections to the families of Peverill, D'Alselin, de la Guerche and Vipont, whose names are linked to Nottinghamshire in the Domesday Book or in records from the reign of King John. The Earl of Derby and his family had ties to the area that stretched back to the time of the Norman Conquest. We do not know who the Sheriff of Nottingham was in the 1190s – frustrating for historians, but very convenient for fiction writers.

While undertaking my research for this book I used a wide array of historical works, a number of which I can heartily recommend to others wanting to learn more about this topic. For overviews of the reigns of the three Angevin kings I used W.L. Warren's *Henry II* (University of California Press, 1977) and *King John* (Methuen, 1978), as well as John Gillingham, *Richard I* (Yale English Monarchs Series, Yale University Press, 2002), whose work also contains one of the rare glimpses into the siege of Nottingham Castle in 1194. For this event Trevor Foulds, 'The Siege of Nottingham Castle in 1194', *Transactions of the Thoroton Society of Nottinghamshire* (Vol. XCV, 1991) and Andrew Hamilton, *Nottingham's Royal Castle* (Nottingham Civic Society, 1991) were also very useful. For information on the ritual year, Ronald Hutton, *Stations of the Sun: A History of the Ritual Year in Britain* (Oxford University Press, 2001) was invaluable. Thomas Ashbridge, *The Crusades: The War for the Holy Land* (Simon & Shuster, 2000) gave me a great deal of the context which I needed for the Third Crusade, while general information on medieval warfare and contemporary attitudes towards it were provided by Maurice Keen, *Medieval Warfare: A History* (Oxford University Press, 1999); idem, *Chivalry* (Yale University Press, 1984); and Nigel Saul, *For Honour and Fame: Chivalry in England, 1066-1500* (Bodley Head, 2011). The legal context of the 1190s – immensely complex as it was – was rendered far more comprehensible by Robert Bartlett, *England Under the Norman and Angevin Kings: 1075-1225* (Oxford University Press, 2000); idem, *Trial by Fire and Water: The Medieval Judicial Ordeal* (Clarendon Press, 1986); Danny Danziger and John Gillingham, *1215: The Year of Magna Carta* (Coronet Books, 2004). As for the daily life of a manorial estate at this time, I used Peter Hammond, *Food and Feast in Medieval England* (Sutton, 2005); Trevor Rowley, *Norman England* (Shire Living Historyies, 2010); Margaret Wade Labarge, *A Baronial Household of the Thirteenth Century* (Eyre & Spottiswoode, 1965); C.M. Woolgar, *The Great Household in Late Medieval England* (Yale University Press, 1999). Henrietta Leyser, *Medieval Women: A Social History of Women in England, 450-1500* (Ted Smart, 2002) and Carole Rawcliffe, *Medicine and Society in Later Medieval England* (Sutton, 1995) provided further context, relating to women's experience and the medical world. For the man himself I looked at J.C. Holt, *Robin Hood* (Thames & Hudson, 1993).

I recommend the exhibition covering medieval Nottingham life inside Nottingham Castle, which was extremely useful, and I advise any budding medievalist to visit the reconstructions at the Medieval Palace in the Tower of London and Great Tower at Dover Castle, where I have been very fortunate to work for the past four years.

This era is rich in incredible stories and I hope this book inspires you to read more of them.

Acknowledgements

I have to say a few words of thanks to the many people who assisted me while I was writing *The Arrow of Sherwood.*

Many friends and colleagues offered encouragement, not least my first readers, Jen Parr, Laura Clark and Claire Chate. Alys Jones provided the brilliant map illustration – I thoroughly recommend seeing more of her work at http://alysjonesillustration.weebly.com. My bosses at Past Pleasures Ltd., Mark Wallis and Stephanie Selmayr, allowed me time away from my research duties so that I could write it, for which, and for enabling me to inhabit so many wonderful historical worlds, I am very grateful. I must also thank Diane Parkin, who edited this work, and my long-term contact at Pen & Sword, Laura Hirst.

Most of all, I want to thank my family, whose constant support and creative thinking is an inspiration. Particularly thanks to Anne & Keith Johnson and Joe Carroll, to whom I dedicate this book.